About the Author

Amalie Berlin lives with her family in Southern Ohio, and she writes quirky, independent characters for Mills & Boon Medical Romance. Her favourite stories buck expectations with unusual settings and situations, and the belief that humour can powerfully illuminate truth – especially when juxtaposed against intense emotions. And that love is stronger and more satisfying when your partner can make you laugh through the times you don't have the luxury of tears.

Juliette Hyland believes in strong coffee, hot drinks and happily ever afters! She lives in Ohio, USA, with her prince charming, who has patiently listened to many rants regarding characters failing to follow the outline. When not working on fun and flirty happily ever afters, Juliette can be found spending time with her beautiful daughters, giant dogs or sewing uneven stitches with her sewing machine.

New Zealander **Alison Roberts** has written more than eighty romance novels for Mills & Boon. She has also worked as a primary school teacher, a cardiology research technician and a paramedic. Currently, she is living her dream of living – and writing – in a gorgeous village in the south of France.

Opposites Attract Collection

Opposites Attract:
Medics in Love

AMALIE BERLIN

JULIETTE HYLAND

ALISON ROBERTS

MILLS & BOON

First Published in Great Britain 2025
by Mills & Boon, an imprint of HarperCollins*Publishers* Ltd
1 London Bridge Street, London, SE1 9GF

www.harpercollins.co.uk

HarperCollins*Publishers*
Macken House, 39/40 Mayor Street Upper,
Dublin 1, D01 C9W8, Ireland

ISBN: 978-0-263-41723-4

MIX
Paper | Supporting
responsible forestry
FSC™ C007454

This book contains FSC™ certified paper and other controlled sources to ensure responsible forest management.

For more information visit: www.harpercollins.co.uk/green

Printed and Bound in the UK using 100% Renewable Electricity at CPI Group (UK) Ltd, Croydon, CR0 4YY

BREAKING HER
NO-DATING RULE

AMALIE BERLIN

To Tina Beckett – A great friend, fantastic writer, and an awesome lady to work with! It's been a blast!

To Laurie Johnson – For giving me the chance to collaborate with a writer I adore, and letting me slip a hippy chick into a book :) You rock.

PROLOGUE

"I KNOW THAT you want to manage this situation yourself, but you do have to relax at some point. Let me and the universe carry the load for a few days."

The fact that most of the resort had been abandoned at the first hint of the approaching storm gave Ellory Star more confidence than she might've otherwise had in what would be an intense situation at best. Only a handful of staff remained—enough to keep the resort running—and a handful of guests trying to get in as much time on the powder as they could before the clouds rolled in. But it wasn't like Mira was leaving the premises. She'd be around for catastrophe, her safety net.

"Enjoy your post-coital vacation, spend time with Mr. Forever, Number Five. I promise not to refer to him any more in any way that highlights the fact that I totally won the New Year's resolution war this year." Ellory leaned over the bar in Jack's suite, where she and Mira were chatting, tidied a stack of napkins emblazoned with the lodge logo, and pretended not to be feeling smug about how totally right she was.

Mira—her sister by everything except genetics and actual family ties—was the concierge doctor for the ski lodge where Ellory was now living and working, and her best friend since they'd set eyes on one another as toddlers, when Ellory's mother had brought her to work at the lodge Mira's family owned. She was the brilliant one, and rational, dependable, smart, and a lot of other good-sounding words that everybody would use to describe Mira and only Mira would ever use to label her.

"You haven't won until you figure out your quest. Your project. The thing you're working on."

A project Ellory hadn't explained. "I should've just bet you I could go without a man longer than you could keep serial dating. Though I haven't seen any contenders for sexy fun since I've been home. So the resolution is safe."

But that wouldn't have served the point of her making the resolution to begin with. Besides, her inability to articulate exactly what was wrong was part of the problem she needed to figure out. She skated through life, largely flying on instinct and ignoring anything that hurt her to the point that she wasn't even sure what hurt her any more. For the past year she'd been running from some pain she couldn't name—because ignoring the reasons for pain didn't mean she didn't feel it. It just meant she felt it blindly.

Her quest had led her home, and left her with the understanding that she had something to work on. Banishing men from her life kept her from sublimating with sex, kept her from distracting herself. She'd spent a decade distracting herself with a string of different boyfriends, and she wasn't any closer to finding enlightenment...or just plain old happiness...than she had been when she'd left home, determined to give her life meaning.

Before things got too deep, before Mira picked up on the melancholy lurking in Ellory's soul, she shifted the subject back to one she knew Mira couldn't resist. "So, I'm going to have to come up with a new nickname for Jack. I could make some 'playing doctor' references, but that's too obvious."

Jack's timely arrival through the suite door was her

cue. "Hey, *Loooove* Doctor," she called, and then shook her head. "Nah, that's not it. I'll keep working on it. Somewhere else now that we've got everything hashed out." She winked at Mira and brushed past Mr. Mira on the way to the door.

Before she stepped out she turned to say something, and interrupted kissing. "Man, I was going to say that I was totally wrong about the resolution—that it just wasn't that Jack was lucky to be the fifth dude but that I believed he was the one…and would have been if he'd been number twenty-five or number five. Now I just want to give you a safe-sex talk!"

When they both laughed at her she smiled and cooed at them both while closing the door, "Oh, Number Five, you'll always be number *one* to me!"

The door clicked before she could get pelted with bar paraphernalia for her pretend Mira-sex-talk.

The universe did like her. Occasionally.

CHAPTER ONE

ELLORY STAR HAD never been a sentinel before, and there were good reasons for that.

But this was where her mission to find herself had led. From the hot, life-laden forests of Peru to Colorado in the winter. To cold legs and a head full of static, hair that stuck to everything, and, of course, to trying to find other people. Correction, she wasn't even out doing the heavy lifting on the finding. She was just waiting for other people to find people.

The universe had a wicked sense of humor.

A tight cluster of yellow headlights flickered in the far left of her field of vision and soon grew strong enough to cut through the gray-blue haze of hard-falling snow.

The rescue team was back!

She turned from the frosty glass inset in the polished brass doors of the Silver Pass Lodge to face the ragtag group of employees she'd managed to round up after the mass exodus. Most lodge employees had families they wanted to get to before the blizzard hit, and nearly all the patrons had left too—the ones who hadn't left were the ones the rescue team was returning with. She hoped.

"Okay, guys, do the things we talked about," she said—the most order-like order she'd ever given.

Usually, she was the last person to be put in charge of

anything, and that was how Ellory liked it. She had less chance of letting people down if they didn't expect anything from her. It probably highlighted some flaw in her character that the only time she was willing to take on any kind of serious responsibility was when her primary objective was guarding her best friend's sexy rendezvous time.

Ellory—gatekeeper to the love shack.

She who kept non-emergency situations from disturbing the resort doctor while she got her wild thing on with Jack, aka Number Five.

Pure. Accomplishment.

She watched long enough to see the first staff member break into motion, placing another log on the already blazing fire and opening the damper so the lobby fireplace would roar to life.

Later she could feel guilty for the amount of carbon she was responsible for putting into the atmosphere today. Right now, her heart couldn't find a balance between the well-being of people around her and the well-being of the planet.

Some lifestyle choices were harder to live with than others.

Those returning would be cold at the very least, and Ellory prayed that was the worst of their afflictions. Cold she could remedy with fire, hot beverages, hot water, and blankets hot from the clothes dryer—even if all those warm things further widened her expanding carbon footprint and left her feeling like a sasquatch. A big, hypocritical, sooty-footed, carbon-belching sasquatch.

And those kinds of thoughts were not helping. She had no room for negativity today. She had a job, she had a plan, she'd see it through and not let anyone down—especially the only one with any faith in her.

One of them should be having wild monkey sex with someone, and as she wasn't having any she'd defend

Mira's love shack to the last possible minute. Be the stand-in Mira today, and do the very best she could for as long as she could. At least until she knew exactly what Mira would have to deal with when it got to be too much for *her* to handle.

When she looked back at the headlights, they'd grown close enough for her to count. Six sets, same number as had gone out. Good sign.

She fastened the coat she wore, crammed a knit cap on her head and pushed her hands into her mittens. Her clothes might be ridiculous since she hadn't yet augmented her wardrobe with Colorado winter wear, and her bottom half might freeze when she went out to meet the team, but at least the places where she kept her important bits—organs, brain—would be warm.

As the snowmobiles rolled to a stop in front of the ornate doors, she took a last deep breath of warm air and pushed out into the raging winter. Wind whipped her gauzy, free-flowing skirt around her legs and made it hard to keep her eyes open. With one hand shielding them from the blast of snowy, frigid air, she counted: ten people, one dog.

Should have been eleven.

Another quick count confirmed that all the six rescuers in orange had made it back, which meant one of the lodge's patrons was still lost in this storm that was forecast to only get worse.

Oh, no.

She'd have to disturb Mira.

People were already climbing off the snowmobiles, rescuers in their orange suits helping more fashionably dressed and slower-moving guests from the machines.

"How can I help?" she called over the wind, approaching the group.

The large man paused in his task of releasing a big

snowy black dog from the cage on the back of his snow-mobile, turned and pointed at Ellory. *"Get inside now!"*

Real yelling? Okay... Maybe it was just to get over the wind.

He unlatched the cage and his canine friend bounded out. The sugar-frosted dog didn't need to be told where to go. Ellory made it to the outer doors behind the massive canine and opened it for him, then held it for people.

It wasn't technically a blizzard yet. It was snowing hard, yes, and blowing harder, and of course she was cold, but she wouldn't freeze to death in the next couple of minutes while she helped in some fashion. And she needed to help. Even if all she could think to do was hold the door.

As the man approached, he lifted his goggles and sent a baleful stare at her, stormier than the weather. With one smooth motion he grabbed Ellory's elbow and thrust her ahead of him into the breezeway, "That wasn't a sugges-tion. Get inside now. You're not dressed for the weather."

"I didn't offer to make snow angels with anyone," she joked, looking over her shoulder at the angry man as he steered her inside.

Stumbling, she pulled her elbow free and pushed through, intent on getting some space between them.

Good grief. Up close, and without fabric covering the bottom of his face or the goggles concealing his eyes, the fact that he was working some kind of rugged hand-some look canceled the effect of winter and made her feel like she was dipped in peppermint wherever she touched him.

Ellory didn't get those kind of excited feelings for any-one ever, not without really working at it. Must be the cold. And now that she was inside, she had things to do besides tingle and lust after Ole Yeller.

A specific list of things, in fact, to look for when check-ing these people out.

As the group gathered around the fireplace and the hats and goggles came off, she got a good look at how beaten down they all were. Exhausted. Weak. All of them, both the rescuers and the rescued. But those who didn't do this for a living, the ones who'd been helpless and still had a missing friend, looked blank. It was the same shell-shocked expression she'd seen on the faces of victims of natural disasters—earthquakes, mudslides, and floods. Being lost in a snowstorm probably counted…

Her people stood around, waiting for her. Follower to leader for one day—no wonder they didn't know what to do. She was supposed to be leading them. Her list of things had *hypothermia* at the very top as the most important situation to remedy.

"Okay, guys, we need to help everyone get out of their snow suits and boots. Get the hot blankets on them. And hot beverages. Hot cocoa…" she corrected. Everyone liked cocoa, and it was loaded with calories they no doubt needed after their harrowing day.

While the employees did as she asked, Ellory backtracked to the Angry Dog Man. He seemed much more leader-like than she felt, so he got the questions.

In hushed tones, she asked, "Where is the other one?"

He frowned, his left hand lifting to his right shoulder to grip and squeeze through the thick coat he wore. "The other one tried to get back to the lodge when these four wanted to stay put."

"Where were they?"

"South Mine."

Ellory winced. The terrain around the mines was left rugged on purpose in the hope of discouraging exploration by guests. The mines weren't safe, and signs announced that, but they could serve as shelter in a pinch. A very dangerous pinch.

"Did you see a trail or any sign of him?" Mira would

want to know everything, so she tried to anticipate questions.

"There is a trail, but it's the one that they followed in. If he's wise and we're lucky, he'll follow it back. There's still a chance that he'll make it back to the lodge while we're out looking for him. If he does, I need you to call on the radio and let me know. It was impossible to take the snowmobiles directly along that trail, but we're going to go back out and look. We'll take a quick peek in the mines between here and there, and hit South Mine again in case he went back to where they all were."

"After the storm?"

"No." He looked back and called to the group, all of whom had dove into the drinks and stew to fortify themselves. "Ten minutes and then we're going back out."

"You can't!" Ellory said, much louder than she'd intended. She tried again, quieter, calmer than she felt. "The storm is going to get really bad."

"We have some time." His voice had a gravelly sound that sent warm sparks over her ears, almost like a touch. That kind of voice would sound crazy sexy in whispers, hot breath on her ear...Raspy and...

"I'm sorry, what did you say? I think I misheard you." Or hadn't heard him at all. God, she had to do better than this.

"Are you a doctor?" he repeated.

"No." It was time for him to figure out she wasn't important, or capable of handling this.

"Where's Dr. Dupris?"

She noticed him looking back at the people in front of the fire, all out of their suits now, which meant time for step two.

Ellory spun and headed for the guests, expecting him to follow. "She's here, but I'm like triage or something. I have a list of things to wake her up for. And we have water heated in case there were any frostbite cases. Also I read that heating the feet would help get the body temperatures up fast. Actually, I have the saunas roaring too if that would help. I just wasn't sure whether or not that would be a bad thing or a good thing, and it wasn't in the books. Do you know?" She didn't stop, just threw the question out and then went on.

Since the staff had handled her warming requests, she headed for the smallest member of the party, a petite, pixie-like woman who wasn't drinking her cocoa…and who held her hands above her lap as if they were hurting.

His stride longer, he overtook her and scooped up a stethoscope as he passed the tray of first-aid and examination supplies she'd laid out and slung the thing around his neck. Catching it caused a brief flash of pain on his handsome features. He ignored the pain, but Ellory noticed. That was her real job: Physio and massage therapy. Just not today.

He wasn't the concern right now. He'd been mostly warm when out there in it, though his cheeks looked chapped from the winter winds…

She reached down to gently lift one of the woman's arms to get a better look at her fingers. "What's your name, honey?"

"Chelsea," she answered, teeth chattering. "My fingers and toes burn. Like they're on fire."

"Socks off, everyone. Time to check extremities." Chelsea's fingertips were really red. Ellory didn't want to touch them, but she didn't really know enough about medicine not to investigate fully. Maybe frostbite started with redness?

Gingerly, she wrapped her hands over Chelsea's fingertips, causing the freezing woman to gasp in pain but confirming that they were indeed hot. This wasn't frostbite. Though that was probably going to be the next stage. "I'm sorry," she whispered, and let go of the hands, her gaze drifting down to where Angry Leader had knelt at Chelsea's feet, which he now examined. Her toes were exactly the opposite in color from her fingertips: an unnatural, disturbing, somewhat corpse-like white.

That might be a good reason to call Mira...

"Is that—?" She hadn't got the question out before he nodded and looked Chelsea in the eye.

"My name is Dr. Graves. Anson, if you prefer. I'll even tell you my middle name later if you need some more names to cuss me with... This isn't going to be pleasant. We have to warm your feet fast," Anson said, his raspy voice much gentler with the woman. "You have the beginning stages of frostbite."

Chelsea's gaze sharpened and she blurted out, "Are my toes going to fall off?" She sounded so stricken every head in the lobby turned toward her.

Ellory's heart skipped.

Anson looked grim and his wind-burned cheeks lost some of their color, but he shook his head. "It's going to feel like it. It will hurt like probably no one but you can imagine right now, but that's how you get to keep them." He didn't sugarcoat it, not even a hint of the usual *discomfort* nonsense doctors liked to say.

Chelsea nodded, her eyes welling.

Anson looked at Ellory again. "Get her pants off. How hot is the water?"

"One hundred and ten on the burners." Ellory answered. That she knew.

He looked surprised they'd been using a thermometer on it. "A little too hot. Add a small amount of cold water to it to get it to one hundred and five and then pour. It's got to be between one hundred and one hundred and five degrees Fahrenheit all the time. Dip out water, pour more in, or swap out the containers to keep it within range. I know that's going to be hard to do in buckets, but it needs to be done as exactingly as possible for a full half-hour." Anson said this to Ellory, who nodded and relayed the orders to her kitchen helpers, then helped Chelsea out of the bottom half of her suit.

By the time Chelsea was down to her thermals, the water had been sufficiently cooled and poured into a large rubber container. Ellory pushed the cotton cuffs to Chelsea's knees and guided the woman's feet into the water.

It hurt. She could tell by the way Chelsea's lower lip quivered, though admirably she didn't cry out.

With all the time Ellory had spent in disaster zones, witnessing human suffering, she should have built up some kind of callus to it by now, but it tore at her heart all the same. "I'm so sorry this has happened to you... We'll get you something for the pain."

"My fiancé is still out there," she whispered, clarifying in those simple words what hurt worse right now.

Ellory put one arm around Chelsea's shoulders, giving her a squeeze. "Let's get your insides warmed up and see if we can beat the shivering." She took the cocoa Chelsea hadn't been drinking and held it to her lips. "We'll help you with this until your fingers stop smarting and you can do it yourself, okay?"

"*Ohh*...chocolate," Chelsea said.

"That's pretty much how I feel about chocolate too." Ellory lifted the cup to the woman's mouth. "Sometimes it's the only thing that makes the stuff we have to go through bearable. Though I do feel like I should apologize for not making it from better ingredients." A nervous laugh bubbled up. "You didn't do anything wrong, that's not why I'm making you drink preservative juice." She was doing that thing again, where she lost control of her mouth because she was nervous.

Chelsea looked at her strangely. "Preservative juice?"

She named the popular brand of cocoa everyone knew, then added, "I'm sure it's fine. I'm just…" What could she say to explain that? "I'm big on organic."

"Ahh." Chelsea nodded, relaxing back in her chair.

Great bedside manner. Most of her patients worked with her for a long stretch of time so they got to know her quirks and oddities, and only had to suffer her help with exercise and a program that their physiotherapist designed. All Ellory did was help them through it and massage away pain, she didn't need to be trusted to make decisions.

Ellory added in what she hoped was a more agreeable tone, "Ignore me. It's a throwback to childhood."

"You were big on organic in childhood?" Anson asked from down where he crouched, examining the feet of another patient. Which meant he was listening, and probably losing faith in her with every word that tumbled out of her mouth.

"Yes. In a manner of speaking."

His eyes were focused on the patient, but it still felt like he was staring at her. "Which is?"

The only way out of this conversation was to pretend it wasn't happening.

Stop. Talking.

Handing Chelsea's cup to another staff member, she said, "Please assist Chelsea with her cocoa. I should assist Dr. Graves." The man needed a different last name. Which she wouldn't bring up. She probably already sounded like an incompetent idiot to them.

She caught up with him kneeling before the last of the rescued, checking extremities.

As she stepped to his side he looked up, locking eyes with her in a way that said he knew she'd heard him and that he wasn't going to press the matter.

Message delivered, he got back to work and the potency of his stare dissipated. "Get all their feet into the water.

But Chelsea's the only one you have to keep in the temperature range."

"What about the sauna?" She rolled with his return to business. As out of her depth as she felt, she did want to do a good job, take good care of them all.

"Maybe later, or if they don't get warm enough to stop shivering soon, but I'd rather you not put them into the stress of a sauna until a doctor is on hand should things get hairy."

Ellory nodded.

"I'm going to check on my crew. And Max."

Hearing his name, the fuzzy black dog currently stretched in front of the fire popped up and looked at Anson.

"Or maybe I'll get him some water first…" He called to the rescuers to check their feet and while they peeled off boots he took care of himself and the big bushy dog.

Ellory organized the helpers with instructions on the water, her shoulders growing tighter and tighter every time she looked through the door or the windows at the worsening storm. After assigning two people to Chelsea and getting them another round of hot blankets, she finally went to find Anson.

And Max—maybe the dog would listen to her concerns.

CHAPTER TWO

"WHAT IF YOU'RE not back in half an hour, when they come out of the warm water? And isn't that weird, a doctor moonlighting as a rescuer?" She'd always considered Mira to be an unusual doctor—fabulous and outdoorsy—so Anson seemed like an anomaly. He had the bossy bit down, at least. But he could be safe and inside during this weather, or out driving his four wheel drive and…smoking cigars. Whatever people did in four wheeled drives, she wasn't sure.

"Dry them gently and wrap them in loose gauze." He answered that first, then added, "I don't moonlight. I work in the ER six months of the year, and the rescue team is my life during ski season."

His admission surprised her. Adrenaline junkie? Extreme sports wackadoo? Both those fit the idea of returning to the outdoors in this weather. Once more, her gaze was pulled to the glass doors. The snow, already heavy before they'd returned, had picked up even worse since. "Are you sure it wouldn't be better for you all to wait until the storm passes?"

The sharpness that came to his green eyes shut down that thought process completely. Right. He didn't say anything. He didn't need to.

Anson turned to his crew instead. "Five minutes." He

pulled a plastic baggie from his pocket and extracted some kind of jerky to give to the big shaggy dog.

One of the group asked, "Where are we going?"

"Blue Mine and South Mine," Anson answered, then looked at Ellory. "Why are you not dressed for the weather?"

"I haven't bought clothes for being home yet, and all the winters in the past decade, I guess, have been in warm places. Before New Year's Eve I was in Peru. It's summer there right now. I wasn't sure if I was going to stay, so I didn't want to buy clothes I might not wear very long. It's wasteful."

He shook his head. "Rent a snow suit when you're going to be out in the elements…what's your name?"

"Ellory. And I have one." It's the one thing she did have, but it was old, hopelessly out of fashion and not nearly as well suited to the winter as the suits these people wore because she didn't wear manufactured materials. So it was bulky, and kind of itchy. And she left it at her parents' after every New Year…so it was musty from storage and…

She didn't need to share that with Anson. He was covered in layers of modern insulating materials, and while she could understand it and tried not to be jealous of his warmth and mobility, he wouldn't understand if she explained. Not that his opinion should matter. "I wasn't going out to stay in the weather earlier, just to meet you all. And I have thermal underwear under this."

Like he would think well of her if she'd been wearing wool and a parka in her short jaunt into the weather to meet them. She was a flake. That's how normal people viewed her. So today she was a flake who didn't dress properly. What else was new?

"Go put it on."

Ellory didn't know how to respond to a direct order like that. And she really didn't like it that the bossiness made her tingle again… Wrong time, wrong place, wrong feelings.

She wanted to blame them on her nerves too, like being nervous amplified all her other emotions, but she couldn't even lie to herself on that. Ruggedly handsome wasn't a look the man was going for—he just had it. Some combination of good genes, lifestyle and that voice gave it to him. She tried to ignore that, and the squirmy feeling in her belly she got when his mossy hazel eyes focused on her.

"Anson." She went with his name, in an attempt to reclaim some power. "It's not just blowing more, it's falling thicker. If you guys get all…frozen and stuff, then you aren't going to help find—"

"There's still time." He cut her off. Again.

Rude. Curt. Terse. That should make him less attractive. That should definitely make him feel like less of a threat to her stupid resolution…

He had flaws. The bossy thing, which shouldn't be hot. What else? He probably wasn't even half as strapping and impressive as his winter wear made him seem. It was just the illusion of beefy manliness from the cardinal rule of winter: loose layers kept you warmer. It somehow amplified the squareness of his jaw and the scruff that confirmed the dark color of the hair currently hidden by his knit cap.

Her heart rate accelerated and her hands waffled at her side. This was not going the way she'd pictured it while waiting and watching through the windows. She didn't anticipate having to try and convince someone not to go back out in the storm, and for some reason she knew he wouldn't care that she was more afraid for the crew than for the missing man.

She could just lock the door and keep everyone safe inside. Except she hated confrontation, and if he told her to give him the key in that bossy gravel voice of his, she'd give it to him. And possibly her undies too.

She could really think of a good way to distract him. It definitely violated her Stupid Resolution parameters, but it was in the name of humanity and keeping people safe. Surely that was a good reason for an exception.

Through all this stupidity, the only communication Ellory managed was skittish hand motions that made her jangle from the stacks of thin silver bangles she loved. Sentinels probably didn't jingle.

He glanced down at her hand and then back up, impatient brows lifting, urging her to say something else. Only Ellory didn't know what else to say.

Winter was his job after all. And, really, she'd spent most of the past lots of years in places where her weather awareness had mostly consisted of putting on sunscreen and seeking high ground during the rainy season. She probably wasn't the best judge of snow stuff.

When she failed to form any other words he started talking instead. Instructions. Things she'd already learned from studying Mira's medical books when reading up on treatment for frostbite and hypothermia. But it was good to hear it from someone who really knew something about it. Anything about it.

He even gave her additional explanations about signs of distress, outside the cold temperature illness symptoms she'd read about—other stuff to look for that would require Mira immediately, and he capped off the instructions with a long, measuring look. "If you're not up to the task, tell me now. I'll get Dr. Dupris down here."

"I'm up to the task." She was, she just wished she wasn't. "Are you? Your shoulder is hurt. I've seen you roll your arm in the socket at least three times since you came inside and you've been rubbing it too."

He closed the bag of dog treats and stuffed it into his pocket. "I'm all right. We'll call if we get stuck. And we've got survival gear on the ATVs."

Movement behind her made her aware that the team had all moved toward the door, ready to go wherever Fearless Leader told them to. They all either ignored what she'd been saying about the danger of going out in the crazy falling snow or were busy building an imaginary snow fort of denial.

Anson held the door and looked at the dog. "Max." One word and his furry companion scampered right out behind them.

It would be okay. People who risked their lives for others had to build up good karma. The team would make it back, and maybe their karma would extend to the still missing skier. Until then she'd do her best—manage the lobby/exposure clinic, keep the fire stoked and the water heated and flowing, and keep those who'd been out in it warm and safe.

After the team returned, and when the head count was official, then she'd get Mira.

Anson Graves's snowmobile crept through the falling white flakes. Theoretically, there should be another couple of hours of daylight left, but between the dense clouds and miles of sky darkened by falling snow it felt more like twilight. Zero visibility. He was half-afraid he'd find the missing man by accidentally running him over.

A trip that normally took fifteen minutes was taking forever.

Anson knew only too well how much longer it would seem for the man who was stuck in the cold, counting his own heartbeats and every painful breath, wondering how many more he'd have before the wind froze him from the inside and winter claimed him.

That's what he'd done.

The blonde at the lodge hadn't been wrong, he'd just wanted her to be wrong. At least half an hour had passed since they'd started the trek to the third-closest abandoned silver mine, and they weren't even halfway there yet. She should be getting Chelsea's feet out of the water and bandaging them by now. He'd forgotten to tell her not to let Chelsea walk...though maybe she wouldn't try.

If they hadn't had to take the long way they'd be there by now. But this was the safest route with the snow drifting the way it was.

If the wind would just stop...

The wet, blasting snow built a crust on his goggles, his eyes the only places not actively painful and cold from the wind. He shook his head, trying to clear the visor, but had to use his hand to scrape it off. He didn't even want to see what was becoming of Max in the back. Snow stuck to his fur like nothing Anson had ever seen.

The only thing he felt good about right now was leaving the four rescues with the hippie chick. Her choice of attire showed a distinct lack of common sense, but she'd picked up on his shoulder bothering him. She was perceptive and paying attention. And he'd seen her hug his frostbite patient. She cared. They'd be safe with her, especially considering the detailed instructions he'd given. She'd be watching them with an eagle eye for any slight changes. Getting Dupris should an emergency arise would be a simple enough task for anyone.

His stomach suddenly churned hard, a split second before he felt an unnatural shifting of the snow beneath him.

He reacted automatically, cutting sharply up the slope, and didn't stop until the ground felt firm beneath him. Damned sliding snowdrifts.

He'd only reacted in time because he'd been waiting for it to happen. After his harrowing experience, snow had become an obsession to him—learning the different kinds of snow, what made it slide, what made blizzards, all that. And since he'd bought Max and had him trained, he'd probably spent more time on the snow than anywhere else in his life. His instinct was honed to it, and he knew to listen to his gut.

Especially when he couldn't see the terrain well enough to judge with his eyes...

But he couldn't trust that his crew would have the same ability, especially with how tired they already were.

Conditions had just officially gotten too bad to continue.

His team had stopped when he'd pulled his maneuver— quickly enough to see how he'd survived it before they tried to follow—but he didn't want them to try it. They'd follow where he led, but he couldn't have any more lives on his conscience.

Grabbing the flashlight off his belt, he clicked it on, assuring that they'd see the motion even if they couldn't clearly see any other details, and gave it a swirl before pointing back in the direction from which they'd come.

Retreat.

He waited until they had all turned around and then started up the slope in a gentle arc to bring up the rear. Not ideal. The best formation had him at the front—taking the dangers first—but at least from this vantage he'd be able to see if anyone fell behind or started having difficulty.

He felt shifting against the cage at his back. Max huddled behind Anson, strategically placing himself to get the least of the cold wind that blasted around his owner, even as the machine crept along.

If it were just him, he'd stay out on the mountain, looking until it was impossible to do anything else, but there were five other human lives under his protection, not to mention his hard-working, life-saving dog.

"I'm sorry, man," he said to the wind.

They had to go back.

He'd have to tell the others they couldn't reach the mine. Yet.

They hadn't gotten far enough to find anyone or signs. Those they'd rescued earlier would just have to understand.

His gut twisted. He'd lost people to avalanches, recently even. But he'd never lost someone to a storm and not found them alive.

Worse, he'd have to lie to those people who'd been through so much. Say he was certain they would pick up the trail again as soon as the snow and wind let up. But the only thing he was certain of was the fear and guilt tearing through him—colder than the Colorado cyclone buffeting them about the mountainside.

Just as Anson had expected, Ellory was doing the job she'd been assigned. She'd been fast out the door when they'd first arrived, but not when they returned.

As quickly as they could, the team shut down their machines, climbed off, and hurried inside. They hadn't been out in the weather that long compared to their hours of searching for the group, but the wind speeds were now enough that the awning over the front doors sounded like thunder as it rippled in the wind. That, coupled with exhaustion, made it impossible to keep warm.

He stepped through the ornate doors to the comforting heat and the smell of burning wood. The fireplace in the lobby still burned actual wood, something that had surprised him when he'd returned to Silver Pass. It was good. Wood fire dried out the air and cut through the damp better than anything but a shower. Anson loved the crackling and the temperatures for those times, like now, when he just couldn't get warm enough. The dancing flames. The red coals. The warm golden light, so hopeful... Hopefulness he wished he felt.

Max looked up at him, made eye contact, and then headed for the fireplace at a trot. He always did that and Anson still didn't know whether it was him asking for permission to do something, or he was just giving Anson a heads-up that he was going.

His crew hit the hot beverages first, the fastest way to heat up your core, leaving Anson to check on his patients and deliver the news.

Ellory had positioned his frostbite patient close to the fire, having transferred her to a fancy brass wheelchair that matched the décor—the lodge kept a few on hand for the really bad skiers—and now sat at Chelsea's feet, gently patting them dry. She'd kept them in the hot water bath longer than he'd told her to. Not great. The tissue was fragile and being waterlogged wouldn't do her any favors.

A hot plate sat on the floor about a foot away, which was new. Somewhere closer to keep the water hot for the footbath.

She was taking that temperature range very seriously at least. Probably keeping it better than the whirlpool baths at the hospital.

"Chelsea's toes are pink now," Ellory called, on seeing him. It almost helped. "Well, almost all the way pink. A couple of her small toes have a bit of yellow going on. We had a little trouble with the water temperature at first, but once we moved the hot plate closer, it got easier to keep it in the range."

"It's not hurting as bad now," Chelsea added in quiet tones, swiveling in her chair to look the lobby over.

She was looking for her fiancé, as they all were, but she was the one who'd be hurt the most if the man didn't make it back.

Anson stepped around and crouched to look at her toes. "No blisters have formed yet, so that's good. You'll likely get a couple of blisters soon, when they start swelling. But we're going to take good care of you, and when the storm passes we'll get you to a hospital."

"What about Jude?" Chelsea asked, letting him know

what she was interested in talking about but not whether she'd heard him at all. Someone would have to repeat the information to her later.

Anson straightened so he could address the group. "The storm has gotten to the point where it's impossible for us to continue searching. I want to be clear: this is just a suspension of the search, not the end of it. I'm sorry we haven't found your fiancé yet."

"Jude." Chelsea repeated the name of the missing skier, stopping Anson with one hand on his arm.

"Jude," he repeated, his pulse kicking up a little higher. He knew why it was important to her, but saying the man's name made it harder to maintain the distance he needed to be smart about this. "Just because we have to postpone going back out to look for Jude, it doesn't mean it's time to give up hope. So don't get ahead of us, okay? You'd be surprised what someone can survive. Those mines are a pretty good shelter. There are also some rocky overhangs between here and where we found you. And some of those might actually be better."

"How could they be better? You're closer to the snow," one of the rescued asked.

He contemplated how much to actually tell them about his experience with this kind of situation. *I know these things, I killed someone with snow once* wouldn't inspire anyone to trust him. This had to be about them, not about his fear or guilt. "Small spaces hold the warmth your body makes better, and the wind can't get into it as fully as it does in the mines, which have a bigger entrance and room for the wind to move around inside. He might still show up here before we get out to him, but as soon as the storm lets up we'll get back out there. It's not time to give up hope." He repeated that, trying to convince himself.

It was time to bandage Chelsea's toes…and hopefully him moving on would make them take the hint not to ask more questions. He didn't have any answers or much of a mind left for coming up with more empty words of comfort. He was too busy trying to ignore the similarities between this storm and *his* storm.

Pulling off his cap and gloves, he squatted beside Ellory at Chelsea's feet, struggling to hold his calm for everyone else. "Do you have some gloves for me to use?"

Ellory ducked into the bag of supplies she'd packed and fished out the box of gloves. One look at them confirmed they wouldn't do. Small. He could squeeze into a medium at a pinch, but large were better. "All right, this job has been passed to you."

To his surprise, she didn't argue at all, just grabbed a couple gloves from the box and put them on. Crouched so close he was enveloped in a cloud of something fruity and floral. The woman looked like summer, and she smelled like spring. Warm. And distracting. He scooted to the side to give her room.

"What is the job?" she asked, looking at Chelsea's toes and maneuvering herself so she could gently cradle the patient's heel in her lap.

He handed the gauze to her and began ripping strips of tape and tacking them to the wheelchair, where she could get to them. "Part of the healing process is just keeping the site dry and loosely bandaged." He gave short, quick instructions, and left her to it.

She unrolled the gauze carefully and began wrapping. He watched, ready to correct her, but she did it as he would've: a couple of passes between the two toes to keep them separate, controlling the moisture level better, and then loosely around the two together.

No matter how out of her depth she looked, she was anything but incompetent. There might even be some kind of medical training there. The cloud of floral scent stole up his dry, burning sinuses and almost made his mouth water like a dog's.

Awesome priorities. Reveling in attraction to some woman while the lost man was freezing. Maybe dying. He definitely didn't have the warm comfort of a fireplace and a wench-shaped blonde to take his mind off his failure to get back to the lodge safely, didn't even know his friends had been saved, so he suffered that additional torment—worry for them in addition to himself.

An inferno of shame ignited in his belly.

Hide it.

At the very least he owed them all a confident appearance. Calm. Strength. Determination.

Meltdowns were something to have alone—a luxury that would have to wait until he was no longer needed.

CHAPTER THREE

ELLORY HAD READ about frostbite treatment so she could anticipate Dr. Graves's needs for that, but she had no idea what his other needs were. She'd kind of pegged the search and rescue team as attracting the kind of adrenaline fiends in it for the thrill, but Anson looked almost as devastated by returning empty-handed as Chelsea had.

With the bandage applied, she switched off the hot plate, scooted it out of the way and stood. What came next? She didn't know, but certainly there would be something she would need to do, and being on her feet would help her react that much faster.

"They still hurt, I know," Anson said to the woman, looking at the toes now hidden by the gauze, the patch of yellow skin surrounded by angry redness hidden. "But most of this might not even be frostbite. The yellow area is, but the good news is that we got to it in good time and it's very unlikely to leave any lasting damage. I won't be able to tell for a couple of days if it's frostbite or the lesser version, which you all have on your fingers and toes... frostnip. We're going to treat yours as if you have frostbite, just to be safe. I'll see what kind of antibiotics Dr. Dupris has in her inventory, and some pain medication."

Good news. She'd take whatever kind of win they could get.

Anson asked the standard allergy questions, got whatever info he needed, and nodded once to Ellory—a kind of *do it* nod. She had been promoted: triage to assistant, or nurse…or whatever that position was.

"I can check with Mira. Which antibiotic do you need?" If she had to, she could no doubt find in Mira's books which kind of antibiotic was good for skin infections, but she'd rather he tell her. She wasn't a doctor. Not by a long stretch. But she knew enough to know that antibiotics were a tricky lot—some worked for everything, some worked best for specific things, and these days a frightening amount were resistant to stuff they used to be awesome at fighting.

"I'm sure she's got some of the broad-spectrum ones, but I don't know how well the drug cabinet is stocked for anything obscure." For some reason she wanted him to think well of her, and she felt more competent even saying the words "broad spectrum." Like proving to him she wasn't a complete idiot was important. Probably something to do with the lecture she'd gotten about her clothes…

She didn't even know the man, had never seen him before today, but as he spoke she became aware of something else: there was a rawness about him she couldn't name. Something in that raspy timbre that resonated feelings primal and violent.

He rattled off a few medication names that sounded like gibberish to her, and she didn't ask him to repeat himself, just hoped she could remember them when she came face-to-face with a wall of gibberish-sounding drug names.

Then she'd come back here and keep an eye on the good doctor with the terrible name, because alarm bells were ringing in her head.

Chelsea suffered the whole situation with more dignity than Ellory could've mustered, and directed the conversation back to what she really wanted to talk about. "If I got frostbite in the mine and I wasn't in the snow, Jude's going to have it for sure, isn't he?"

"Nothing is ever certain." Ellory said it too quickly. It sounded like a platitude. She shook her head and tried again with better words. "You can't compare your situation to his for a couple of reasons: women don't hold heat as well as men do, and your boots are different. Even if they are the same brand, the fit will be different. If his have more room inside than yours they'll hold heat better. If he's taken shelter in a smaller space than you did, like Anson… Dr. Anson…was saying, he could just be warmer…"

Anson pulled out the footrests on the wheelchair and carefully positioned Chelsea's feet on the metal tray. "Find a pillow for her."

Ellory knew he was speaking to her, even though he didn't look at her. She hurried to the main desk and the office behind, where she knew she'd find some. When she presented him with two slender pillows from the office, he put one under Chelsea's feet and rose. "Would you like the other pillow to sit on?"

"Yes." She made as if to rise and Anson put his hands out to stop her. "No walking. No standing. When you need to go to the bathroom, someone's going to have to go with you. Right now, I've got you. Luckily, you weigh about as much as a can of beans…" He caught her under the arms and lifted. Ellory slid the pillow beneath and then stood back as he returned Chelsea to her seat, lifting a brow pointedly at him when she saw his shoulder catch again and a wave she could actually name cross his handsome features: pain. His shoulder definitely hurt.

She really had to stop thinking about how hot he was. It wasn't helping at all. It wasn't breaking her resolution to think that the untouchable doctor rescue guy was hot, but it might lead her to other thoughts. It also wasn't her fault that his eyes looked like moss growing on the north side of a tree…deep, earthy green blending to brown. Was that hazel or still green if she looked…?

He was staring at her. It took a couple of nervous heartbeats for her to realize that it wasn't because he was a mind-reader.

Oh, yeah, she'd made the *Ahh, your shoulder does hurt* face at him. Because it did. He'd made the pain face, she'd made the *ahh* face, and now he was making the scowl face.

He didn't know she was sexually harassing him in her mind.

While she was trying to decide what she was supposed to be thinking, the man pivoted and walked straight through the archway leading to the rest of the resort.

Where was he going?

Crap.

She should have gone after the medicine by now.

He was going to disturb Mira, maybe make her leave the love nest and come down here.

"I'll be back in a few minutes, Chelsea," she babbled, and rushed after him in a flurry of flowing skirts and jingling bracelets, but she was too late to see which direction he'd headed. The elevators all sat on the bottom floor, where she was.

The man was a ninja. A cranky, frosty ninja.

Ducking into the stairwell, Ellory tilted her head to listen, hoping he wasn't outside earshot. The plush carpeting that blanketed the hallways and stairs made it hard to tell which way he'd gone. "Anson?" Tentative call unanswered, she stepped back into the hallway.

Okay, so he didn't go upstairs by any means, he wasn't heading for Mira and Jack's suite.

Mira's office? He did want antibiotics for Chelsea. She turned to the right, the shorter hallway, gathered her skirts to her knees so they'd stop the damned swirling, and ran.

No yelling. Yelling disturbed people. And every single person in the lodge, except for maybe the two upstairs sheltered from all this information overload in their love nest, were disturbed enough with the current situation.

One turn and then another, she reached the final hallway just in time to see Anson reach the end and turn toward the wall outside the clinic.

Before she could call out to him, he reared back and slammed his fist through the drywall.

The loud slam and cracking sound stunned her into staring for a couple of seconds. Long enough for the pain to reach his brain and make him pull his hand out of the hole while the other gripped his poor shoulder. If it hadn't hurt before he'd done that...

"You broke the wall," she muttered as she trotted forward, no longer running. She was not at all sure how to respond to this masculine and aggressive display. She didn't know anyone who hit walls when they were upset. Generally, she kept company with people who avoided violence. "I have the keys to Mira's office, we can get whatever you need for Chelsea. I've been keeping an inventory of supplies."

He finally turned to look at her and she saw it again—he wasn't just upset. She saw desolate, blind torture in his hollow eyes. It robbed her of any ability to speak.

Whatever she'd thought earlier about his motivation behind taking this kind of work, she was now certain: It had nothing to do with being an adrenaline junkie or any kind of fixation on the dream of being the big hero. This mattered to him. This *hurt* him.

She did the only thing she could, reached out and touched him. Tried to ground him here with her.

Contact of her palm with his stubble-roughened cheek sharpened his gaze, bringing him back from wherever he'd gone.

"Don't worry about the wall. We'll fix it. Everything will be okay." She whispered words meant to soothe him.

It took him a few seconds, but his brows relaxed and he nodded, looking down at the bloody knuckles on his hand and then at the wall. "That was pretty stupid. She's going to give me hell, isn't she?" He mustered a smile while simultaneously pulling his head back from her hand.

He didn't want her touching him… Okay. It's not like they really knew one another, and some people just didn't like to be touched.

It wasn't about her. It wasn't judgment on her.

Ellory pulled her thoughts away from the vulnerable nerve he'd accidentally struck and played along, faking a grin with her tease. "You have no idea. She's going to make you cry like a baby."

His smile was equally slight, but it was a start. And it reminded her of where she should make him focus. Sobering, she reached for his hand but didn't touch him, a request, open palms. "Can I see it?"

Okay, that might've been a test.

She'd been rejected more times in her life than any person ought to be—it wasn't anything new to her—but the second she'd found out that he was a doctor he'd become her partner in dealing with this and keeping Mira out of it. She needed him to actually connect with her and be her partner in it. And a good person didn't abandon her partner when he was hurting.

When he placed his large, bloody-knuckled hand in hers, her relief was so keen she had to fight the urge to squeeze and wind her fingers in his. He didn't shun her. Recoiling was about something else. He didn't find her lacking.

Nice skin, and considering she hadn't had any male contact since she'd come back from Peru it wasn't surprising that she wanted to relish the contact a little bit.

She forced herself to examine his knuckles before he caught on, paying careful attention to the cracked and rapidly swelling skin. "Can you move your fingers for me?"

He made a small sound as he got his fingers going, but his fingers moved smoothly at the knuckle, despite the swelling. "Well, we both know that it's an old wives' tale that you can't move something that's broken. Can't know for sure that it's not, but it looks good. Sorry, have to do this…"

Still holding his injured hand for support, she stroked her fingers over the abused skin, just firmly enough to feel the structure. She knew it hurt, he stopped breathing until she stopped touching it. "Don't think it's broken. Everything feels intact. Could be some hairline fracture, though. Guess we'll have to take a wait-and-see approach on this, along with poor Chelsea's toes."

Breathing resumed, and he pulled his hand back, nodding. "I don't think it's broken either, but I'm a fan of X-ray…"

"Come on. Let's get this cleaned up, then we'll get Chelsea's medicine into her, and I'll go and tell Mira what's going on so she can join the fun later. While the storm is here, you two will keep watch over our patient guests in shifts so she can have time with Jack and you can have some rest. Welcome to your first rotation at Silver Pass Blizzard Clinic, Dr. Graves."

"Time with Jack?" he asked, as she turned toward the door.

Ellory fished the keys from her coat pocket, unlocked the door and stepped inside, flipping on one set of lights as she went. "The past six months have been really hard for Mira, not that she'd admit it to anyone. Her fiancé was a louse. They broke up and the universe rewarded her for choosing to take care of herself."

"Jack from the avalanche, or do you mean her reward is having to do jack-all?"

Ellory peered at him. "Have you never heard the name Jack before?"

"I have and I've met a guest called Jack. But it's also a noun or an adjective." He followed her into the clinic. "Your manner of speaking is unusual. I'm looking for landmarks."

She decided not to comment on that—he didn't seem like a big talker and she had jobs before her. She talked strangely. She dressed wrong. Blah-blah-blah.

"I've been making notes of the supplies I took to the lobby. We'll just write down whatever we need, I'll go tell Mira and you can get the medicine for Chelsea. We should probably start charts for everyone too, but since your hand looks like hell, you tell me what you want it to say and I'll do the writing."

Anson followed her, enjoying the floral wake. The tropical scent reminded him she'd said something about Peru earlier. "Were you on a medical mission before you came here?"

She unlocked the drug cabinet and opened the doors, then flipped on a light above it and pointed at the bottles to direct his attention. "Medical mission? Oh, no. You mean in Peru. No, I was at a…" She looked sidelong at him, her expression growing wary. "I was at an ayahuasca retreat."

The word was familiar somehow, but between the pain in his hand, the pain in his shoulder and the headache he'd been nursing since he'd decided to turn the group around he couldn't place it. "I know I should know what that is, but it's eluding me."

"It's a place you go to have…" She stumbled along, clearly hedging and not really wanting to tell him.

People who avoided a direct answer had something to

hide, either because it embarrassed them or they expected disapproval. Which was when he remembered what ayahuasca was. "Ayahuasca is a hallucinogen, isn't it?"

Her sigh confirmed it. "It's not like LSD or hard drugs. It's a herbal and natural way of expanding your consciousness. I went there for a spirit quest under the care of a shaman—someone who knows about use of the plant and how to make the decoction properly. Someone who could help me understand everything I needed to know beforehand. And before you say anything, I'm not a drug user. I don't smoke anything. I only drink alcohol once a year— champagne on New Year's with Mirry. And nothing else remotely dodgy the rest of the year." As she spoke, her volume increased, along with the tension between her brows. "My body is a freaking temple, Judgy McGravedigger."

Anson lifted both hands, trying to put the brakes on the situation before she got really angry. Obviously he'd hit a nerve, she'd gone from quiet and somewhat babbly to angry because he'd called it a hallucinogen. "I'm not judging, but I am curious. And I agree your body is a temple."

Smooth.

When she turned back to her task he focused on the cabinet again and the array of medicines, and changed the subject. "Well stocked."

She went with it and didn't comment on his completely unacceptable remark about her body. "Mirry's a planner. She likes to be prepared for anything. She's always been good like that, never lets anyone down." A clipboard hung inside the cabinet, but where he'd expected to see an inventory sheet had been clipped a single piece of notebook paper, a list of supplies in a scrolling, extravagant script. She picked it up and began writing again.

Mirry? Always been?

Ellory wasn't a nurse…

Sister? "Are you Ellory Dupris?" Anson put the two

names together as he plucked one bottle of antibiotics from the shelf and set it on her clipboard so she could get a good look at the spelling and dose of medication.

"Ellory Du…? Oh, no. My name is Ellory Star."

She scribbled down the medicine then put the bottle into a little plastic basket. "You look for any other medicines, I'm going to get the supplies to clean your knuckles up." Before she headed away she turned back to him with a little pinch between her brows. "I'm sorry I made fun of your name. It wasn't nice. But in my defense it's kind of a terrible name. You should change it. Pick something more positive."

Pick something? "You picked Star, didn't you?"

"Yep."

Okay… He'd think about that later. "You do work here, though."

"Licensed massage therapist, which is my primary occupation, I guess. I've completed training and passed boards to be a physiotherapy assistant in Texas, but I haven't done any office work on it or taken boards here. The closest I came was a mission where the leader had back trouble and I helped her with the daily exercises her actual treatment prescribed…helped her handle being out in the field," she answered, fishing a badge from under her sweater and answering the question that he'd been working toward.

Anticipating. She really was perceptive. And the occupations fit. But then again, she could've said artist, pagan priestess, or tambourine player and he would've believed her. So, a massage therapist who called the owner's daughter and resort doctor 'Mirry.'

He plucked another medication from the cabinet, the mildest prescription-level pain medicine Mirry…Dr. Dupris…had in stock, and put it on the clipboard. "I put another medicine there for pain for Chelsea. Frostbite pain is monstrous."

Shrugging out of his coat, he pushed his sleeves up and stepped over to the sink to wash his hands, paying special attention to the puffy and bloody knuckles. He gave his fingers a few more slow flexes. Burning. Tenderness. But no bone pain. He knew about bone pain, just as he knew about frostbite pain. So she was right, even without having that information at her disposal. Good eye.

"Oh, my God, that's all you..."

He turned away from the sink, hand still under the water. "What's all me?"

"I was hoping that the coat was puffier than it seems to be."

He briefly considered not asking her for clarification, but he needed all the information he could get to keep up in conversation with this woman. "Why were you hoping my coat was puffy?"

"You're seriously beefy. Shoulders a mile wide, muscled. It's going to make working on you hard. I was hoping that some of that was your gear, your coat...I've got pretty strong hands and upper body, but you're going to be a tough case." She'd put a tray on the table, an array of antiseptics, gauze, tapes and ointments on it, and then went to write the medicine on her special clipboard.

"No, I won't. I don't need to be worked on." He didn't mention the compliment. Best ignore that attraction she'd all but said was mutual.

"How's it feeling?"

Good. She wasn't going to push the subject. "Nothing broken but the wall and my self-control. Bruised. Some abrasions..." He dried his hands on paper towels and wandered toward the table. "Maybe a mild sprain." He'd hit the wall hard.

"After you give the medicine to Chelsea, I want you on my table."

"Ellory, I don't need it."

"Suffering for no reason doesn't make you tough, it makes you stupid." She made a noise he could only consider a verbal shrug, "Your shoulder needs working on. If you want that thing to heal up so you can get back out there to find Jude when the snow lets up, let me help you."

He should've seen that coming. Her vocation was one hundred percent hands on, and from what he could tell by having observed her, she was on a mission to take care of the world.

The idea had some appealing qualities. Not the least of which the prospect of having her hands on his body… She might be dressed like a crazy person, considering the season and latitude, and conversing with her might be like running a linguistic obstacle course, but strangely neither of those things made her unappealing. And neither did the revelation about her spirit quest.

But he didn't really deserve comfort, and it was possible that his shoulder would calm down on its own in a little while.

"Maybe later. I should stick around the lobby. Keep a watch on them and the weather."

"Have you seen the radar? The storm is going to be with us for a while, hours and hours. We'll leave one of the radios with your people in the lobby and they can call us if…" The lights flickered, stopping her flow of words and her hands. When the power steadied and stayed on, she continued, "We're going to lose electricity."

"Maybe. We should see about making preparations, on the off chance…"

"It's not an off chance, Anson. It happens in every bad storm that hits the pass. Summer. Winter. Doesn't matter what kind of storm. It's not the whole town, but the lines to the lodge are dodgy, always breaking or going out for some reason. Tree limbs. High winds. Accumulation of heavy snow or ice…"

"I thought you were just in Peru."

"And before that Haiti. And before that the Central African Republic. Before that Costa Rica. But I was born and raised in Silver Pass. I needed to come home after my retreat, and Mira offered me a place to work. I have a history with the lodge. I know what I'm talking about. Nothing ever changes here. The power *will* go out."

"What does a massage therapist do in those places?"

"Dig ditches. Build dams. Distribute food, clothing, or whatever the mission is. And I help at the end of the day when people are worn out and hurting from all the manual labor." She disappeared into the office, and after some mucking around in there came out with a file folder, some forms, and another clipboard. "And there have been a few projects where I ended up with the same project leader, and I think she took me along as much to help keep her on her feet as to help with the actual project."

She left him to clean and dress his hand and made some notes in Chelsea's chart.

She'd grown up at the lodge, which explained why she was on such intimate terms with the owners. "You knew Dr. Dupris growing up?"

"Yes, and before you dig further she's my best friend. I love her more than anyone else in the whole world and if I'm upsetting you by making you help with the skiers, or making you let me help you, you're just going to have to get over it. She's having some much-needed downtime, and I'm going to take care of her people. Right now you're one of them, Dr. Graves. So suck it up, get the medicine into Chelsea and meet me at the massage therapy room. It's three doors down. There's a sign." She locked the drug cabinet and then turned and tossed her keys to him.

He instinctively caught them with his right hand, and regretted it. The combination of flying metal hitting his throbbing palm and the quick jerk of his arm tweaking his shoulder doubled the pain whammy that followed.

"Fine." Not fine. Annoyed. But as annoying as it was, she had a point, and if she could help, he'd make use of her.

"Lock the door when you leave. And turn off the lights. No wasting fossil fuels."

At least she didn't gloat.

CHAPTER FOUR

WHEN ELLORY KNOCKED on Mira's door, she wondered if she would be interrupting something she didn't want to interrupt.

Not usually one to be shy about sex, Ellory could only blame her squeamishness on the fact that being around Anson was making her think naughty thoughts, and now she was acutely aware that she wasn't allowed to follow through with them.

She hadn't specifically said her resolution not to date included no hook-ups, but she was trying to break that cycle as she'd spent her adult life sublimating her desire for love with lots of sex. Safe, sterile sex. So in the spirit of the resolution it had to include hooking up with handsome, inexplicably surly, dog-owning doctors—because Anson and his mile-wide shoulders were the best Fling Contender in Silver Pass.

She scrambled out of the stairwell on the top floor, already avoiding the elevators so she didn't get trapped when the power went off, and jogged down the corridor to Mira's Stately Pleasure Dome.

In the plus column, Anson would never want to date her, so her Stupid Resolution wasn't in danger. He'd already remarked on finding her strange—unsurprising as most people who didn't move in her circles found her odd. Add to that him now thinking she was someone who would use the spirit quest as a reason to go to the rainforest and take drugs…

But none of that came close to touching the biggest block: the anguish she'd seen in his eyes earlier didn't leave room for much thought of carousing.

Even if sex was a really good way to generate heat when the power cut out during a raging blizzard.

Also? Sheer entertainment value. Something else she'd ignore from here on.

None of that helped her figure out how to talk to Mira without being afraid that she was interrupting something special. More special than any sex Ellory had ever had… another reason she was weirded out about it.

Mira had found love. Real love… It wouldn't just be sex Ellory interrupted, it'd be making love—which was probably sacred.

Or, as she'd like to think of it, making wild, reality-shattering love so potent it could mess with physics, the future, the past, and maybe illuminate all those dark places in her heart where negative thoughts and bad feelings liked to hide.

She'd been looking hard for that for the past decade, but it was elusive.

She stopped in front of the carved white door of Number Five's fancy suite and did the unthinkable: She knocked. "I'm sorry, Mirry, I have to talk to you."

The sound of stumbling and doors closing preceded the door opening, and her decidedly disheveled best friend appeared in the frame. "Hey. Is everything okay?"

Bedhead. That glazed look that came with passion that's been unexpectedly shut down. She'd definitely interrupted love…

"I'm so sorry. I just want to keep you informed about what is going on, and there's some stuff. But I want you to know that I'm handling it, and Anson too. I'm not handling Anson…well, I am a little. But not in a sexy way. I'm still being faithful to my resolution." Ellory stopped talking. That's not what she was supposed to talk about. "The blizzard."

Mira, gaze sharpening with understanding, unsuccessfully tried to hide a smile smug enough that Ellory knew she'd be getting teased to hell and back if Mira weren't likely in a hurry to get back to Jack. "Good to know you're handling Anson. What about the blizzard?"

"We've got missing people. Person. One. The others, the rescue team got back. They were suffering moderate hypothermia but we've got them warmed up and are keeping a close eye on all four of them. One of them has either stage one or stage two frostbite on her toes, Anson said. Did you know he's a doctor too? He's been treating her. We went and got medicine from the clinic, and I've written down—"

"I'll get dressed…"

"No!" Ellory grabbed her arm to keep her from getting away. "It's okay, really. We're doing great…except for the missing man, and you can't help with that right now. One of the guests who was with the rescued group tried to get back to the lodge on his own, and he didn't make it back before the storm, or yet, and they weren't able to locate him before the storm got too dangerous and the visibility too bad. It's impossible to go out right now. I knew you'd want to know, but there's nothing you can do about it right now. Later or tomorrow, if you want to come check on everyone, that'd be great. Anson is tired. I'd feel bad making him do like a seventy-two-hour shift or something."

"Where are they?"

"Still in the lobby in front of the blazing fire, but we're relocating them to the fireplace suites. The lights flickered so I figure we're going to lose the power and then the central heat will go…so I'm corralling everyone into the fire-place suites, employees too. Doubling up occupancy and stuff. Everything is as under control as it can be, there's nothing else you could do. Well, unless you know how to fix drywall."

"What happened to the drywall?" Mira, unlike every-one else in her world, didn't have any trouble keeping up with Ellory's mind—which could be counted on to bear off in another direction without warning during pretty much every conversation. But especially those fraught with emo-tion and where something unpredictable loomed.

"Anson punched it. There's a hole…"

"This isn't sounding all that under control, Elle."

"I know it sounds all kinds of chaotic, but that's because I'm condensing hours and hours into a few minutes. He's sorry about the drywall, but he's very upset and worried about Jude."

Mira nodded slowly, taking it all in. She didn't even have to ask who Jude was, she just kept up. "The lost skier…"

"I brought you this." Ellory fished a spare radio from her pocket and handed it over. "I know you'll want to be con-tacted super-fast if there is an emergency. They're all tuned to the lodge emergency channel, and they'll be spread out among the patient rooms and rescuers, so anyone in need of help can get it fast when the power goes out."

Ellory's faith in Mira was boundless, and generally that faith extended to the confidence Mira would mirror her own faith. Not many people did that. No one, actually. Not right now, at least. But for a few seconds while Mira con-sidered the radio in her hands, Ellory's faith wavered. "I can do it, Mira. I won't let you down. I promise."

"I know. I know you can. I was just thinking about whether I'm taking advantage…"

Relief warmed her and she relaxed, a smile returning. "You're not taking advantage of anyone, except maybe

Jack." Ellory shook her head, covering her friend's hand as she teased. "And don't worry about the hole in the wall. I'll get Anson all patched up and then I'll make sure that he fixes the wall or gets billed for putting his fist through it when everything is up and running. And speaking of running, I need to. I have him on my table."

"Anson?"

"He hurt his shoulder."

"With the wall…"

"Well, it was hurt before that. But he made it worse with the wall." Ellory smiled and gathered up her skirts. "Don't worry, I'm just going to work on his shoulder. Not breaking my Stupid Resolution! You're still losing this year, Dupris!" And since the wing was deserted and she wanted Jack to hear, Ellory bellowed, "But that's okay, your Karmic Love-Jackpot Sex Machine Jack sounds like a good consolation prize!" She backed down the hallway, smiling as Mira's cheeks went pink.

Karmic Love-Jackpot Sex Machine was a much better nickname than Number Five, even if it took forever to say. Any man should be proud to bear that title.

Anson unlocked the door to the massage room and stepped inside, flipping on the lights. It was warm in there. Warmer than anywhere else he'd been in the lodge, except rooms that had *steam* in the name.

He pulled the top of his snow suit off again and let it pool at his waist, then took a seat while waiting. Like everywhere else, it was a deeply comfortable room, with plush chairs, stacks of fresh towels, a line of oil bottles and lotions…and the lingering scent of sandalwood and eucalyptus. A hedonist paradise.

Luxury. Comfort. And he was getting a massage when he should be out looking for the lost skier… No, nothing at all wrong with that.

Ellory had a point about him being in top shape for when the snow let up, but he was wound so tight it'd be a miracle if she could get him to relax at all.

He even felt guilty about wanting to relax a little. His rational mind knew how big this storm was, that if they were lucky it would be over in a day, and that he couldn't spend all the time until then on watch for a break. There'd be no break until it was over. Resting and taking care of the patients until then was the correct course of action.

He'd be doing something, but he wanted to do something more active.

And doing anything kept him from having too much time to think about what the man was going through while *he* was warm, safe, and…resting.

He stood and headed for a shelf with candles. Light the candles, save time.

He also lit a stick of incense propped in a holder, because that probably had some kind of peace-making mojo she would insist he needed.

When he stumbled over a remote control, he turned on music from a well-hidden stereo system.

By the time he'd gotten everything powered up, the door opened and Ellory walked in, pulling back her long, wavy, sun-kissed locks as she did, and twisting them into some kind of knot at the nape of her neck.

"So you do want a massage." She smiled. "Got the candles going for mood lighting, the incense, the music…"

"I was helping. Speeding things up." And now he was making excuses. He shut up.

"Yes, you were helping, but I'm pretty sure there's only one lightning-fast method of instantly relaxing." She closed the door, locked it, set her radio on the counter and began stripping. Off came the coat. Then her sweater…which left her wearing a small white T-shirt that had risen up enough to give him a view of the curve of smooth hip to waist before her arms came back down and she was once more covered. "And while that was completely inappropriate, it was payback for earlier. Don't worry, we're not doing that."

Despite seeing him at less than his best, and witnessing him put his fist through the wall—which he really wasn't proud of—the little eco-princess was flirting with him. He smiled, felt it, thought better of it and stopped. No wonder the woman liked to go to tropical places. Golden, shapely, and not at all what the media would classify a beach body… in the best way.

"Why are you getting undressed, then?"

It might have been years since he had a massage from anyone other than a lover, but he was sure that the only person who got naked was the one getting ministered to.

"I don't want to get oil on my clothes." She tossed the sweater onto the couch. "I'll keep my skirt on and the thermals beneath, but the sweater's sleeves are baggy and tend to drag. Oil would ruin it." A brief pause and she gestured to the opposite corner of the room. "There's a changing room through there, just strip down and wrap a towel around your waist. Underpants on or off, up to you. And I'll get…"

What she was saying registered and he shook his head, moving to sit in a chair, "I don't need to change. It's just my shoulder."

"Okay. Take off your shirt, then. And your shoes. You're the only one who didn't have your toes checked when you came in."

"I don't need my toes checked," he muttered, that directive enough to pull him out of the fantastic place his mind was going. Perfect little beach body didn't need to gawk at his ugly feet. But now that he'd seen what was beneath the baggy sweater, he wanted to see what was beneath the flowing skirts.

"Shirt," Ellory repeated, done arguing with him for now.

She'd work on his shoulder, get him to relax, and then get him on the table. She couldn't fix his shoulder without having full access to his back. It was all connected. Not that she was going to bring that up with him right now. He was a doctor, he knew full well how anatomy and muscles worked together. He was just being a pain in the butt, and there was no reasoning with a pain in the butt. Logic didn't win in an emotional kerfuffle and after seeing his display of testosterone earlier she could definitely say he was having an emotional kerfuffle he didn't want to talk about.

Out of the corner of her eye she could see him complying. Arms up, material moving... She didn't look yet. He may have lit incense, and there might be enough essential oils in this room to gag an apothecary, but with his suit open and body heat escaping, all Ellory could smell was Eau d'Yummy Masculinity.

All she needed was to start undressing him with her eyes. That would lead to her undressing him with her hands, and then her Stupid Resolution would be shot.

Distract him. She should talk about something.

"So, you ever been south of the equator?" And that sounded like another come on. Because he'd turned her hormones on.

"No, and I've never done drugs with a shaman either."

"It's not like that."

Eucalyptus. That was a manly smell, and it would overpower the warm, salty awesomeness pouring off him. She snatched up the bottle of oil, a couple of towels and headed his way. "Do you want to lie on the table?"

"No."

She rolled her eyes, and didn't even try to hide it from him. He countered with a brow lift. "You can reach my shoulder from here." He did slide forward in the chair so he was sitting at the front edge at least.

In an effort to save his snow suit from the oil, she shook

out two towels, draping one over his lap and tucking the other into the wad of insulated material at his waist, then stepped between his legs and reached for the oil.

"The skin on your shoulder isn't bruised, unless it's such a deep bruise that it hasn't come out yet. Is that the case?"

"Doubt it."

"Okay, how did you injure it?"

"Lifting Max. He is good at his job but he doesn't have the greatest problem-solving skills. Got stuck, couldn't jump out…"

"So you picked up a huge dog that probably weighs more than me." She rolled her eyes again. "Next time, just get his front feet or something. Picking up half a dog is less likely to injure you than going whole dog."

"He's my dog. I don't like to see him scared or in pain. I'm a little sore, it's no big deal. I'd do it over again."

"Fine. Anyway, it doesn't look like it's more than muscle strain." She drizzled the oil on and spread it around, carefully avoiding looking at his face. Looking a man in the eye was like challenging him, and she wanted him to feel comfortable, not put on the spot. Besides, if he was feeling as vulnerable about this Jude situation as she knew he was, then he wouldn't want her seeing it. "What should we talk about?"

Anson shook his head minutely, but didn't answer right away. Not until she'd started working her thumbs into the corded muscle on his shoulder. "Your spirit quest." He grunted the words.

Ellory didn't particularly want to talk about that either, but a small amount of explanation could keep him from thinking she'd just gone down there for some excuse to 'do drugs with a shaman.'

"I needed to try and figure something out, and I believe we're our own best healers. Your mind and your heart can heal you if you let them. I didn't want to see a psychiatrist and tell her things I already know, and have her give me some pharmaceutical that might do more harm than good, a pill to dull and pollute. I wanted to get through it on my own."

"Did you?" he asked, and did honestly sound interested. She didn't hear the censure she'd expected. And to his credit he hadn't yet asked what her issue was, maintaining some respectful distance from that subject.

"Not all the way. But I figured out that I needed to come home to get right. It gave me a starting point, and it also filled me with wonder for the universe… It's amazing that the earth gives us plants that allow for this kind of experience. I wish I understood better, but there's too much going on when you drink it. The shaman said it detaches your consciousness from your body, which sounds all woo-woo and like astral projection—something I'm not sure I buy. But I'm glad I went, despite having more questions than answers. Sometimes the biggest part of solving a problem is figuring out what the right question even is."

A soft pained sound escaped when her thumbs hit a particularly knotted area. He tried to cover it with words. "Did you go alone?"

"No. I went with my last boyfriend." She tried to ignore how final that sounded, like the last one she'd ever have and from here on out was a lifetime of loneliness. "He wanted to learn to hold those kinds of rituals so he could lead people in their own quests up here in the States, some retreat in Nevada he wants to work at. But I don't feel like his heart was in it for the right reasons. He was after money, not to help people. That's no kind of cause. So I left him there and came home. Been trying to work on my quest alone since I got back." She paused long enough for him to look up at her, establish fleeting eye contact, and asked, "Do you want to talk about Jude?"

Anson frowned. "There's nothing to say. He's still out there, and I'm getting a massage…"

"So you think you're letting him down."

"Of course I let him down." The admission came through gritted teeth, which either meant her thumbs were causing enough pain to make him grit his teeth or the situation was.

She stopped the deep kneading there and stepped forward until his head touched her chest. "Rest against me, I'm going to rub down your back, stretch those muscles out some. That will make it easier to work on your shoulder."

"That plan has me pushing my face into your breasts." He tilted his head back to look up at her as he said it, but his teeth stopped clenching, which she could only consider progress.

"Consider that a bonus." She smiled, "But if you ask for a happy ending when your shoulder is feeling better, I may punch you somewhere you wouldn't want me to punch you."

He smirked. "That could be anywhere. I'm not a fan of being punched."

"Just of punching. Which is how I know you're feeling worse than you let on."

He leaned forward, burying his face in the valley of her cleavage, and sighed. Still not wanting to talk about it.

"No motor-boating while you're down there either," she said, trying to draw him out of it a little. And it was easy to flirt with him. She hadn't seen a real smile from him yet and it surprised her how badly she wanted to.

Her teasing was rewarded with a little chuckle she felt a rumble through her chest to her belly, and his arms relaxed, elbows on his knees, his hands lightly cupping the outsides of her thighs. The innocent touch set off a wash of good tingles more powerful than his face on her chest. She'd long considered the back of the thighs an erogenous zone…

The tension in his spine lessened. Better. An even better sign that she'd be able to get him to smile later, when she could see it.

Another drizzle of oil and she pressed her thumbs into the muscle knotting the back of his neck, and stroked down along his spine, making little tight circles with the pads of her thumbs when she encountered a knottier area on his spine.

"How are you working on your quest?"

He still avoided the too-personal question, but kept her talking.

"Meditation. Exercise. Aromatherapy."

He laughed for real this time.

She was going to choke him. "Oh, hush, Doctor Man. You know that smell is one of the most powerful memory triggers?"

"So you're trying to recover a memory?" he asked, the chuckle fading from his voice.

"I don't know," she whispered, now that he'd started circling the subject she didn't really want to talk about. But lying was equally distasteful to her. She thought for a bit and tried to tell the truth while not exposing her tender underbelly. "This will probably sound all depressing, and I'm not depressed—I just haven't really been happy for a long time. Not truly happy or content. Doesn't matter what I do, even the highs I've gotten from volunteering and doing good things don't do much or last very long any more. It's started to feel like penance, and I don't know why." Which was part of it, but it still left her feeling vulnerable. She'd been hiding this from everyone.

Anson leaned back again, putting enough space between them to look her in the eyes.

Exposed. She felt exposed the way he looked at her, and aware of an unpleasant cold feeling in her chest. She looked away. "You want realigning."

* * *

Anson couldn't read her expression, but he knew a thing or two about living a penance-filled existence. There was such vulnerability to her honesty that it hit something inside him and made him want to help, to fix whatever was making her unhappy. She put on a good show. Had she not said those words to him, he might never have guessed.

"I need realigning," he repeated, no longer sure he was speaking of his spine.

"Right here." She pressed on the muscle that had seriously bunched up just below his shoulder blades, the pain proving her point. "T7 and T8 vertebrae. I can fix it if you get on the table."

She wanted to help him, and he'd let her. Maybe it would help her feel better too. "Fine, but I'm leaving the thermals on."

Her smile reappeared, though now he didn't know how real it was and how much was for show, even though he believed she wanted to help. She stepped back, pulling the towels with her and giving him room to move around. A pause to remove his boots, then he stretched out face down on the padded vinyl table.

Before he could protest she swung one leg over his waist and he was caught by warm thighs and an overwhelming desire to roll over. Her small hands pressed into the muscle on either side of his spine, walking up and down a few steps until the vertebrae reseated with a loud crack.

Task done, she patted his back, climbed down, and left him thankful she couldn't see what the intimate position had done to him.

It wasn't Ellory's practice to molest people she had on her table, but the feel of his solid heat between her legs made her breathless. She grit her teeth to keep her mouth shut, struggling to control the rapid breathing from the surge of hormones.

No matter that he'd spent the better part of ten minutes with his face pillowed on her breasts, he didn't seem bothered by her straddling, as she was. Although she wanted to talk to him about the situation that had put his hand going through a wall, maybe talking should wait... She continued working, tried to ignore the glide of the firm male flesh beneath her hands, and focused on the task.

By the time his arm was moving easily in the socket, the muscles worked to pliancy, he'd fallen asleep. She heard the slow, rhythmic breathing and ducked under the table to where his face perched in the padded donut-shaped headrest.

This happened a lot. Get someone to relax deeply enough, they fell asleep. And that was when they weren't exhausted and worried from all the hours spent in the horrid climate and stressful conditions. He needed sleep so she wouldn't wake him until he was needed.

Moving to the end of the bed, she pulled his socks off and swapped the oil for some lotion to rub into his tired feet, which was when she noticed them. Missing toes, two on one foot and one on another. He had no pinky toes. Her heart skipped.

Frostbite pain is monstrous.

His words came back to her, brought tears with them that closed her throat. He knew that pain. No wonder...

She slowly bent his leg at the knee so she could see the top of his foot, and get a better look at the damage.

The scar extended far up the top of his foot, stretched out, pale and thin. An old scar. A very old scar, considering how far growth had caused it to migrate from his toes.

He'd been a child when it had happened.

CHAPTER FIVE

ANSON FELT SOMETHING touching his feet and snapped awake. Lifting and turning to look over his shoulder at the woman at his feet was harder, his movements sluggish and stiff. "God, what did you do to me?"

"Relaxed you." Ellory laid his leg back on the table and kept one hand on his foot. He wished she'd move away from them. "Your muscles will be a little slow to respond for a few minutes. You should drink a lot of water today too."

"Water?"

"Toxins."

He shook his head, not awake enough to run the mental obstacle course yet. Instead, he concentrated on lifting up and rolling over until he was sitting on the table.

"Toxins in your muscles get released with deep tissue massage. You should drink lots of water, flush them out. Or tomorrow you might have some mild flu-like symptoms."

"I thought the massage was supposed to make me feel better."

"How's your shoulder?"

Frowning, he tentatively lifted his arm and rolled it around in the socket to check. No catch. Sore still, but no catch meant no shooting pains, which was better than it had been.

He didn't answer her. Waking on the table he'd had no intention of climbing onto had left him feeling disgruntled and angry. And, pushy thing that she was, she'd had to get at his feet even though he'd told her they were fine...

"Frostbite pain is monstrous?" She pointed at the missing toes and looked up at his face.

He nodded. "You don't have to take care of my feet, you know. You can see there's no frostbite there."

"The scar has stretched and moved back from the toes."

He nodded again. She was already getting there. He'd just see how far she could take the logical path without his assistance.

"How old were you? Still in elementary school, I'd say. Unless you still had really tiny feet in high school and they only recently exploded like peppermint in your herb garden."

Anson assumed that meant peppermint grew fast. The fastest way to get her to get off this subject was probably to answer her. "Yes." It was an answer.

And judging by the way her eyes grew damp, it was enough of one.

How the hell had this gotten so out of his control?

"Socks," she said suddenly, and sniffed, then popped into the changing room for a moment. When she returned it was with thick cotton socks, which she pulled apart, threading her thumbs into the toe of one and beginning to work it onto his right foot. "Your feet wanted different socks, and you shouldn't neglect your feet in this weather. Doubt you have any to change into. I usually put these on my patients when they have achy feet and want a wintergreen treatment. Thick warm socks while the rest of your body pains are getting worked on, it's nice."

Anson let her get one sock on, since she'd already started and he was moving with decided sluggishness, and then moved his feet out of her reach and held his hand out for the other sock. "You don't have to take care of me, Ellory."

"You're sad. I don't want you putting your fist through anything else."

"I'm not going to. I'm not sad. The fist through the wall did what I needed."

"Which was?"

"Pressure release. And it helped."

"Your anger maybe, but not your hand or your shoulder. And it didn't make you feel better about being inside and warm while Jude is out there. If you need to talk about it, you can talk. We're in this together, and you're helping me with our patient guests, so I want to help you too. Plus..." She stepped away from him and grabbed the sweater she'd discarded earlier, not finishing her sentence.

"Plus?"

"I don't know." She pulled the sweater down over her head, untangled her hair from the knot she'd twisted it into, and let it fall around her shoulders. "This."

Before he could figure out what she was up to, she'd stepped over to the table, wrapped her arms around his middle and squeezed. She cared, just as she had cared for Chelsea. But it felt good, gentle and warm, and gave him an overwhelming desire to bury his nose in the hair atop her head.

He resisted by tugging her back just enough that she looked up at him. The look in her eyes was anything but pity. Suddenly, all he wanted was to taste her. For a few seconds the world receded—he gave in to instinct and covered her mouth with his own. A small surprised sound tickled against his lips, but she tilted her head at the first brush of his tongue against her lips, opening her mouth to him.

Her scent might've been floral, but her mouth was sweet and fruity, just the barest hint of tartness that made him think of berries. Ripe, juicy, and summer-sweet.

And this was winter.

The disparity seeped through the subconscious need to consume her, and he lifted his head, reluctantly breaking the kiss.

Her dark brown eyes were even more heated than her pink cheeks looked. Those lush lips parted, as moist and inviting as her quick, shallow breaths.

"No, no…" Ellory whimpered, when she realized he was backing away. Every inch of her screamed for more. One kiss would not violate her Stupid Resolution.

Neither would two kisses.

And if he kissed her again now it could still count as one.

Her hands slid up his torso until scruffy beard tickled her palms and she could urge his mouth back to hers.

His tongue stroked into her mouth and she let go of his cheeks and wound her arms around his neck, sagging closer, resting against him, chest to chest.

Strong arms came around her, catching her when every thrust of his tongue made her knees threaten to buckle.

A kiss more intoxicating than a keg.

"This is not good," he whispered against her lips, just as she was about to start tearing his clothes off.

She was confident enough to call him on that one. "Liar. It's better than good."

So much better it was impossible for her brain to begin comparing it to every other kiss in history, none of which had ever made her come close to losing control.

"Okay, not a good idea," he corrected, his voice holding a needy rasp that made her wonder how it'd feel against her ear with sexy whispers.

Which was definitely in the vicinity of violating her Stupid Resolution. "Yeah, maybe."

"Why are you still hugging me?"

She tilted her head and laid it on his good shoulder. "Because you need it. You're in pain and you're a good man. You're worried about..." She jerked her head back and looked up at him again, realization forming due to her mouth running wild again. Ruining everything.

"What?"

"You have a cause." She snatched her arms back and took two big steps back from the table.

"No, I don't."

"You're trying to make the world a better place," Ellory clarified, the realization making her exceedingly cranky.

"I am?"

"Yes, you rescue people from the winter! You have a driving goal! You have a mission in life!" Her stomach hurt. The man was definitely a danger to her Stupid Resolution, and her stupid quest and her stupid everything...

"You are such a strange little thing..."

He didn't get it!

"You're my type!" She pointed a finger at him. "And I'm not supposed to be dating!"

"I haven't asked you out, sweetheart."

And he didn't get it so much that he was joking around.

Ellory's cheeks had flamed to life when she'd surged away from the table, like she had just discovered she'd been kissing a big hairy spider. "This isn't 1957. Women can ask men out."

His joking eased her enough that some of the wariness left her eyes. She just seemed unreasonably irritated by the fact that he spent half the year helping people who got in trouble in the snow. Especially considering her activities prior to coming to this little special wintery haven had all been aimed at helping people.

He shouldn't rile her up more. He should put a lid on this situation, say whatever it was that would make her relax. But she'd hugged him, she'd rubbed his feet, and then she'd kissed him back… She was so insistent on taking care of everyone, it was kind of nice to see that she had an unreasonable side.

Donning his best flirting smile, he popped his brows up a couple times. "Are you asking me out, Ellory?"

"You're not listening! I can't date you. I have a resolution!"

"You have a resolution, and I'm jeopardizing it by having a cause—which I really don't think I have."

"Yes, you do. And, *yes*. That's… Well, no…" She took a breath, her mouth screwing up in a way he was probably not supposed to find cute. "Having a cause is my type, but that's not the only part of my type." A few seconds passed as she looked to the side, brows pulled together, thinking, thinking… "Never mind. It's just that you're very good looking, and you smell like sex and chocolate…and Sunday morning. And now you have a mission to help others. For a second all that messed up my brain."

He could sympathize—his brain felt equally scrambled. The difference was, he liked it. And he *really* shouldn't. Also, her description of his scent was probably the most outlandish and fantastic compliment he'd ever been given. That overt honesty charmed him as much as her manner of speaking amused him. He shouldn't be feeling this good. His job was unfinished and someone was out there waiting for the cavalry…

Remembering that took the spirit out of it for him.

"But the last piece is that you're like…a normal man."

"And you like weird men who want to be shamans." He filled in.

"I like men who would like me. And you aren't the kind of man who'd like me," she explained, and her declaration grew stronger with every version she repeated. "I'm not your type. So we would never date. You'd never date someone like me. So it's okay. It's okay! Everything is okay. Sorry. I don't process information quietly very well. It's kind of got to be out loud or it doesn't happen. I don't know why. Because I'm strange! Oh, thank all the gods."

Anson opened his mouth to ask what she was going on to decide that she was not his type but a hurried request for help crackled through the radio, a voice he recognized.

He grabbed the radio, "Go ahead, Duncan." The most experienced EMT on the team, Duncan led it during the warm months, but stepped aside in the winter when Anson was around with his miracle dog.

One of the rescued was having trouble breathing. He got the room number where the patients had all been relocated, pulled his snow suit on—it was the only clothing he had with him—stuffed his feet into his shoes and took off out the door. While he talked, Ellory blew out the candles, turned off the lights and grabbed her keys.

Anson made a note to rile her up again later when the power went out…that could serve as hours of entertainment. Ask a question, make a statement, and then just watch her start spitting out random words that would eventually make sense.

Conventional wisdom did say that to learn to speak a foreign language fast, submersion was the key.

The regular fireplace suites were all situated in the same place on the floor plan for each level of the lodge, blocks of four stacked up for several floors.

The patient guests had been split into two groups and settled in side-by-side suites on the second floor—the closest to ground level, which was taken with communal and recreation areas, like the clinic and therapy rooms. With the frostbite to her toes and Anson's ban on Chelsea walking, she couldn't go anywhere without a wheelchair or being carried, so it made sense to locate them close to the ground in the event that the power went out and there were no elevators working. Easier to carry or roll her up one set of stairs than five.

Anson said the gibberish names of two different medicines as they passed the office, and where to look, then left her as he took the stairs to get to the person in distress.

She hadn't written down the medicines. She'd have to do that. This inventory thing could get out of hand fast, and she couldn't let Mira down. His kiss had done a brain scramble on her. So much for resolutions. She hadn't even thought to protest when he'd gone all smoochy on her.

She was officially a weak-willed kiss pushover.

A kiss pushover who was obviously being given more responsibility than she should be.

Ellory had never been an important part of any medical team in a medical crisis before. The knowledge that the rest of Anson's crew was there helped her keep her cool, but her heart still pounded. If she failed to live up to people's expectations now, someone could die.

One of the orange-clad rescuers stood in the hallway, meeting her with an open door, which she rushed through. Anson was already at the window with Duncan and one of the patient guests, who was clinging to the windowsill, his head hanging out into the storm. Snow blew in around him, but even above the roar of the wind she could tell how labored his breathing was.

The group rescued consisted of two males and two females, one other couple, and with Chelsea's missing fiancé Jude still out in the wind, Chelsea was sharing the suite with Nate, brother to the other woman, and odd man out.

"He insists the cold air is easier to breathe," Duncan said, briefing Ellory on what was going on. They'd moved a chair to the sliding window so he could sit and breathe… but in Ellory's estimation it wasn't helping.

"Looks like that thing that happened with me last year," Duncan said, more to Anson than to her now.

How many years had Anson been doing this?

"Damage done to the respiratory system from the cold," Anson filled in, looking at Ellory's stash of medicines and supplies and then pointing to the inhaler she carried. "Pop the seals and shake it hard."

He listened to Nate's lungs again, leading him through breaths that were supposed to be deep but which ended up rasping and wheezing loudly.

"Had you been sick before you got here, Nate?" Anson asked, the concern in his eyes enough to worry Ellory. She prepped and shook the inhaler harder and faster.

When the man chose to nod rather than speak, she had a clue about how serious the situation was.

Questions flew about allergies, Nate answering with shakes and nods of his head. He couldn't do anything but try to breathe.

Did he have any allergies? Yes. Food? No. Medicine? Yes.

In less than a minute Anson had gotten enough info to feel safe about giving the man the inhaler. He'd also started preparing some kind of injection.

"Nate, Duncan is going to pull you back into the room. I want you to breathe out as much as you can, Ellory is going to puff the inhaler by your mouth and you breathe it in deeply."

Anson looked between her and Duncan, making sure they knew their jobs. She liked it that he didn't repeat himself, didn't give them any extra instructions, just trusted them to handle things. It might not be the right call for every situation, but even she could handle an inhaler.

On the count of three, they all stepped in. While Duncan supported most of Nate's weight, Ellory watched him breathe out, holding his gaze. When he'd gotten out as much as he could, she gave him two puffs of the inhaler as he struggled to breathe in. Anson pushed Nate's sleeve up and injected something into the man's triceps, which he then rubbed to disperse.

His skin was very pale, maybe even a little bit blue—another skin color she could add to the shades that terrified her, right after the shade of Chelsea's poor toes.

Anson flipped the cap closed and handed the needle to Ellory, turned Nate's chair and helped settle him back into it…still near the window but not with his head hanging out.

Long terrible seconds ticked as Anson listened to his chest again, coaching him through the breaths as they slowly began to come easier.

She found herself breathing deeply, trying to breathe for the poor man, and noticed Anson doing the same thing. A quick look around the room confirmed it. They all breathed slowly, deeply, in unison, five other sets of lungs trying to do the work of one who struggled to breathe. All worried. All invested. All hoping it helped somehow. She felt part of something good, like she did on her missions, and it was probably silly since all she'd done was be the gofer and puff an inhaler. Still, it felt good.

As Nate's breathing stabilized, everyone else's returned to normal… And that was what she had trouble letting go of. Not the drama and the fear of his fight for air but how for a few seconds all anyone had cared about was helping make Nate's world better. It didn't matter what kind of lifestyle these people led, they were still people. She didn't even have to wonder what her father would've wanted to happen in those seconds. He wouldn't have batted an eyelid if Nate had died. One less consumer, one less parasite devouring the planet while giving nothing back… She could almost hear the tirade.

Anson closed the window and came around, hand held out to Ellory. She put her hand in his, not thinking about what he wanted. It seemed like the natural thing to do. The warm squeeze of one hand, the other relieving her of the inhaler, cleared up what he wanted. Quickly, she let go of the medicine and Anson, and stepped back from the group.

"Respiratory infection?" she heard him ask Nate, who nodded. "If you're not completely over them, it's not a good idea to go out and exert yourself in the cold. Remember that."

CHAPTER SIX

FOR THE NEXT half-hour Ellory watched Anson listen to the lungs of the other patient guests, and then he made his crew breathe for him as well. He gave the same speech at least four times. Prolonged exposure to severe cold could damage nose, sinus, throat, and lungs when someone was healthy, let alone when they were getting over an infection or illness that had damaged them—as had been the case with Nate. She did very little but follow, watch, and listen.

Well, that and look the man over.

She wanted to kiss him again.

The world was coming apart at the seams, winter and wind and random acts of crazy nature, someone stuck out in it, someone's heart breaking, friends in anguish, and Ellory herself caught in a full-on lust-o-thon with the man who'd taken charge of keeping everyone alive.

The only thing saving her had been the dog. He'd joined their tour of rooms as soon as they'd stumbled over him, and now he kept her company.

She spent most of the time crouched beside the big black fuzzball, petting him and whispering to keep herself occupied. Noting the changes in the rooms. She hadn't been in the fireplace suites in a long time. They'd been remodeled since she'd last been there. They were a blend of the new and the old, modern classy mixed with the comforting classics. But everything was secondary to the fireplaces.

Max was fascinated with her opinion on the décor and the superiority of the lobby fireplace to the ones in these rooms. They were top of the line, the logs looked every bit the real thing, and the hidden burners fed by gas and flames that wound through the wood...but it wasn't the same.

He agreed, wood definitely was better. "You're right. I should probably do some research and find out which one is the worst for the environment. But if we're using a hominess scale rather than the Scoville scale—or is that just about how hot peppers are?"

Real fire and all, but it didn't smell the same. And it didn't talk to you, make comforting noises when the lights went out and the only thing to listen to was the wind.

Anson was saying something...talking treatment. More drugs, no doubt.

"What about the saunas?" Ellory snapped back into the conversation, standing in a room with just Anson, her buddy Max, and the last two members of his crew.

All of them looked at her.

"Steam is good for soothing the respiratory system." She shifted to one foot, half-afraid the people in the room were going to give her hell for even suggesting something natural compared to whatever came from a pharmacy and had the backing of the FDA. "It'd bring in moisture to what's been dried out. And we could put some therapeutic oils into the mist. Maybe some eucalyptus and rosemary... stuff that's anti-inflammatory and good for decongestion?"

Anson smiled at her but shook his head—nicely contradicting himself. "It's not a bad idea, the steam and oils actually sound quite good if you've got the quality oils for it. But moving them into the sauna might put more stress on their systems than would be beneficial. It can dehydrate and they're all probably more than a little dehydrated as it is." He looked at the other two. "Are we pushing liquids?"

A small conversation occurred about drinks and Ellory cut back in.

"We could just do it in a bowl and tent a towel over, a breathing treatment without getting everyone awkwardly naked together in the sauna. And I have good oils. Nothing synthetic, of course."

The lights flickering again had everyone looking up, breath held to see if they went out for good.

"Unless the power goes out and we can't effectively heat water," she muttered, more to herself than anyone else, and suddenly felt chilled by the prospect.

The power would go out. It wasn't even a question of whether or not it would happen, just when. With a little shiver she wrapped her arms around herself and rubbed her upper arms through the coat, which just wasn't pulling its weight heat-wise. Though to be fair, it was probably impossible to keep her body temperature as high as she was used to having it with the clothing she had to choose from.

When the lights firmed up and stayed on, Anson continued his organization. "Get your helpers to start heating more water, and go find something warmer to wear. You're going to need it when the lights go out."

"I'm wearing the warmest clothes I have. I promise."

Anson rubbed his forehead, his words coming in short, clipped phrases. "Get everything set up. Water heated. Oils measured. My guys will run the treatments. Then meet me in the corridor. Be quick. I want to get this done before the power goes."

When had he gotten cranky? With the way things had turned out with Nate and the others, she'd have expected his mood to have improved, but in the last five minutes it somehow plummeted. Her clothes worried him that much? The loss of power?

"Enough for your crew and you?"

"Yes. Not me, but the crew."

"No one listened to your lungs," Ellory pointed out, feeling suddenly cranky herself. He hadn't let anyone look at his feet earlier, granted there hadn't been any *new* frostbite damage to look at, but he also had a problem he hadn't wanted them to see. Was he hiding something else by not letting anyone listen?

"Ellory." He waved a hand, cutting off her train of thought as well as the lecture that had been brewing, "See to it and meet me in the corridor when you're done."

With that, he was gone. And Max went with him.

Of course, Anson just stood in the hall and waited for her, like looming was his favorite pastime. Like she wasn't going to hurry, or maybe she was going to dilly-dally.

Ellory looked at him every time she passed, hurrying to and fro to gather the necessary ingredients for the steam bowls. Big metal bowls. Big fluffy towels. Eucalyptus, rosemary and lavender oils.

She couldn't read his scowl, he could be worrying about the power, but no doubt there was something else—something she'd done, the way his brooding and gorgeous eyes tracked her.

She hurried through her prep, counting drops into empty bowls, left instructions for the amount of boiling water to be added, then hurried to meet him before he had an aneurysm. "So, what's the plan?"

She could think of a good plan. A fun plan. A plan guaranteed to make him relax. A plan involving more kissing. A naked plan! But that would be a violation of her Stupid Resolution.

"To get you properly dressed," Anson answered. Of course he couldn't say Undressed—she'd told him about her Stupid Resolution.

"I told you, this is all I have to wear."

"What about Mira? Doesn't she have anything you could borrow?"

"Mira?" she said. "She's lean, toned and svelte. Have you looked at me, Anson?"

He took her hand and tugged her toward the stairwell. "I've looked plenty when you were ditching the sweater and wearing that…snug T-shirt." It sounded like he had some mix of pleasure and irritation at the memory, but at least she didn't have to actually say she was curvy like a mountain path, he got it. Mira's acceptable clothing wouldn't fit her.

"Where are we going?"

"Your room." He paused. "Where is your room?"

Bossy Man wouldn't be put off this until he saw it with his own eyes. "Fine. But you're not going to find anything more suitable." She tugged him toward the stairs up. "I'm not in the usual staff rooms. I have a guest room because I came late in the season and the staff rooms were already full."

She took the stairs at a jog, letting go of his hand so she could gather her skirts and avoid tripping and falling on her face. His shoulder was hurt. If she fell, no one was carrying her to safety.

Most of the employees being local was the reason there were so few of the staff on hand for this little adventure. The only ones here were actually living in the staff quarters—those folks stayed even when Mother Nature and Old Man Winter got into a spat.

And she was Mira's best friend, which meant she also probably got a nicer room than she might've otherwise—Mira knew how her living spaces always ended up. It just didn't bother her.

Over the last couple of hours she'd not only decided she wanted a vacation from her Stupid Resolution, she'd come to the conclusion that it was a good idea. Like eating a little bit of chocolate once in a while when dieting helped avoid going nuts one day and chewing your way through the donut counter at the bakery. Moderation was always a good thing, right?

She stopped just outside her door. If she took him in there, he'd know just how big a mess she'd become since coming home, and sex would really be off the table. "Anson, my room is messy. You could just trust me, you know."

"I can handle messy." He held out his free hand for her key card.

She could just say no. Put her foot down.

Make it seem like she was hiding something really nefarious in the room…

Or she could let him in and get it over with.

Since she'd come home her habits had grown out of control. But it wasn't until this second that she realized how out of control she'd become again. Until faced with the prospect of wanting to make a good impression, of having someone look into this intimate glimpse of her life, and the judgments that she knew would follow.

If nothing else, this trip into her obsessively green existence would help her keep her Stupid Resolution. Find the bright side. Embrace optimism.

Be cranky later.

Find some company that sold environmentally friendly vibrators… That should've been her first purchase when she'd come up with this Stupid Resolution.

With a sigh she grabbed her badge, which pulled double duty as her room key, unlocked the door and stepped inside before turning to look at him. She stopped him following by putting her hand to his chest. "I don't have that many clothes. I could just bring them out to you here."

* * *

Anson looked her in the eye, and she looked away. Scared. Was she afraid to be alone with him in the room now? Not something Anson often experienced. People trusted him—which he could argue wasn't the smartest option given his track record—but it still bothered him that she looked afraid. "I'm not going to hurt you, Ellory. My hand hurts, my shoulder hurts…we're locked in here during a blizzard. It'd be extremely stupid for me to try something ugly right now."

She nodded, but the glance over her shoulder cleared it up for him. "When I said it was messy, I meant that I'm… I'm working on a problem I have."

"Your spirit quest?"

"Actually, no. That's something else. I think." She looked nervous again, then groaned. "God, how many problems do I have? I thought I'd gotten over this one! I was fine when I was away, but I come home and then I fall right back into a decades-old pattern that I hate."

Anson reached over and flicked on the lights, illuminating the room behind her, then steered her inside.

He had gone to college, so he'd lived with slovenly people before. When someone warned him their living space was messy, he usually had an idea what to expect.

That's not what he saw when he stepped into Ellory's room.

There were no clothes on the floor, no empty cups lying about or any real disorder that he could see.

But it was messy.

There were trays on the floor all around the room with different kinds of tiny plants growing in them. "What are those?"

"Sprouts. Please don't step on them," she muttered, stepping around to the closet to wrench the door open, apparently in a hurry now to get this over with.

"I thought you didn't know if you were going to stay? You're already sprouting plants for...a garden?"

He followed her toward the closet, which required some careful stepping: She also had those rickety wooden drying racks located anywhere the air blew into the room from the central heating.

Her hands went up in unison, shrugging to the ceiling. "Eating. They're mostly alfalfa sprouts. I eat them a lot. They're great in salads and sandwiches and Mira likes them so I grow enough for both of us."

"I see." He wanted to ask why, the contradiction between the at times flighty but always proficient way she'd handled herself and the situation so far would've made him want to help even if he hadn't been undressing her with his eyes earlier. But it was another distraction. "Clothes?"

She reached into the closet and pulled out skirt after skirt after gauzy skirt, then wadded up something that looked even sheerer than what she was wearing...and threw it behind her.

"What was that?"

"Nothing!"

And yet her voice seemed to say, *I have candy I'm hiding behind my back that I took without asking.*

The whole thing took a comical turn and Anson found himself unable to keep from smiling at her. Definitely the type of woman every horny man wanted to play strip poker with—hot, and with an astounding lack of guile. "You know, I could reach around you and get it."

She grunted and held her hands up in front of her, which did not deter him at all.

"You don't need to see it."

"Is it a nightie?" He had no business asking that, but the bright peach blush warming her golden skin made him want to tease her more. And possibly convince her to model it.

"It's a belly-dancing outfit."

There was no way to contain the laugh that confession pulled from him. It was the last thing he'd expected her to say. "Do you have a tambourine in here too?"

"It's good exercise, and you can do it anywhere. And it's fun! And it doesn't require special equipment…"

"Just outfits."

"I made them so that doesn't count."

This flighty eco-princess thing was serious business to her. And the mix of sweet, eccentric and vulnerable worked for her. Ellory was definitely one of a kind—a bright spot in the storm.

"You're the first man I have ever met who thought it was funny that I belly-dance."

"I might change my mind if you want to belly-dance for me." He forgot all about the reason for dragging her off to her room. Now all he could think of was: the hot blonde hippie chick was also a belly-dancer.

It was like hitting the idiot frat boy lottery.

He really didn't deserve to see her belly-dance.

And that really wasn't going to stop him from trying.

"I'm sure you could convince me that it's not funny. I have a very open mind. And I like art."

The humor of the situation finally got through to her and she laughed then shoved at his good shoulder. "You don't deserve to see it."

That struck a nerve, and his stomach felt hollow for the space of a couple of heartbeats before he realized that she didn't know what misery he'd caused in his life, so she had to have some meaning he didn't get. "Why not?"

"Because you think I'm an idiot." Her sing-song manner of telling him off made him feel guiltier.

Except that was one thing he was not guilty of. "I don't think you're an idiot."

"Then you think I'm a liar."

"No, I don't."

"You just dragged me up here to make sure that I didn't have anything more appropriate to wear after I told you several times that I was already making the best of things. So you have to think I'm either an idiot or a liar." She closed the closet door and crawled onto the bed again, her only route around him now that he'd blocked her from the closet and the rest of the room was some kind of cross between greenhouse and launderette.

"I don't think either of those things. I left you in charge of my patients, I trusted you to take care of them, and I completely approve of your breathing treatments. You also helped my shoulder, so I think you're probably very good at your job."

"Then why? If you wanted to come to my bedroom, God, Anson, all you would've had to do was say, Hey, want to get naked together? I've got this penis and I'm not doing anything with it right now. Want to see if it's a good fit!?"

Her terrible lines made him laugh again. "You do have the best pick-up lines I've ever heard." And would never in his life use, even if someone paid him and guaranteed that they would work. "You were right, though. I don't deserve to see you in that belly-dancing outfit…or to have any of the thoughts I'm having."

"Why not?" She tilted her head as she looked up at him, an intensity to her expression that made him want to tell her the truth.

"Because Jude is out there. I left him out there."

"So you punishing yourself makes him warmer?"

He knew how ridiculous it sounded, so he shrugged. It was the noncommittal kind of answer that usually got people to drop something when he didn't want to talk further.

"You know, I may not have much to show for what I've done with my life so far—I don't have land, a house, a car. I don't even have a winter freakin' wardrobe." She hooked a finger in his belt loop, which kept him from stepping away, kept him focused on her.

"No. You're unconventional and not at all materialistic. I respect that."

"That's not what I'm getting at. I've been places. And I've seen suffering…" She stopped and swallowed, those expressive brown eyes letting him know she relived those bad memories when she recalled them. "I've learned that the people who survive, they're the ones who remember pretty quickly how to find joy in life. The others might keep living for a little while, but if they give in to the tragedy that has hit them, part of their soul dies. And soon enough they die too. Your body can't continue without your soul."

"I've heard the sayings. A burden shared is a burdened halved. All that. They're nice ideas…but do you expect me to go and tell those people jokes and make them laugh?"

"God, no. The last thing they needs is to think you're not taking this seriously. You have other resources, though. If you take joy where you can find it, that doesn't diminish your worry about Jude, or the unfounded guilt you're feeling because he's out there and you're not. It's okay for you to smile, and even if I protest about you teasing me about my belly-dancing, it's a good thing. And not only do you need it, but it's like an alternate fuel source. Good feelings can keep you going so you can actually get out there and look as long and hard as you need to in order to find him. You need it."

"Like I need hugs?" It was hard not to agree with her when she was standing right there, somehow making him feel better.

She nodded, and when he smiled rewarded him by lifting her sweater and the other layers she wore beneath it. His gaze dropped to the soft little tummy and he watched her slowly roll through the abs, activating one at a time to produce an undulating wave that…wasn't even a little bit funny but still made him feel good.

CHAPTER SEVEN

THE TOP OF his snow suit was still open, and while the branded insulated clothing she tried ever so hard not to covet might keep him warm, where it stood open down the front heat poured off him. She could probably go outside in her ridiculous clothes and survive the terrible winter if she cuddled up with the man.

For a second she remembered that the cold had hurt him, though. He wasn't invulnerable. In fact, she was increasingly certain that he was more vulnerable than he could even admit to himself.

She dropped her sweater and stepped forward, taking the opening given to slip her arms inside the suit with him and wrap them around his waist. Just one more hug. One more squeeze. One more pressing together of two bodies in need. He wouldn't mind…

It took Ellory tilting her head back and chancing a look up at him to make sure he didn't actually mind, though. His arms had come round her.

What she saw on his face made her belly flutter and her heart race—terrified and excited. He had that look, the one that split time equally between her eyes and her mouth. The man was going to kiss her again, thank all things holy. She wasn't out on this ledge by herself, the idea appealed to him too.

He had been to her room, had seen the disarray that went with her everywhere, had had a glimpse of the chaos she was currently swimming through, and he *still* wanted to kiss her.

Maybe.

He might be looking at her mouth but he was taking his sweet time about it.

Another look from eyes to mouth, and now the kind of frown someone only used when they were either concentrating or...

"If you have to try this hard to psych yourself up to kiss me, then forget it!" She let go, pulled her arms from the warmth inside his suit and made to step around him—using his belt loops again, though this time to keep from falling since he had her blocked in.

Before she got her first foot placed, his hands were in her hair, catching her head as he leaned down and covered her mouth with his own. His fingers, which had just a hint of roughness, massaged the back of her neck and sent goose bumps racing down her arms, neck and chest.

The first kiss had been good. An appetizer, a bite snuck from dessert before the main course. But this meeting of the mouths sent a tremor racing even more potent than the first streaking through her. If she bathed in champagne, Ellory couldn't imagine a more potent eruption of tingles dancing over her skin.

Instinctively, her fingers curled into the loops she'd snagged and she pulled closer, using him as an anchor.

She didn't even have the will to make excuses regarding her abandoned resolution. All she knew was the heady pleasure of soft lips contrasting with the light scrape of stubble, the strong arms that had wound around her, and heat.

He tasted even better than he smelled—better than anything she'd ever had in her mouth. Sex and chocolate, yes, sinful and decadent. But there was no hint of the indolence of Sunday morning now. Some time in the first heartbeats after his lips had touched hers, an urgency had taken them both.

His tongue stroked against hers, deep in her mouth, and her belly clenched. Desire licked through her, so strong it was all she could do not to tear the suit off him, get her hands back on that firm, glorious male flesh.

Firm and demanding, his hand slid under her sweater, seeking skin, fingers splaying across the small of her back. He felt it too.

She was ready to rip her clothes off, his clothes off... permanently swear off clothes! All she knew was that she'd never had a kiss bring her to life before. Make her forget her problems. More importantly, she'd never had a kiss turn her on without her actively trying to get turned on by it...and picturing kissing her daydream man in her head.

She opened her eyes, hoping to see that intention mirrored back at her, but the room was completely dark.

The power had gone out.

"Told you," she whispered, pulling his head back down so that she could punctuate the words with a soft little kiss. "Lights went out, or I went blind."

He chuckled against her mouth, even though he knew he had to stop this. After one more kiss... Sliding his hand out from beneath her sweater—where it had no business being anyway—he wrapped his arms fully around her, crushing her soft body to him, soaking up every sensation, every piece of information he could before he gave up kissing her...

She wanted him as much as he wanted her, but she was a distraction...and a comfort he didn't deserve. It was unjust, at least right now. Maybe after the storm passed, after they had found the man and returned him to his loved ones alive…maybe he could pick up this raging attraction again. After he earned it.

He lifted his head, swallowed, and slid his hands on her shoulders so he could put her away from him a little bit. "How are we going to get out of here without stepping on your garden?"

His reason for coming to her room had been… "And the snow suit!" He cleared his throat, glad she couldn't see him yet. And that he didn't have to see her. The passion he'd glimpsed on her face the first time he'd given in to temptation and kissed her was almost too much to bear. The power being out now was a blessing. "Where's the snow suit?"

"Under the bed." She sighed the answer and crawled onto the bed at his side. "Stay there until I get the light." Apparently she'd picked up on his shifting mood. Which would make things easier.

Some clatter followed, and then the sound of cranking as she wound the eco-friendly lantern and cast the room in blue LED light. "Go sit down, I'll get it out. I'll bring it to the fireplace suites with us, but I am not wearing it unless we lose the fireplaces. It's really itchy and bulky and ugly."

Anson stepped over a few of the shallow sprout trays, made his way to a chair and sat to watch her crawl under the bed and carefully drag out a canvas duffel bag, somehow managing to keep from upsetting anything in this kooky ecosystem she'd built in her room.

When she righted herself, her cheeks glowed once more. He'd have said it was exertion that had caused it if she looked at him anywhere but the eyes.

Embarrassed.

That hadn't been his intention, though considering the way he'd dragged her to her room and questioned her ability to dress herself…okay, maybe he could understand the feeling. "It can't be that bad."

She shrugged and dragged it toward the door.

Rising from the safety of his chair, Anson took two big steps over the Ellory obstacle course until he stood in front of her, making her pause in her exit, and once more wrapping himself in that fruity floral cloud, and grabbed the massive duffel bag at their feet. "I'll carry it."

After dropping off Ellory's duffel in the suite next door, Anson entered the one saved for him and Max and found the big furry Newfoundland lying by the fire some thoughtful person had already lit, trying to keep ahead of the cold. His faithful companion stood and ran to meet him, tail wagging.

"So this is where you've been." He talked to his dog a lot. After he crouched and gave the big lover a good scratch, he found his way to the sofa and sat, leaving Max to return to the fire. As great as he was in the snow, he loved a fireplace.

Anson couldn't blame him, but after the trip to Ellory's room he knew one thing for certain—she gave out more heat than gas logs.

And he had no right to that heat.

On his last round to check on the rescued, Chelsea had shown him a picture of Jude. An engagement photo. Two smiling people with the future shining in their eyes...and he hadn't had the heart to ask her anything else about her missing fiancé.

He didn't need more motivation to want to find the man. So much of this situation echoed his own wintery nightmare. What he wouldn't have given for the fire in those days when he'd been so cold he hadn't wanted to move at all. The gaps between his snow suit and his skin had allowed the heat to build in pockets, and those pockets left the second he'd moved and the material had pulled tight.

All his hope had filled these small spaces, and all it

had taken had been a muscle twitch to dispel it. Right now Jude was holding onto a thread of hope growing thinner and more brittle with every frigid breath he'd drawn since this morning.

A knock at the door brought him back to the present. Max lifted his big shaggy head and looked at the door. A couple of sniffs of the air and the search dog's big tail began beating the carpet.

No calls had come through on the radio, so it wasn't an emergency. He'd like to ignore it. Go to sleep. God, he was tired…

Anson peeled himself from the sofa and made his way to the door. Max beat him there.

"I see how it is." He ruffled Max's ears and pushed him back so the door could swing open.

Ellory stood behind a stack of sprout trays, arms straining to carry them. Her warm brown eyes met his over the spring-green shoots, and she smiled. He couldn't see her smile, but he saw the apples of her cheeks bunch and merriment in her eyes.

She kicked the duffel bag he recognized, and the stuffed thing flopped through his doorway to land on his feet. Heavy. Big. It took up as much room as at least two of his suits. Max sniffed the hell out of it.

"I need to bunk with you," she said, the strain from carrying the trays down several flights of stairs and long corridors showing in her voice.

Anson grabbed the bag and hurled it further into the room, then grabbed the edges of the bottom tray to relieve her of her portable garden.

"No. Your shoulder is hurt. Just move." She refused to let go, but since the way had been cleared she stepped forward to come in.

"No," he repeated back to her, and lifted, forcing her to let go. Once they were in the room, he placed the trays on the counter. Which was when he noticed two other bags swinging from her shoulder. She didn't travel light…

She closed the door and dropped her bags.

"Let me guess," he said, looking at the sprouts. "You're here because you changed your mind about that belly dance."

"Nope." Ellory looked the tiniest bit guilty then. "I can't bring myself to have a wasteful fire all to myself. And no one else would understand if I brought the sprouts and crashed in their pad. They'll be ruined if I leave them in my unheated room. I don't really know anyone else well enough to include them in…this. And…well, you kissed me. You like me. I like you." Max barked at her. She hadn't paid him any attention yet, and he wasn't having it.

"And I like you too, Maxie." She caught his front paws in the chest and roughed up his ears with the kind of affection usually reserved for someone's own pet. "I'm sorry I left you out. Go and tell Anson you want me to sleep over! Go tell him!" She pointed at Anson and Max dutifully ran to him, tail wagging hard enough to clear a table, tongue lolling out of his mouth. Happy panting.

"What about your resolution?"

"I'm not asking you to marry me, Anson. I'm not even asking you to curl my toes and make me forget that my enviro-OCD is out of control again, or whatever else is wrong with me that made me think coming home would fix it." Edging around the sofa, she dropped her other bags on the floor and took a seat there in front of the fire. "I just want to share space. And maybe I'd like to spend some time around a wild man who puts his fist through walls… and his dog."

As soon as she said the word "dog" Max came and flopped down on her, then rolled so he was on his back and his head propped on her thigh, all but demanding belly rubs. Anson briefly considered doing the same thing to her other thigh, but having it known that his dog had better moves than he did was just too much for his ego to handle today.

"Max clearly wants you to stay." Anson wanted her to stay too, he just wasn't into admitting that right now.

"We should move the bed over by the fire." Ellory didn't sit yet, but Anson did.

"It's not that cold in here. For people dressed better. You should put on your suit."

During the hour since Anson had kissed her lips and made her feel like she was drowning in champagne Ellory had devised a plan.

Or, well, she'd *un*-devised part of her plan. The whole point of her resolution had been to remove distraction and give herself the attention she'd normally pay to a relationship, so she could work on herself. Figure out what was wrong with her. Figure out what she wanted to do with her life. Traveling was getting old. She wanted to settle down, but she didn't want to lose her ideals in order to build a life.

Tearing off Anson's clothes and dragging him to bed wouldn't change any of that. It wouldn't solve her problems. It wouldn't make them worse. If anything, it made her more acutely aware of the fact that they were waiting for her. And they would still be waiting for her when the skies cleared and the power came back on, and Anson was no longer stranded here with her.

"Or we could go to bed and be warm under the blankets. I brought my quilt, it's really warm and snuggly." Temptation lit his eyes, but was chased out by that deep scowl she'd come to loathe. "Or you could go to sleep by yourself and I will go spend time with Mira and the patient guests. She's come down, by the way. You've got some free time to sleep if you want it. You look like you need it, and if you aren't into chasing away demons for the next few hours in the manner we'd both enjoy, then you should sleep."

She thought a second and added before he could protest, "Better now than when the storm clears and you have to go back out after Jude."

"No argument here." He untied his boots, kicked them off and stripped out of the suit as he walked to the bed.

Ellory watched until he was under the blankets in his thermals, at which point Max gave up his spot by the fire and went to curl up on Anson's feet on top of the fluffy duvet.

After she spent some time making sure everyone got fed, she'd get some sleep too.

On the couch. She'd already made enough moves on the man. The next move was his.

Ellory awoke after a long night of lumpy sleep on the couch, burrowed beneath her quilt with her head propped on one of the cushions and Max panting in her face.

"Good that you woke up. I think Max was about to wash your face. With his tongue," Anson said from where he sat, using her duffel stuffed with the snow suit from hell like a beanbag chair in front of the fire.

The dog's tongue was exactly the last thing she wanted on her face this morning. But after the way the night had gone, and the fact that she was sleeping on the couch when she'd much rather have been sleeping beside big warm Anson…well, Ellory didn't wake up feeling chipper.

Rolling over so she faced the couch back, she pulled the quilt over her head to block out the smell of dog mouth and ignored both of them.

When the power had gone out, Mira couldn't be kept out of things any more, so in theory Ellory didn't have anything to do this morning. No duties to perform, nothing to organize. And as guilty as it made her feel to be glad about that, she figured she'd probably handled things as well as she could for as long as she could. Two straight days of organizing and keeping everything under control was too much responsibility and decision-making for her.

Besides that, yesterday had felt like it had been weeks long.

And today still felt like yesterday, however that worked out.

The smell of food filtered through the quilt now that Max wasn't breathing on her face. Eggs. He was making eggs somehow. Could you cook with gas logs?

She closed her eyes tighter and tried to ignore the scent. Her stomach growled.

"The storm is still going." Anson spoke again, apparently not satisfied with her attempt to cocoon herself away from all contact. "But the kitchen staff brought up breakfast. Scrambled eggs and toast."

So he hadn't cooked.

But someone else had. Someone she wasn't mad at. Someone whose food she could eat.

She was mad at Anson? The realization startled her enough to bring her up out of her quilt.

She took inventory. A frown, but nothing teary going on in the eye department. A desire to hide out, sleep some more and guilt him over his great sleep... A martyr complex about her own sleep, which had been anything but restful.

She *was* mad at Anson.

Weird. She rarely ever got mad at anyone. So rarely she couldn't remember the last time she'd gotten angry about anything. When someone disappointed her, she usually just got sad, and then moved on.

No matter that she'd playfully threatened to punch him

yesterday, she had never engaged in any sort of violence. But now? She might be able to do something aggressive. Like throw something at him. Pelt him with scrambled eggs.

Well, she just wouldn't think about him. Do whatever needed doing. Ignore him.

Mira probably needed help anyway, and she'd have to sleep at some point…so maybe Ellory wasn't off the hook anyhow.

She crawled out from beneath the quilt, stood and shook it out, then carefully folded it before draping over the back of the couch.

"Not speaking to me today?"

No. Not speaking to him today. She pretended he was talking to the dog and went about getting her stuff together. She dug a fresh skirt from her bag, and then another… As they weren't as substantial as yesterday's barely substantial skirt, she pulled them on over the unflattering long thermal underwear she'd been wearing since yesterday. She hadn't brought any clothes-drying racks with her, naturally. And there was no hot shower. No sunshine. Because winter sucked, and winter in Colorado sucked even more.

She pulled on a fresh sweater, yanked from out of her collar the braid she'd worked her long hair into before sleeping, and went to wash up.

However they'd been cooked, she'd eat the damned eggs. Whatever realizations she might've come to last night seemed much harder to follow through with this morning. It took concentrated effort not to wonder where the eggs were sourced—or any of the other ingredients.

They were probably from chickens full of hormones, just like she'd felt she was since the grave doctor had grumbled into her life: full of hormones.

Sighing, she grabbed a handful of sprouts from the bin

from the third-day ready-to-eats, rinsed them and sat at the table, her back to Anson.

This would teach her not to prepare ahead of time for these types of situations. With the predictable nature of the power to the lodge, she should have been making and storing granola bars and trail mix, dehydrating fruit—just doing something besides growing sprouts…

Max came around and rested his chin on her knee, giving her big sad eyes.

Okay, half of a sandwich for her and half for Max. She pulled the sprouts off his half and handed it to the dog, who took the sandwich and ran off to eat it.

"He has already eaten."

Well, he'd just eat more.

Ellory took a bite of her sandwich in silence.

"Did I do something to tick you off?"

Yes. Probably. She just wasn't sure what it was.

Maybe it was the rejection. Or the double kiss and run. Or the couch.

"I'll take the couch tonight." He pulled out the other chair at the table and sat where she couldn't ignore him as effectively.

She finished with her current bite before even trying to answer. It'd be the height of irony to be killed by foods that she usually avoided because they were bad for you. "Don't bother. I'll find another room." There, she was even proud that she managed to speak in a completely level and natural-sounding voice.

Anson gave a low whistle, leaning back in his chair until it tilted on the back legs, and linked his hands behind his head. "You really are mad."

CHAPTER EIGHT

MAX CAME BACK for more and Anson set himself back upright, snapped his fingers and pointed to the fire, and the dog obediently went to lie down.

Ellory took a big bite of her terrible sandwich and considered giving the rest to the dog.

"Did something happen that I'm not aware of?"

"Probably."

"Did I talk in my sleep?"

"I don't know, I didn't spend the whole night watching you sleep," she snapped, getting more and more worked up as he pumped her for information—obviously not feeling the same courtesy to refrain from badgering her that she extended to him. "I might be struggling with my compulsiveness about my carbon footprint and about what I eat, but I'm not a psychopath, a sociopath, or any other path that I can't think of right now."

"Did you have a bad dream?"

Not deterred.

Why was he not deterred? Did people yell at him all the time? Was this how he liked to communicate?! "I don't know. I don't think so. I don't think I slept enough to dream anything of significance." Ellory pushed the plate away and went to get more sprouts. Eating the sprouts didn't feel like punishment.

"The couch is uncomfortable." He offered another incorrect guess.

"More comfortable than the ground," she muttered between fresh, crunchy bites.

"What does that mean?"

"It means I sleep on the ground all the time. So if I can learn to do that, I should be able to sleep on a cushy couch in front of a fire. Well, a fake fire. The hissing sound it makes...and this place smells like gas to me all the time, even though I know the gas can't be leaking—the fire would burn it up."

"So the gas kept you awake?"

Like he could fix that if she confirmed it bothered her. Ellory thought about doing what he liked to do—go silent and brood or punch things—but talking about the fireplace was better than talking about the real problems. "Yes. And some other stuff."

"What stuff?"

"I really don't want to talk to you about it. You've seen enough bad things about me, and to give you credit you're handling it better than most normal people would."

"I haven't seen any bad stuff about you," Anson said softly, shrugging. "You keep saying that I'm normal. The insinuation being you're not normal."

"Yep, that's the insinuation." She stopped there, shrugged and shook her head. The only word that came to her was even more negative than usual. Broken. She felt broken, and with no idea how to fix herself. No idea how to learn to be content...

"Quirky. Free-spirited," he filled in when she didn't finish the thought.

Ellory grunted, stuffed some more sprouts into her mouth and resisted the urge to throw them at him. She might not have anything remotely natural to eat if she gave in to the urge to smash them in his face. "Stop sucking up."

"Something must have changed in the night."

But somehow, as they talked, she got less irritated with him. Even though she didn't want to tell him anything. Which was when it became clear. "I came home for a reason, because I have to figure out what is wrong with me and fix it. Instead, I had some kind of compulsive relapse, and I told you about it! I told you more than I've told anyone else about it. I haven't told anyone what's going on with me. I told Mira that I needed to spend time working on myself, but not why. But I've been open and all that with you. I hoped that you would open up to me too. But you didn't. You won't even admit that you are upset about anything. I can't help you if you won't even talk to me at all."

Anson righted the angle of his chair and linked his hands on the table, his eyes staying fixed on her even if she couldn't read them right now. "What makes you think you can be of any help to me? Or that I need help in the first place?"

"Please," she intoned, running a little water into a cup so she could water her sprouts and at least be busy doing something while he gave her the third degree. "I'm on a quest too, even if I'm not currently 'doing drugs with a shaman in the jungle.' I can recognize a fellow traveler when I see one. You have the look. You're searching for something…"

"The only thing I'm looking for is for the storm to pass so I can actually go out and search for that man."

She said the man's name even if she knew how it made Anson react. "Jude." Immature of her to say it, but she couldn't help herself.

"Yes, Jude." He bit the name at her, his voice finally rising from the calm, detached doctor voice he'd been using on her. "And I will be fine again once I can go out there and find him."

"Fine. You're fine. You're perfect and great. You punch

the wall every time it storms." She poured the rest of the water into the sink and ate another pinch of sprouts for good measure.

"Do you feel better?"

"No, of course I don't feel better! You can't make me *un*-mad at you by basically saying I'm dumb for being concerned about you." She shook her head, eyes rolling. He was just being obtuse on purpose, she knew he was smarter than this.

Max stood up in front the fire. Now that voices had been thoroughly raised, he was becoming upset. Ellory watched him rise up to sniff Anson's face, and when satisfied he was okay come to sniff her. "Down." She lowered her voice and petted his head then shoved him gently but firmly to the floor.

When she spoke again, she kept her voice level, for the sake of the dog. "For the record, I'm not mad about the couch, it was a symptom. Not mad about the food. Not the weather. Not the hole in the wall. I'm mad that I shared something with you that I haven't shared with anyone—even my best friend. I thought that we were bonded or something after yesterday. But I felt lonelier last night than I think I ever have while in the same room with someone. So, yes, I'm not feeling my sunny self. I'm disgruntled and I'm going to find somewhere else to stay. I shouldn't have invited myself to begin with. I'll be back for my stuff."

She stepped behind the chair she'd been sitting in and scooted it back under the table—keeping things as tidy as she could was the only way to deal with the amount of clutter she traveled with. Then she slung on her coat, dug into her bag for clean socks and her boots, and left barefooted. She'd put her shoes on in the hallway, or somewhere else she couldn't feel him watching her, glowering at her. Somewhere Max didn't follow her around, looking worried.

So he didn't want to sleep with her. So what? Lots of

men didn't want to sleep her. And he didn't want to talk about how he felt about Jude or how he'd lost his toes. That was his personal business. Her focusing on his emotional well-being was probably just her using him as an excuse not to focus on her own emotional well-being anyway. And a danger to her Stupid Resolution. The heart of her resolution was about fixing herself...and there was no difference in the level of distraction between dating a man and fixing him.

She didn't want to tell him anything about her past, though, which was stranger than anything else. She was like an open book, or she tried to be. People asked her questions, she answered them. She didn't lie. She didn't conceal. Not usually. She had flaws and she embraced them or tried to change them, but she didn't hide them. Until now. Until this problem.

She hadn't been lying to Anson when she'd said she wanted to be content, she wanted to be happy. She just didn't know what exactly was standing in her way.

All she did know after this morning was that she needed to talk about it. As much as she didn't want to give her best friend something heavy to carry when she was supposed to be enjoying new love bliss with Sex Machine, she had to tell Mira as much as she knew.

She could only hope that putting the words together would give her access to the information her conscious mind had trouble getting at.

Ellory made her way through the circuit of rooms, knocking on doors, checking on staff, and worked her way back to the patient guests' rooms, with Chelsea's room her last stop. Mira was there, the two of them in front of the fire, talking in low tones to avoid waking Nate.

She snagged a chair from the table and as quietly as she could moved it over to where the two women sat, forcing as much chipper as would be appropriate, and making her greetings in whispers, then added to Mira, "Your relief is awake, so you can go off duty and get some rest again. Where's Jack?"

"I can stay a little longer." Mira gave her a long look, no doubt picking up on her fake chipper. "Jack has already gone back up to the suite, you just missed him."

"I wasn't really looking for him," Ellory admitted, "Just thought you might like to get back to him." And then she focused on Chelsea. "How are you this morning? Is there anything I can do for you?"

The small woman shook her head. "I'm hanging tough, as Jude likes to say. Dr. Dupris and I were talking about how we knew we were in love."

"Oh." Another conversation that she couldn't really participate in, though at least this time it wasn't because she was being excluded.

She just didn't have anything to add. She had never been in love and she'd never claimed to have been in love, but who kept track of that kind of thing? Would Mira put it together? Should she be ashamed of that? Was that something she should admit?

Now she'd found something else she didn't want to tell anyone. All this hiding had to stop.

The other two repeated their tales for her. The way his voice could make her heart flutter, the way her belly flipped when he looked at her, spending the whole weekend in bed together and refusing to even answer the phone and be apart for a minute… Stories full of smiles and epiphanies, details burned into their memories.

Having shown her the way to tell this particular kind of story, Chelsea fixed her with a hopeful smile, expecting a similar one.

Ellory could only shrug. "I don't have a story like that." When both women looked a little sorry for her, she added, "I have sexy stories, but this is probably not the time for those. I also have lots of feel-good stories about weighing malnourished children when they were finally starting to put on weight. I can tell you about the sounds of the rain forest at night and stories about food I stopped asking for details on…because it might involve bugs. They're good stories, just not the 'I knew I loved him when' sort."

Mira was a wonderful doctor, she knew just when to push and when to hold the line, and although the smile she gave Ellory said she would get it out of her at some point, she gave her a pass because of the people around.

Mira tried to change the subject, and Ellory wanted to let her, but she had joined their conversation for a reason and it seemed like as good a moment as any.

"Mir, I haven't been entirely honest with you, hiding something…which is probably making it worse."

Mira glanced at Chelsea and then looked back at Ellory. "Do you want to go somewhere else to talk?"

There was a suggestion in her tone, and Ellory realized only then that it might give Chelsea a bad impression. "Chelsea's already seen some of it," Ellory murmured, and then looked to see if the woman wanted them to go somewhere else.

"What did I see?"

"I apologized for the cocoa," Ellory said softly, then refocused on Mira. "You know how a few years ago my attempts to…be environmentally responsible got a little… out of control?"

Mira nodded, a thoughtful frown on her features. She summed it up in one word. "Preservatives?"

She meant the cocoa. Ellory nodded. "And, well, the sprouts. The clothes washing in the bathtub and drying on racks in my room, never using the lights or…well, the electricity in any way I have control over…"

"Is that why you wanted to come home?"

Mira sounded confused, which Ellory couldn't blame her for. She ran on instinct more than anything else, probably because she had such a hard time identifying what she actually felt at any particular time, let alone being able to explain it.

"That was the spirit quest."

"Right." She nodded, and like a good friend and doctor she asked questions, gathered information to make a treatment plan. "How long has it been bad?"

"Mostly since I came back. I didn't know exactly what I was working on at the time of my spirit quest. I just was looking for…contentment, and an indication of what I was supposed to be doing with my life. The only answer I got was that I needed to go home…so home I came."

A knock at the door preceded Anson and Max strolling in, there to check in, no doubt. Her stomach bottomed out, and she looked everywhere but at his eyes.

"I just wanted you to know, in case I've been extra… eccentric lately." She focused back on the two women, and Max came to nose at her hand until she petted him. "But we can talk later. I'm sure Dr. Graves wants to…do his rounds."

With everyone in a holding pattern until the storm let up and no emergencies currently happening, Anson and Max had nothing to do. Except wonder about Ellory. And why she'd fled upon his arrival. How could she be that mad at him?

"Actually, if you don't need me, I have something to discuss with—" Anson didn't get through the statement before Mira waved him off.

Time to put an end to this quarrel, whatever it was.

By the time he got Max out the door, Ellory was nowhere in sight. He hit the stairs on the chance that she'd gone back to do that moving she'd threatened him with.

How had she gotten so wrapped up in his life—in his mind—in twenty-four hours?

When he'd lain down last night, it hadn't been with the intention of hurting her, or making her sleep on the couch. Hell, he hadn't even meant to sleep so long, just a nap to recharge. But his body had had other ideas.

He and Max caught up with her and followed a few steps behind, all the way to their shared suite and in behind her. She went for her bags first.

"Put those down." Anson gestured to the couch. "We don't want you going anywhere, Max and I. You want to talk. Let's talk."

"Is this some kind of trick? Don't think I won't move just because you make it sound like Max needs me." She blotted her eyes with her sleeve, turning her face away from him as she did. Crying? What had escalated things to crying level?

"No trick." He closed the door behind him and decided to give her a moment to breathe. "Let's move the mattress in front of the fire, like you wanted." Physical things were easier to take care of, and the action gave him time to think.

Moving the couch and furniture out of the way was easy enough. By the time he'd moved to the bed she'd joined him, and together they lugged the unwieldy thing to the cleared spot in front of the fire.

Max thought it had been put there for him, naturally, and ran over to lie down in the middle.

"No, Max. Go lie down." Anson ushered the big dog off the bed, then bent to unfasten his boots so he could shed the snow suit and be a little more comfortable on the floor bed. It also gave him an excuse to get under the quilt with her once she'd settled with it. "What were you three talking about?"

"I already talked a bunch."

"Okay. Me first." He pulled her against his side and anchored an arm around her waist. "When I was ten I was lost on the big mountain for several days with my mother during a storm," he said without preamble, since it seemed like the easiest way to start this story.

She looked up at him, her eyes going unfocused beneath frowning golden brows. Not really looking at him—that was the look of someone searching her memory. Did she remember hearing the story? Had he become a tale told to frighten local children into right outdoor behavior? It was something he never talked about, so the idea had never occurred to him.

"Did you hear about that?"

She shook her head. "Maybe...I'm not sure."

His relief surprised him.

"We crawled under a ledge to get out of the snow. The ledge wasn't small, but it was very close to the ground. Too close for us to do much besides lie there on our backs and wait for the storm to pass. It took a long time. By the time it was past I was drifting in and out of consciousness. My mother...she died."

Ellory looked down to where his legs disappeared beneath the blankets and with one hand she found his closest foot. By chance it happened to be the one with the most damage. The one she'd been looking at in the massage room before he'd kissed her.

He felt her hand curl around the remaining toes and squeeze, but she didn't say anything. She just rubbed his disfigured foot, which he'd really rather she not touch at all—he didn't like anyone touching his feet.

Before he could stop her, she'd snagged the top edge of the sock and pulled it down and off his foot. Anson had to work not to say anything or stop her. Not that she was going to say or do something cruel, but he just didn't like how exposed it made him feel to open up about this stuff, to let someone see the mark of his shame.

She wouldn't know that part. He hadn't told her everything.

"You touch everyone," he said as her hand curled over the decades-old scar.

"Yes. I touch everyone." She finally spoke as she caressed his foot and leaned her head on his shoulder. "People need to be touched in order to be healthy. Touching heals and..." She started to say something else but stopped short.

He'd finally started to understand most of what she said without asking for clarification, but when she left off thoughts entirely, he still needed help. "And what?"

The woman was like an exotic creature he had no chance of understanding if he didn't ask all the questions that other people would leave alone.

"That's how I express love."

That sounded like a declaration. Only it couldn't be, they barely knew one another. And she touched everyone. Compassion. She meant compassion.

"I can't imagine how alone they're all feeling right now, even if they're in it together. Especially Chelsea. The man she loves is still out there because he wanted to save her. I want her to know that I feel for her and that there are people here who want to help her through this if she wants the help," Ellory murmured, but she didn't sound like herself. "Sometimes it's harder for someone to hear words than just to offer your touch and presence for them."

Like she was touching him now. It was still all about how he was doing, making him feel connected to someone and better, whether or not he deserved her compassion.

"It's good. I had teachers in school who made a point of telling some...well, a good number of the students to touch their patients."

"All book, no heart?"

"Something like that."

She may be all heart. Based on their fight earlier, he

knew she wasn't just sad for him and the patients. She was struggling too. He held back telling her more, and pretended it was in case he should need to barter the information with her later, because he really needed to know why she was crying. "Why were you crying earlier?"

Her eyes warmed again, giving Ellory warning that tears were imminent. She laughed. "So annoying, you can just mention tears and they spring right back up." A sniff and she swiped her eyes again, mentally cursing her lack of control.

"Only when you've stopped crying because you're avoiding what upset you." The gentleness in his voice helped. At least it pushed away the embarrassment she felt as the result of tearing up.

"Mira and Chelsea were talking about being in love," Ellory began, trying to find words that fit what she felt so she'd actually know what she was thinking. "These moments of insight when they knew they were in love..."

Anson's arm came around her again and gave a squeeze—encouragement to talk, not that she needed encouragement, she just needed words. It was sweet anyway.

"Started thinking about someone you lost?"

If only that were the case...

"No. I realized I never loved any of the men I have been with. Not one of them. I never had that realization of love." She couldn't look at him. The confession sounded terrible enough to her without seeing disgust or something worse in his mossy green eyes. "Which is horrible, I know. And makes me sound like a—"

He shushed her. "It doesn't make you sound like anything."

"Not something bad? Because you'd think I would've loved some of them, they were all perfect for me in some way. We were..." She started to claim they were just alike, but the words sounded false. "We had a lot of the same ideas and beliefs. And they were always doing something good. And they taught me…"

Anson let her work through things at her own pace. She tended to work through things out loud, and he suffered her pauses with patience she only recognized when she'd fallen into her thoughts long enough to make him prompt her. "Elle?"

"I know why I've fallen apart since I came home."

He could hear the disgust in her voice, and it was all Anson could do to keep from dragging the information from her.

"What did they teach you?"

"They taught me their habits. We usually lived someplace where simplicity was the only option, and I just did whatever they did. If they had fruit salad in the morning, that became my routine too."

The sigh that came from her was so forlorn his first instinct was to change the subject. Don't make her dig that deep—he hadn't dug that deep for her earlier. The difference was he knew how he felt, he knew what had happened, he knew what he'd done. He'd examined it all so many times the memories barely made him feel anything any more—except shame.

But it was clear her process was one of discovery. Not something to be shut down. Clean out the wound so it can heal.

"Whose habits are you following now?"

"My father's. And they keep invading what I do. Like when I was apologizing for the cocoa. That was a habit he gave me."

"How so?"

"When I failed to follow the rules in some fashion, his favorite punishment was a diet of junk food. Because if I behaved like the rest of the parasites on earth, I should eat what they did so at least I'd not live very long. Some kids got grounded, I got fast food, the greasier and more processed the better."

Anson felt his mouth fall open. The psychological warfare of that made it horrifying. Other kids would rejoice to eat candy and snack foods, but if she'd been raised believing that they would kill her—and that her father wanted to her to die young because she didn't live up to his expectations... That was a special kind of twisted.

"There are a bunch of ways to live the kind of life I need to live, but I come here and I fall into this pattern of extremes. It's ridiculous that the place I love more than anywhere on this earth turns me into a basket case. I want to stay, but I don't know how I can if I can't get control of this. Figure out how else to be. Relax my rules. Or actually just figure out what *my rules* really are. Right now, central heat feels like a gateway drug! It's not even something I can control here, but it's like some slippery slope that's going to make me give up my beliefs or compromise my ideals. So I push to the other extreme, as hard as I can, and..."

Her words died, but he knew it for what it was now: where her epiphanies dried up. She burrowed closer to him and he tightened his arm, for once uncertain of what to do, or even to say to help her.

Max finally picked up on the tension in the room and invited himself to the bed with them, where he could plop his big heavy head onto where their knees met.

Ellory took it as a request to be petted, and obliged him, comforting the dog who wanted to comfort her. It was exactly what they were doing—a cycle of comforting and no one fixing anything.

"Change one thing you're doing," Anson said, the only solution he could come up with that didn't involve putting his fist through something living and infinitely more deserving than the drywall.

"What thing?"

"I don't know. The sprouts. Get rid of the sprouts." It was the first thought that came to him.

"But I like the sprouts."

A gust of wind rattled the window, timely and a reminder. "Get a new snow suit, one you'll actually wear." There was a ski shop downstairs. She could do that immediately, which would give him some peace of mind.

"We're not dating, but how is that any different than me just adopting your habits?"

"It's not just my habit. My habit is an orange reflective snow suit. A regular suit is the habit of everyone who hits the slopes during a Colorado winter." He strenuously avoided using the word 'normal.' She didn't need those kinds of comparisons right now. "You get a suit so you'll be better protected, and you'll be changing something small. And I'll do something for you in return. I'll do…spirit quest stuff. Just no drugs."

"Ugh, stop calling it a drug. It's a natural decoction," she grunted, pulling back so she could look him in the eye. "You'll do spirit quest stuff if I get a new snow suit?"

"That's what I said." It might not solve anything, but it was something that they could do that might let her feel like she was helping him too, which balanced the margins. She didn't need to know his margins could never actually be balanced.

"You could also look for a job once the storm passes. I know a few centers I could recommend you to."

"I don't know if I want to work at a center. Regimented schedules are hard for me."

"Okay. Then make some plan. Come up with what your ideal situation would be if you decided to stick around." He wanted her to stick around, God help him.

She laid her head back down on his shoulder and resumed stroking Max's snout so he'd stop making big sad eyes at them both. "What are you going to do for uphold-ing your end?"

"You tell me. Where do we start?"

"Meditation."

The rest of the day passed at a lazy pace. No emergen-cies dragged them out of their meditation, and Anson only really left when it was time for him to make another round to check on everyone. Just because no one was in a state of life-threatening duress it didn't mean he slacked off on his duties. They all ate together, and Ellory managed to make something that didn't send her into an OCD tailspin. Mira provided a key and Anson helped her pick out a snow suit from the shop—not too big but big enough to hold in some heat—and set his mind at ease.

When watching the fire got old, they spent time in front of the window, watching the snow swirl and blow.

And he held her hand. All the time. When they were alone in the room, Anson held her hand. She always had known that touch healed, reminded you that you were part of something bigger, a way to share strength. She'd always believed those things, even if she didn't feel it as deeply as she wanted to.

But as they sat by the fire, saying nothing, his support flowed into her and carried away the loneliness she'd been feeling since…always.

As night came, Ellory felt content for the first time in a long time. It probably wouldn't last. Maybe not even the night, but it was a start—like glimpsing the end of your journey while still on the mountaintop, with days of hard travel still to make.

With their thermals still on, they stretched out for the night, Anson's big body behind her, matching her bend for bend, his arm around her waist. "Wake me up if you have bad dreams," she said over her shoulder, then settled down to the smile-inducing feeling of his nose burrowing into her hair.

"I should get it out of the way. Braid it."

"Don't you dare," he mumbled, his arms tightening.

CHAPTER NINE

ANSON LET HIS eyes close and tried to make his body relax. She felt too good, she smelled too good—especially in this position, where he got the sweet, natural scent of her beneath the long sun-kissed honey locks he'd like to wrap himself up in.

So he'd managed to avoid kissing her today, which didn't mean much considering where they'd ended up anyway. People who weren't already feeling intimate didn't cuddle. Two people who just happened to be sharing a bed and who didn't want more than that...they lay with as big a gap as they could between them.

"This is a joke," Ellory muttered, pulling thoughts right out of his mind. "I can't sleep like this. If you don't want me, if you don't want to want me, or whatever, then I should sleep on the couch."

"You're not sleeping on the couch." And, by God, neither was he. Anson sighed into her hair, keeping his arms around her.

Ellory looked over her shoulder at him. "You know what I would be doing right now if we *were* dating and you were being this big of a brat?"

"I'm not being a brat."

She snorted and then beneath his hands he felt her tummy do that roll thing again, which pushed his thoughts further down that path they should not travel.

"You're the brat."

She rolled her tummy again. "Did you know there are a whole bunch of ways to move your tummy and your hips? It's about controlling muscles, not just the abs but accentuating the movement of the hips and the curve from waist to hip."

"You're playing dirty."

"I haven't even begun to play dirty." She laughed and then did something with her hips that rubbed that firm round little tush against his groin. In an instant he was hard, and just like that he stopped caring whether or not he deserved her attention and the amazing womanly body pressed against him. He had it. If Fate was making a mistake, then Fate would be to blame.

Except…

"I don't have condoms."

"I do!" She scrambled out of his reach and leaned off the mattress, one hand on the floor so the other could reach her bag and drag it over. The position gave him the best view of her backside, and before this second he'd have never said thermal underwear was sexy.

"Your thermals are too snug. They're supposed to be loose to keep you warm…"

"Shhh." She flung condoms at him, and then started peeling those thermals off, starting with the top.

The room was fairly warm, but as the shirt whisked over her head, he could see that she was a little chilled. The shirt landed on the floor and she was about to strip right out of everything else, her thumbs in the waistband of her leggings, when he grabbed her by the hips and dragged her back to him on the bed.

"I get to take those off." After he kissed her. After he got to explore the gorgeous flesh he'd already been granted the pleasure of.

* * *

As he slid her beneath him, Ellory reached for the hem of his shirt, pulling it over his head. While her confidence might be hit or miss in other areas of her life, one thing she'd never had a compunction about was nudity—her own body or the nude bodies of others. With the kind of life she led, there were a great many communal activities, and her actual between-missions job was massaging frequently naked bodies...

Since the minute Anson had yelled at her and dragged her inside from the cold, she'd been trying not to think naughty thoughts about him. Seemed like forever had passed since then. She might not have the most accurate concept of time, but she was pretty sure that her massage of his shoulder and back had lasted three whole years. And in the intervening years since she'd had him on her table— yesterday—she'd missed the sight of him.

As soon as the thermal top was off, she did what she'd been itching to do since the start and ran her hands over his chest, lightly scratching her fingernails through the whorls of dark hair that danced over his glorious torso.

"You're beautiful." She hadn't meant to say that, but the smile he gave her made her glad it had slipped out... so glad she almost said it again. Instead, what came out was, "Let's take off your pants!"

Anson laughed again and pinned her hands above her head, levering himself over until his deliciously manly chest and belly flattened to her own.

But one kiss, and the playfulness was gone. The third kiss was the charm. In the space of a single heartbeat her thoughts turned as chaotic as her body became needy.

Heat.

Hunger.

And on the horizon the likelihood of hurt. Nothing good

could come of this. It was not dating. It wasn't a relationship. It wasn't anything except the moment.

Forbidden fruit, the allure of what could never be.

His tongue dipped into her mouth and he let go of her hands so he could lean off her again and remove her bottoms, every inch of flesh exposed burning with awareness.

Under any other circumstances she couldn't have him and he would never want her. But right now he needed someone to lighten his load and she needed to feel connected to someone—that's what they'd be to each other.

Being the leader meant keeping up appearances to those who looked to him for something. All Ellory could think to look to him for right now was some relief. And maybe being able to save him from something, since she couldn't freaking figure out how to save her own damned self.

She was just the life raft.

And that was okay because under any other circumstances she wouldn't…well, she probably just wouldn't want to want him. The idea of actually not wanting him was so far removed from what she felt right now that she couldn't even really picture it.

He kissed and licked his way down her chest, with detours to kiss and suck. When his teeth scraped her nipple she thought she'd come apart, the growing tension the only thing that held her broken pieces together.

Even knowing this man was a recipe for betraying herself and her way of life. A gorgeous man with a cause, and standing. And who knew what else? His lifestyle was a complete unknown. He could be the picture of everything she'd hate. But with the way he made her feel she had to consider that he'd still be someone she'd change herself for. Her mother had changed for the love of her father. Even as a child, Ellory had understood that.

She'd tried to change and make her father love her too—but he still didn't. He never could, just like Anson never could. She'd never been able to fit into her father's world, and she couldn't fit into Anson's. The best she could manage was a short stay in this twilight zone version of it. The lodge was a deserted island, a bubble away from the rest of the world.

So he wasn't really a violation of her resolution. This wasn't dating. It was sex.

The desire she felt for him might leave her feeling like a virgin on the cusp, but it was still just sex. Just sex. Much-needed sex, sure, but still… Just. Sex.

As he kissed and licked his way over her belly to her breasts, the extreme appetite she'd developed for him took over. Lifting her legs, she hooked her big toes into the waistband of his thermal pants and dragged them down, causing his erection to spring free.

Her toe tracked over a scar on his thigh, which she registered…something to ask about later, when stopping wouldn't kill her.

Everywhere his mouth touched her skin became heated. Something she'd never experienced with her past lovers—this need. She ached to the point that the whole thing was becoming unpleasant.

One hand shot to the side, where she thought he'd dropped the foil packages, and half felt, half banged around on the floor. "Condom…condom." She panted the word. When he lifted to look at her, there was a question in his eyes.

"I don't doubt you'll remember. And this isn't a date. And neither of us thinks so, right?" And with her brain functioning at half-power she added, "I'm not supposed to have babies."

He reached for one of the condoms she'd pelted him with, bit into the foil, placed it over the head of his shaft and unrolled it with one stroking fist. The bruised knuckles even thrilled her. There was something incredibly erotic about watching his muscled arm complete that motion, and she was never so happy to have massaged someone in her life—gods only knew how this would go if his shoulder still hurt like it had.

His hands fell onto the mattress at either side of her and he lowered himself until they were pressed together again, his sheathed heat between her legs, though he made no move to enter her yet. "Why aren't you supposed to have babies?" The words were an effort for him to speak, every one carrying an edge of tension and urgency.

Had she told him that? "Uh. Well…because I'm not supposed to be alive."

She grabbed his head and tugged his mouth back to hers, needing his kisses like she needed air. He pulled back long enough to look at her, a question on his handsome, scruffy, three-day bearded face, but to her relief he didn't ask. Instead, he reached between them and glided the head of his erection over the little nub begging for his attention, and then drove into her with a single thrust.

She arched, lifting her hips from the bed, pushing against him in such blatant wantonness she kind of shocked herself, but he wasn't moving yet—just holding her, pinned by his big body and the frowning concentration in his eyes.

"Don't look like that," she muttered, wiggling her hips again to try and spur him on. "What's wrong?"

"You will explain yourself to me after we're done." He gritted the words through clenched teeth.

Ellory groaned then slid her hands down his back to squeeze his clenched butt as he held himself motionless inside her.

"Say it."

"No." Already flushed and wanting, the heat that stole

over her face now was of a very different sort: anger. She was mad at him again. "This is cruel."

"Say you will explain it when we're done or we're done now."

"No."

He began pulling away. The madman meant it!

"*Fine*," she growled, now really wanting to hit him. "I'll tell you but this is blackmail."

The savage smile he gave her made her want to hit him even more, but he pressed forward, filling her again and then establishing a rhythm she was too thankful for to remember to be angry.

Bracing her feet against the bed, she lifted her hips to push at him and he took the hint, rolling with her, letting her be on top. There would be no more withholding anything from her if she was in control.

She'd just stay sitting up, it was a little bit of distance because he was a big hunky jerk and he didn't deserve the full-length loving.

But within a few measly heartbeats she'd leaned down to kiss him again, and his arms locked back around her waist, chaining her to him so tightly that she could feel the instant their heartbeats synchronized. Not every beat, but as they moved it became obvious to her that they were meant to be there together—two heartbeats that overlapped for short intervals that gradually became one thunderous, unified hammering as they built to a climax so fierce and pure she could have cried.

Ellory believed in fate, and that sometimes things were meant to be. She and Anson, here in this moment, was bigger than her pitiful needs, desires, or resolutions. Their hearts beat together.

She could only pray hers kept beating when they came apart again.

* * *

The curtains had been drawn before they'd gone to sleep, the extra layer of wind protection also keeping it mostly dark in the room.

So it wasn't the light that woke Ellory. It was the foreign sound of the fireplace clicking off. That hadn't happened since they'd moved into the suite. The wind had been blowing hard enough that the thermostat in the fireplace fought constantly with the wind to keep the room warm.

But not Ellory. She had a big warm man behind her, wrapping her in heat, and a big warm dog on her feet, keeping them warm.

Max lifted his head to look at the fireplace, which gave her an opening. She rolled to face the sleeping doctor, who had at some point put his shirt back on. She found the hem and slid her hands inside over the firm male flesh and the crisp tickle of hair against her palms.

Anson awoke to the feeling of Ellory pushing his shirt up. His chest was bare by the time his mind cleared and he lifted his arms enough to let her push the warm material over his head.

"I need skin. Why did you put these back on?" she grumbled, her voice just a little bit raspy from sleep. Sexy.

Just like that, he woke up.

She nudged him until he rolled to his back and she rolled with him, straddling his hips in a position that reminded him of last night's activities and made his body respond—intentions forming.

Wiggling around a little, when she was satisfied with the bare chest-to-chest position, her head turned to press her cheek into his shoulder and her nose up under his chin. "Just so you know, we can have morning sex and it still doesn't mean we're dating. We're still not dating, we're just comforting each other."

"So your resolution is intact?"

"Mmm-hmm."

He grinned, his hands stroking over her bare back, having not really had the time to luxuriate in her body when they'd been together before.

The sound of silence cut through the sexy haze settling over his brain. No hissing from the fireplace.

No wind.

No wind!

Light reflected up onto the ceiling in a pink band above the curtains.

"The storm..." He rolled her off him immediately and stood up to look out the window. Deep snow, at least five feet, had been dumped on them, but it was calm now and reflected the soft pink hue of sunrise.

Ellory joined him at the window, pulling her thermals back on. He didn't look, he was still waiting for his body to catch up with his brain and give up on the idea of sex so soon after it had become ready for it.

"It's over?" she asked.

"We can go back out."

Ellory looked toward the brand-new snowsuit laid out like a deflated person-shaped balloon on the sofa. She'd already purchased the thing, not wearing it would be even more wasteful than wearing it. Plus, if she wanted to go out with the team and help look for Jude—which she really did— she'd have to put it on.

While Anson was on the radio, waking everyone up, Ellory got dressed in her new gear.

"You have to eat something before you go out there."

"The kitchen staff are going to make breakfast now," he said, turning to look at her by the door. "Where are you going?"

"I was going to talk to Mira for a minute before we go

out." She said the words casually, hoping he wouldn't pick up on her meaning until she was actually out with him and he couldn't…

"You're not going."

Do that…

"I want to go." He should know how badly she wanted to go considering her getting dressed in the new—and worrisomely awesome—snow suit. "I want to help."

"I know you do." He sighed, scrubbing a hand over his face. "But Mira is going to need your help. Chelsea isn't going to want to leave, but with the snow past, you can get her and Nate to the hospital. Have Mira call for a chopper or maybe another crew to come up. Do they have a snow coach or something here? Multi-passenger? Preferably enclosed. I'd rather keep Nate out of the cold wind as much as possible and Chelsea can't wear her boots while her toes are swollen."

Ellory frowned. "Mira's a doctor too, you know. She can handle this stuff. Plus she knows how things work here and I don't. If I come with you, I can maybe get places you couldn't. I'm smaller."

"How big is Jude?"

Okay, she didn't know how big Jude was. He could be Anson-sized for all she knew. "Probably bigger than me."

"It's dangerous out there. I don't want to have to worry about you too."

"If I stay with you—"

"Ellory? I'm not having your life on my hands too. That's how it is out there. I have to find the one who is lost and keep my crew and Max safe. That's seven lives on my shoulders. I'm not adding to that weight with one more person who won't be of any help and who I don't need."

She flinched and hurried out the door before he could say something else negative. No, she didn't know what she could do, but it was doing something. An extra pair of eyes would be helpful. When she was just here, just waiting for them to return, it had been bad enough when she hadn't even known him.

Even when someone was as on the ball as Mira was, it took time to ready the snow carriage to transport patients down the mountain. If they waited until tomorrow the workmen would've had time to inspect the cables leading from the resort down to the town, but just jumping into an aerial carriage and hoping for the best would've been colossally stupid after the couple days they'd had.

Since Mira was doing the organizing, she waited with Chelsea. "How are you doing?" She dragged a chair up to Chelsea's wheelchair and sat, offering a hand should the woman need some support.

"Bad," she admitted, and then took Ellory's hand. "I know that I need to go to the hospital, and Nate needs to go too—we probably all need checking over, but I want to stay. Even with the power situation as it is, I just want to be here for the instant that they find him."

Her hand felt dry and tight, still chapped and rough from her time in the storm. Spotting a bottle of lotion across the room, Ellory stood and went to get it. She made a conscious decision not to check the chemicals, poured some into her hands and set about rubbing it into Chelsea's hands, working the muscles as she went.

"I pray that they find him today, but if they don't, we'll make sure you get regular updates."

"Regular updates?" Mira said from behind her, having entered quietly. "Absolutely. I've got my cell and I will call your hospital room several times a day to keep you up to date." She gestured to what Ellory was doing and asked, "Almost done?"

"Yes, just rubbing the lotion in. Are we ready to go?"

"They're out plowing the lot now and someone shoveled a path to the snow carriage, so we can go as soon as we're ready."

Anson had a plan, but he didn't have a good feeling about it. Normally, out on the mountainside, doing his job, he felt peace. There was purpose to it, the extreme focus and need to push himself cleared his mind of anything else. Even the cold air he breathed exhilarated him.

Today every breath burned, both going in and out. Which was how he knew it was in his head and not him coming down with whatever Nate had been ignoring for his ski vacation.

There was no thrill from zipping around the mountainside on his snowmobile, though he usually loved it. Snowmobiles triggered avalanches easily, and because the day before the snow front had arrived had been sunny and warmer than usual, it had weakened the snow supporting the thick, deadly mantle they were all riding around on. Even without them making any mistakes or pushing any limits, that layer of snow could slip at any time.

Six people on his crew meant he had enough to split up in to three teams and work on the buddy system, driving far enough apart that if the ground started to slip it was less likely that both searchers would be swept away in the snow, and all were wearing locator beacons in case the worst happened. Even Max had one on his collar.

Anson looked behind him in the mirror again and caught sight of his buddy, and then Max's big head filling up the rear view, panting in that way that looked like a smile.

Having the Newfoundland with an insanely talented nose made their searching easier.

Anson stopped outside South Mine, got one of Jude's

shirts from a plastic bag he carried, and opened Max's cage. By the time his search buddy reached him, Max was already snuffling the shirt and taking off for the mine. Both rescuers grabbed their lights and followed him inside, but the dog didn't stay.

Jude wasn't in there.

He sniffed in a circle in the entrance, and then headed back outside to sniff the air, looking for an air trail to follow.

The wind was blowing from the northwest—the direction of the lodge—and Max got nothing. No excited yips that would indicate he'd found a trail.

Anson pulled his radio off his belt and called it in. "Search team one at South Mine. It's clear."

The radio crackled and it became immediately clear that Ellory was still considering herself part of the search, even if he hadn't let her come out.

"What does that mean? Where are you going now? Did Max pick up which way to go from there?"

She didn't even know how to use a radio properly.

"No, he didn't. Would've been hard considering the storm, hard winds and deep snow."

"Oh."

He heard the disappointment in her tone. And since he'd already disappointed her once today he added, "If he found a scent, it would probably mean Jude was outside in the snow, and that would be bad news. The other teams are going by foot through the woods to try and pick up his trail where we couldn't search. And to hit the cave between. We're going northeast."

"But that's away from the lodge."

"I know. I'll call when we've reached the next stop."

He ended the communication and stashed his radio again, getting Max back into his cage to go.

He'd probably given her false hope. If the other two

teams didn't find Jude where the snowmobiles had been unable to travel, it was unlikely they'd find him alive. Everything else was outside the direction he should have traveled, which was why they were heading off in the wrong direction.

That's where he and his mother had gotten lost: Down the wrong side of the mountain.

CHAPTER TEN

TWILIGHT HAD ENDED thirty-seven minutes ago, which meant it was officially dark. So dark Ellory could probably see the Milky Way if she looked long enough.

They were supposed to stop searching when it got dark. It was a rule. The other two teams that made up Anson's crew had returned to the lodge, but he and Marks? Still. Not. Back.

Ellory didn't need to ask why they weren't back yet. Anson was pushing it to the last possible moment in order to find the missing skier. Or past the last possible minute...

Because they hadn't found even a trace of Jude. Yet. Yet, yet, yet. She mentally scolded herself for her pessimistic thinking. As angry as she'd gotten while waiting for them to return—and being mad at Anson again just underscored the fact that they were incompatible—she knew Anson would be beating himself up more than she could ever stand to do.

With the snow that had fallen the risk of avalanche was incredibly high. The teams had managed to trigger two different small slides today without getting trapped in them, which was why they didn't bring in a helicopter for air searching yet. They'd been lucky that the slides had happened in areas where there weren't caves or mines where Jude could be hiding.

Headlights bouncing off the blue night-time snow told Ellory they were back, and no one else would have to say boo to him about being out there after dark. She was going to confront his handsome and well-toned ass, and she didn't even like the idea of it.

In her new suit—which she loved even more after a couple weeks of Colorado winter in equatorial clothing, she stayed inside the breezeway leading to the lobby, opening the outer doors from the inside when Max got there, and then again when the bipeds caught up.

"It's dark," she said to Anson, who stepped past her and into the lobby, making a beeline for the fire she'd kept stoked for them. "You are supposed to be here before it's dark. When it's still light out. To travel safely...*more* safely. Two slides! Two in one day."

She put a bowl of warmed water down on the floor for the dog then grabbed two big mugs of cocoa she'd been keeping warm and forced them on both men. "Drink this. And say you will be back earlier tomorrow."

Anson took the cocoa thankfully and drank it down fast enough that she once again felt compelled to apologize for giving him food with preservatives in it. Maybe they'd preserve him longer if he got trapped in a freaking slide tomorrow. "We checked in."

Sure, but after dark, and the only way that would've comforted her was if he'd also kept up a steady stream of running chatter on the radio while they'd been driving back, so she'd know from second to second that he'd still been alive. "Not recently."

"Elle, I can't talk and drive at the same time. It's treacherous out there."

"Yes. Yes, it is." She puffed and took a seat, making herself calm down before she actually did yell at him. He looked haggard, worse than he had that first time she'd seen him, and he'd been grappling with the idea that he had lost his first person on the mountain overnight. And put his fist through the wall.

"Tomorrow more crews with their own dogs will be here. Mira called up everyone she could think of when we were getting Chelsea and Nate down to the hospital. We passed power crews working on the poles and the power should be back on tonight or tomorrow," she informed him. "Two of her toes had sprung big blisters this morning, so they've confirmed that she has stage-two frostbite on two of her toes. But they've got a treatment plan and said it's very unlikely that she'll lose them."

He nodded, still grim but happier to hear some good news. Because the window where they could hope to find Jude alive was rapidly diminishing. She couldn't even think about what that would do to him.

"The original rooms in the lodge, the first ones built, still have water heaters that run on natural gas. Mira showed me today and we all had baths. You can have a hot shower to warm up. I'll take you to the rooms. But the rooms are pretty cold. No fireplaces there so dry, dress and get back to your real room so you don't get pneumonia or something."

She led them to the rooms they'd been using, steering Anson toward one and leaving Marks for the other, pointing out that fresh towels had been put on the bed for him. And repeating her warning that he not dawdle.

"Are you okay?" she said to Anson, as they and the dog stepped into the room. She'd lit candles in there earlier. They'd been burning since the first staff member had gone to shower, so the room was not nearly as chilly as she'd expected. Max hopped onto the bed and lay down.

Anson sighed and shook his head. The admission surprised her. "I don't think he's alive. And what a coward I am. I didn't want to come back here and have to tell Chelsea. The others… I know they're all close. I can tell the other two…"

"They all went down together. No one wanted to wait here."

"Because I can't find him?"

Ellory stepped over and helped him with his suit, knowing how stiff and useless your fingers got when you'd been in the cold too long. "No, because they want to be with Chelsea and Nate. And Mira and I both promised them that we would contact them if the situation changed, and Mira is taking lead on contacting them several times a day anyway, just so they expect to get updates and all that. Waiting is murder."

"You have no idea."

She wanted to ask, but the wound seemed too raw right now. Instead, she just continued helping him undress. And once he was in the shower she undressed too and joined him under the spray. It was dark so she couldn't see what he was feeling by looking at his face. The best she could do was distract and comfort him.

If she was honest, that wasn't all it was. She needed a little comfort too.

By the end of the second day of searching the power had come back on, returning them to the twentieth century, but the broadband was still out, making rejoining the twenty-first century still a goal. Anson and Ellory remained in the fireplace suite they'd been using for the extra heat the gas logs provided. And she didn't feel at all bad about the carbon—not because she was adopting the habit of her current boyfriend, he wasn't her boyfriend, but he needed the heat. He needed it, and that was enough to keep her from focusing on the negative.

By the end of the fifth day, no matter what she tried she couldn't get him warm when he came in.

The hearty and thick lentil stew she'd made didn't warm him.

The showers he took were so hot they left him a vigorous shade of pink, but still didn't manage to cut through the ice that had settled in his core. When he stepped out of the steamy shower or bath he got cold again.

Worst of all—the sex failed to heat him up too.

Bleak, fast, and over too soon, Ellory felt blistered by the haunted look in his eyes, even at climax. She'd have sworn he didn't want her there with him at all if every night he didn't wrap himself around her on the mattress that still rested before the perpetually burning fire, and burrow beneath the thick duvet and her quilt.

Even when the heat he surrounded himself with made him sweaty and miserable, he still shook when he slept. He still said he was cold.

The sex was supposed to help him sleep, but it didn't. He remained stiff behind her, except for the constant low rumble of shaking that seemed to come from his chest and shoulders.

They both avoided mentioning the elephant in the room: everyone's worry about how long they would be able to search for Jude, and when would it be called off or considered pointless?

Putting the thought out of her mind, she rolled to face him, her hand coming to cup his cheek and force his eyes to open. "You have to relax."

"I'm trying." He licked his lips. "I know I should be sleeping so I can be my best tomorrow, but I just really want to get back out there right now. I'm not even sleepy."

"Do you want a massage?"

He shook his head.

She didn't offer sex again, it hadn't worked the first

time and with his head as screwed up as it was right now he didn't need to venture into anything adventurous and kinky in search of relaxation.

"Meditate with me."

"Elle, I can't concentrate right now."

"You don't have to concentrate." She pulled away from him, though it took effort—he didn't want to let go. "I'm not going far." The words were ones she might've said to comfort a child. Grabbing the quilt from on top of the duvet, she shook it out. "Sit, legs crossed."

His arms loosened.

To his credit, Anson didn't sigh. He didn't roll his eyes. He sat up and did as she asked.

Ellory wrapped the quilt around his back to keep him warm and then climbed onto his lap, wrapping her legs around his.

"Is this some kind of sex meditation?" he asked, wrapping his arms around her waist as she settled against him. The tremor he was unable to stop made it feel vaguely like cuddling a big manly vibrator.

A shake of her head. "No. It's much simpler than that." She combed her fingers through the hair at his temples and kept his face facing forward. "All I want you to do is look me in the eyes. Watch the light of the fire, and just be. You don't have to do anything. I don't expect anything from you. It's not so hard to look at me, is it?"

"It's incredibly easy to look at you," he breathed back, but his brows were still pinched, like he was concentrating. "But how is this meditating?"

"It's supposed to make you feel safe…and connected. Do you feel safe?"

He gave her one of those smiles that contradicted his pinched brows.

"How about connected?"

"I feel connected."

That one she believed, but he needed to relax his brow if he had any hope of this working. She pressed one thumb between his brows and gave that muscle a firm rub until it relaxed, ran him through some breathing techniques and then settled her arms around his shoulders.

Her neck relaxed a little, causing her head to tilt to one side, and stared deep into deep green and hazel eyes, saddened at the bleakness there.

He mirrored the action, keeping their eyes aligned.

She kept her voice gentle, wanting nothing more than to soothe. "We're sharing energy. It's like physics. Entangled particles. We will just sit and be together, share breath, share heat, share touch. You will look into me, and I will look into you. And when our particles are good and entangled, no matter where you are on the mountain, doing this terrible job that needs to be done, you can share my peace and hope when your well has run dry, and I can share your burden."

He swallowed, but he didn't argue. She half expected him to declare the exercise stupid and pointless, but surprisingly his arms relaxed until they were more looped around her than holding her.

If there was one thing Ellory knew how to do, it was relax. She could cast off her conscious mind with astonishing ease, having learned long ago how to escape into her imagination.

Pulse and respiration slowed, relaxation extending from her body to her eyes. The focus went past the firelight dancing in his mossy eyes, and images started to emerge. First blurry, then crisp. A home in green fields, babies with eyes like the forest, and fuzzy black puppies. She saw the green fading from his eyes, the dark fringe of his lashes turn sparse and grey, and love that grew strong.

She saw everything she'd always said she never wanted, and knew it for what it was: the biggest lie of her life. The bond she felt with him, the aching need, that was love. She loved him. This was that moment that Mira and Chelsea had been describing, where her heart swelled and… She remembered she couldn't have that future. She couldn't have him, but she couldn't even begin to understand how she would ever be strong enough to walk away from it.

Anson shook her.

Something cold and wet splashed on her chest, and she realized she was crying. Her breath came in broken hiccups and she let go of his shoulders. "I can't do this." Her having some kind of a breakdown wasn't the purge he needed to start healing. It was hers. How many purges did she have to have to reach the bottom?

"Why? What just happened?" His voice firmed with intention, focus, and he kept his arms locked around her waist. "What are you afraid I'm going to see?"

"I don't know." She pulled back hard, and turned to crawl off him and away. Just get away.

He let her go, sounding bewildered but not following. "You do know. What's wrong?"

"I don't know," she repeated, and only stopped once she reached the farthest corner of the mattress, her back to him, on her knees, struggling to calm herself.

This was supposed to be for him. Metaphorical, a way of releasing tension, not anything real. If this was how he felt…

She gulped the air, smelling the sharp ping of the natural gas from the fireplace and focusing on that smell, using it to clear her head. This was supposed to be about him, not about her…

"Talk. You said you put things together in words. Talk." His words came from right behind her, and his arms came around her waist again, pulling her back to his chest and then into his lap as he sat. "You're not going anywhere. You said we're having a spirit quest, so if you really believe that then you either know something you don't want to know, or you just figured something out. Tell me."

She had to say something, and blurted out the first words that came to her mind. "You find people who are lost…"

"I find people who are lost," he confirmed, and waited for her say more. Think it through.

But right now it wasn't about making connections. That one statement unlocked so much more. So much she didn't even really want to think about, let alone put into words. Or what she could even tell him without freaking him out.

That she knew she loved him?

That she knew she wanted him?

That she'd change every part of who she was just for the chance to be with him?

That she wasn't even supposed to be alive, so how could she be with him?

She wasn't supposed to be able to have a family and make more people, more consumers, add to overpopulation. She couldn't settle down, stop going out into the world on her missions to try and make her accidental life a happy accident instead of being the waste her father had always said she would be.

As she felt the firm heat against her back she realized he'd stopped shaking. At least she'd managed that…

She'd never loved any man because she'd always dated men she wasn't especially attracted to—the ones who wouldn't tempt her—and if they were from the places she frequented they understood her lifestyle.

She couldn't even let herself think about the possibility of having her own family. It was wrong. It confirmed every bad thing her father had said about her. It made him right, and it hurt too much. Daydreaming gave her hope, but it was false.

But somehow Anson had slipped past her defenses and

she wanted to change, be someone that he could love. Become someone real.

She had to say something, and she couldn't lie to him.

Instead, she whispered the only thing she could. "I don't want to tell you."

He didn't say anything right away, just held her and nuzzled into her hair until she relaxed against him.

"Is it too hard to say?"

"I don't want you to know."

He stilled. "You don't trust me?"

"You find people who are lost," she repeated, not knowing what else to say, "but you can't find me, Anson. There's nothing to find."

The sigh that preceded his words said as much as his tone. "There damned well is someone to find."

"I don't want to hurt you."

"Is this about what you said the other night? I forgot about that. You aren't supposed to be alive?"

She went quiet again, trying to sort through it. But the epiphanies that had given her the bum's rush dried up with her gaze fixed on the wall. His heart beat against her back slow and steady while hers hammered so hard her lungs felt they would bruise.

"My father and mother didn't ever want to have children. The world is overpopulated, and people who are trying to change should lead by showing the way. They shouldn't have kids because it helps offset all the people who have lots of kids and all that."

"Why did they?"

"Accident. Mom got pregnant and her conscience wouldn't let her have an abortion. So I'm this black mark on Dad's record. I make him a hypocrite."

"He said that to you?" Anson asked, the incredulity in his voice making her look back at him.

"Honesty is the best policy."

"It's not the best policy when it makes your kids feel…I don't even… I can't even think of what you…"

"I'm fine. I just I don't want to mess up. I need to do better than they did. Not ever get pregnant, or have the strength to do what has to be done if I do. I shouldn't have the opportunity to make more lives to burden the planet with, or burden the planet in any other way either. So I try…"

He flipped her around so she landed on the mattress on her back. He leaned over her, his expression thunderous. "You're not a burden on the planet. If your parents actually said that…"

"Oh, not my mom. She never… Just my dad. He has very strong morals."

Anson might've put his fist through the wall once or twice in his life, but he didn't take out his aggression on people. Ellory's father? He'd make an exception for that man, if he ever met him. "What did you think of when you ran away from me just now?"

"Nothing. Nothing important."

"You tell me right now."

"It's not important. I know why I was supposed to come back here now. That's what is important."

She reached for his face, trying to distract him or soothe him, when she was the one who needed soothing. He pulled her hands away from his face and laid them on her chest, holding them there, holding her beneath him. "You want to know why you're not happy? That's why. No one can be happy under that weight. That lie."

"I was supposed to come back here and find you."

"So I could tell you that what they told you was bull?"

"No. Stop thinking about that. It's not important. What's important is that you're lost too. You find people, but you're lost. Someone else has to find you."

CHAPTER ELEVEN

ANSON KEPT HER pinned beneath him so she couldn't get away—it felt like that kind of a situation, where one wrong move and she'd be gone from him. "You can't be okay with this. It's not an okay situation. You can talk to me."

"You can talk to me too. I've told you so much about myself, but I know very little about you. It has upset you, even though that's silly, so now you want to talk about it. But there's other stuff that upsets you and you never talk about that stuff. I've told you, like…everything about me. If you can't tell me anything, then whatever connection… whatever is going on between us is just a joke."

He didn't want to talk about that stuff. He wanted to talk about this stuff. This *I'm supposed to not be alive* stuff. "If I tell you that stuff, will you talk about this too?"

She looked at him for several long seconds and then nodded. "If you tell me about the important things, about how you feel about Jude and why it's so personal, and I want to know about your toes…and your mom—were you with her when she died? You tell me that so I don't have to keep trying to badger it out of you, and I will tell you what you want to know. You can't just try to shut me up with kissing or some other method. If you keep bottling things up, eventually you're going to put your fist through another wall."

"That was before we were together."

"It was when you needed someone to talk to and refused to talk to anyone."

Anson sighed and leaned off her, pulling her with him as he rolled onto his back. He liked this position. His arms could go around her and her hair was loose, not lain on or pinned down in any fashion—he could touch it without accidental pulling and he found that soothing.

She did warm him, and he finally noticed the tremor he'd been feeling in his guts had stopped.

Being with her—fed by her, held by her, loved by her— were all comforts, but being challenged by her, being worried about her, was what turned up his internal furnace and finally warmed him.

Telling her the whole truth would make her feel differently about him. Maybe not negative—not telling her was doing that already—but would she take his guilt on? She'd said as much before she'd started inexplicably crying.

"Me not telling you that stuff, how I got stranded on the mountain, it's not that I think you wouldn't understand. I know you would understand, you're probably the most empathic person I've ever met…"

"Then why? It hurts me that you won't tell me. And, more importantly, it hurts you."

"That's not more important." He bit the words out, then stopped and took a breath. He didn't want to yell at her, upset her more. It was his frustration talking. And the fact that he needed to know why she'd started crying, what dark thing she'd thought about herself. She couldn't carry that darkness, it *would* hurt her. Change her. "What makes you think I don't deserve the burden I carry?"

"You're a good man."

He shook his head, and she must have felt it because she lifted her head from his chest and looked up. He kept his eyes on the ceiling, though, not looking her in the eye might be the only way he could get through this.

"You're a freaking hero!"

"I killed my mother."

She went utterly still in his arms, even to the point she stopped breathing. He felt her heartbeat increasing beneath where his palm flattened against her back, keeping her close.

"I don't believe you."

But her behavior said she did believe him. He gave her a little shake and she started breathing again, though more shallowly and faster than normal.

He had to tell her now. And he couldn't look at her when he told her. Rolling again, he managed to get her on her side and lie behind her, where he could once more bury his face in her hair. It was soft, and her scent comforting.

"We were on our yearly ski trip. I was ten."

"Where?"

"Here." He answered the question then continued. "A storm was coming. We, my mom and I, had stayed out until the snow started coming down too hard. She said it was time to go down, go back inside. I said one more run... And before she could grab me I took off down the back side of the pass. If I was going to get in trouble for disobeying, then I was going to get the most mileage out of that punishment I could. That side of the pass, the steep side...no one had let me go down every time I'd tried. They all said it was too advanced for me."

"Did you fall?"

"Of course I did. It *was* too advanced for me. I gave it a good run, made it about two-thirds of the way down before I wiped out on a rock while going too fast. Fell. Slid the rest of the way down the slope. Broke my leg. Thigh. Femur."

"Where your scar is?"

He'd seen her examining it before, she'd touched him

everywhere, but he'd been pretty good about distracting her when she'd been working up to the question. "Yes."

He waited for her to absorb that. She thought through things out loud usually, and no way was he going to do this again. Do it once, do it right, put it out of his mind. That meant letting her have questions as they went.

"Did she find you?"

"She caught up to me when I was on my back, facing downhill, screaming. We were completely alone—if someone had been around they would've heard the screaming."

She started squirming, trying to turn herself around. He didn't want to look her in the eye right now. "Be still." He squeezed then pressed a kiss into the crook of her neck. And then another. And then behind the ear. Sex between them was explosive enough that he could put an end to this conversation for now, continue kissing her, work her up... She'd give up talking but then he'd just have to deal with it again another day, and he wanted answers right now too.

"So what happened? A broken femur can't bear any weight. Was it a straight break? You must have hit... It was here at the pass? I don't remember hearing about this."

"I'm a few years older than you. I was ten. So you were..."

"Six."

"Most six-year-olds don't keep up with the news."

She nodded and sighed. "So it was that big boulder toward the bottom of the insane slope...the one that juts out and is all sharp? I used to think it was a tooth that the mountain had. Mountain tooth."

"That's the one," he confirmed. "Tooth works. And, yes, I couldn't put any weight on it. She wasn't a large woman, so the best we could do was me pushing with one leg while she pulled me. The storm was really picking up, the sky got so dark it could've been night, but she managed to find a tight overhang, a ledge close to the ground. She crawled in then dragged me in after her."

Her fingers twined with his, showing the support he'd known she'd show him. It was easier to accept the support from her hands than to see it in her eyes.

"The first night was the worst. So cold. We couldn't even really huddle together for warmth because of how shallow the space was. My leg hurt so bad. She fished a toy from my backpack and used it like a puppet, told me stories...

"We thought the storm would break in the morning. I was losing consciousness in spells that day, so it was a better day for me. I try not to think about what it was like for her."

She managed to roll over when his arms relaxed, taking advantage of that small window before he could stop her. Her hand pulled free of his and she used it to brush his hair back from his face, her palm soft, and in that moment he knew she loved him. Which meant he had to tell her what he'd caused so she could know what she was getting into. If he told her he loved her before telling that, it'd color and corrupt her thoughts.

"From there, the story is what I've managed to cobble together from what other people have told me and what I remember. When the storm stopped on the third day I was completely out. I don't remember that night or morning at all. I imagine she tried to wake me. I didn't actually wake up until several days later in the hospital, which was a couple of days after my final surgery. There was one to repair my thigh, the pins needed to set the bone and remove some tissue that had died. And the second one was to remove toes that had succumbed to frostbite. Only one on the healthy leg, but the broken one got it worse. Probably because of restricted blood flow to the area."

"I didn't put that together. I saw the scars..."

"I know." Part of being loved by Ellory meant she touched him everywhere. She hadn't simply stroked her fingers over that scar, she'd kissed it on multiple occasions. She just hadn't known it was all connected.

"How did they find you?"

"She'd tucked her outer jacket over my legs to try and keep them warm..."

"Femur breaks are terrible..."

"Yes. And lots of blood pooled. She was a doctor too, an ER doctor, so she would've known how dire my situation was becoming. After doing what she could to keep me warm, she crawled out and tried to make it up and over the mountain."

"Did they find her?"

"Yes. She'd frozen before she reached the top. Being three days without food and water...she just wasn't strong enough to make it. They followed her trail back to find me."

She combed his hair again and pulled him down until his head was on her chest and she could continue the petting. He should argue with her about it. He didn't deserve her comfort. If he had to relive it while finding Jude...who had left his friends to try and get help, just like his mother had done...he deserved to feel miserable.

"What you're feeling now? Everyone goes through it. It's the bottom."

"Rock bottom?"

"When you're on a quest, you have to purge all the bad stuff before you can start to heal."

Healing. She was so sweet. He wouldn't heal, and he didn't want to. He deserved whatever punishment his mind, or the universe, as she liked to say, deigned to dish out. There could never be redemption for what he'd done. There just was no way to make up for it. His mother was gone.

She'd always be gone. His father had lost the woman he loved, and it was *his* fault.

It was his weakness that kept him from pulling away from her. Just another sin, a mark of his cowardice. The search was pulling him back into the void he'd suffered in his darkest days during recovery, and Ellory was his lifeline. If she was pulling away from him, he had to keep her with him. At least until he found Jude and could afford the time it would take to lose his damned mind properly.

"What are you thinking?"

"That I need this," Anson muttered. He shouldn't, but if she knew…maybe she'd stick with him a little longer.

"This? Do you mean to feel bad?"

"No. I mean this." He slid his hand over her skin until it settled over her breast, and the soft firmness that instantly changed, the nipple growing hard to poke the hollow of his palm.

Before she could ask anything else, he pulled her under him, slid an arm under her neck and kissed her. He could lose himself in her—his only way to keep from thinking. Burying himself in her was his only form of meditation, her soft body, her tender heart, and the brief, blessed oblivions she could give him.

"You owe me words, Ellory Star."

"I know," she whispered, still touching his face. "Can we save it for tomorrow? I'd really like it if you would just kiss me right now."

Day fourteen of searching since the storm had passed.

Nothing had been the same since that night—except in every physical way.

Another long hot shower, though she didn't join him wasting the water any more. Their showers got longer and longer—more and more wasteful—when she was with him. And she wanted to ignore that little voice that insisted she was making herself into whatever she needed to be to fit into his lifestyle. But she didn't really know what his lifestyle was—in her mind it was the worst it could be for her. Becoming the antithesis of all the things she'd believed in her whole life…even if it would make life easier and keep her from being this obsessive crazy person, it felt like exchanging one set of bad habits for another.

At least if she listened to that annoying little voice right now, she could feel confident that she wouldn't be manufacturing more guilt for herself later when she finally did figure out what she was supposed to do with herself, how she was supposed to find a way out from beneath the crushing guilt, and find contentment. It was all hard enough without having to think about the things she'd been conditioned to do. Habits, even while tiring and tiresome, were easier than the uncertainty.

Another hot and hearty meal to cut the chill and fortify him. He ate too fast, so did she—it was simply nutrition, tasteless no matter how she tried to make it good, and they both needed to get back to that mattress, their only comfort.

She'd tried to explain to him that her father's distance and disapproval had driven her to live the best life she could, and that while she could see why it upset him, she thought she'd turned it into something positive. Or she'd always thought that until now. She'd tried to explain it until they both were so frustrated with one another they stopped talking altogether.

She didn't know what to say or how to help him. She wanted to help, and she'd made early attempts to try and tell him he couldn't live his life with that kind of blackness in his heart without it consuming him. He'd nodded, repeated it back to her, and disregarded her advice.

As soon as they found Jude, Ellory was going to break it off. It would be an acceptable time then. She wouldn't be abandoning him when he needed the support she absolutely knew he did need. But afterwards…breaking up was just what had to happen.

It already hurt so bad to be with him that she was trying to soothe herself when they went to bed as much as she was trying to soothe him.

Those all-too-brief moments of bliss when they were together carried her through the next day. Well, almost through. Like a drug, the more she had of him, the quicker the effect wore off until she needed more. She'd had friends who had gone down dark paths—had watched them spiral down, and when lucky, their recovery.

It was the only mental comparison she could make. Withdrawal. How bad would it be to recover from his touch? Would she have any chance of staying on the wagon if she stayed in town where she had access to her drug of choice?

She should start looking now for a new mission. Some exotic new location, people she could actually help and feel good about herself again. Somewhere she didn't have to work so hard to figure out how to live… If she were in some remote village away from all modern conveniences— where they struggled to provide running water— she'd live simply and have no way to be a planetary burden.

They were just finishing dinner when someone knocked at the door.

Mira?

"Graves?" A low man's voice called.

"It's Frank." Anson stood up and answered the door. "Are we going back out?"

Frank Powell was his supervisor, and he had taken over managing the search operation once roads up to the lodge had been cleared enough to get additional search teams in.

Wishful thinking. Ellory saw it on his face the moment she joined them. They weren't going back out.

Frank stepped inside and closed the door. "No, not tonight," he answered first, and then dipped his head to her. "Evenin', Ellory." They'd met many times in the past two weeks as she'd made it part of her job description to bring food to the base of operations they'd set up in one of the conference rooms.

Her visits had never been wholly selfless. With all the tooling they did about the mountains on the snowmobiles, she was in a constant state of anxiety that a slide would happen and bury them all. Showing up with food or drinks gave her an excuse to be there and hear any information, and sometimes to just hear Anson's voice come through on the radio and know that he was okay. Or as okay as he could be.

She was about to offer food when the older gentleman turned to Anson. "I wanted to come tell you in person— word's officially come down that the search for Wyndham is being reclassified as a recovery mission."

They'd been waiting for this moment, but her heart still sank. She may have only been a few feet away from Anson but hurried over to him and slipped her hand into his.

"There's still a chance," he said, for once not accepting her comforting touch. His hand pulled free and he scrubbed it over his face, trying to wipe off the lie he'd just uttered. They all knew better. Jude could've never survived two weeks in the cold without food or water. He couldn't have survived one week, and probably not even a few days. He was gone, and had been for probably the whole time they'd been searching.

Frank knew his words for what they were—grief. Grief for a man he had never met. Grief for a man he felt like he'd let down. Grief for himself… His normally booming voice was gentle, gentler than Ellory would've ever thought he could make it. "You know that's not true, son."

Anson stepped away from both of them, and Max, sensing the discord in the air, stood up where he was in front of the fire and went straight to Anson's side, ducking his nose and pushing forward until Anson's hand cupped his head.

Anson took the request and petted his trusty companion. Which was good. At least he was touching and taking comfort from someone who loved him.

"Most of the outside teams are leaving and we're re-working our plan," Frank continued. "You and Max should be on duty where you can help the living. I want you to take a couple of days to rest and then report for regular duty."

Anson folded his arms and shook his head. "No. We need to see this through, Max and I. We're not off the search team." The dog moved in front of Anson and sat, a silent and calm sentinel doing what sentinels did. Protective instinct. Ellory couldn't blame him. Hers were running on high too. She just couldn't pull off the calm sentinel routine like Max did. She'd have said something if she knew what to say.

Was she supposed to back him up? The search was killing him, but not searching? She had no idea how that would affect him.

The next day, while Anson was disobeying orders, Ellory did what any sensible kind of almost-girlfriend would do when confronted with a man in pain: she dug around for information about him on the internet. Found his father's name and that he was a doctor still practicing in San Francisco. Found his mother in an article talking about the rescue, and a memoriam set up to remember her by her old hospital.

None of it was particularly insightful, though she did find one gem: an old photo attached to the rescue article showing exactly where Anson had been found, the place they'd hidden and where his mother's trail had led the rescuers back to. And she found something else: a young

Frank to one side, caught in mid-gesture as he'd crouched and pointed into the dark space.

God bless Frank and whoever had taken the picture. They might as well have left a road map for her.

CHAPTER TWELVE

SINCE HER DISCOVERIES had come early in the morning, by noon Ellory had rented a snowmobile and set off on one of the lesser-used trails of Silver Pass. Thanks to the article and the photo she'd found, she was pretty sure she knew right where Anson and his mother had weathered the storm. Maybe there was some trace of the time they'd spent there. His toy? Marks on the stone…something. Even just a simple understanding of what it was like to be in there would be a start.

Even Ellory knew she was grasping at straws, but aside from grilling Frank—which would no doubt be the next step if she didn't find anything in the overhang—it was the only idea she had that might help her help *him*.

The slope Anson had crashed on in his childhood wasn't marked for guests to find easily these days, and she really didn't know if that had always been the case or if it was something that Mr. Dupris had done after the accident. It was maintained and usable—if you knew what you were doing and how to get there. But all signs led to other slopes.

She knew she'd found it when she started seeing the warning signs.

Stopping the snowmobile at the top of the slope, Ellory surveyed the way down, trying to decide whether there was a safe route to the bottom or not.

With the machine idling in low gear, she heard some short staccato sound echoing through the pass.

She killed the engine and immediately realized what it was: frantic barking. Max…it was Max. But the echo made it impossible to follow.

If Max was barking like that, then something was really wrong. Anson should be calming him down.

Her heart skipped. If Anson wasn't calming him down…

This rugged part of the pass was the most remote, the most dangerous… Her instinct told her that down the crazy run was the direction to go.

The cold air suddenly felt suffocating. Adjusting the face mask and goggles, she started the machine again and took a chance with the machine in the trees. If she went slowly, she could make it down that way. And it couldn't get out of control and end up rolling too far if there were trees in the way. She'd just crash into one, and hopefully not be going that fast when it happened.

Now wasn't the time to stop trusting her gut.

As carefully as she could with any speed, Ellory wove between the trees in a wide zigzag down the slope. The further down she went, the louder the barking got.

About halfway down she realized the barking was getting quieter again.

She'd passed them.

She turned the beast hard toward the cleared slope and worked her way to the tree line.

About a hundred yards up the slope she saw a snowdrift and the black dog in stark relief against it. He was barking at the snow between periods of frantic digging.

Avalanche dog.

She scrambled off the machine and up the slope as hard and fast as she could. *"Anson!"*

When Max saw her, he barked more frantically and ran

to meet her, grabbing her sleeve and half dragging her toward the snow she clawed her way up and over.

If he was in there…as long as the barking had been going on…God, she knew someone died in avalanches every couple years. They'd already lost one in a slip this season.

Rounding the drift to where Max dragged her, she saw a hole dug into the bank and Anson's head. Max had got to his head.

"Anson!" She strangled on his name, a barely controlled sob almost choking her.

His head turned and he looked at her. Alive. Alive and awake. No neck injury…he could move his neck.

"We'll get you out." She began pushing the snow off the mound holding him down. Max joined in again, digging beside her.

"It wasn't a real slide…there was a weird cornice…"

She didn't have time to look around and figure out what the hell he was talking about. The only thing she could think of was getting through the heavy wet volume of snow and pulling him free.

"How long?"

"I don't know." He sounded tired. She knew he was tired.

Her goggles fogged from the tears streaming from her eyes, so she tore them off and used the cup like a shovel. She should have had a shovel…

"Tell me what you're feeling."

"The snow is heavy," he said, but as she dug through several feet and lessened the load on his chest, he began to breathe more easily.

When his hands were free, he held them up to her. "Pull."

Taking both his hands, she leaned back as hard as she could, putting all her weight into the pull. Max pulled too, grabbing Anson's hood and giving quick powerful tugs that made her worry about his spine.

He slid free enough to use his legs, and soon he was out with her and Ellory grabbed for his hands, tearing through the buckles to get his gloves off and inspect his fingers. Red. Still red.

She fell at his feet, and shoved his still wobbly body back into the snow so she could rip one of his boots off. The foot with the most toes had red toes. She checked the other. Two red toes, red feet.

"I'm okay," he said, but he still didn't sound okay. She didn't believe him, not one bit. But she couldn't leave him with his boots off, so she shook the sock to make sure no snow had gotten on it, and helped get his boots back on before she even tried to look him in the eye.

"We're going to the hospital." She looked up now, at the cornice that had fallen on him. "Is your snowmobile under there?"

He nodded. The fact that he wasn't arguing with her about going to the hospital actually did worry her.

"Max will just have to walk with us. I have one, down the slope a way. We'll go slowly."

"How did you know to come?"

"I heard Max."

"You were out already?"

"I was…looking. For something." She wasn't going to tell him precisely what she'd been looking for, and she wasn't going to ask why Anson had gone looking for Jude on this slope. She had the idea that they were headed in the same direction, but neither of them was emotionally ready to talk about it yet.

He moved stiffly and slowly, but when she took his arm again to get it over her shoulder, she realized he was shaking again. Really shaking. The kind of intense shivering the body did to warm itself. Hypothermia…and more than a mild case.

"It's not far." She held him as best she could and they wove a sliding path for the machine, Max keeping pace with them.

When she got him on the machine, she dug into the back and pulled out an insulated jug of hot tea. "It's ginseng and honey for energy." She didn't drink the preservative-laden cocoa, and was trying to get herself back to the habits that had had to be abandoned when things had gotten hairy during the blizzard. "It will warm you some."

Anson took the tea and drank. First a few sips, then more deeply.

When it was half-gone he handed it back. She capped it back up and stowed it in the back compartment.

Max looked around for his cage…but since it was on the buried ATV she said, "Come, Max." Hoping he'd follow them.

"Track," Anson said, wrapping his arms around her middle. The tea helped a little. He wasn't shaking so hard now that she thought he would lose his seat on the machine.

Even so, as a precaution she took a moment and cross-buckled the straps on his gloves, securing them together with his arms around her waist, in case Anson passed out while they rode. The last thing he needed was to fall off and add head trauma to his hypothermia…

Max barked once, she repeated the command, "Track, Max. Track." And then fired her rental to life and started back the long way she'd come.

Too many hurdles had been thrown at her in the past month, she couldn't keep up or even keep track of what she was supposed to be worrying about from moment to moment. Jude. Anson's emotional state. Her carbon footprint. Whether the dog would keep up with them. And now whether Anson had frostbite. Again. Never mind how she was going to cope when she had to go…

She and the universe were going to have to have a long talk after this was over.

Anson had never actually been covered by snow before, not to that extent. Had the situation been any different, had it not been for Max, had Ellory not been mysteriously out on the mountain on a machine she hated…

He'd have to ask her about that later.

Right now, sitting in the examination room at his emergency department, waiting for X-ray results to be read, he was glad he'd banished her to the waiting room.

If he had, in fact, broken ribs, as he suspected he had, then she couldn't know. She'd try to use it to keep him off the mountain, and that couldn't happen.

Technically, the doctor checking him out—a colleague he worked with during his six months of the year when he wasn't on winter duty—was supposed to report his injury to Frank, who would then suspend him from duty. But Anson had gotten hurt while on his own time, since he'd been ordered off the search and had been actively disobeying. And he could ride around the mountains on his snowmobile without much physical exertion. When he found Jude, he'd just have to call for someone else to recover the body.

He owed it to Chelsea and the rest of the group to find the man. He'd looked her in the eye and told her he'd bring Jude home. He'd bring the man home. And on the way out, when this exam was over, he'd stop by Chelsea's room to let her know he wasn't giving up.

Twenty minutes later, having been given a lecture he could've done without, Anson had been zipped back into his suit and in a wheelchair, being wheeled back out to the waiting area. Hospital policy, blah-blah-blah. He could walk, but considering he was getting by without being officially reported to superiors he decided not to push his luck.

Ellory stood as soon as he was wheeled out and came over to take over the pushing. "Are you ready to go?"

"I want to see Chelsea first. But I have to ride there in this chair…stay in it until I have officially left the hospital after being seen."

She wheeled him through the sliding doors toward the elevators. "I know where it is."

"How do you know where it is?"

"I checked while you were being treated. I had a couple of hours to do it." She waited until they were alone in the elevator to ask him more questions. "What did they say is wrong?"

"They said I'm all right. It wasn't the best thing in the world to have happen, and I'm very sore, but it's not going to kill me. They said to make sure and force a cough once an hour, which is what I expected."

"Why?"

"Because when your ribs are hurt, you don't want to breathe deeply. That can cause some people to get pneumonia. But if you keep coughing regularly, it keeps your lungs clear."

The elevator dinged and she pushed him out and to the left, not mentioning to him that she'd actually gone to check in on Chelsea once while waiting for him and going nuts with worry about him. Mira was watching Max, so Ellory hadn't even had her furry support system with her to distract her for her wait. Rescue dogs, while service animals, aren't in the same class as personal service dogs— like seeing-eye dogs—who can go anywhere.

She didn't even feel bad about not telling him that she'd gone to see Chelsea. He wasn't telling her everything, and he'd not let her go into the examination room with him.

Because this wasn't a relationship. This wasn't a relationship. This wasn't a relationship.

Maybe repeating the words again and again would make them finally sink in. She was not his girlfriend. He didn't love her, he couldn't love her. It was never going to happen. This was not a relationship.

As she pushed him into Chelsea's room the woman sat up in her bed, eyes wide and round as she looked at him.

"You look like hell," she informed him. "Looks like this search is wearing everyone to the bone. Maybe you should let someone else do the searching for a while."

He shook his head then commandeered the wheels of his chair to wheel right up to Chelsea's bed, where he could reach over and take his patient's hand. "I'm all right. Max the wonder dog and Ellory got me out of my little accident."

"What happened?"

"On the back side of the pass there's a place about midway down the slope, a geographical oddity where there's flat ground beneath a short, slanted overhang…short in terms of mountains. I stopped the snowmobile there because it was flat and Max needed to water some trees… It was a dumb place to stop. The mantel slid and dumped snow on me, knocking me down but not sweeping me away. It wasn't enough for that. Not even a proper avalanche, more like all the five feet thick blanket of snow off a big slanted roof dropping on you unexpectedly."

"You were lucky," Chelsea said, her expression soft. Ellory wished she could see inside Anson's head and read the emotions there as easily as she could read Chelsea's. She felt guilty that he was still out there.

Anson shook his head. "Max dug the snow out before I suffocated and then barked loud enough for Ellory to find us."

Ellory didn't know what to do or say. He wouldn't want

her comfort here in front of people, and she didn't really know what to say or do for him right now to help.

Chelsea settled her gaze on Anson, still in his chair. "When the storm passed your crew were the only ones who could search for Jude, but they came to visit the other day, and told me how there was no way he could have survived in the snow this long. That it was turning into a recovery mission."

Something else Ellory didn't know was how Chelsea managed to speak so steadily. Now that Ellory knew what it meant to love a man, and remembering the panic she'd felt when she'd realized Anson was under the snow…

"It doesn't matter if you find him today or in two weeks now. It's not worth dying over. They said I'll be here for a few more weeks at least, maybe even until spring arrives and the snow melts… If there's no chance that he's alive…" Chelsea's throat finally closed, stopping her words.

There was absolutely nothing she could do or say to help either of them. She opened her mouth to say something, though she had no idea what would help, when a knock behind her had her turning and stepping away from the door.

Sheriff, a deputy, and Frank.

Her stomach bottomed out. The presence of three officials together…

They must have found him.

"Jude Wyndham has been found."

Anson heard the voice, heard the words, and carefully turned the wheelchair he'd been confined to so he could face the doorway and whoever had walked into Chelsea's hospital room.

Sheriff Leonard. Deputy Gates. Frank.

"Where was he?" Anson asked, even though he knew that they'd come to tell Chelsea. One look at her face confirmed for Anson that she wasn't able to ask the questions she'd later need the answers to.

"Montana."

Montana. He searched his mind for the name of different peaks and valleys in the area, and came up with nothing. "Where is that? I don't think I'm familiar…"

He noticed Frank looking at him. Frank, his boss, who didn't know he'd been hurt today. Not like it mattered now that Jude had been found.

Frank kept the censure Anson knew he was due out of his voice and his words at least. "The state."

"Montana," Anson repeated, and then again, this time in unison with Chelsea and Ellory, "Montana?"

"How did he get so far away?" Ellory asked.

He couldn't have walked that far during the storm or after without someone noticing. Only an idiot wouldn't walk west or east to get out of the mountains if he was lost. The area was developed well enough that he'd have stumbled over a road and gotten help before he made it all the freaking way to Montana.

"I don't understand. How did he get to Montana?" Chelsea repeated the sentiment.

"By car. He and a woman were picked up in a bank, trying to cash a stolen check they'd tried and failed to cash in Canada," Sheriff Leonard said.

"A woman?" Chelsea asked, her voice rising in pitch.

"Maybe we should speak about this further in private," the sheriff said gently to Chelsea, but Anson didn't need further explanation. He got it.

A look at Ellory confirmed that she was still as confused as Chelsea was.

"Elle?" He said her name softly, getting her attention. "Let's leave them to speak with Chelsea." He tilted his head toward the wheelchair handles, silently asking her to push him out of the room.

She stepped behind him, and after giving Chelsea's hand a supportive squeeze wheeled Anson out of the room. Once out of earshot of those still inside the room she stopped and crouched beside him to whisper, "What were they trying to say to her?"

"That he was never lost in the pass." He said the words gently. "The stolen check he and some woman were trying to cash? They were probably Chelsea's."

"He planned it? He abandoned them out there in the cold and…stole from them and left?" Her voice rose, much as Chelsea's had done. Not only was she shocked that someone would do that, she was angry. Anson could recognize the emotion, even if right now he was surprised to find he didn't share it. He didn't actually feel anything.

"Looks like it. Let's get out of here." He nodded in the way they'd come.

"They could've died…" She continued to speak quietly as she pushed him out of the hospital and on to Mira's car, which she'd borrowed to bring him to the hospital, listing the man's offenses as they occurred to her.

She left him sitting at the patient pick-up and drop-off area to get the car, and Anson took his chance to cough and clear his lungs. It hurt. And she'd insist on staying with him tonight to take care of him if she knew what was going on with him.

A half an hour later, following Anson's directions, she pulled off the highway onto a one-lane road that had recently been plowed. "What do I do if we meet someone?"

"We won't meet anyone. My house is the only one out here," Anson mumbled, "but I have a service to come plow the lane for the big snows."

The road wound through trees on either side, thick enough that Ellory wasn't sure whether or not there was a ledge anywhere in sight. She drove slowly, afraid of sliding into a ravine in the dark.

It didn't take long to break through the trees to a blanket of barely disturbed whiteness. The lane, which she now realized was more of a long driveway, sloped down and back up, following a gently undulating terrain toward a very small house.

Really small.

"Anson, is part of your house underground?"

"No. It's a micro-house. I thought you'd be familiar with them."

"Of course I am. I guess I just thought…with the size of your dog…" Teeny-tiny environmentally friendly house? Who was this guy?"

"Does Max even fit in there?"

It had been a really tough day, but this discovery was a bright spot.

"He stays mostly in the living room. Sometimes I think it's a glorified doghouse, like when it rains and he gets that wet-dog smell. The bedroom is in the loft, which you get to by ladder. That took some getting used to for him. We lived in an apartment when I first got him, he got used to sleeping with me…and then suddenly he couldn't even get near me when I slept. I think that's why he's been so possessive about sleeping with us…"

He didn't go on at length about much, but the man did love his dog.

He opened his door and climbed out, so she did the same, intent on seeing him safely inside and getting a gander at the interior.

On the tiny porch stoop he fished his keys out of his pocket and let himself in, disabled the alarm, and then looked back at her. "I saw the weather while we were at the hospital. You should probably head back to the lodge now. It's going to get bad again in a little while."

Before she'd even gotten her toe over the threshold he'd slammed down the unwelcome mat? "You aren't coming with me?"

"I really just want to sleep. In my bed."

They may have found Jude, he may not have been on the mountain in need of rescue and all that, but there was an unpleasant sort of hanging feeling left over. At least if they had found him dead, there would've been resolution, a completed task, a way of honoring his promise and all that.

This way? It was just over. It was just done, and as calm as he acted he couldn't be okay with the way things were.

"Are you feeling like punching the wall?"

"No," he said softly.

"What about Max?" And what about her? Was this the end? Now that there was no finding that monster on the mountain, it was just a switch he could flip and be done with her?

He didn't answer as immediately. "He could stay with you tonight if you don't mind, and I'll pick him up in the morning."

Stay with her. Somewhere he wasn't.

"I could stay." She tried again, and barely cared that she sounded pathetic, even to her own ears. "Mira could watch Max. I know she wouldn't mind."

His eyes were tired, his shoulders not nearly as broad and weight-bearing as they usually appeared. Much too quiet.

"You want me to go." The words were out of her mouth before she actually thought about saying them. "I don't feel good about it. About leaving you here without any-one, even Max."

"It's not that I want you gone, but I'm tired. The idea of crawling into bed and sleeping a day or twelve appeals."

He'd slept with her every night for more than two weeks, but now that Jude had been found...alive...

"Are we supposed to be glad he's alive?" she asked finally. "Because I don't think I am. I've never wished anyone dead or anything, but before, when we were looking for a guy who'd tried to be a hero and save his loved ones, I so wanted him to be found alive. Now I just want to go to Montana and drown him in his own jail toilet."

Anson nodded, though his expression remained sedate. Too sedate. It was worse than when she'd been trying to get him to talk about how Jude being lost affected him. At least then he'd had some kind of emotional expression. He'd put his fist through the freaking wall, so she had at least known he'd been upset, even if he'd denied it. Now, though, now he just seemed numb. And numb scared her.

Whatever he was feeling had to have been worse than what she was feeling. He'd been the one out there searching, reliving losing his mother, overwhelmed by guilt… But he wasn't going to share it with her.

Everything he said, including the stuff only said by his body, let her know he wanted space. Who was she to deny him?

Ellory covered the short space that separated them and leaned up to kiss him.

He tangled his hand in her hair and kept her close, even if he didn't hold her like she wanted…his kiss warm and full of feeling even if she hadn't been able to see it when she'd looked at him, or heard it in his voice.

Maybe she was just reading too much into things. He could just really need some sleep. Maybe tomorrow he'd feel like talking.

CHAPTER THIRTEEN

Anson wasn't sitting about in his underwear, refusing to shower, drinking too much beer, and punching his walls full of holes.

And that was the best thing he could say about his response to the news about Jude.

Jude.

Judas. Was that the man's name? He was going to have to look it up. At some point.

Max, on the other hand? Pretty much doing half of that list. It was next to impossible to get him off his fireside doggy bed. He didn't eat, not even his beloved jerky treats. There had been exactly zero hours of play since their return home. And he got really disgruntled when Anson forced him to go outside.

It looked like mourning to Anson, and probably because his new person was gone. Ellory. He hadn't seen Ellory in several days, and Max hadn't seen her either.

With a sigh Anson peeled himself off the couch and retrieved the phone. He'd call her, let the dog talk to her or hear her voice, and maybe that would help.

She answered just as the call was about to shuffle off somewhere else—the front desk? Voicemail? Anson had no clue where unanswered calls went at the lodge.

When he heard her voice come down the line his chest

squeezed, which set off a coughing fit before he'd managed to say a word.

"Anson?"

He cleared his throat. "Ellory. Sorry."

On hearing her name, Max got up from the bed and nearly knocked Anson over. "Max wants to talk to you on the phone."

"Max wants to talk to me." He heard it in her voice—she might as well have called him the bastard they both knew him to be.

The massive Newfoundland standing on his hind legs and putting weight on Anson's upper body got him moving toward the point. "If you wouldn't mind. He's been really depressed. Won't eat or anything." He pushed the dog off him and walked to the couch. At least there Max could crawl up on the seat beside him and maybe not break his cracked ribs the rest of the way.

He punched the speaker button and laid the phone on the coffee table. "You're on speaker."

"Hi, Maxie-Max," Ellory crooned, and the dog's tail went wagging with enough force Anson thought his legs might bruise. The big furry head tilted in that confused and interested way he had and he looked up at the loft, then behind him, smelling the air. But he couldn't find Ellory.

"Want a jerky, Max? Tell your big dumb jerky-face who loves you very much. I'm sure he'll give you a jerky. Jerky? Jerky?"

Every time she said "jerky," the dog got more and more excited while she left Anson abundantly clear on exactly what kind of jerky she was talking about: not the kind his dog lived for.

"Just a second," Anson said. "Keep talking, I'll get the stuff."

He stood and walked into the kitchen, leaving Ellory to psych up his dog into eating.

When he came back, she was saying "jerky" so fast and so frequently that the word had stopped sounding like a word. But Max still took the piece when Anson offered it to him.

"He's eating," he yelled, to get over the sound of her silly jerky song. Then he picked up the phone and switched off the speaker. "Thank you."

Asking how she was would be the right thing to do, she'd been upset about Judas too. But asking her that would certainly open the door for her to ask him, and he just had no answers to give her on that score.

Ellory made her way back through her bedroom obstacle course to sit on the bed. After the storm the lodge had started filling up again. She could be working right now if she wanted to. Guests had returned to the lodge and the slopes as soon as the slopes had been prepared and the power had come back on.

By now someone would've overworked an ill-used muscle or joint. Injured themselves...something. But she just didn't have the desire. She was exhausted from worrying, trying not to worry, trying to pretend she didn't care, etcetera—so she didn't worry Mira or work herself up into such a state about Anson that she made herself crazy.

"I'm just a symptom," she said into the phone, after silence had reigned for entirely too long.

Anson spoke with caution, because this whole business was awkward. "A symptom of what?"

"He doesn't miss me so much as he has a big chapter of his life unfinished."

"Finding Jude?"

Ellory nodded, then actually spoke out loud because this wasn't video conferencing... "He spent weeks of his life looking for someone who never got found. He needs closure." And she did too.

And just like that she knew what she had to do. She'd never gotten to her destination that day. Only the universe knew whether or not she'd find anything of his time in the tiny cave. Maybe getting to find someone where he'd lost his mother would help him move on too.

"There isn't going to be any closure about that. Though I think they are extraditing him to the area, so maybe we could go and find him at the jail."

"He needs to find someone. Anyone will do. I'm going out on the mountain in my old crappy snow suit that doesn't keep very warm compared to what my beautiful new suit does."

"Elle…"

She ignored the warning in his voice. "I'm going back to where you got trapped. Take Max there and come and find me. When he finds me, he'll feel better."

And maybe he would too.

Before he could say anything, she hung up, dropped her phone, and crawled under her bed to retrieve the snow suit from hell.

On the plus side, if she froze to death out there, when they found her, everyone would get a good laugh out of how ridiculous she looked.

If it weren't for the fact that he was generally against killing people…

Anson's snowmobile was still buried on the slope where he was going to find Ellory, which meant he had to go slowly enough on the rented thing for Max to keep up.

Unlike the weather that had plagued them for the past several weeks, the day was bright, sunny and warm enough that the snow held high in the trees was dripping and dropping off, forcing him to take the long way around to where he knew to begin the search.

When they got near the area where Max and Ellory

had pulled him from the snow, Max took off and left him speeding in something other than the safest manner in order to keep up with him.

On the other side of the big mound of snow sat another empty snowmobile.

Max sniffed it and then ran back to Anson, to and from until he'd gotten the machine throttled down and had climbed off. Footprints led down the mountain, the snow being still deep enough in this area that she'd left deep leg prints in the snow.

And if she was in the old-fashioned snowsuit, it would not be water-resistant, so she'd be cold. Anywhere her body touched snow would be wet, and that wetness would sink in toward her body fast.

"Dammit, Ellory," he muttered to himself, and led Max to her abandoned snowmobile, tapping the seat twice and giving the command "Find."

Max didn't even smell the seat—it wasn't like he couldn't follow the tracks she'd left. He tore off down the mountain after her, barking and so excited that Anson felt bad for having kept the big guy away from her.

It had taken Ellory an hour of digging in order to make an opening in the snow big enough to crawl through into Anson's tiny cave. She got about halfway in before her suit caught on a jagged piece of rock hanging down. Ellory felt it rip as she backed up, deepened the hole with a couple more shovels of snow, and finally made it inside.

He hadn't been kidding when he'd said it had been a tight fit.

With how long it had taken her to get to the area and make it inside, she half expected that he'd get there just before her feet disappeared inside and drag her out.

She looked toward the light. Feet inside.

Very dark.

Rolling to her side, she got a small flashlight out of her pocket and flicked it on to shine around the creepy interior.

Now that she was there, she felt the strangest feeling of peace—like she was right where she was supposed to be, when she was supposed to be there. Though she really had no idea why, aside from providing Anson the closure he and Max both needed.

Closure. So final. She shivered.

With effort, she shifted to a slightly taller area of the overhang and managed to roll over. That left the area she'd dug out open for Max or Anson, or anyone else who decided to come crawling inside.

If she had been Anson's mother, when they'd crawled in here she'd have put her son on that side of the cave. It was smaller, would've kept him from moving around too much with his broken femur.

She shone the light around, looking for anything he might've left behind...some evidence of having been there...but she didn't see his toy or his backpack. She didn't even see any marks on the rocks where he might've passed the time.

But she did see a dark little cubbyhole opening in the rocks.

And something shiny sparkled in the dirt beneath the hole.

Rolling back to her cold belly, she crawled over to that side again and stuck her mittened hand into the cubbyhole.

It went deep, all the way to her elbow before her hand touched bottom. Weird.

She patted around, trying to decide if that was maybe a place that air had come in and had maybe made Anson colder during his wait. There was no outlet she could feel, and with the snow blanketing everything outside no air came through either.

When she began working her arm back out of the hole,

something bumped into her knuckle and she cried in alarm and jerked her hand out. A few seconds of listening confirmed it—no sound of movement came from the dark and suddenly dangerous-seeming cubbyhole.

What had it felt like? Animal? No... If it had been an animal, it would've bitten her. She looked at her mitten. Intact. No pain in the hand in it.

Dead animal? Felt way too solid for that. When she didn't hear any movement, she took a deep breath and shoved her hand back inside. This time her hand curled over the object immediately and she extracted her arm from the hole.

She fished a toy from my backpack and used it like a puppet...told me stories.

Ellory looked at the plastic army man in his camouflage fatigues and black flat-top haircut and really wanted to cry this time.

He had peeling paint on his legs and back, but his molded plastic face was pristine.

The sound of barking cut through the air, letting her know Max was on his way to find and save her. She stuffed the doll into her suit, and then looked around. Where had that shiny thing gone...?

She flashed the light around in the area she'd seen it, didn't find it, and then started roughing up the dirt in the area as well. Silver Pass wasn't just called that because of the silvery white snow that fell in great quantities. And she'd discovered a tiny silver nugget once...

By the time her flashlight caught the reflection again, she'd almost worked up enough dirt into the air to send a dust bunny into asthmatic convulsions.

A delicate silver chain. She lifted it out of the dirt and her breath caught as the chain grew taut and a good-sized oval pendant hopped free from the earth.

Correction: oval locket.

Giving it a quick wipe, she pulled one mitten off and found the seam with her thumbnail, popping the catch.

The picture inside had been through however many seasons of snow and ice. The colors had faded. Her throat burned.

She knew the eyes looking out from the picture.

Anson caught up just in time to see Max's fluffy tail disappear under the overhang of rocks where he'd known Ellory would be.

"You found me!" he heard her say, her voice animated. "Good boy!" And then, a moment later, "Anson?"

"What?" He folded his arms, not in the mood for this.

"Can you call him back out? It's hard to crawl around in here."

He shook his head, feeling an epic eye-roll coming on. "Come, Max. Out!"

Many long seconds passed before his oversized dog crawled back out, wagging his tail so hard he could have cleared land with it. Completely happy.

"You too. Come, Ellory. Out!"

He saw padded black boots first. The dog might've been able to squirm around and crawl out head first, but Ellory didn't have the room in there to do it.

The further out she got, the less angry he became. Her snowsuit, if it could be called that, looked like a quilt. An actual quilt...but canvas, and possibly made from army surplus duffel bags, and maybe even circus tents? And the best part: some kind of purple and yellow checkered canvas.

She came up butt first, and when she turned around it was all Anson could do not to laugh. On her head? A knitted cap in of many colors—as if if it had been made using a little bit of every yarn in the store, and topped with a puffy ball. He had to remind himself he was mad at her for going in there.

"I can see why you don't often wear that snowsuit." He laughed a little, the sound would not be contained. "Must be hard to bear the envy of all around you when the skiers get a look at that magnificent creation."

She ignored him, though her cheeks looked quite pink by this point beneath the smears of dirt she'd undoubtedly picked up in the tight little cave.

Instead, she crouched and petted Max again, making much of him in a way that made Anson feel a little lonely, truth be told. She hadn't tried to hug him, though, to be fair, her arms were so padded it didn't look like she could put them all the way down. Wrapping them around anything bigger than Max would be a feat.

"Elle?" he prompted, when she'd avoided looking at him for long enough that it became apparent she was procrastinating. "Did you think that me finding you here would help or something?"

"Did it?"

"My mom is still gone. Max can be distracted and move on from a...really awful experience by giving him a win... but..."

"But you're smarter than that," she said, squeezing the dog one more time and then standing up. "When I devised this plan I pictured you crawling inside, finding your toy... and I hoped it might help you."

"My toy?"

"The army man your mom used as a puppet to act out stories for you."

He'd never told her it was an army man. "Did you find...? Was the toy in there?"

She smiled and unzipped her crazy snowsuit, reached inside and pulled out his army hero action figure. Something in his gut twisted as she held the toy out to him and he felt the light plastic weight of it in his hand for the first time in twenty-five years.

"Sargent Stan." He said the toy's name and then stepped back to a bank of snow and sat, not feeling like his legs could support him suddenly. "Why would you even think to do this?"

She followed and knelt before him, pulled off her dirty mittens and stuffed them into the open monstrosity she wore so she could clean Sgt. Stan's face with her fingernail. "I know you already know what I'm going to tell you, but I think you still need to hear it."

He looked up from the doll at those warm brown eyes and nodded, not trusting himself to speak.

"You can't find something on the mountain that you didn't lose on the mountain."

It was like talking to her in the first hours they'd met. He knew she was saying something that she felt was important, but he needed some landmarks to try and run this linguistic obstacle course. He nodded, slowly, hoping she'd elaborate.

"I internet-stalked you."

He nodded again, still waiting.

"Your mom was an emergency room doctor."

"Yes." He could understand that statement.

"And so are you."

He nodded.

She added, "And you save people from the fate that befell her when she…saved you."

Max sensed his growing discomfort and came to sniff at his face. Anson leaned back and gently shoved the dog's head to his lap to pet.

Ellory added, "You lost her on the mountain. But you didn't. She died here, but she was found, and because she was found, you were found. She had a funeral."

All he could do was nod.

"She's not here, Anson. Because you didn't lose her on the mountain. Not really. But Sargent Stan…" She repeated the toy's name and then laid her hand on Max's head to pet him too. "You did lose him here. And now you have him back, and the memory of your mom doing whatever she could to make you feel better…"

Her voice strangled at the end and she looked away long enough to swipe her cheeks. When she looked back he saw her tears had streaked the dirt and muddied her up a little. Any other woman he knew would stop and clean her face at this point, but Ellory didn't and he suddenly knew why: dirt was natural. Like the material of her insane outfit. Natural and real, like she was.

"I went there to find that because I feel like he's your totem. And because I really do think that Max needed to find someone…"

"He did." Anson murmured, not sure how he felt about all this. Or what she meant by totem, but all he could see was his mother's hand holding Sgt. Stan. He wished he could remember what she'd said…

"I found something else. Something I didn't expect. You didn't tell me…"

She slipped one hand into her pocket and when she pulled it out it was closed around something.

"I told you the whole story…all that I know, at least." He kept his eyes off the toy, it was too emotionally charged and he was barely keeping himself together. And he was afraid to look at whatever was in her hand.

"Then it's another piece to cobble together," she whispered, and opened her hand and held it out to him.

Dirt-covered and tarnished, his mother's locket rested in her little hand.

He couldn't move. And when he didn't reach out for it Ellory popped the thing open with her fingernail and showed him the portrait he knew was inside: the one of him and Mom when he'd been a spaghetti-sauce-covered monster toddler, and she'd pressed her cheek to his for a close-up picture all the same. All smiles.

"You have her eyes."

He nodded, and swallowed, finally reaching for the piece of jewelry.

"She left her totem to protect you. Before she left. The rescuers probably just didn't see it." She paused and then added, "You can't control what other people do, that's what I learned from this Jude mess. You can't control anyone but yourself—whether they do something awful like Jude, or whether they're true heroes like your mom. All you can control is how you respond. I get why you're a doctor and why you and Max risk your lives for others." She stood and backed away from him, focusing on getting her dirty mittens back on, so he almost missed it when she whispered, "She'd be proud of you."

His mother would be proud of him, something he had heard from other people in his life, but had never believed. But when Ellory said it…he did believe it. And he suddenly wished he had something he could say to her that would help. He'd been so focused on Jude and Chelsea, on how the search had made him feel, he had neglected tending her in the way she tended him… She was still hurting. He'd done nothing to diminish it.

"I wouldn't try to clean it too much," she said, breaking through his thoughts. "The picture is fragile, and any chemicals that would remove the tarnish would probably ruin the photo. Plus…"

"Dirt is natural?" he asked, teasing a little.

"It is, but I was going to say…maybe there's still a trace of her. Even a particle. Maybe even protected by the tarnish." And then she shrugged, and turned toward the tree line and slogged off through the snow. "Which is also natural. Tarnish… Or you could ignore me."

"Doubtful." He closed the locket, unzipped his suit and stashed the precious cargo in an interior pocket. "Where are you going?" He zipped back up and stood to follow her.

"Lodge." She reached the trees and turned up the hill, using them like posts to help pull herself up through the snow. "It's cold."

And she was wearing the world's most ridiculous snowsuit. "Is it wet?" he asked, hurrying to catch up to her so he could link elbows and they could pull up the steep slope together.

"Yep. It doesn't hold water out as well as..." She looked at his face and stopped speaking, probably noticing how displeased he was with this little tidbit. Out in the cold, freezing for his benefit...

He let the silence go on between them for a few minutes before asking, "Are your feet cold?"

"My feet are fairly warm. Not wet, three pairs of wool socks. Boots two sizes too big."

When they'd made it far enough up the slope to reach the snowmobiles, she pulled away from him and climbed on hers. She waved a mittened hand at him and called, "Take care of yourself and Max," then turned around and zoomed across the slope, heading back for the lodge and leaving Anson to try and catch his breath.

His chest ached, though not from exertion or even from his cracked ribs.

Her farewell had sounded an awful lot like goodbye.

CHAPTER FOURTEEN

"SHE LEFT."

Anson stood in the doorway of Miranda Dupris's office, staring at the woman. "What do you mean, she left?"

"I mean she isn't here any more. She doesn't work at the lodge any more. I told her we'd be happy to have her here for the whole year, guests don't just get hurt when skiing, but you and I both know that as much as she loved being here, she has her code and that code requires space." She paused and looked at him. "As well as no central heating. She's been making small changes, but she's still very against central heating."

Okay, so it had taken him a couple of weeks to figure his life out, what he wanted versus what he did. But he hadn't expected her to run away in the meantime. Winter wasn't even over yet. "Did she go back to Peru?"

She could be anywhere!

Mira shook her head.

"Do you know how to contact her?"

"Of course I do."

Best friend, guardian at the gate, torturing the guy who'd hurt her best friend. Right. He deserved that. "Will you call her, please?" He tried some honey, because what he really wanted to do was hose the woman down in vinegar. And shake her.

"What do you want to say to her?"

Definitely shake her. Except if he was going to be part of Ellory's life, he couldn't go shaking her best friend. And they obviously stuck together. Tight.

"I don't need to be vetted before you'll let me talk to her. Trust me."

"You hurt her," Mira said, and then sat down at her desk, hands linked as she fixed him with an unrelenting stare.

Anson sighed, closed the door and went to sit down.

If he had to jump through hoops to reach Ellory, it was his own damned fault. "I did."

"You don't understand, you made her break her resolution and then you hurt her on top of that."

"I understand. Believe me." He had to say something to convince her. "I don't know if she will want to take me back, but I have to talk to her even if it's just to tell her one thing. And if I have to go all the way to Patagonia to do it, I will go all the way to Patagonia."

Mira said nothing, just watched him.

"I love her, Mira."

"Is that what you want to say?"

"That, and I want to tell her something about her father."

She sat up straighter, brows surging to her hairline. "Did you go see him?"

"Yes, I did," Anson answered, then frowned, "After I told him what I'd come to tell him, he refused to tell me where she was. I didn't expect him to know, I just wanted to highlight this fact in a completely obnoxious manner."

An hour later, after he'd relayed a blow-by-blow account of his meeting with Ellory's parents, Anson left with a Main Street address in hand and the urge to shake Mira again.

He'd spent the whole time thinking Ellory had left the country, and she was just in town.

* * *

A brass bell at the top of the main door rang and Ellory popped her head round the corner from the back room. "We're not open for business yet," she called, but all other words died in her throat. Anson stood in the doorway wearing actual clothes, nothing orange in sight.

Jeans that fit his muscled frame well. A worn leather jacket hung open, revealing a flannel button-down over a navy thermal top.

He'd shaved.

His hair was combed back and not hidden beneath a knit cap.

And he had a plant with him.

Max, his perpetual companion, didn't stand on ceremony and obviously didn't feel any of the awkwardness the humans felt. He danced around the counter in that happy wagging-tail way of his to greet her.

Ellory greeted Max before he destroyed the place with his big swinging tail.

"Max," Anson grunted, "You're stealing the show, buddy. Go lie down." He snapped his fingers and pointed to the fire, which was enough. The big black Newfoundland all but pranced over and flopped onto the old worn wood floor of the building Ellory had leased from Mira.

Her heart in her throat, Ellory looked back at the man, and only then realized she should say something. "Thank you. For the…the…spa-warming gift."

"I wanted to get flowers but apparently you can't buy flowers that are locally sourced in winter." He approached the counter and thrust the potted fern at her.

She took the pot, careful not to accidentally touch the man, and set it on the counter. "It's really nice. Reminds me of the rainforest. Besides, cut flowers just die anyway. Nice of you to bring it by."

"I actually don't have any clue if the plant is a viable

substitute… You're supposed to bring flowers when you apologize to the woman you love."

No preamble. He just laid it out there so boldly that her mind went blank.

"You can't control what other people do, right? That's what you said. You can't control what other people do…or think or anything. Just you, how you react."

"Right," she whispered, her hands starting to shake. The blasted bracelets jangled, and he noticed.

Before she could hide her hands, Anson reached out and took both of them, his thumbs on top to stroke the backs of her hands. "I visited your father."

"Oh, no… Did you hit him?"

"No. I wanted to, but he's a miserable old cuss, and nothing I can do will ever change that." He said the words slowly, like she hadn't already come to that conclusion on the mountain.

"I know that now. And I hate to say it, but Jude taught me that lesson."

He nodded, seeking her gaze and holding it for the space of several heartbeats. She loved his eyes…

"That's why you left us? So I could figure everything out? It wasn't because you stopped loving us?"

Us. She knew he meant him and Max, not the two of them as a couple, but it was still cute how he was hiding in language a little bit.

"I never said I loved you." Having her hands in his gave her the confidence to torment him a little. It had been at least twelve years since she'd seen him on the mountain… a couple of weeks ago. Twelve really long years.

"Yes, you did."

"No, I didn't. I definitely never said that."

He shook his head, looking at her like she was crazy. "You did too."

"I never ever said that to anyone but my parents and Mira. Never. Not once."

"Well, I heard you say it." He let go of her hands suddenly and reached across the counter, his hands folding over her shoulders to pull her toward him as he leaned in to meet her. No working up to it, no flirting and coyness, he just kissed her like a starving man, like it was all he could do to keep from dragging her across the counter into his arms.

She did it for him. Ellory's arms stole around his shoulders and she hooked one knee on the counter to climb over. Warm hands slid to her waist and he helped drag her to the front with him, and right onto the floor, only deepening the kiss when he got her well and truly plastered against him.

By the time he came up for air the worried look she'd seen in his eyes was gone, and he smiled. "And there you said it again."

"Did not." She grabbed his head and pulled him back down, not caring at all whoever happened to walk by the big glass windows on the old general store she was converting, and that they might see them making out.

Though she was really glad that she'd taken several days to clean and restore the hardwood floors with lemons and beeswax. Which reminded her…kissing and making out hadn't been their problem. They were really good at that.

"Say it," he grumbled. "I know you love me. You might as well admit it."

Ellory sighed and then nodded. "I love you. But that doesn't mean we're compatible."

He snorted softly. "Are you and Mira compatible?"

"Of course we are."

"You're totally different. And you still fit together. You and I? We're not that different, and we fit together. I can prove it."

"You cannot prove it."

"Things you'd do to improve the house and property—greenhouse, doghouse, solar panels everywhere, and a thermal well into the earth to get the heat without a drop of carbon in the atmosphere. How am I doing?"

She laughed up at him. "Proud that you figured that out? It's pretty obvious."

"I'm a smart guy, what can I say?"

"I can't really tell you if I like your little house or not. You never let me inside, smart guy."

"Okay, yes, I have made some mistakes. But you will love it, as much as you love me and Max."

"But I still never said that."

"Everything about you says it. Mira said you moved out of the lodge. Where are you living?"

She pointed up at the ceiling.

"Above the shop?"

A nod. "Spa."

"Is it furnished?"

"Mmm it has a futon…and a fridge. And a pot-bellied stove."

Because she hated central heating.

"What made you decide to stay?"

"What I realized in your cave." She started to look a little nervous then, and chewed her lip which made him want to kiss her some more.

"About my mom?"

"Sort of." She started wriggling to get out from under him, but Anson knew better than to let her get away again.

"Look at me. I just told you I love you. What can you possibly be afraid of?"

"You don't know how successful I've been with wrangling my compulsions."

"Tell me."

"I'm about half as obnoxious as I was." Ellory said, shrugging. "It's not going to happen overnight, and I don't want to just become whatever you want me to be. I want to be what I want to be, and I need some time to figure that out."

"Okay. If you want to wait, I can wait." He leaned down and brushed his lips against hers. "So is this a grocery?"

"Do you see fresh fruit? It's a spa, maybe a wellness center. There will be some natural remedies available, oils and decoctions for different common ailments—like muscle soreness, and the respiratory flush we used on our patient guests. And some other natural stuff. Like deodorants without propylene glycol and other bad chemicals. Meditation, yoga, and primarily treatments."

"Treatments?"

"Massage therapy…remember? And with Mira's old contacts there are a few serious ski competitors who will likely be bringing their physio orders here."

"How have the epiphanies affected your stance on children?"

She opened her mouth to say something and then shut it again, her shoulders creeping up.

"You don't know?"

"I didn't want to think about it," she confirmed, though with less energy than she'd spoken with up to that point.

It was better than her saying outright she wasn't allowed to have them because she wasn't supposed to be alive to breed a bunch of new people into existence. "Afraid it's too far off your new paradigm?"

"New paradigm?" she repeated, and then shook her head. "No. More afraid I might turn mean, like my father. What if my child, no matter how well I try to raise it, turns into the world's biggest polluter and consumer?"

"We won't let that happen." He'd slipped that "we" casually in there and watched her smile return before adding, "So long as you don't make them wear that snowsuit."

"You haven't asked me to marry you yet." She laughed, getting Max's attention.

Anson shoved the big furball back before they both got licked on the mouth. "I'm working up to it!" When Max would not be dissuaded from licking them, Anson stood and pulled her up from the floor, then set her on the counter where he could kiss her safely and add, "But, it's going to be a lot easier to ask now that you've already said yes."

She laughed against his lips. "I did not!"

"Yes, you did. I heard you. Plain as day."

Flinging her arms around his neck, she kissed him again and then peeked around him toward the entrance. "We have to lock the door. Because it's definitely time I give you the tour of my futon." With a bounce in her step she scampered to the door and then back to take him by the hand. "Just so you know, it's a naked futon tour. We like to keep things natural around here…"

EPILOGUE

"NO CHAMPAGNE."

Ellory Graves drank once a year. Once! But not this year. She looked at her new husband, who had spoken the words, and made a face at him as he shooed off the waiter carrying a tray laden with sparkling flutes of bubbling liquid amber yum-yum. They'd been married since Thanksgiving. True to his word, he'd waited until she was ready for the ring, which happened to be a few months after she'd been ready to make a baby...

"I brought a sparkling apple cider."

He flagged down another waiter, leaving Ellory to slowly spin on her bar stool, hand resting on her rounding belly that had finally reached the point where none of her shirts seemed long enough.

Mira was a few months further along than she was. Ellory had decided she could have one baby and not ruin the planet. And since every child needs a sibling...and Mira was making a baby...

"I'm almost afraid to make any resolutions this year," Mira said. "Like nothing can live up to the last year, so stop making them while we're ahead!"

"No way. We need a goal. I need a goal. Can we hold the resolution to midway through the year when the babies are out and we need to lose weight? Because you're looking mighty round, Mirry."

Jack stepped around his wife and laid a hand protectively on her belly. "Don't listen to her. You're perfect."

"Shut it, Sex Machine. I am trying to get out of doing work for the first half of the year!" Ellory laughed, leaning against Anson. It still felt surreal to her—the most negative and contrary resolutions they'd ever made had turned into blessings bigger than either could have imagined.

The universe really had a wicked sense of humor.

Although, if making negative resolutions was the way to ensure big changes in your life, she was done with that. Her life was perfect. No changes welcome!

"I'm going to learn how to turn flax into linen," Ellory said, snagging the sparkling cider and waiting for Mira to lift her glass. Nice and innocuous.

The countdown had started. She felt pressure on her back, spinning her stool so she faced him. "Leave the lady alone," Anson said, his lips right at her ear. "She's got her first New Year's kiss with her husband to attend to." He waited a beat, tilting his head to catch her eye, then added, "*Hint.*"

He regularly made her laugh, and she knew their child's life would be full of love and laughter. Neither of them would allow anything into their lives that threatened that contented bubble of happiness they'd wrapped around their home.

Graves wasn't even a bad last name in the right context. A love they'd both go to their graves to protect? Good context, and Anson had the perfect example of it.

When the crowd hit one, he swooped in and delivered a kiss full of promise and acceptance. Her favorite pastime.

And it was even good for the environment.

* * * * *

A STOLEN KISS WITH THE MIDWIFE

JULIETTE HYLAND

For my sister – my confidante and co-conspirator.

Here's to more fun and crazy days!

CHAPTER ONE

CERTIFIED NURSE-MIDWIFE Quinn Davis refused to look out the window, even as a few of the other nurses gaped at the orange blaze on the horizon. The wildfire had been burning for almost three weeks; she didn't need to see the damage. Quinn knew what the fire looked like, knew where it was heading, knew what was at risk.

"I can't believe it's still burning."

"I heard it's less than fifteen percent contained."

"No! I was listening to the news this morning, but I changed the station before they talked numbers."

It was twenty percent contained. Quinn had been monitoring the blaze since it began, but she kept the news to herself. She didn't want to join the conversation. Didn't trust herself not to break.

If she could only drown out their words.

She had a patient in labor; she couldn't afford to be distracted right now. At least, not distracted any further.

Quinn slid into a chair and tried to block Rhonda and Sherrie's exclamations from her ears. Both nurses commuted in from the south. This fire wouldn't touch them—not directly. But no one in this area of California ever truly believed a wildfire couldn't reach them.

Georgia stuck her head into the lounge. "Rhonda, Olivia is at nine centimeters."

"Guess that puts us on deck." Sherrie turned from the

window and nodded to Quinn as she and Rhonda left to tend to their patient.

Quinn was grateful that work had called them away before they'd asked her about the destruction in the hills.

Or if she was worried.

Her phone pinged with a text message from her landlady, asking if she was safe. She managed to type a short affirmative without tearing up—barely. The evacuation notice for Quinn's neighborhood had shifted from voluntary to mandatory during her shift. A sob pressed against the back of Quinn's throat, but she refused to let it out.

Tapping her foot against the small table in the lounge, Quinn rolled her neck from side to side and tried to think of anything besides the bungalow being in the fire line.

It was just a place...

But it wasn't. The longest lease Quinn had ever signed before she'd seen the bungalow was for six months. During her decade as a traveling nurse, she'd lived out of two duffel bags. She didn't get attached to places—or to people. She'd learned the hard way that just because she connected didn't mean others did. Picking up and moving was ingrained in her.

Or, it had been, until the position at St. Brigit's had opened.

Maybe this was punishment for her giving in to the desire to finally claim something as her own. For painting walls and pretending the bungalow was really hers. *No!* She would not let her brain accept that possibility.

Quinn also refused to look at the opportunity to work with her best friend as anything other than a blessing.

She'd planned St. Brigit's to be a temporary place, too—a year-long contract at best—but something about that bungalow had called to her.

Or maybe it was being back in California.

When her landlady had told her she'd wanted a long-term tenant, Quinn had readily agreed.

Still, she hadn't bought new furniture. Renting had seemed safer. Easier to dispose of if things didn't work out.

Yet, the bungalow, even with its rented furnishings, had felt like hers. *A home.* She'd never felt at home anywhere, not even as a child. She'd seen so much of the world but never found a place to really call hers. It didn't make sense that it was happening here—the home she'd escaped as soon as she'd graduated college. But no matter how much Quinn pushed back, the seed of a possible forever here in California had refused to slow its bloom.

But now her home was turning to ash.

She swallowed against the tightness in her throat. The yearning for a home, a real home, was uncomfortable. Maybe her biological clock was ticking—a primal desire urging her to plant roots so she could start a family—but that seemed too superficial. Coming back to California had felt different than she'd expected.

She felt different.

Why now? There'd been upheaval in her life before. So many times. And it had never made her want a home or a family. Quinn shifted. Trying to find a comfortable position on the plastic lounge chair was a lost cause, and her body was restless.

She absently rubbed the skin on the finger of her left hand. She'd worn James's engagement ring for less than three weeks before he'd confessed to cheating on her with one of the other itinerant nurses. The worst part was that she hadn't even been all that surprised. Her birth mother hadn't wanted her. Quinn hadn't lived up to her adoptive parents' dreams—so why had she thought James would be different?

She hadn't been angry, hadn't yelled or thrown anything. Quinn couldn't even remember crying. She'd simply packed her bags and moved on. A wildfire in the hills of California—something she'd seen far too many times growing up—wasn't unexpected, but it was throwing her out of sync.

It was her own fault. She knew better than to surrender to sentiment.

Quinn bit her lip and wiped her hands on her thighs as she tried to push away the image of her home on fire. Squeezing her eyes closed, she crossed her arms and willed the tears away.

Before rushing into the birthing center last night, why hadn't she thought to grab the things she'd packed a week ago? She'd boxed the few items that she cared about and carefully stowed them where she could snatch them up in less than ten minutes if the evac orders came down. She should have brought them with her.

"If your face gets any longer…"

A hot cup of coffee pressed against her fingers and Quinn lifted it to her lips without opening her eyes. The black coffee was bitter, and a bit burned, but the caffeine kick was what she needed. And she was grateful for any distraction.

"Seriously, Quinn. What's going on?"

A knee connected with hers as Milo slid into the chair across from her, and Quinn ignored the tingles that slid along her leg. She was tired, worried, and her emotions were tangled. That was the only reason she was reacting to Dr. Milo Russell this morning, she told herself, ignoring the fact that she'd felt those same tingles yesterday morning…and every other day since she'd walked into his arms at the airport eight months ago. Such a simple welcome that had shifted everything in Quinn's soul.

Almost a year later and she still couldn't explain the feelings.

Or why those emotions hadn't made her pack her bags and flee.

Luckily, Quinn's brain was too full of other worries to let that one take residency in the front of her mind today. Not that it ever wandered away for long, though...

Opening her eyes, Quinn tipped her cup at Milo as he took a seat beside her on the lounge chair. His jade eyes bore through her and she barely kept herself from leaning into him. Milo was her friend. Her best friend. He was the reason she'd leaped at the opportunity to work at St. Brigit's.

Sure, he was gorgeous. *Stunning.* His deep dimples were the stuff of legend. She'd heard more than one single lady talk about what it might take to get those dimples to appear outside the birthing center. But Quinn never swooned over anyone. Not over her cheating ex-fiancé and certainly not over Milo. At least, that had been true until she'd moved back to California. Now she yearned for any contact with him.

Quinn and Milo had always just been Quinn and Milo. They'd been best friends since grade school when Quinn had refused to name the person who had started the epic food fight. She'd stood in the principal's office, refusing to out the new kid, when Milo had marched in and declared that he'd thrown the first nugget. In truth, neither had thought tossing a few hard chicken nuggets would result in pandemonium and pudding on the walls—but they'd cleaned it together. And they'd had each other's backs ever since.

Even when wanderlust had taken her to the other side of the country or the other side of the world, she and Milo always kept in touch. Video calls, emails and social media had meant they were only ever a GIF away. He was the one constant in her rambling life. Always there to make her laugh, to bounce ideas off about her next move, to make her happy.

He'd always just been her friend Milo and working together at St. Brigit's was a first for them. She'd enjoyed every minute of it, even if she was in a constant battle to get her body to stop substituting friendly feelings with romantic ones.

"My neighborhood was placed under mandatory evac." She ignored the shake in her hand as she lifted the coffee cup to her lips again. One of the packed boxes was filled with pictures of her and Milo, his sister, and his mother. Diana Russell had never made Quinn feel unwelcome—despite being a single mom and a hardworking physician—unlike Quinn's own family. If that box of memories was lost… Quinn mentally kicked herself. She was *not* going to travel that well-worn path again this morning.

"Do you need to leave?" Milo leaned forward and the soft scent of his cedar shampoo blended with the smell of her coffee.

What was wrong with her? Before she'd returned to California, she couldn't have told anyone anything about Milo's shampoo. Though she could have told them that the scrunch of his nose meant he was concerned. And that a twitch in his left cheek meant he was holding in a laugh, but a twitch in his right cheek meant he was angry.

Maybe the lines between friends and more had blurred long ago…

They'd spent almost all their free time together since she'd arrived, enjoying the opportunity to be together in person rather than on the screen. He'd helped paint her bungalow, and they'd watched silly romantic comedies while sharing giant bowls of popcorn. But he'd never mentioned wanting more.

And Milo always knew what he wanted.

Focus!

Shaking her head, Quinn shrugged. "Molly's in labor. You know her history." Molly had struggled with infertility, and she and her partner had had more than their share of losses over the past five years. After so many disappointments, they'd adopted a son a few years ago—a gorgeous little boy they were both devoted to—and had been stunned when she had conceived naturally.

"I think Molly would understand." Milo gripped her fingers.

The simple gesture made Quinn's heart rate pick up, but she didn't pull away. She didn't have the strength to put distance between them today—even if she wanted to. Glancing out the window, she shuddered. "If I left right now, I wouldn't make it home before the roads closed. I'm just mad I didn't throw stuff in the car before I left last night."

She forced her gaze away from the orange glow creeping along the hills. Her home was really in danger. The place she'd felt called to might vanish.

"Why not?" Milo's lips formed a soft smile that any other day would have sent her belly tumbling with need. "The reports coming in—" He caught his final words.

She knew all about the reports. Knew that if it had been Milo's home, he'd have already prepared a five-page emergency plan. Heck, he probably had one anyway.

Her chest constricted. Plans provided safety and security. But they could be weaponized, too.

Used to control.

Her hair, her room, her clothes, her activities had all been controlled—micromanaged. Her mother had kept a weekly calendar on the fridge. It was adjusted every Sunday morning—but only with activities deemed important to her parents. And deviation was *not* allowed.

Quinn had learned to hide her true self. To build walls to protect that precious self. The world hurt less if she kept the well-constructed barriers in place.

She'd done what had been expected of her. It hadn't mattered that her toes screamed through another ballet practice. It hadn't mattered that she'd absorbed the cutting remarks with a smile and the criticisms without argument. Walls hadn't provided happiness, but they had kept her safe. Besides, a false smile achieved more than tears.

She'd been the docile daughter until she'd refused to let her parents control her career choices. That one rebellion had led to her being cut out of their lives—all because she'd wanted some say about her future.

But that one mutinous act had granted her freedom. The right to pick up and move to where *she* chose. To cut her hair. To dress how she wanted. To never have a planner!

And when she had her own family, they were never going to feel like their life was scheduled. Her children, if she ever settled anywhere long enough to meet someone and have children, were going to know her love didn't depend on following a plan.

"I figured I had at least another day or two." Her throat closed as she fought off tears. She never cried in front of anyone—and she wasn't going to start today. Plus, denial was easier than focusing on disaster. But Milo wouldn't understand that. He was always at least three steps ahead of everything.

It was too late to do anything about it now, though. "I'll be fine," she assured him. "You know me. If necessary, I'll find a new place." The thought of moving again made her heart sink. That was new...and not welcome.

Leaning forward, Quinn squeezed his hand.

Why was she always reaching for him?

"Maybe somewhere that gets snow," she quipped, pulling back, "where the summers don't make me worry about melting into the pavement."

Milo's lips turned down. He'd never liked her talking about new places. He'd cheered when she'd announced that she wasn't going to work in her parents' law firm, but then he'd frowned when she'd said she was leaving California. He always frowned when she mentioned moving. She wasn't even sure he was aware he did it.

Though he hadn't frowned when she'd told him she was coming home to join him at St. Brigit's. The memory of his bright smile on that last video call still sent thrills through her.

She hated his frown—hated causing it. Her fingers itched to smooth away the small lines at the corners of his eyes. "Want to see if there's a clinic in Alaska that needs a midwife and stellar ob-gyn? We could buy some snowmobiles and race around the Arctic."

His mouth moved but no words came out. Quinn could feel the heat in her cheeks as Milo's gaze met hers. She hadn't meant to ask that and certainly hadn't expected how his stunned silence would cut across her.

"Quinn…" The question she should never have asked him hung between them as his voice died.

Concern coated Milo's features and she feared pity. That was the last thing she needed or wanted.

Especially from him.

"I'm kidding, homebody." She laughed, hoping it didn't sound as forced to him as it did to her. Maybe Milo would chalk it up to her fear and exhaustion. "I know I'll never get you out of LA. One day you're going to run the maternity ward at Valley General. I've seen the planning boards." She patted his hand.

Milo carefully managed his life. He never jumped from one contract to another. The man developed a plan. And he followed it.

No chasing a shiny, unexpected adventure.

"Enough about me." Standing, she downed the rest of her coffee. "What we should be worrying about is if those winds shift and we have to evacuate the birthing center."

"Quinn…" Milo stood and pulled her into a quick hug.

The heat from the brief connection evaporated before Quinn could blink. But the ghost of his strong arms clung to her. She wanted to step back into the embrace. She wanted to run from the room. But her feet refused to follow either order.

"It's okay to be worried about both the center and your house. I know what that tiny, falling-apart bungalow means to you."

Crossing her arms at her chest, she glared at him. "No knocking the bungalow, *Dr.* Russell. We can't all live in a fancy downtown high-rise." It was her normal retort, but her tone was sharper today. The pain of not having a home, a family, a place to belong to, stabbed her. And somehow she'd lost the ability to bury that emotion behind her walls.

"I'm sorry," Milo muttered. "That was beyond a poor choice of words." A dimple appeared in his left cheek as he stepped up to her.

They were at work, but with the stress of the day, all Quinn wanted to do was to lose herself in Milo's arms. Let him hold her to see if that would make the stress and pain float away. They were close friends; everyone knew it. No one would raise an eyebrow if they found them embracing. But Quinn's heart wanted more.

And she wouldn't risk that.

Quinn's parents hadn't wanted her. She and her brother, Asher, hadn't talked in years. Even her ex-fiancé had found her lacking less than a month after getting down on one knee. If her relationship with Milo changed, would his need to plan everything out clash with her desire to go with her gut?

Their different approach to life worked while they were friends. But if she lost him, Quinn would be completely alone. And she couldn't stand the thought of losing the one person she'd always been able to count on.

She just couldn't.

Putting a bit of distance between them, she held up her empty coffee cup. "Thanks for the caffeine rush." Ignoring the flash of hurt that crossed Milo's features, Quinn moved for the door. He clearly didn't understand why she was being awkward, and there was no safe way for her to say *My heart's confused—sorry.*

Swallowing a pinch of panic, Quinn dropped her coffee cup into the recycle bin. As it hit the bottom, she looked over her shoulder. "I need to check on Molly."

Whatever was going on with her when she was near Milo needed to stop. They were just friends. Best friends. They'd stuck together through their awkward teen phases, all their different jobs, her failed engagement and the end of his short-lived marriage. No one knew her better. No one made her feel more grounded.

More cared for…

Her chest seized. Quinn was just lonely, longing for a place of her own. Her heart was confused. It was reaching for the comfortable. That was all.

Milo's arms were heavy as the light scent he associated with Quinn lingered in the air around him as he stared after her. She was hurting and needed a friend. Why had something that had always been so easy become such a challenge once she'd started working with him at St. Brigit's?

What if she noticed how his embraces lingered a bit too long? How he had to fight to keep from leaning his head against hers? That he longed to be near her?

It had taken over a decade for them to land in the same place at the same time. But the excitement he'd felt when she'd stepped into his arms at LAX eight months ago hadn't been grounded in friendship. He'd wanted Quinn Davis for years. He wasn't sure when the friendship they'd shared had transformed for him, but it was there in every bright smile and subtle touch. Yet she'd never indicated she wanted more. And losing her friendship wasn't an option.

He'd worked up the courage to ask her out once, years ago. But when he'd arrived with flowers, she'd been dancing with her roommate, screaming about signing her first contract with the traveling nurse agency. She'd looked so beautiful and happy. Milo had claimed "best friend telepathy" as he'd passed her the sunflowers and congratulated her on the new job.

Then he'd locked the question he'd wanted to ask deep in his heart. She had talked about putting space between her and California since elementary school. And he'd been determined to never throw a wrench into those plans. Dreams and goals were important—his father had taught him that.

Milo wanted Quinn to be happy. Wanted her to get every stamp in her passport, no matter how much he hated the distance between them...

He swallowed the desire that was his constant companion. Now wasn't the right time to ask Quinn out.

And it wasn't ever going to be right.

St. Brigit's was just a stopover for Quinn. He knew that. Every time he sat on her lumpy, rented couch, it was a reminder that this was a landing zone after a decade on the road. And he knew the road would eventually call to her again—it always did.

It didn't call to Milo, though. He loved California and never considered relocating. His mom and his sister were in California, as were all his goals.

Still, every so often, Milo would catch a look in Quinn's eyes or a touch of a smile that made him wonder if she'd also considered exploring the possibility that there might be more between them. His brain screamed that he was imagining it, but he couldn't kill the pang of hope his heart felt each time. Last week, their hands had brushed as they'd walked to the movie theater and she'd smiled at him in a way that had Milo barely managing to prevent the words from flying out of his mouth.

These thoughts, the bloom of heat in his belly when she was near, the dreams he woke from, still feeling as though he was holding her close—he'd always been able to suppress them. But now, working with her every day, the thought that she might complete him—might patch the empty space in his soul—was growing ever stronger.

But that void had existed long before he'd met Quinn. It had been ripped open the night his father hadn't come home from the store with the supplies for his science project. His mom had done her best, but Milo had been so lonely.

The comfortable conversations he'd had with his dad hadn't been the same with his mom. He'd missed the feel of their complete family. The hole his father's passing had created still ate at him and he clung to his few memories and the emotions they stirred in him.

But if his short-lived marriage had taught him anything, it was that another person couldn't fill the void of his father's loss. That was far too much to ask. And that disaster had proved that impulsive acts just caused chaos.

And heartbreak.

Milo had always been impressed with Quinn's ability to start over. To pick up and leave the past behind when a new opportunity presented itself. She saw a new thing and ran toward it, confident that the details would sort themselves out. He let his eyes wander to the fire on the hills in the distance and sighed. But if she'd planned better, packed her car when the fire blazed closer last night… He let the thought float away.

As a kid, he'd left everything until the last minute, especially school projects. The week before he died, his dad had bought him two small whiteboards. He'd written Short Term on one and Long Term on the other—just like the headings on the boards his dad kept in his office. Then he'd explained that he wanted Milo to at least plan a few things out.

But Milo hadn't. And the night before his science presentation was due, he'd panicked because they didn't have the supplies he needed. His father had marched him upstairs and taken the money for the supplies from Milo's piggy bank, telling him he would have to do what he could but he was not to stay up past his bedtime.

While Milo had started the research, his father had gone out for supplies. A drunk driver had collided with him as he'd left the grocery store. Poster boards for Milo and flowers for his mother had been found in the car and dutifully delivered by a policeman days later.

Milo, suddenly lost, had been a mere shadow of himself. Adrift in a world where the man who'd made him feel tall, important, special, had vanished. In the grief-filled days that followed, he'd finally started using the planning boards his father had given him. The routine they'd provided had eased his pain. It never entirely vanished, but he found that rigidly structuring life left him open to fewer surprises. It gave him a bit of control in the chaotic world.

Milo was never going to be that person who had no idea what the next six months would hold. Where Quinn needed freedom, he required control. She wasn't going to stay in California, and the goals that would make him whole were set in stone.

And he was so close.

Milo made his way over to the window. Smoke had descended over LA a week ago, but the light of the fires had stayed away until now. A bead of worry moved through him as he stared at the glow just beyond the horizon. Wildfires were an all too constant threat in California and he'd experienced life with voluntary evacuation notices a few times. But he had never received a mandatory evacuation notice.

Would Quinn's house survive? He hoped so. He remembered questioning her decision to rent the rundown property when he'd helped her move her limited belongings inside almost a year ago. She'd just smiled and said she'd loved the place.

They'd spent weekends painting the gray walls of her bedroom a bright blue and her kitchen walls the color of the shining sun. If coffee didn't wake her up, the sunflower color would. Milo hadn't teased her that bright colors were out of fashion—at least according to his interior designer sister—because Quinn deserved to have walls whatever color her heart desired. He'd never understood her mother's refusal to allow Quinn to paint her childhood room, even when Quinn had offered to pay for all the supplies. But there was a lot about the Davis family that Milo hadn't understood.

The only problem Milo had with her bungalow was its distance from his place. It was forty minutes away from St. Brigit's on a good traffic day.

Forty minutes away from him…

Maybe it had been ridiculous to think she'd want to be neighbors. But he'd looked for places near him as soon as Quinn had told him she'd accepted the position at St. Brigit's. He'd plotted the best areas and done a ton of research for her. She'd signed her lease on the bungalow without ever looking at any of it. He knew she'd always trusted her gut over research, but had thought she'd want to be closer for the short time she was going to be in LA. It had hit him surprisingly hard when she'd chosen somewhere so far from him.

She'd signed a two-year lease on the two-bedroom bungalow. He should have rejoiced. But then she'd rented all her furniture. And his small piece of hope that she'd stay had died. He'd counted on having two years. But now, if the bungalow burned, would she leave again?

Even with her lease, Milo had started looking for hints

that she might run off on another adventure. The nursing agency still sent her job advertisements, and he was aware that she talked to her clinic colleagues about the travel opportunities when they arose. Her excitement was contagious, and he knew at least one nurse from St. Brigit's had put in an application.

But she'd asked him to go to Alaska— No, Milo corrected his heart, Quinn had joked about finding a place somewhere else if her home turned to ashes. She'd just thrown him in—probably without thinking. After all, her cheeks had burned as soon as the question had left her lips.

He'd teased her about her tendency to blush for years and when her cheeks lit up, he'd wanted to lean forward and rub his hands over them. To pull her close.

Instead, his tongue had refused to mutter even a basic response. And then she'd confirmed that it was only a joke.

Which he'd known…

So why was his heart still wishing she'd meant it—even if he never planned to leave?

Pushing a hand through his hair, Milo tried to rope in his wayward emotions. An offhand comment when Quinn was stressed didn't mean anything.

But what if it did? What if it was a sign she wanted more from him too? The loose plan he'd thought of for asking Quinn out formed at the back of his brain again.

Why was it refusing to stay buried?

"Molly's crowning and the baby won't drop!" Rhonda shouted from behind him. She was gone before the lounge door slammed shut, giving him the perfect excuse to bury the lingering questions and thoughts, and focus on his work instead.

"I can't," Molly sighed and leaned her head back.

"You can. Just breathe. And when the next contraction

comes, I need you to push with all your might." Quinn kept her voice level as Molly let out another low cry.

She'd been pushing for over an hour and was growing tired and frustrated. Quinn dropped her eyes to the baby's heart rate monitor. It was still holding steady, but the longer Molly's son refused to enter this world, the greater her chance of needing an emergency cesarean.

"I'm tired." Molly's voice ached with exhaustion.

"I know," Quinn commiserated, but only for a minute. Her nursing mentor, a former army medic, had taught each of his students that sometimes a patient needed a command. Meeting Molly's gaze, Quinn channeled her inner drill sergeant. "Your job isn't done," she reminded her. "So, Julian, help Molly sit up a bit. And Molly, get ready to bear down."

Molly's partner helped her up and rubbed her back. He whispered something in her ear, low enough that Quinn couldn't hear him. Whatever the words were, Molly set her lips and nodded at Quinn.

Good. She needed Molly focused. Bringing life into this world was hard work, but Molly could do it.

The monitor started to beep and Molly's face screwed tight. "Oh, God."

"Here we go. Push!" Quinn ordered.

Molly let out a scream as she held on to Julian's hands, but she didn't stop pushing.

And Quinn breathed a sigh. *Finally.* His little nose and lips were perfect. "Good job, Momma. One or two more pushes, and we should have him."

The air shifted next to her and Quinn knew Milo had joined them, but she didn't look up. She'd asked Rhonda to grab Milo after they'd passed the forty-minute mark of pushing. If the baby hadn't descended... Quinn swallowed. The baby had—that was all that mattered now.

Quinn was pleased that Milo's presence wasn't needed, but she knew he wouldn't leave now. Not because he didn't trust her ability to safely deliver a child, but because he cared for each of his patients. And Milo tried to be present for as many births as possible. Quinn liked to joke that he lived a block from the birthing center so that he could welcome as many little ones into this world as possible.

"Looks like I got dressed in my fancy scrubs for nothing."

Quinn could hear the smile in Milo's voice as she focused on Molly's little one. This was the part they all loved. The reason every midwife and ob-gyn entered the profession. There was no better joy than to watch new life enter this world. Sharing a few minutes with loving partners becoming first-time or fifth-time parents... It never got old.

The monitor beeping picked up and Quinn offered Molly a quick smile. "One more time, Momma."

Molly's eyes were a bit watery, but she gripped Julian's hands and pushed as the next contraction cascaded through her. "Fine!" Molly bit out. "But I am definitely telling his first date about how much trouble he put me through."

"That is every parent's right. I think it's in a handbook somewhere," Milo agreed.

Quinn laughed and then smiled as the tiny guy slid into her arms. He was perfect. Ten little toes and fingers, and a set of very healthy lungs, as evidenced by the fact he immediately erupted in a screech.

Perfect.

For just a moment, Quinn wished the child was hers. It was a need that she was having trouble ignoring lately. But it encompassed so much more. A desire to find someone. To walk through life with another, someone who'd try to keep a straight face while she crushed his hands and brought their child into this world.

Someone who would choose her, just as she was...

As she laid the still-screeching little one on his mother's chest, Quinn grinned at her patient. "Congratulations, Molly. You're a mom—again."

Molly and Julian were good people, a loving family. Surely their hearts were big enough to include the new baby *and* their adopted son, even if he didn't share their DNA. Unlike her own parents...

The placenta was delivered with no complications as Molly and Julian bonded with their newborn—each counting his toes and fingers—before letting Milo take the baby to check him over while Quinn took care of Molly.

A few minutes later, Quinn watched as an exhausted Molly kissed the top of her son's head and then kissed her husband.

"He's beautiful," Quinn said with a smile. It was true. Their little man was adorable—like all new babies.

Molly let out a sigh. "He is. So beautiful. He looks a bit like Owen. I know technically people would say that's not possible, but look at his little nose." Molly's fingers traced a line down the boy's nose and laughed. "Such a cute nose."

Julian kissed his wife. "I agree. Though maybe that is because all baby boys seem to look like little old men when they're first born." Julian laughed and pulled out his cell phone.

A small boy appeared on the screen a few seconds later. "Am I a big brother? Am I?" Owen beamed at the baby on his mother's chest.

"Yes," Molly whispered. "This is Adam—your little brother." She let out a yawn and waved to her oldest.

Julian took over, his smile wide as he looked at Owen. "Mommy is tired, but Grandma is going to bring you to visit in a little while."

"Promise?" Owen queried.

Quinn wondered if the small boy was worried. At four, a bit of sibling jealousy was to be expected, and he was likely too young to understand that his world had altered forever. *Please*... Quinn sent out a silent prayer to the universe that it was altering for the better.

"Promise." Julian gave him a thumbs-up. "I love you, big brother."

Quinn sucked in a breath as her heart clenched. She needed to leave—now. Molly was fine, and the family needed some bonding time, anyway. She wanted to believe that was why she was ducking out. But Quinn had never been good at lying—particularly to herself.

The echoes of her past chased her as she exited the birthing room.

This wasn't her life. The reminder did little to calm her racing heart. Molly wasn't her mother and Julian wasn't her father. These parents would love both their children equally.

They would.

She'd wanted to return to California, had felt drawn here. Working with Milo had been the biggest draw, but LA was also her hometown. Where she'd been raised. She had hoped that maybe enough time had passed. But in the short time she'd been home, she'd realized the pain of her childhood refused to bury itself in the hole in her soul.

Rolling her shoulders, she tried to find a wave of calm, but it eluded her. Her parents had struggled to conceive, too. After years of trying, they'd adopted Quinn—a newborn abandoned at a fire station.

If they'd loved her then, Quinn had been too young to remember. Her brother, Asher—the miracle child they'd always wanted—had been born when she was not quite two. Overnight, Quinn had become an interloper. If they could have returned her...

Leaning against the wall, Quinn inhaled a deep breath, trying to fend off the past. Today had been too emotional. But the tiny part of her heart that wasn't happy on the road, that craved permanence, that got louder with every move... And screamed loudest when she was near Milo—

"She looks just like my mother." The soft coo of a new mom walking past with her newborn sent Quinn spiraling further.

Every time someone had commented on how her jet-black hair and dark eyes were so different from her family's blond hair and baby blues, she'd wish her mother would laugh it off. Make up a great-grandfather. Or say that she was her daughter by choice instead of by birth—other adoptive families believed that. But no matter how hard Quinn had tried to follow the family's strict rules, to abide by her parents' wants and desires, it hadn't been enough.

Instead, Carolyn Davis would calmly explain that Quinn wasn't really hers.

Not hers...not a full member of the family.

When her parents had died in a car crash right after she became a nurse, she found out that they'd left everything to her brother. She hadn't even been mentioned in the will.

Though they'd never been close, her brother had tried to make it right. Asher had divided the estate evenly. Quinn hadn't cared about the money or the real estate—her parents had stopped supporting her financially the day she'd declared that she didn't want to be a lawyer. She'd realized that that wouldn't have gained her acceptance, so why give up her dreams of being a nurse?

It wasn't his fault, but Asher had gotten the things that mattered. The letters. The keepsakes. The acknowledgment. Quinn shouldn't have expected anything. Still, part of her had hoped that one day she might be welcomed into her own family. With her parents' passing, that dream became impossible. And to not even be mentioned in the documents they'd meticulously prepared in case they died unexpectedly, was a wound she still didn't know how to mend.

Then she'd lost her brother, too. Not physically. At least, she didn't think so. But Asher had stopped returning her phone calls and picked up the reins at their parents' law firm. Their lives had always been separate, but without their parents between them, she'd hoped they might be friends, or at best, not competitors. She'd been disappointed—again.

But she'd found her place—at least professionally. Nursing was her calling and she'd never regretted choosing it. She'd carved her own path, focusing only on the step right in front of her. But nursing didn't take away her desire to be accepted, to be loved, to have a family that wanted her—just as she was.

"Molly and Julian are going to be excellent parents, and their boys are going to keep them busy." Milo's words floated over her.

"Of course they are." Quinn opened her eyes and looked toward the door where Rhonda was hanging the welcome stork. The spindle-legged creature was hung on all the doors, and Quinn's heart ached with the worry that she might never experience that joy. She was less likely to find it if she moved every year—or sooner. "I'm fine."

Maybe if she repeated the phrase, it would bloom into truth.

"I didn't ask." Milo leaned against the wall and wrapped an arm around her shoulders.

At least he hadn't directly called out her lie. Pushing away from the wall, Quinn offered him a smile, doing her best to make it seem unforced. "You were going to." She tapped her head. "Best friend telepathy."

Milo grinned. The dimple in his cheek sent a tiny thrill through her. Between working with him and hanging out with him, it was getting harder to keep the lines of friendship from blurring.

Particularly when she didn't want to.

Hurrying on before he could add any commentary, Quinn knocked a finger against her watch. "I'm off duty. So, I'm going to—" Her words died as she remembered that she couldn't go home.

"You want to crash at my place? I'm off, too."

His heat warmed the cold that refused to leave her. But if she said yes when her emotions were so close to the surface, it could be a disaster. "No." The rushed word was clipped, and her heart sank as Milo's nose scrunched.

He was worried and hurt, and there wasn't a good way to walk her tone back. She hadn't meant to hurt his feelings.

Trying to sound bright and cheery, Quinn offered, "I'll crash here, and one of the on-call midwives can have a date night!"

Someone should.

Bumping his hip, she ignored the gibe and added, "I'll certainly be on time for my next shift. Maybe even early, given the commute."

Milo nodded, but the ghost of hurt still hovered on his face. "The commute will certainly be quick."

Pursing her lips, Quinn watched him go. Longing pushed at her chest, ordered her to chase after him, to tell him she'd love to go home with him. In so many different ways…

But that was why she couldn't do it. He was her friend. If their dynamic changed, she could lose so much.

But what if she gained everything?

Until she could quash her heart's cry, she needed to keep a bit of distance between them. No matter how much it hurt.

CHAPTER TWO

QUINN'S DARK HAIR spilled across her cheeks, her breaths were slow and her feet hung from the couch. Pulling at the back of his neck, Milo sighed at the sight of the crumpled pillow she was using. He'd taken more than one nap on that monstrosity. She was going to wake with a stiff neck.

If she'd come home with him last night, she'd have been comfortable, well rested. *Cared for.* But he knew Quinn's independent side well. She'd been taking care of herself for most of her life. But she didn't have to do *every*thing herself. Relying on each other was an important part of any friendship. She could ask him for anything. Anything.

Besides, there was independence and then there was stubborn. One night on that couch was more than enough. If the evac order hadn't been lifted on her home by the end of their shift today, he was going to find a way to make her agree to stay at his place until this was over.

His heart rate picked up, and Milo wanted to slap himself. He should not be happy that she might have to stay with him.

Get hold of yourself.

Her home might be engulfed in flames at this very moment. A sobering thought…

Milo's hand shook as he reached for her shoulder, but at least she couldn't see it. "Quinn." She'd never been a quick riser. He set one alarm and never allowed it to snooze, but Quinn relied on at least three. A small smile touched her lips and she rolled toward him—as much as the couch would allow anyway. "Milo, I want…"

I want… What? He wanted to know the final part of that statement. Desperately.

She wasn't really awake. And he knew that dreams offered scattered bits of information. After all, Quinn had been a regular fixture in his dreams for years. And since her return, those dreams often woke him with decidedly less than friendly thoughts.

But that didn't mean he was a feature in her dreams. She could be dreaming of painting, cooking or any of the multitude of activities they'd done together over their two decades of friendship. Still, the small bursts of hope cutting across his heart refused to be quashed.

What if she was dreaming of more too?

He didn't have time for introspection this morning. Gripping her shoulder, he shook harder. "Quinn."

Ainsley Dremer's husband had called to report that his wife was in labor. She'd worked out a plan for a home birth, but the midwives they'd worked with were currently dealing with mandatory evacuation orders. St. Brigit's standing rule was that two midwives attended home births, but no midwives other than Quinn were available. So, Milo was going to act as the second.

If the fire expanded, their patients might have trouble reaching St. Brigit's. He knew the first responders were doing their best, but months of drought had created the perfect landscape for the fire to grow. And grow it had.

According to the news, homes in Quinn's area had been destroyed, though he still didn't know for sure that Quinn's bungalow had been one of them. He didn't want anyone's house destroyed, but Milo especially wanted Quinn's house to stay safe. That way she wouldn't have an excuse to leave.

She belonged here…with him.

Why the hell wouldn't that thought disappear?

Warm fingers grazed his and heat rushed through Milo's body. Those little touches meant far more to him than they should. But that didn't stop him from craving them.

"Milo?" Quinn's lips turned up and her cheeks pinkened as her eyes landed on him. "What time is it?"

"Time to get to work!" Milo winked, hoping his face didn't show the multitude of contradictory emotions floating through him. "Ainsley Dremer is in labor. Sherrie and Heather are both dealing with mandatory evac orders, so you and I are up to the plate."

Quinn flinched as she straightened and rolled her shoulders.

"This couch isn't built for long-term slumber." Milo barely resisted the urge to reach out and rub her shoulders, even though he'd performed the action dozens of times over the years—after long study sessions in college or in the weeks she'd be passing through LA before heading off to her next contract.

It was a simple gesture. One a friend could easily offer. But it felt far too intimate when his body craved so much more than just a friendly touch.

"I've slept on worse." Quinn's hand ran along her neck as she massaged the knots out. "Nothing a few pain tablets and a hot shower won't fix. Though only one of those is an option this morning."

It was her standard reply. She'd said the same thing after sleeping on the floor of a makeshift hospital in Haiti during a cholera outbreak. She'd also joked about the tiny cot she'd fallen into while living in a rural area of Maine where the roads nearly vanished in the winter. The woman seemed capable of falling asleep anywhere, but that didn't stop muscles from complaining, no matter how much she tried to hide it.

At least he was prepared this morning. Milo reached for

the glass of water and passed her two pain-relief tablets. Then he held up a small bag with a toothbrush and toothpaste. Small comforts went a long way.

"Milo—" Quinn smiled "—you're the best."

The small compliment sent more than a few shivers down his spine. She was being Quinn. His wonderful, amazing, best friend. But it wasn't enough.

Hadn't been enough for years.

"The service here is going to be hard for my next locale to live up to." Tipping the water bottle toward him, she grinned. "To friends."

"Friends," Milo repeated, bitterness coating his tongue.

Her "next locale." Such a simple phrase. *An expected phrase.* This was just a waypoint. And he needed to remember that.

He tried to force his voice to sound normal. "I am pretty amazing." Milo wished he had more caffeine in his system.

"And so humble." Quinn laughed as she set the water bottle down and grabbed the bag of toiletries. "How far along is Ainsley? Sherrie was her primary. Thankfully, she said Ainsley's pregnancy was textbook."

Home births were rising in popularity in the US, and Milo fully supported them. But he did not recommend them for women with possible birthing risks. Milo loved that St. Brigit's offered both options for his patients. Just like his mother's clinic did.

His heart compressed a tiny bit. He hadn't worked at that clinic in nearly five years. St. Brigit's was great, but it wasn't Oceanside Clinic.

No place was.

And five years ago, when his mother had married Felix Ireman, another ob-gyn at the clinic, the place had taken on an even more homey feel. Milo'd spent most of his teen years volunteering at Oceanside and, during his undergrad years, had even sketched out an idea to add a natural birthing center, which they'd started building the year he'd worked there.

Oceanside Clinic was special and he'd only experienced the feeling he got when he stepped into Oceanside at one other place. Valley General.

Three weeks before his father had passed, he'd had a meeting at Valley General. He'd taken Milo along so he could interview a surgeon for a science project. The one Milo had put off.

As they were leaving, his father had slowed next to the chief of obstetrics' office. He'd smiled at Milo and said, "One day, this will be my office." The memory of the confidence in his father's voice still caused goose pimples to rise on Milo's skin.

It was the clearest memory he had of his dad. His father's voice might have been lost to the waste bin of memory, but that day, that perfect day and all its feelings, Milo remembered. His dad had never achieved that goal—but Milo would. And each morning, when he walked through the door, he'd feel close to his dad again.

"Milo?"

Ignoring the ache in his chest, Milo focused on Quinn's original question. "She is forty weeks and two days. When her husband called, the contractions had been holding steady since a little after three. So it's showtime!"

Milo glanced at the window. The sun wouldn't rise for another two hours, but the glow of orange still lit up the hills in the distance. "Ainsley and her husband are a few miles from the voluntary evacuation zone."

Quinn's eyes hovered on the hills through the window. "Did the winds shift overnight?" Her lips tipped down before she shook herself. "I meant…are they expecting them to shift? Morning brain."

The attempt to cover her worry didn't fool him. Of course she was wondering if her home had survived the night. And he didn't have an answer for her. But rather than pull on the first thread, he addressed her second question. "Have to ask someone more versed in fire control than me." He knew the department's director was in regular contact with the city fire brigades and that conditions had been deemed safe enough for them to head out.

Quinn moved toward the bathroom. "Give me five minutes to take care of necessities, and then we'll be on our way." Before she closed the door, Quinn added, "And don't eat all the croissants. I saw the bag behind your back."

Milo laughed. "I make no promises."

Their director opened the door to the employee lounge just then. "Dr. Russell, if the fire shifts and there are complications with Ainsley Dremer's delivery, I've instructed Kevin to run you south to Oceanside Clinic."

The bag nearly slipped from Milo's hands as he tried to steady the beat of his heart. *Oceanside.* Did they really expect the fire to shift? And if so, why were they not directing Ainsley and her husband to either head to St. Brigit's now or to go south to Oceanside? Plans and routes ran through Milo's head.

"Dr. Russell?" Martina stepped into the room, lines crossing her forehead.

She met his gaze then let her eyes wander to the window. "They aren't anticipating the fire shifting. We would never risk anyone's safety. But it's always good to have a backup plan."

"Of course," Milo agreed. Plans were how he lived his life. He just hated the small bead of want that always pressed against his soul when he thought of the Oceanside Clinic. He'd loved working with his mom, but with each passing year, his connection to his father slipped farther away, making him more determined to get the job at Valley General. For a kid that had been his dad's shadow—to not even remember his dad's voice…

Pain rippled down his neck as he tried to recall it, but it refused to materialize. Valley General offered Milo an opportunity no other place would. If he could reestablish that connection to that last blissful day they'd shared, then maybe the loneliness he hadn't fully conquered since would dissipate.

It might vanish completely if Quinn stayed. Suddenly his body was on fire for a different reason. He couldn't go down this path. She'd mentioned her "next locale" less than fifteen minutes ago.

"Didn't realize we would need to go that far south. Caught me by surprise. That's all."

Martina nodded. "Ainsley and her husband are halfway between here and Oceanside. Easier to head south from there. You know how it is. No one can afford the city rents. And since you still have visiting rights at Oceanside, it makes the most sense."

He'd maintained his position as a visiting physician at his mother's clinic, but only in the event of an emergency or if his mother and Felix were unable to work. Thankfully, that had never happened. Though, if his mother kept talking about him coming back, he might need to end it. She knew what Oceanside meant to Milo, and she also knew about his dreams for Valley General. "Glad it's finally come in handy." Milo lifted his cup of coffee. "Quinn and I will be ready to go soon. Is there anything else you need from us? We'll probably be with Ainsley for most of the day."

"Since you asked… Dr. Metri is looking over a few résumés for the open OBG position. When you get back, I'd like you to look them over, too. See if there is anyone you think would make a good addition to our team. There's even one from a senior Valley General ob-gyn. Guess she's looking to slow down a bit."

Valley General. An open senior position.

His tongue stuck to the roof of his mouth as he glanced

toward the door where Quinn was getting ready. Working with Quinn was one of the top highlights of his career. He'd assumed she'd be the first to leave, but could he leave before her?

Mercy General had approached him a few weeks ago about a potential senior OB position. The opportunity would've enhanced his résumé for any potential opening at Valley General, but he'd passed. His credentials were already impressive, and Quinn might never make it back to California once she left. Their working relationship had an expiration date, even if neither of them discussed it, and he just wasn't willing to cut things short.

Valley General! his brain screamed. *It's only ten miles up the road.* But his heart was less willing to celebrate the potential coup. Still, he could look at the résumés.

"Of course." Milo nodded and smiled as Martina walked out. If a senior OB was looking to leave Valley General, perhaps he could accelerate his plan. It would make Quinn's transition back to the road easier to accept.

Maybe keep him from making a fool of himself, too.

"What's up?" Quinn asked as she grabbed the white bag from Milo's fingers. "You look like you're planning something."

"How can you tell?" Milo grabbed a croissant from the bag.

She hit his hip with hers as she raised the pastry to her lips. "The far-off look and rubbing your chin. It's cartoonish but adorable."

She'd been able to read him like that since they'd been teenagers. It was comforting, but what if she saw the swirls of emotion directed at her? Milo's throat tightened as he purposely removed his hand from his chin. "I see."

Quinn's fingers burned as she gripped his wrist. "It really is a cute trait. So, what are you planning?"

"Nothing major." Milo started for the door. "Martina

wants me to look over a few résumés. Apparently, one of them is from a senior OB at Valley General."

Quinn fell into step beside him. She was tearing off pieces of her pastry, but her eyes had a faraway look in them. "So, you're plotting how to become their replacement at Valley General?"

"It's not plotting." Milo sighed and hated the flash of hurt that hovered in Quinn's eyes before she strode past him.

Following her to the van bay, Milo opened the back door as their driver, Kevin, started the engine. "I'm sorry. But 'plotting' sounds so much more sinister than 'planning,' which is what I always do. Stay the course." He chuckled, but it sounded false, even to him.

Quinn nodded as she finished her croissant. "Plans can shift. You're the only one writing them in stone."

"What is that supposed to mean?" Milo's stomach hollowed as her gaze met his. Their ability to read each other could really be a curse.

"Milo." Quinn raised a brow. "Ever since Bianca left, Valley General has become your obsession." She leaned her head against the wall of the medical van as it turned out of the parking lot.

"Planning is not an obsession. It gives you control." Milo frowned as Quinn's dark gaze held his.

"Control doesn't—" Quinn bit her lip so hard he feared she was tasting blood, but she didn't continue the well-worn argument.

Quinn moved with her heart; she didn't look for stepping stones in her career. And she didn't understand why he was so focused on Valley General when St. Brigit's and Oceanside had made him happy, too.

He'd been lost after Bianca's infidelity less than six months into their impulsive Vegas marriage. It had been ridiculously cliché and completely out of character, but when

Bianca had said it would be nice for them to be bound to each other forever, it had called to the lonely place inside him.

They'd been together for almost a year at that point, and he'd considered proposing, but the time hadn't ever seemed right. Still, he'd rationalized that they'd have done it eventually, so he'd said yes and they'd walked down the aisle.

And in the end, not waiting, not planning, had cost him. He might not be able to remember his father clearly, but the image of his ex in bed with another man was certainly seared into his brain.

He'd stepped off the path he'd outlined and chaos had erupted. In less than a year, he'd gone from married doctor to the source of gossip, particularly when Bianca had announced her pregnancy less than three months after she'd left him.

Luckily, his mother had offered him a position at Oceanside. He'd spent a year there regrouping, and the memory of his father at Valley General, and how right everything had felt in that moment, had begun to consume him. He needed to make it a reality. *He did.*

Quinn kept her eyes closed, but he could see the twitch of her lips. She wanted to say something, probably wanted to run through the pros of letting his heart lead. But it was. It was leading him to Valley General.

It was ironic for a traveling nurse to seem so invested in him staying in one place, something he'd kidded her about a few times. She liked to say that it would be nice if one of them settled down.

Why couldn't it be her?

Ainsley and her husband, Leo, met Quinn and Milo at the door with forced smiles. "Who would have thought we'd be bringing a babe into the world as it burns?" the mom-to-be quipped nervously.

"Well, this isn't California's first drought. We'll be fine. I'm sure," Leo said, kissing Ainsley's head, his gaze not leaving the smoke that was much heavier than even Quinn thought it should be.

They'd checked as they'd driven, and the voluntary evacuation zone was less than fifteen miles north of Ainsley and Leo's neighborhood. Unless luck shifted for the firefighters, this area was going to be under voluntary evacuation orders eventually. Quinn hadn't known much luck in her life, but maybe today...

Ainsley gripped her belly with one hand and the doorknob with the other.

"Breathe," Milo offered as he stepped up beside Quinn.

"I...know." Ainsley's eyes were firmly shut as she forced the words out. When the contraction loosened, she met their gazes and stepped aside. "Sorry. Welcome to our home."

"It's not a problem." Quinn smiled as she gripped the strap of her midwifery bag and stepped across the threshold. A birthing pool was ready in the center of the living room, and a pile of towels lay next to it. But it was the stack of boxes sitting next to the front door that caught Quinn's eye.

"I thought it might be good to put a few things together... if..." Leo's words were soft as he looked from Quinn to the boxes. "It's mostly baby stuff and paperwork. I've almost put them in the car a dozen times today. Every time I start, I think I'm tempting fate if I do, then worry that I'm tempting it by not. Crazy thoughts while my wife is giving birth, right?"

Quinn understood Leo's rambling logic. She offered the expectant father a smile. "I think you should go ahead and pack it." There was little that a partner could control during a birth. Quinn had seen more than one spouse spiral as they tried to find something to do to help.

And she couldn't push away the bubble of fear in her

mind that wanted to scream at her for not doing the same. Her boxes may have turned to ash, but Leo and Ainsley's were still whole.

When Leo hesitated, Quinn added, "You can always take them out later. But if you don't do it, you're just going to keep worrying. And Ainsley will need all your focus soon."

Leo stared at the boxes for a moment longer before looking down the hallway to where Ainsley was pacing. Then his eyes moved to the center of the living room where Milo was pulling supplies from his medical bag. "You're right. Can't hurt."

Moving toward Milo, Quinn set her midwifery bag next to his. The supplies in one kit should be enough, but each practitioner carried their own bag when they went to home deliveries.

"Nice job. Having those boxes in the car will relax Leo a bit." Milo's voice was low as he checked the oxygen and syringes from his bag. Every person she'd worked with had an item or two that was always triple-checked. For Milo, it was oxygen and syringes. For her, it was the maternal and infant resuscitators—items she always prayed would stay packed. "You have a gift for finding the right words."

"Thanks." Quinn nodded. The tiny compliment was nice, but did little to fill the hollow in her stomach that just wanted to know if she still had boxes. If the few precious items she loved were intact.

"It'll be okay." Milo's voice was soft as he kept an eye focused on Ainsley as she paced the hallway.

"What if it isn't? What if everything is gone?" She wanted to kick herself, but there was no way to reel the words back in. Now was not the time or the place.

"Then we buy new things." Milo looked at the oxygen tank for the third time. "And make new memories together. Like helping bring a baby into the world while a fire rages on the doorstep."

Together. Such an easy word with so much meaning. How did he always manage to find the right words? A calmness pressed through her as she stared at him. Milo always put people at ease. It made him a wonderful friend and a great doctor. How many people would have thought to bring water and pain tablets to make the start of her day easier?

But it was more for her. Quinn knew that. Milo grounded her. He was her point of reference. The haven she knew she could come home to anytime, but also the one who would always cheer her on as she found her next adventure.

She wished there was an easy way to return the favor. She might not understand his connection to his father, but she could see how important it was to him. Yet she was terrified he wasn't living his life, not really.

How could he when he was so focused on a memory?

But maybe her desire to run from nearly everything about her past was what fogged her brain— Right now wasn't the time to focus on that. When her mind was more at ease, and less prone to jumping to inopportune thoughts about her best friend, Quinn would find a way to at least mention the cons of running a large unit like the one at Valley General.

He'd miss things like home deliveries and spending extra time with patients—and Quinn didn't think that would make Milo happy.

Was a memory enough to carry him through? Was it worth it?

"I'm going to go wash up and see how far along Ainsley is." Quinn tapped Milo's shoulder as she grabbed her box of gloves and headed for the kitchen. Her fingers tingled from the brief contact, but she ignored that feeling as Ainsley came to stand beside her.

"How far apart are the contractions?"

"About four minutes." Ainsley's face contorted a bit as

she gripped the edge of the counter. "Nope, three and a half."

Quinn held out her arms and gestured for Ainsley to grip her forearms as she breathed through the contraction. "Three and a half minutes is good. Breathe. As soon as this one ends, let's see how far along you are. Then, if you want to get into the birthing pool, now would probably be a good time."

"Okay," Ainsley whispered as she released her grip on Quinn's forearms. She looked at the pool and let out a sigh as they walked toward her bedroom. "I planned to spend most of my labor there. But when it started, walking felt better. Leo spent so much time setting it up for me."

"Labor often throws plans out the window." Milo's grin was brilliant as he joined them in the hall.

Quinn shot him a quick look as she followed Ainsley into the bedroom. He was quite willing to grant everyone else the grace to change their plans. Shame he couldn't offer the same grace to himself.

"Dr. Russell is right. If you want to keep walking, that is fine. Leo will understand." Quinn kept her voice level as Ainsley slid onto the bed, which had been prepared with medical-grade covers and protective layers. Many mothers planned out their home births for months. And they became very attached to specific ideas that might have to be adjusted or just weren't what they wanted during labor. There was no shame in changing plans, though.

"I hope so." Ainsley lay back and gripped her belly as another labor pain started.

That one hadn't taken three minutes. "Milo!" Quinn called.

"This…one…is…bad!" Ainsley's face contorted.

She was likely moving into transition labor. There was going to be a little one here shortly.

Milo stepped to the door and took in the scene before him. "I'll get the bags."

As the contraction ended, Quinn checked Ainsley. "Nine centimeters. It won't be long now. I think we need to just stay here and not worry about the tub."

"Here...works." Ainsley shook her head as another contraction started. "Leo?"

Milo returned, dropping the bags next to the bed. "I'll go grab him."

Before Milo could leave, Leo stepped into the room with a police officer.

Quinn felt her heart drop. Milo caught her gaze and she saw fear in his eyes too, though he didn't adjust his position. If the officer was here, the winds must have shifted again. Luck really wasn't on their side, but Milo clearly wasn't going to panic.

"See, we can't leave." Leo's whisper wasn't low enough.

Milo's face paled, but he moved quickly. "I'll go get the stretcher and Kevin." Milo nodded to the officer as he darted from the room.

"No." Ainsley's lip quivered. "Please..."

"Sorry, ma'am." The officer nodded. "But the fire is moving faster than expected. This area is under mandatory evacuation and you need to leave. *Now!*" He tipped his head toward Leo. "I need to see to the rest of the neighborhood."

"Leo." Quinn kept her tone firm as she looked between Leo and Ainsley. "We are headed to Oceanside Clinic. Meet us there."

"I can't leave my wife." Leo's cheeks were red and tears coated his eyes.

"We do not have room for you in the van. Dr. Russell and I need to focus on your wife. Plus, you need to get those boxes to safety." Quinn was surprised her voice was so steady, but she was grateful.

Adrenaline was coursing through her. She'd been in several crisis situations—though never this close to home.

And never fire.

At least it was Milo here with her now. They worked seamlessly as a team, and this delivery was going to be difficult just because of the circumstances. If anyone could handle delivering a baby while on the run from a wildfire, it was Milo.

"I need you to go, so I can take care of your wife and baby." Quinn walked over to Leo but didn't touch him with her gloved hands. She needed to remain sterile. "Ainsley needs all our focus, and she needs to know that you are safe and will be there to meet her at Oceanside."

"Give me a kiss and then go!" Ainsley said, her voice strong despite the tears slipping across her cheeks.

Leo shuddered, but he walked to his wife and dropped a kiss on her forehead. "Race you south, sweetheart."

"I'm right behind you." Ainsley's hands were shaking.

Quinn knew she was trying to hide the contraction. If Leo knew how much pain she was in, how close their child was to this world, he'd never leave. She glanced at her watch—less than a minute since the last one. Transition labor was the shortest phase, and she wished Ainsley had spent just a bit more time in it.

Ainsley laid her head back as Leo left. "I have to push."

No! Quinn rechecked Ainsley, and fear skittered across her skin. They needed to move her. But Ainsley was right, the baby was crowning.

"We need to move." Milo's voice was controlled as he pulled the stretcher into the room. His nose was scrunched tight.

How close is the fire?

"She's crowning. How much time do we have?" Quinn asked, then looked back at Ainsley. "I need you to do your best not to push for me. Don't hold your breath," she added as crimson traveled across Ainsley's cheeks. "Pretend that you are blowing out a candle."

It was a trick Quinn had learned in Puerto Rico during a category four hurricane. They'd had to deliver patients in near darkness with the howling wind pulling at the roof. She'd used it a few times to slow quick labor since, though never in such dire circumstances. She didn't like having to use it during a crisis again.

"All the time we need." Milo smiled, but Quinn saw his jaw clench as he maneuvered the stretcher closer. He was lying.

Dear God.

Her lungs heavy, Quinn forced herself to breathe evenly. They needed to get Ainsley, her baby and themselves to safety. "Okay."

Milo gripped Quinn's arm and looked at her gloved hands. Lowering his voice, he motioned to the stretcher. "I'm not gloved. If I move her, are you okay to handle delivery?"

"Of course," Quinn stated. "But we could stay until she delivers. It won't be…"

Milo's gaze softened, though he barely shook his head.

"Dear… God…" Ainsley muttered. "I need to push."

"Breathe for me until it passes." Quinn held her finger up, mimicking a candle, and breathed with her. Everyone needed to be calm for what was coming next. This trick worked around sixty percent of the time in Quinn's experience. The longer they waited…

As the contraction receded, Quinn let out a soft sigh. If they were going to move her, it had to be now. "Dr. Russell is going to get you onto the stretcher. Then you can push. I promise," Quinn reassured her. Ainsley nodded, but Quinn could see the fear dancing across her features. Her birth plan had just gone up in smoke, and the disaster that had seemed a bit distant was now on their doorstep.

"All right, Ainsley." Milo's voice was low and steady as he slipped an arm under her shoulders. "Wrap your arms around my neck—just like you see in the movies."

Ainsley let out a tight laugh and did as Milo instructed. "At least I'll have a story to tell this little one."

"She'll love hearing about it, I'm sure. At least until she's a teenager." Milo winked as he put his other arm under Ainsley's knees and lifted her quickly. He wasn't even breathing deeply.

Quinn had seen him work through difficult deliveries—always focused on his patient—but this delivery was one of a kind…she hoped. During her travels, she had witnessed more than one medical professional stumble when the world seemed intent on putting every obstacle in the way. But Milo was in complete control.

As he clicked the emergency belt into place, Ainsley let out another ragged breath and lifted her knees. "I can't stop—"

Quinn understood. Eventually, the body refused to delay the birthing process. At least she was on the stretcher. "Give me a push then. Just don't use all your force. We're saving that for the van."

"I wish… Leo…was here," Ainsley muttered.

"He'll meet us at the…" Quinn's voice dropped away as they stepped out the front door. The orange glow was just over the hill.

Dear God…

"The smoke…" Ainsley coughed as Milo raced them toward the van.

Wrenching the doors open, Milo lifted the stretcher and motioned for Quinn to get in. "Let's roll, Kevin!" Milo's voice cracked as the first bit of strain broke through his composure.

The doors slammed shut, and Quinn repositioned herself to be able to take care of Ainsley. The van started moving, and Quinn braced her feet against the doors the way they'd been trained to do in an emergency situation.

She'd been through a few instances where a home birth became critical and they'd had to transport the mother to the hospital. But the world hadn't been engulfed in flames then. Quinn took a deep breath as the world now dimmed to just her, Ainsley and Milo. She couldn't control anything about the fire.

The van's siren echoed through to the back, and Quinn met her patient's gaze. "Okay, Ainsley. Time to go to work."

In no time, Quinn was holding a beautiful, perfect and very angry baby girl. As her screams erupted in the van, Quinn smiled and laid the baby on Ainsley's chest. "Good job."

She finally let herself start to relax as Milo cleaned the baby as much as was possible given the circumstances. The baby was here and safe. Ainsley's delivery had been textbook—minus the evacuation.

Everything was fine…

As soon as that happy thought exited Quinn's mind, Kevin slammed on the breaks. Quinn lost her footing. She tried to grab herself, but the edge of the gurney connected with the side of her temple.

Pain erupted up her arms as her knees and palms connected with the floor of the van. "Oh!" Quinn blinked, trying to force the black dots dancing in her eyes away.

"Quinn!" Milo's fingers were warm and soft against her forehead as he reached for her. "Hell, Kevin!"

"Sorry!" Kevin shouted as he threw the van into Reverse. "A tree limb fell across the street. Hold on!"

"Is she all right?" Ainsley's voice was taut as the tires squealed again.

"She's going to be fine," Milo said with more certainty than he felt. The cut above Quinn's eye was bleeding, but her pupils were focused. He wasn't sure what the world outside looked like, but he *was* certain he didn't want to know given Kevin's muttered curses.

"Of course I am." Quinn's smile didn't quite reach her eyes, and Milo was stunned when she offered Ainsley a thumbs-up before grabbing gauze and pressing it against the wound. This was the woman who ran into crisis situations, who was comfortable—or at least didn't mind—small cots in areas damaged by natural disasters or ravaged by disease.

He'd seen her in action at St. Brigit's, but the true core of strength running through Quinn hadn't been visible until now. No wonder her nursing agency still sent her open positions, and the contacts she'd made while serving with Doctors Without Borders regularly called or texted her.

"How bad is it?" Quinn leaned forward, "Give it to me straight, Doctor." *And* she was trying to put him and Ainsley at ease, even as blood dripped from the bandage she was holding.

The side of his lip tipped up as he pushed a strand of her dark hair back. She was something else.

"The cut is going to need stitches, but it could have been worse." Milo swallowed as he grabbed another sterile pad and pressed it over the one that was against her forehead. If she'd fallen differently or if the van had hit the tree Kevin had swerved to miss…

Focus on the now!

Milo leaned back and sighed. "Well, this has been quite the day."

"Nothing preps you for running from a wildfire." Ainsley kissed the top of her baby's head and pushed a tear away.

"Nope." Quinn's voice was steady. "But I've served in several crisis zones, and it helps to focus on what you can control. And you did beautifully, Ainsley."

"My heart refuses to stop pounding." Ainsley let out

a nervous chuckle. "You and Dr. Russell make this look easy."

"I am just following Quinn's lead. This is, fortunately, my first time running from a crisis." Milo offered a playful salute, hoping he came off as collected as Quinn.

"But he's fantastic in all situations. There were multiple times when I was with Doctors Without Borders when I wished Milo had been there to help stabilize a tense situation." Quinn grinned as she pressed another gauze pad to her forehead. "And apparently head injuries make me talkative. So, Momma, what's her name?"

Milo tried to focus on the conversation floating between the women as the van raced south, but he kept coming back to Quinn's words. Had she really wished for him to be with her while she'd been working with the humanitarian medical group?

Or was she just trying to project calm in this rapidly changing situation? And why did the idea of serving in such a manner send a thrill through him?

Milo sucked in a breath and ignored the subtle glance Quinn gave him. They needed to get Ainsley checked in at Oceanside, and then to figure out their next steps. And those steps involved getting back to LA, with the fire blocking multiple routes, not addressing the unwelcome desire to follow up with Quinn on her statement.

CHAPTER THREE

"IT'S A GOOD THING you kept your town house in Oceanside," Quinn said, leaning against Milo's shoulder as he put the key in the lock. They smelled of smoke, and it had taken them nearly twice as long as it should have to reach Oceanside. Then Milo had insisted that she let him check the cut on her forehead after they'd gotten Ainsley and her daughter checked into the Clinic and said a brief hello to Milo's stepdad, Felix.

Now she had six stitches above her eye, and she couldn't remember the last time she'd been this exhausted. She'd been in tense situations multiple times during her career, though, so Quinn knew from experience that her brain was too wired to let her drift into oblivion.

Her stomach growled—another function the body forgot about during stress.

When had they last eaten?

"Tell me you have food in the fridge!"

"Nope." Milo swung the door open. "It's fully furnished, since I rent it out most weekends as a vacation spot. But the rent doesn't include food. Luckily, it's not due to be occupied for the rest of the month. Wildfire concern caused my last two renters to back out."

Her stomach roiled with emptiness, but she ignored it. Focusing on her hunger wouldn't make food magically appear. "At least I can get a hot shower," Quinn sighed.

"And our Thai food should be here by the time you're done. I ordered it while you were saying hi to Felix."

"You are the best!" Quinn wrapped her arms around his neck without thinking. Today had been hell, even though it had ended well on all fronts. She didn't care that they were both starving and in desperate need of showers. She just wanted to hold him, to remind herself that they were fine. Her body molded to his as Milo's strong arms pulled her closer.

Her day's fears melted as he held her. This was where she wanted to be *so badly*. Her fingers itched to run through his short hair. To trace her lips along the edge of his jaw and see what happened. Sparks flew across her back as his fingers tightened on her waist.

If she held him any longer… Quinn swallowed. This embrace had already gone on for too long. She needed to stop this before Milo started to think she was crazy.

Her cheeks were warm as she pulled away. "I promise not to steal all the hot water."

"Wait." Milo grabbed her hand.

Her body vibrated with need as Milo ran his fingers along the bandage on her forehead. His touch burned as she stared at his lips.

So close, and yet so far away.

"The bandage I put on seems watertight." Milo's husky tone raced around her.

"Since you put it on less than an hour ago, I would hope so."

Was he looking for reasons to touch her?

"Yes, but it's important the wound doesn't get wet." His words were so matter-of-fact.

Of course they were.

He was a good physician and her oldest friend.

But just for a moment, she'd thought he might need to touch her, need to be near her, to hold her, too.

"I should clean up." Her throat was dry as she pulled away, but Milo didn't stop her again.

When humans were stressed or escaped catastrophe, they often sought comfort in the arms of another. A reminder that they'd lived to fight another day. She'd seen it happen when she was serving in areas that had been hit by earthquakes and floods. It was standard. But Quinn had never felt the urge to seek out that comfort—until tonight.

Until Milo...

Milo cleared his throat as he started to follow her. "There should still be some of Bianca's old clothes in the back closet. They got left behind when we separated, and she never picked them up. I'll see if I can find something you can wear."

Bianca... That name sent a cold splash down Quinn's spine. Quinn had never gotten along with the woman. She'd tried, but Bianca always seemed cold to her—unwelcoming. But she'd been Milo's choice, so Quinn had kept her mouth shut.

When he'd called to tell her that they had gotten married in Vegas, she'd cried for almost a week. For a man who planned everything, she'd been stunned that Milo had run off with Bianca for the weekend—even if they were overdue for a vacation after their residencies—and to get married on a whim?

Quinn had also been hurt that he hadn't at least told her beforehand. She'd have video-called to support him. Even if she'd thought Bianca hadn't been worthy.

She'd been right about that and hated the small part of her that had been happy when Milo had told her it was over. He'd been hurt—and happy shouldn't have been an emotion she'd felt. But maybe a small part of her had wanted him even then. Quinn was certainly not going to examine that thought tonight.

Milo was the best part of her life. He had deep roots in

this state, and he deserved someone who would walk beside him as he followed his plans.

Someone who supported him.

And Bianca had not been Milo's match even before she'd cheated on him.

Quinn's throat closed at the realization that she wasn't his match, either. Her parents had ensured she'd known exactly where her faults lay. Too flighty. Too needy. Impulsive. She led with her heart. She'd always support Milo's dreams, but checking off items on a list, trying to control everything? That wasn't something Quinn could do.

She should be happy just being best friends with Milo. Her heart skipped around him, but she could put it back in its place. Maybe returning to California had been a mistake. But she'd felt called here. Like she needed to come home—at least for a little while.

It was a feeling she still couldn't explain, but Quinn had always chosen new locations and jobs by what felt right. And working with Milo had felt right—still felt right.

So why was it so hard?

Turning on the shower, Quinn quickly stripped off her scrubs and tried to push away the thoughts of the man just outside the door.

How does Milo kiss?

She shivered despite the heat of the water.

"Quinn?" Milo's voice raced across her and goose pimples rose on her skin. "Can I put the clothes on the counter?"

"Yes." Her tongue felt thick, but she forced the word out.

"Quinn?" Milo's voice echoed in the small bathroom, and Quinn held her breath. What was he going to say?

Part of her brain screamed to be bold. To stick her head around the curtain and suggest they conserve water. But that was just the craziness of the day talking.

Quinn had never been bold in her relationships. She always looked for the reasons why they would fail. Even when James had proposed, she'd wondered when her world would upend…though she'd expected it would be longer than three weeks.

Her guard had been up ever since.

No matter how often she told her brain to stop, it always tried to identify any signs that a partner was getting ready to leave her.

When would they throw her out of their life?

If her parents could discard her so easily, then anyone could.

She'd become an expert in identifying the subtle shifts in people. Noticed the moment the nurse she'd met in Puerto Rico discussed moving and asked her opinion as an afterthought. Her brain had tweaked the first time the oil manager she'd dated in Alaska canceled a date and mentioned his full schedule. So Quinn had ended the relationships. Better to leave first.

If you left first, the hurt wasn't as deep. Her family had drilled that lesson into her. But that did not lend itself to sultry risk-taking.

When he didn't say anything, Quinn worked up her courage. "Still out there?"

"Food is here." Milo's husky voice drifted over the curtain, an emotion she couldn't place deep within it.

Quinn wondered if he'd wanted to say something else.

Get it together!

"Remember, you promised not to use all the hot water," Milo joked.

"Well, I'd be done faster if you'd take your leave." She heard him chuckle and forced her shoulders to relax. They were both exhausted from the day, burning through the last reserves of their adrenaline. After they'd showered and had food, their bodies would sleep for the next ten hours.

Focus. Stop letting adrenaline control your hormones.

She raced through the rest of her shower and quickly

dried off. Pulling on the shorts he'd left on the counter, Quinn's heart raced as she held up the green tank top. It had a built-in shelf bra, which meant that she wouldn't have to put on her smoke-scented bra, but it was a much lower cut than she usually wore.

It would have looked great on Bianca. She'd had full breasts and a curvy frame. On Quinn's athletic figure, it was much more likely to highlight her lack of assets. She sighed as she pulled it on.

Then she began to remove the bandage on her forehead. Stitches needed to be kept dry and uncovered for the first forty-eight hours, but she'd needed to shower to wash away the day's grime and smoky residue.

Between the dark circles under her eyes, the wet hair, the borrowed clothes and the cut, Quinn looked less than desirable.

Which was fine.

But she also felt downright pathetic. Were the borrowed outfit and the smoky scrubs the only things she had to her name?

"I'm going to eat all the pad thai if you keep hogging the bathroom!" Milo called out.

The ghost of a smile pulled at her lips. She'd told Milo that she'd had nothing when her parents had disowned her following her admittance to UCLA's school of nursing. He'd put his hand in her hand and said, "Nope. You have me."

"You better not!" Whatever tomorrow brought, she could handle it. As long as she had her friend by her side.

Milo's gaze fell on her as she stepped up to the kitchen counter. Heat tore across Quinn's skin, but she refused to acknowledge it. "I will not apologize for eating all the food if you're just going to stare at me. I know I look like I need a belly full of food, followed by ten hours of sleep."

"You always look perfect." Milo grinned. "Or at least presentable."

Presentable... That was a word.

"Well, hop into that shower so we can dig in." Picking up one of the boxes, she nodded in the direction of the bathroom.

Why was he just standing there? Did she look that bad?

"Go shower, Milo. I promise there will be enough here for you to have dinner."

"I'm counting on you to share." He paused right in front of her.

His face was so close. What would he do if she lifted her head and kissed him? Just as Quinn started to follow through, Milo stepped back.

"I plan on taking the quickest shower ever!" Milo raced down the small hallway.

Quinn let out a breath as she stared at his retreating form. His smoky scent still clung to her senses. Grabbing plates from the cabinet, she began to set their dinner out. Anything to try to keep her mind from wandering to thoughts of how he might kiss.

The shower shut off in record time, and Quinn jumped. She could do this. It was just Milo. Except there was nothing *just* about Milo. At least, not anymore.

Presentable. He'd called her presentable!

What the hell, Milo?

Perfect, wonderful, sexy—all of those were descriptions for Quinn. *Never* presentable.

He wanted—needed—to get back to her. Today had been an emotional roller coaster. When he'd watched her fall, his heart had stopped. It had only been a minor cut, but his need to hold her, no matter how unprofessional, had been overwhelming. He'd barely managed to keep it together.

He needed a plan. Plans gave him peace, a sense of order—control. He could follow a plan. Quinn was at St.

Brigit's for at least another few months. Maybe she'd stay if he asked her to. Was that what he wanted?

Yes!

True, she loved being a traveling nurse and working around the world. But life was here. Could he ask her to give that up? *Sure.* But should he? Maybe not. Yet suddenly he wasn't sure that he cared.

As that selfish thought rolled through him, Milo promised himself he'd find a way to broach the topic. Not tonight. Their day had been too hectic. Their emotions were still packed too tightly with adrenaline and fear to really know what they wanted. And even if he did know, Milo needed to sort out the best way to approach all of this.

Coward! his brain shouted as he toweled his short hair dry. His heart knew what he wanted.

But Quinn always left. She chased adventure and never stayed in one place for too long. What if they started dating and a new job—a better job—materialized half a world away?

Could he handle losing her?

He shivered as the silence of the town house registered. They were all alone. That wasn't new—yet the lack of distractions felt dangerous. His stomach skittered.

It was just him and Quinn. His tongue was tied around her, and his body wanted to act. When she'd walked out in that low-cut green tank top, Milo had ached to pull her to him. His fingers had pulsed with the need to run along her sides. He'd had to grip the side of the kitchen counter just to keep from rushing toward her.

How could he address these racing thoughts with Quinn?

No immediate answer came to Milo as he dropped a shirt over his head. He would think better after dinner and some sleep. Maybe tomorrow? No. He wouldn't rush this. It was Quinn. So the plan—if he used it—had to be perfect.

"Did you eat it all?" Milo picked up an empty container

on the counter. Then he froze. The table was set and Quinn was pouring wine. The shorts he'd grabbed for her hugged her derriere and highlighted her long, slim legs. His mouth watered as he imagined trailing kisses up her thighs. "I figured we'd just eat out of the paper cartons."

Quinn's dark eyes met his and her lips pulled up into a smile. "We spent the day outrunning a fire while helping a new baby into the world. I think that calls for actual plates and a glass of wine. You'll have to get another bottle for your next renters."

"It's fine." Milo walked to the table. His property manager always dropped off a bottle of red for the occupants. Milo would let him know that they needed another. It was the least of his concerns as Quinn's knee knocked against his.

Her shoulder-length hair was damp, and she was wearing borrowed clothes, but she was perfection. Her high cheekbones had a few freckles that his thumb ached to trace. How could he ask her if she'd ever thought of changing their relationship? If her heart had yearned like his for something more?

They ate in silence. The tension made Milo ache. Or maybe he was imagining it. After all, they hadn't eaten anything other than a few granola bars since their croissants this morning.

Once her plate was empty, Quinn leaned her elbows on the table, propped her head in her palms, and stared at him. "We have a problem, you know."

Milo smiled. "We do?" Her full lips were calling to him. If she brought up the emotions charging the air around them, would it save him from having to find the right path to address their relationship? No. Thinking it through still held more appeal. Rushing only messed things up.

How many times did he have to prove that?

"Dishes!" She winked and pushed back from the table.

"Dishes?" Milo's head spun. "Dishes?" He hadn't meant to repeat the question, but his brain was incapable of finding any other response. He was thinking of kissing her, of changing everything, and Quinn was thinking about dishes?

Could he have misread the situation more?

Quinn leaned over and pecked his cheek. It was an innocent action. One she'd done hundreds of times over the years. "Yes." Her gaze held his as she gathered the plates and rose. "If we'd just eaten from the cartons, the cleanup would be so much easier."

"But the dinner would have been less satisfying," Milo murmured, standing, as well.

Like that peck?

It wasn't what he wanted. What he craved.

"Exactly!" Quinn's smile sent a thrill through him. "I've eaten off disposable plates in so many places. You don't realize what a luxury such simple things are until they aren't an option." She yawned, raising the plates over her head as she tried to cover the motion with her arm.

Milo took the dishes from her hands and laid them in the sink. "We've had a long day. I think they can wait until tomorrow."

She leaned against the counter, millimeters from him. "Today was certainly something."

Pushing the hair away from her left cheek, Milo nodded at her stitches. "And you got a permanent souvenir."

"A minor flaw. At least I'm presentable."

"No." Milo shook his head. "You are gorgeous." Without thinking, he let his fingers brush the softness of her cheek. Her skin was cool, but his fingers burned as he—finally—traced the line of freckles on her jaw. "Breathtaking. Smart. Courageous." *Sexy.* He barely caught that word. Over the years, he'd tried to combat the negativity he'd heard Quinn voice when she'd talked about herself. If only she could see what he saw. But tonight, so much more rested on his compliments.

Before his brain could comprehend what was happening, Quinn's lips connected with his.

Milo's arms wrapped around her waist and he pulled her to him. He didn't want any distance between them. Her fingers slid up his neck, ran through his hair, and Milo felt the world shift.

This was right. Quinn in his arms, her lips pressing against his. It made all reason leak from his brain.

Her mouth opened and a whole new level of sensations pulsed through him. She tasted of wine, Thai food and perfection.

His Quinn.

Wrapping a hand in her hair, Milo deepened the kiss. loving the small moans escaping her lips. He'd wondered how she kissed for months. Years…

Quinn…

Need pulled at him.

She pulled back a bit, her lips swollen. Her eyes were hooded with desire as she ran a finger down his jaw. "What are we doing?"

He couldn't read the expression floating through her eyes, and the first trace of doubt ripped down his back. What if she was just reacting on the adrenaline from today?

"I don't know. Maybe making a mistake." Those were the wrong words. *Again.* He'd wanted this for so long, but her kiss had been so unexpected, so unplanned. He needed a plan—needed to know that she wanted more than just one night.

He knew Quinn didn't move from partner to partner. But he also knew she never stayed in one place too long, and he was tied to California. The day had been crazy. What if…

"I—" Quinn stepped out of his arms. "Right." She shook her head. "Long day."

His arms felt heavy without her.

Why couldn't he say the right things?

"Quinn." Milo started toward her, but she put the counter between them.

"I'm going to…" Quinn looked to the back rooms. "Bed. Yep. I am going to bed. It was such a long day. I'm not acting like myself. Sorry."

Quinn rushed off before Milo could find a way to fix the mess his overthinking brain had caused. "Quinn." But she'd already fled down the hallway and closed the bedroom door.

"Dammit!" Milo gripped the counter, his brain too wired, too focused on Quinn, to let him sleep. Grabbing the wine bottle, he poured the last bit into his glass and stared at her closed door. Tomorrow… They'd sort all of this out tomorrow. At least he had a few hours to figure out a plan.

Quinn pushed a tear away from her cheek as she stared at the shadows cast by the rising sun along the beach. She'd left Milo's town house quietly, wishing there was some way she could make it home on her own. But her vehicle was back at St. Brigit's, almost two hours away.

How could she have been so stupid? It must have been the long day. And Milo telling her she was gorgeous. Leaning close…touching her cheek…

His compliments and touch had flooded her system. Flowed into the cracks her parents' harsh words and James's betrayal had worn on her soul. For just a moment, she'd believed Milo had been thinking the same thing she had been.

Quinn never let her guard down. She kept her shields up with everyone.

Everyone but Milo.

She could still feel the brush of his fingers along her

cheek if she closed her eyes. *Gorgeous*. Had anyone ever called her that?

The emotion and desires that had raced through her since she'd landed in LA had propelled her forward with just a few compliments. Milo had always seen the best in her, looked past the flaws her mother and ex-fiancé had constantly pointed out. She was being needy, and she'd misread Milo's concern after a long day.

She wasn't bold with her partners. So Milo's rejection was the first she'd experienced—at least, before anything had actually happened. That was the only reason it burned so deeply.

She scoffed as the lie tripped through her brain. The truth was that it hurt because it was Milo. Because no matter what she tried to believe, Quinn wanted more.

And she hadn't even been able to seek refuge in her bungalow. Couldn't pretend to be busy for a few days while she licked her battered emotional wounds. Instead, she'd lain in bed knowing he was on the other side of the wall. So close and yet so far away.

Quinn hugged her knees as she buried her toes in the sand and stared at the ocean waves. She hadn't managed much sleep, but at least she'd worked out a plan to address last night's indiscretion. It would be easier if Milo didn't bring it up. She'd dated several men who would have let it go, but that was not Milo.

Milo planned everything. He'd want to talk about what had happened—make sure that she was all right. And he was going to apologize.

Shame tore across her. That was the part Quinn feared most. The "I'm sorry I don't feel the same. You're my best friend." She could hear the entire speech already, and the last thing she wanted was pity from Milo.

"You know, I tore through the place, afraid you'd started walking back to LA without telling me."

She started before offering a smile that Quinn prayed looked real in the early light. "How often do you get to watch the sunrise at the beach?" She gestured to the incoming waves as she accepted the travel mug of coffee he held out to her.

"You could have left a note." His voice was gruff as he slid down onto the sand beside her. He was grumpy this morning.

Not that she could blame him.

"A note? To walk four hundred feet from your front door to the beach?" She hit his shoulder with hers. If her plan was going to work, she needed to act as naturally as possible. "Really, Milo. I've come down here early before. Nothing has changed."

She said the final words and took a deep sip of her coffee, refusing to let her gaze leave the waves. He'd been her friend for decades and knew her better than anyone. If she looked at him, he might see the hurt pooling in her soul, and she couldn't let that happen.

"Nothing?" Milo's voice was soft. "We kissed last night."

"Actually, I kissed you." It hurt to say the words, but she kept her tone bright. For a minute last night, he'd responded to her. For that brief flicker, everything in her world had seemed right.

Quinn shook her head. She couldn't think of this now, not while sitting beside him. Not if her plan was to work. "I guess racing through a wildfire made me lose my head, huh? Flighty Quinn!"

"I hate it when you call yourself that." Milo's voice was ragged.

He'd loathed her family's nickname and despised the fact that she'd adopted the moniker. But that didn't make it untrue. Quinn never stayed in one place too long. She made decisions based on a feeling in her gut, not rational thought. If a job felt right or didn't, she acted.

Even if everyone said it was a bad move.

She flew from relationships before she could get hurt, too.

That made it impossible to settle down and start a family.

Why wouldn't that chirp in her brain shut up? Quinn didn't have the close family she saw so many of her patients were blessed with. She'd never felt truly part of one, so she shouldn't miss it.

But she did.

And that was an ache that Milo's presence soothed.

But he'd pulled away from her last night. She wasn't sure that pain would ever vanish, but she couldn't lose Milo. He was the closest thing she had to family. She couldn't—wouldn't—risk that because her heart wanted something more. "At least now when people joke that they can't believe we've never kissed, we can say, 'Oh, we did once. We're just better as…friends.'"

She'd practiced that line before the sun rose this morning. Even with all that rehearsal, her voice still shook a bit.

"Better as friends," Milo murmured.

"Do you think I'm wrong?" She did look at him then. Wished he'd contradict her. But Milo just stared at the incoming waves.

He hadn't shaved. The morning stubble along his jawline gave him a rugged look that made Quinn's stomach clench. Why did she have to be so attracted to him?

"You're all control and I'm all heart. You're planted here and I have rented furniture. We're opposites—perfectly balanced, but opposites." She kept waiting, hoping he'd interrupt her. He didn't. "I love St. Brigit's, but eventually…" She shrugged as she watched the waves crash against the beach.

"You do love finding new places." His head rested against hers as the sun cast its brilliant rays across the water.

You could ask me to stay…

She kept that desire buried deep inside. No one had ever asked Quinn to stay. Her family hadn't cared when she'd left for college and never come home. The men she'd dated had hardly batted their eyes when she'd taken a new position and packed up her things. Even James had barely blinked when she'd handed back his ring, no pleas for forgiveness or claims that he still wanted her. No one ever seemed to want her to stay.

"You have a world of adventures left," Milo said with a sigh as he straightened. Then he smiled and threw an arm around her shoulders. "And my life is in LA."

Quinn wanted to yank his arm away from her. Maybe that would stop the longing flowing through her. But he'd always touched her like that. In small ways that didn't mean much, even if she now wished they did. Leaning her head on his shoulder, Quinn sighed. She'd always planned to leave LA.

Hadn't she?

She'd rented her furniture but signed a two-year lease. The contradiction hadn't bothered her at the time. But leaving when her contract was up didn't feel like seeking adventure. Now it felt like running.

Maybe distance was what she needed, even if it was the last thing she wanted. If she stayed, she'd eventually make the same mistake she'd made last night. Let her feelings get too close to the surface and kiss him. She couldn't stand the thought of Milo pulling away again. That might just destroy her. For now, she would soak up as many of these moments as she could get. Maybe they'd be enough to last a lifetime.

Milo hadn't known the heart was capable of breaking before you actually dated someone. But as they walked the short distance back to his town house, that was the only description for the aching hole deep in his body. Quinn's actions had been impulsive. Brought on by yesterday's extremes.

He blew out a breath. How was he supposed to pretend that her touch hadn't electrified his soul? By remembering that this was just another stop for Quinn on her adventures and he was just lucky to be part of it. The reminder did little to quench the pull of need racing through him.

As they reached his door, Milo inhaled. The scent of the ocean gripped him. California was home. He'd never be the man who could pick up a phone and say yes to a job halfway around the world. He needed plans, schedules, five-year goals.

And he had those. All anchored in LA. He should focus on them. But right now, it was only Quinn that his brain wished to think of.

Quinn's ability to jump to a new adventure, to explore the next big thing, impressed him, even if he didn't understand it. But the realization that she would pack her bags again—maybe not today, or even this year, but someday—ripped him up.

He'd thrown his arm around her this morning because he'd wanted to touch her. To sit beside her for a few more minutes. As if his touch could anchor her. And because he was terrified she'd run from him after telling him that their kiss had been impulsive. When she'd leaned her head against his shoulder, it had taken every bit of his willpower not to kiss the top of it.

Her phone was ringing as he opened the door and she raced for it. Good, he needed a distraction.

"Hello?"

Milo walked over and poured himself another cup of coffee. He wasn't sure there was enough caffeine in the world to get him through the rest of the day. But he had to act unaffected by their morning chat. Otherwise, she might pick up and leave sooner—and Milo needed more time with her.

"Really?"

A smile tore across Quinn's face and Milo grinned despite himself. A happy Quinn thrilled him. No matter what happened between them, he wanted her to smile like that all the time. She clicked off the phone, and he raised an eyebrow.

"That was Martina. They're advising patients outside the LA city limits to seek care at our community partners, so they don't have to find a way around the evacuation zones—just to be safe. That means, until the all-clear comes through, all patients south of the city are advised to go to—"

Milo gripped the coffee cup, trying to ignore the twist in his gut. "Oceanside Clinic."

"Yep!"

"You seem surprisingly excited about this." He wanted to kick himself as Quinn's lips turned down.

Why was his brain refusing to find the right words?

"Sorry, Quinn. I didn't mean to make it sound like you were happy about any of this." Milo turned and started fixing another pot of coffee. At least his property manager stocked the cabinet with coffee and tea for the tenants. Otherwise, Milo would have been even more prickly this morning.

"You're right. It is a terrible time. But I've never gotten to work with your mom and Felix, assuming they want a few extra hands. Martina says we should exercise extreme caution in returning."

"I am certain my parents would love to have you help out."

And me, too.

His mother had tried repeatedly to get him to spend more time at the birthing center he'd helped design. She didn't understand his need to follow his father's dream, no matter how many times he'd discussed it.

It had led to a few tense arguments when she'd pointed out how happy the Oceanside Clinic made him. She was right. Milo enjoyed being there. But the closer he got to Felix, his mother's husband, the further his father slipped away. He was desperate to recapture the feelings he'd had so long ago.

Oceanside made him happy, but it would never bring him the same feeling he'd had with his father. He wasn't willing to give up that dream.

He couldn't.

"Are they as easy to work with as you?" Quinn's eyes were bright as she sidled up beside him and inhaled the scent of the brewing coffee.

"Easier," Milo remarked. It was the truth. His mother and Felix were the best physicians he'd ever worked with. The year he'd spent in their clinic following his divorce had been the happiest of his career—until Quinn had arrived at St. Brigit's.

Quinn's hip bumped his, and his body sang with the brief connection. "I'm not sure anyone is easier to work with than you. Any chance your mom might have scrubs I can borrow? She is almost as tall as me." Quinn folded her arms. "And we need transportation."

"Let me get another cup of coffee in me, Quinn. Then my mind will work a bit better. The sun's barely been up for more than an hour, in case you've forgotten."

"Nope," Quinn sighed. "I haven't forgotten." There was such a weariness to her statement.

Was she not as okay as she was pretending to be?

They'd always seemed to know what the other was thinking. But he couldn't stop second-guessing himself. Then she grinned, and Milo pushed the bead of hope from his mind. She was just Quinn. His perfect, fly-by-the-seat-of-her pants, explore-every-new-option, best friend, Quinn. And somehow that had to be enough.

CHAPTER FOUR

HIS PARENTS' CARS were already in the staff parking lot when Milo and Quinn's Uber driver dropped them at the back door. Quinn had traded the low-cut tank top from last night for one of the T-shirts he stashed at the town house for the few times he came down to surf.

His gray T-shirt was too big for Quinn. But she'd tied the corner of it, so it hugged her waist. It was a simple look, and it made his mouth water.

He needed to get control of himself. He'd lain in bed all night, aware that she was only a wall away, desperately trying to will his mind to do anything other than relive that kiss and his overthinking, disastrous words.

Or fantasize about what could have come next.

"Quinn!" His mother raced for them and wrapped her arms around Quinn. They'd always been close, and he knew that Quinn had come to Oceanside several times since she'd moved to LA. They'd even come together—though not to the clinic.

When his mom stepped away from Quinn, she hugged him. "It is so good to see you—here, too." Her breath was warm on his chin as she kissed his cheek. "This is..." She paused, her lip wavering slightly. "Nice."

It wasn't what she'd meant to say. And Milo didn't have any problem hearing *This is where you belong.* It wasn't.

But for the next few days or so, some of St. Brigit's patients were likely to show up at Oceanside.

"It's good to see you too, Mom." Milo threw an arm around her shoulder and squeezed it firmly before following her inside. "I fear we do not have anything other than us and our midwifery bags."

"Felix and I have scrubs for both of you. He drove his car today, so you can take mine back to LA."

"We can't—" Milo started.

"Are you planning to make Quinn walk back to LA, then?" His mother laughed as Quinn smiled.

"I... I hadn't figured that out yet." The phrase felt weird.

His mother's eyes widened. "You didn't spend all night working out the details?" She playfully put the back of her hand against his forehead. "You don't *feel* feverish."

Milo's gaze flitted to Quinn before he shook his head. "Nope. Yesterday was a bit of a beast. You may not have heard, but we outran a wildfire." His voice didn't sound as relaxed as he'd hoped. "I fell asleep as soon as I laid my head on the pillow."

Quinn's eyes flashed as the lie slipped from his tongue.

Rubbing his arms, Milo looked past his mother and Quinn. There was no way he was going to mention he'd spent the night replaying Quinn's kiss. That his brain had been incapable of focusing on anything substantive since their early-morning beach conversation.

"Well, lucky for you, I do have a plan." His mother wrapped an arm around Quinn. "Ladies' changing room is this way."

"You okay?"

Felix's deep voice made Milo jump. "You startled me!"

The lines deepened on Felix's brow. "Are you okay?" he repeated.

There wasn't much that got past Felix Ireman. He'd married Milo's mother not that long ago, and Milo and his sister, Gina, had been thrilled to welcome the man into their small family. But Milo wasn't going to talk to Felix about his roaring emotions for Quinn.

Substituting another concern, he shrugged. "I'm worried about my patients. Some of the staff will probably go to Bloom Birthing Center to help our patients that live north of the city, but it's a stressful time for everyone."

Felix nodded, though Milo suspected he didn't quite believe him. Luckily, Felix wasn't one to pry. "Well, we're glad you're here. Did your mother mention that Dr. Acton's husband was transferred last month, and they're away on a house-hunting expedition in Ohio? She'll be hard to replace."

The statement hit Milo in the chest. "I'm sure you'll find the right person," he said, turning to find his own set of scrubs before Felix could raise the subject of Milo returning to Oceanside.

Quinn and Milo had been assigned to the birthing center and Sherrie had joined them from St. Brigit's. At least Milo's parents' clinic was well equipped to handle the influx of patients.

Soothing music played in the hallways. The walls were painted a light gray, but Gina, Milo's sister, had ensured the effect was calming, not sterile. Having an interior designer in the family had clearly come in handy when Milo had developed the plans for the birthing center.

Quinn could still remember his excitement as he'd laid out the basic plan when they were undergrads. He'd even asked Quinn to sketch a few of the ideas for him, even though her drawing skills favored landscapes.

The architects had adjusted the design, but the basics of what Milo had imagined were all here. She'd been in Hawaii when they'd broken ground on the facility, and on the island of Tonga when they'd held the ribbon-cutting ceremony, so she'd only seen it in pictures.

It was perfect. A calmness settled through her that was so at odds with the craziness of the last day. This place was lovely. A truly great accomplishment. And yet, Milo hadn't stayed long enough to see the ribbon-cutting two years ago. Quinn shook her head.

"Something wrong?" Milo's voice was soft as he stepped beside her. What was it about places where babies were born that made everyone, even the midwives and doctors who routinely saw births, lower their voices?

Yes, her heart screamed. So many things were wrong. He didn't want her. He wasn't working in the center that he'd helped design. And she felt like this was home.

All those things bothered her, but that final piece struck her harder than she'd expected. She'd worked many places. And enjoyed something about all of them. But she'd never walked into a birthing center, hospital or field hospital, and felt a sense of peace. A sense of rightness.

Like this was where she was meant to be.

It was ridiculous, of course. This was Milo's place, even if he didn't work here.

Yet…

He'd do well at a large facility, maybe even run Valley General's OB unit for a few years, but this was the place he'd come home to eventually. She knew it deep in her soul.

She belonged here, too. But she didn't know what that meant for their friendship after last night. *If anything.* But she couldn't push the feeling from her heart.

"Just marveling at your work." Quinn sighed as she looked at him. Her arms ached to reach out to him. To smooth the creases from his forehead. At least at work she could focus on keeping a professional distance.

"It's more my mother's work and my sister's interior

decorating. I think it could use a splash of color. Maybe not bright yellow, but…" Milo's words ran out.

He rubbed the back of his neck before smiling. He was trying to be normal, too. Maybe in a day or two, it wouldn't feel so awkward between them—though she knew that was just wishful thinking. Nothing would ever be the same.

At least not for her.

"No picking on my kitchen." Her throat seized. What if her kitchen was gone? "That color makes me happy."

Straightening her shoulders, she forced the subject back to the Oceanside Clinic. "But this is your accomplishment, Milo. It wouldn't be here without you."

Milo's lips turned up as he looked around. "It is nice."

Nice? Was that the word he associated with it? This place was wonderful. A birthing center that gave mothers more choices in their delivery options, run by OBs, with a surgical suite tucked out of sight in case of emergency deliveries. Already a few hospital administrators from California, Ohio and Texas had visited to see if they could mimic Oceanside's successes. *Nice* didn't begin to cover this achievement.

The buzzer at the front of the building rang out and she was grateful for the interruption. "Incoming." Quinn smiled. She loved deliveries. New life was the best part of her job. And it was the perfect distraction.

A woman wearing a floral-print dress walked in holding the arm of a tall man who was clearly more distressed than his partner. "Hello." The woman smiled and gasped in a breath as she started to work through a contraction.

"We're having a baby!" her partner nearly shouted.

Quinn smiled. "Are you sure?" She walked over to the woman and playfully looked at her belly.

"I think so." The woman let out a giggle and tapped her partner's side. "You have to let go of me for a few minutes, sweetheart." She rose on her tiptoes and kissed his cheek.

He laid his hands over her belly, and Quinn's heart leaped at the simple motion.

This was what her life was missing. Family.

Her friendship with Milo was nice—better than nice when things weren't so tense between them—but it wasn't the sense of belonging she experienced with her patients. Wasn't what her soul yearned for.

Pushing the feeling away, she gestured for the mother to follow her while her partner checked them in. The young woman looked back at him, and Quinn squeezed her hand. "Dr. Russell will settle him down. I promise."

Milo was already talking to the father while the admitting nurse kept passing him electronic forms to sign. By the time the father was ready to join them in a few minutes, Milo would have soothed all his worries.

If only Quinn could soothe away her feelings that way, too.

"You're not Dr. Russell or Dr. Acton." The man looked around him. Milo could see the happiness and hope bubbling through him. All new parents seemed to wear that expression. But there was a layer of fear beneath the surface, too. Many first-time parents were fearful, but anxiety poured from this man as he bounced on his heel and kept his gaze on the hallway where his partner had disappeared.

"Actually, I am a Dr. Russell. Dr. Milo Russell. I'm an OB, like my mother. I'm filling in for Dr. Acton while she is out today. And you are?"

"Trey Kenns."

The man bit his lip as he stared at Milo. Keeping his voice low, Milo leaned closer. "Trey, your wife will be fine."

"Fiancée." The man's fingers trembled as he electronically signed another document. "We…we…" He sighed loudly. "None of this was planned. But it's amazing."

Milo blinked. He'd attended more than one birth where

the partner didn't seem as thrilled about the birth as he'd thought they should be. But this man was clearly excited... and terrified. "What wasn't supposed to happen?"

"Carla and I were best friends. *Are* best friends." He looked toward the hallway where his fiancée had disappeared. "Took me months to convince her that we should be..." He pushed his hair back. "Sorry, I ramble when I'm nervous. I never planned to have children. If I lose her..."

Recognition flew through Milo. "You lost someone in childbirth?"

Trey nodded. "My mother and baby sister. It's been years, and I know the technology is better. But you ever had someone that meant the world to you?"

Yes. And she was with Trey's fiancée right now.

Milo nodded. "She'll be fine. I promise. Quinn Davis is one of the finest midwives in the world. And that is not me exaggerating. She's served all over the globe. Carla is in excellent hands. And if, for some reason, we need it, we have a surgical suite for emergency C-sections, if necessary. But less than six percent of birthing center deliveries result in C-sections. She and your baby are in excellent hands."

Slapping Trey on the back, he motioned for the soon-to-be dad to follow him. "I think Kelly has had you fill out all the paperwork for admittance. Why don't we go see how Carla is progressing?"

Quinn stepped out of Carla's room and wiped a bead of sweat from her forehead. Milo started toward her without thinking. Carla had been in labor for most of the day, but Quinn hadn't raised any concerns to him. The two times he'd checked on her, Carla had been progressing slowly, but progressing.

"Everything okay?" Milo saw the tightness in Quinn's shoulders. They'd been running on full steam since Molly's delivery. How was that only two days ago?

"She's finally at seven centimeters. With any luck, Carla will move into transition labor soon. But she's been laboring for almost twelve hours already. Not counting the six hours she did at home. She's getting tired."

Milo knew that was an understatement. Carla had to be exhausted. A woman's ability to deliver after a long labor never failed to impress him, but if she got too tired...

"Are you worried?"

He hadn't lied to Trey. Quinn was an excellent midwife. She'd been on multiple tours with Doctors Without Borders, spent more than a decade as a traveling nurse, and always seemed to find her way to where she was needed most. She'd delivered babies all over the world and in conditions far less comfortable than this. Her instincts were almost always spot-on.

"No." Quinn shook her head. "At least, not yet. If she doesn't move into transitional labor in the next hour or two, I may adjust that statement."

Milo nodded as he leaned against the wall beside her. His skin vibrated at the closeness, and his palms ached with the desire to reach for her. Holding her hand, putting an arm around her shoulder or her waist—anything. Even after what had happened this morning, he couldn't stand the idea of being away from Quinn. Thank goodness, they were at work or his heart might just give in.

Putting distance between them would probably be a good idea. And a hell of a lot easier if they weren't working and staying in the same apartment. But Milo didn't want to change things. Maybe when she took off for parts unknown again, he'd find a way to adjust. Right now, though, he couldn't bear the thought of it.

"How is Trey?" He'd only seen Carla's fiancé a few times as he'd run for ice chips—literally run! One of the floor nurses had warned him to use his walking feet, and Milo had laughed.

"They are adorable," Quinn breathed. "They have been best friends since high school. I swear they even seem to be able to read each other's thoughts. Just like..." She turned her face from his and let the words die away.

Just like us...

The unspoken words hung in the space between them. Milo swallowed the lump in his throat as he tried to force air into his lungs. He should say something, but his brain disconnected from his tongue as the silence dragged on.

She cleared her throat. "Anyway...they started dating about nine months ago." Quinn grinned as she tried to rub the knots out of her neck.

"Ah." Milo chuckled. "Well, they seem very happy." He hated the twinge of jealousy pooling in his gut. He just needed to focus on his goals, his plans, focus on the feeling they gave him. Except, for the first time, planning out his life didn't offer him any comfort.

"Breathe," Quinn ordered Carla as Trey held her hand.

Milo had entered when Carla had started pushing. The baby's heart rate had dropped the first time she'd pushed. Early decelerations often happened when the baby's head was compressed in the birth canal.

The heart rate had stabilized, and it hadn't happened again. But Milo was on standby, monitoring for any sign of fetal distress. He had also ordered the surgical suite readied—just in case.

He was probably overthinking this delivery, but the hairs on the back of his neck were rising. He'd promised Trey that Carla would be fine. A promise he made to all his patients, but the reality was that labor could be dangerous. There was a reason it was still the highest cause of death for women in underdeveloped countries. Technology lessened that burden, but it didn't decrease it altogether.

Milo had lost a few patients during his career. It was impossible to work in this field for years and not have at least a handful of deliveries go wrong. But today was not going to be one of those days.

"The next contraction is coming, I need you to push, Carla." Quinn's voice was tight as she looked at the maternal and fetal heart rate monitors. "Dr. Russell."

That sent a chill down his spine. During deliveries, Quinn maintained an informality with him. Except when there was a problem. Then he immediately became "Dr. Russell." It was her tell. He wasn't even sure she was aware of it.

His eyes flicked to the heart monitor. The baby's heart rate had shifted from early deceleration to variable deceleration. The baby wasn't getting enough oxygen.

"Carla, I want you to lay back until the next contraction comes." Milo nodded to Trey. "Help her lie back."

"What's going on?" Trey's voice was shaky as he looked from Quinn to Milo.

"The baby's heart rate is fluctuating in a way that I don't like," Milo said. "The little guy has been holding steady throughout labor, so adjusting your position a bit might be enough to give him the room he needs."

"And if it doesn't?" Carla's voice was firm as she gripped Trey's hand and looked at Quinn.

"Then Dr. Russell will perform an emergency C-section." Quinn's voice was low as she stared at the monitors.

She looked at him, and Milo saw the steel in Quinn again. But a subtle peace pressed against him. They were partners, maybe not romantically, but for the first time since she'd walked away from him last night, Milo felt like he could truly breathe.

She held up one finger. This was where their closeness, their friendship, and the layers beneath it collided. The benefits of being able to read each other so easily. Quinn was willing to let Carla push one more time, but if the baby's heart rate dropped again, they'd transfer her to the surgical suite. He nodded and she turned back to their patient.

"All right, Carla. Push on the next contraction, but if your baby's heart rate drops, Dr. Russell will get ready for a C-section."

"My baby?"

"Can be here in less than fifteen minutes, if necessary," Milo stated as he watched the monitors.

"Don't tell him I said so, but Dr. Russell is one of the best in the business." Quinn smiled as she fake whispered the compliment.

He felt his lips tip up. Quinn didn't issue false praise. Her confidence in him sent a wave of strength through Milo. She'd never doubted his ability to accomplish anything. She'd always been his biggest cheerleader. Maybe they were opposites, but they complemented each other—she was right about that.

"Try to breathe regularly," Milo instructed. The baby's heart rate shifted, and Milo exchanged a look with Quinn. The rate hadn't dropped nearly as much on that contraction as it had on the previous one, but it had fallen. They needed to get Carla and Trey's son out now.

Quinn nodded at Milo, and he took a deep breath. "Carla, we are transferring you."

"This wasn't part of the plan." Trey's voice wobbled as he watched Quinn prep Carla's bed for transfer.

"Trey, a nurse will be back to get you in a few minutes." Quinn pulled Carla's bed forward.

Milo didn't have time to comfort the man, but he offered a small smile to Carla's fiancé.

Trey dropped a light kiss on her forehead. "I'll see you soon."

"I'll be the one on the operating table." The love radiating between them was so apparent.

"Here we go," Quinn called as she guided the bed out of the room.

Fifteen minutes later, Milo listened to the monitors as he lifted Carla's son from her exposed womb. The umbilical cord was wrapped around the boy's neck and his skin had a blue hue. Milo unwrapped the cord, but still, the little guy made no noise.

"He's not crying." Trey's voice echoed in the room.

"Trey…" Carla's voice wobbled through the curtain separating them. "Why is he not crying, Quinn?"

"Give the little guy a minute. He's been through a time." Quinn's voice was low but comforting as she took the newborn from Milo, wrapped him in a warm towel, and started rubbing his back.

Come on, little one.

Milo kept his eyes on Carla's incisions and his ears tuned to the baby and Quinn.

After what seemed like an eternity, but was probably no more than a few seconds, the tiny man let out one of the angriest wails Milo could ever remember hearing. Quinn's gaze met his as she laid the baby on Carla's chest.

"He's got a full head of hair." Quinn grinned as she looked from Carla to Trey to Milo.

There was no one he'd rather be in a delivery room or surgical suite with than Quinn. No one he'd rather be with anywhere. Milo let out a breath and smiled as he finished closing Carla's incisions.

Looking over the curtain, he stared at the small family. Trey looked at them with such love that Milo felt his chest clamp. He loved helping deliver new life, and he'd never felt envious of anyone before, but as he looked from Carla and Trey to Quinn, he was surprised by the twinge of the emotion pulling at him.

Maybe her kissing him had been impulsive, but Milo suddenly didn't care. In that moment, she'd wanted him. There were tons of adventures they could have together in California. Milo just needed to find a way to make her want to stay.

With him.

CHAPTER FIVE

"IF THIS GOES on much longer, we will need to get a few more clothes," Quinn joked as she dumped the small load of laundry on Milo's leather couch. Her shoulders were knotted, and she flexed them twice before picking up the gray T-shirt Milo had loaned her. Between monitoring her phone for any word that she could return home, and trying her best to act normal around her best friend, Quinn's entire body felt like it might snap.

Milo picked up another shirt and started folding it. "That is true, but this has been nice, too."

Quinn raised an eyebrow. Nice? That was not a description she'd use to describe the last three days. Though last night, when they'd watched a movie, it had almost felt like old times.

Except it hadn't at all... Her heart had screamed as her brain tried to rationalize the hour and a half she'd spent wondering if she was acting normal enough. Or too normal. Or any of the other myriad thoughts that had run through her head.

This was what needy felt like, and Quinn hated it. Her mother had called her "needy" if she broke any rule or asked to do anything other than approved extracurricular activities. Her wants were too much. And each time she'd failed to follow her parents' exacting rules, she'd been belittled. Her schedule and her life had never truly been her own.

Even the drawing classes she'd begged for had only been granted after her art teacher had told them she was skilled. However, instead of taking classes at the local community center, her mother had set her up with a private art teacher four times a week. The thing Quinn had loved most became a controlled item on her schedule, not an activity she could actually lose herself in.

Yet as each day of uncertainty with Milo dragged on, Quinn wished she had some way to manage the chaos.

But would it ease the uncertainty or make her feel trapped?

Softly exhaling, Quinn forced those thoughts to the side. "'Nice'? How do you figure?"

Milo dragged a hand across the back of his neck. "Quinn…"

His deep voice sent a tingle down her back. He leaned toward her, and she held her breath. The drop of hope that he might kiss her had refused to die. It was ridiculous, and if she was able to spend more time away from him, then she might be able to bury it completely. But as his green eyes held hers, she couldn't quiet the want pulsating in her chest.

"I like spending time with you." Milo's words were soft.

Quinn let out a nervous laugh. She liked spending time with him, too, always had. He'd never made her feel unwanted…until two nights ago. Her stomach flipped as she focused on the laundry again. "Milo, we are always together. *Literally.* We work together, and you were at my bungalow almost every weekend."

"Yes." Milo's hip connected with hers. The touch was too much and not enough all at once. "I had to come to the bungalow," Milo continued, oblivious to the turmoil roiling through her, "you never came to my place."

"That is not true." Quinn's head popped back. She'd

gone to his place when she'd first returned. And been anxious from the moment she'd stepped into it until she'd left.

The downtown high-rise unit looked like something out of a design magazine. Its light gray walls were devoid of pictures. Flower vases, filled with fake arrangements, hovered in the corners, adding the appropriate hints of color against the perfectly oiled hardwood floors. It screamed success. But it wasn't personal.

Her mother would have loved the place. She'd have oohed and aahed at the full-length windows that overlooked downtown. Complimented the well-thought-out vases and minimalistic decor that made the space look bigger than it was. *Upscale...* That was the description she would have used.

Quinn had felt out of place in her torn blue jeans and T-shirt. A lackluster accessory to Milo's life on the fast track to success. After all, what did she have to show for the last ten years? All her worldly possessions had fit into the two canvas bags she'd carried when she'd landed in LA.

Sure, her bank account was healthy, but it couldn't afford the rent for a downtown unit like Milo's. Not that she'd told him that. The few places that he'd scoped out for her had been nice, but they'd also been too much for her—too upscale.

"Really?" Milo's lip quirked. "I don't think one time counts, Quinn."

Why was he pushing this?

He'd always seemed fine coming to her place. "I was there at least twice." When Milo playfully rolled his eyes, Quinn shrugged. "It's too clean!"

"You're complaining about my cleanliness?" Milo laughed. "Should I have had dirty laundry draped over the couch or dirty dishes in the sink? Somehow I don't think that would be very enticing."

His voice shifted; its deepness almost felt like it was

stroking her. The gleam in his eye and the dimple in his cheek sent thrills through her.

Was he flirting with her?

It was a ridiculous thought, but as his gaze held hers, she almost thought he was.

"No!" Quinn lightly slapped his shoulder. And her fingers burned from the brief connection. She needed to stop touching him. But that was an edict her body refused to follow.

"I should've picked a different adjective. It's perfect. Airy." She put a finger to her chin. "Picturesque. That is the word for it. I worry that if I spill anything, I might destroy the esthetic. Then I won't be invited again."

Milo's strong arms encompassed her. And before she could catch herself, Quinn leaned her head against his shoulder. "You are always welcome at my place, Quinn. Always and forever."

Forever. A term Quinn never associated with anyone.

No, that wasn't true.

She'd always associated it with Milo.

Milo's fingers moved along her back, and Quinn sighed. This hug was dangerous. His heat poured through her as she cataloged each finger's small stroke. She inhaled, letting his scent rip through her.

Milo…

She looked up and met his eyes, but he didn't release her. His gaze hovered on her lips.

Or maybe she just wished it would.

She tried to force her feet to move, but they were unwilling to follow her brain's command.

She sighed as Milo smiled at her. Just a moment longer…

"Quinn—"

Before Milo could finish whatever he'd planned to say, Quinn's phone rang. Grateful for the distraction, she pulled away.

The area code sent waves of excitement and dread racing down her spine. This was the call she'd been waiting for. But her fingers cramped as she stared at the answer button. The oxygen had evaporated from the room. The issues with Milo…the fire…all of it was just too much.

She slapped the phone into his hand. "I can't answer. Please."

Milo pursed his lips then lifted the phone to his ear.

Before he could do more than just say hello, Quinn bolted. It was childish, but she needed a moment to prepare for whatever Milo learned. Prepare for where she'd go if the tiny number of personal items she'd treasured were gone.

Her toes hit the sand of the beach and Quinn leaned over her knees. "Get yourself together. Get yourself together. You can handle this. You have to."

Quinn repeated the mantra to herself over and over, trying to put her feelings back behind the walls she'd carefully constructed since her childhood. Why were they cracking now—when she needed them the most?

Milo clicked off the call and looked toward the door. Her shoes were still there, so she couldn't have gone anywhere other than the beach. He couldn't blame her for not wanting to hear the message. Though the recording hadn't said much, the fire was now under control in her area and residents could return starting this afternoon.

Miranda had also called to let them know that St. Brigit's was no longer referring patients to other clinics. They could head home to Los Angeles.

He just didn't know exactly what home looked like now.

But they'd figure that out together.

He headed for the beach.

Quinn was standing at the edge of the ocean, her back to him. He stared at her for a few minutes. Her shoulders were tight, and he knew that he'd added to that strain. But everything had shifted and he didn't want it to go back to normal. Not with Quinn.

They belonged together. She knew everything about him, they completed each other's sentences and the first call they made when their worlds exploded was always to one another. Maybe his brain had overthought her impulsive kiss, but Quinn moved with her heart.

And it had reached out to him.

There were still a few months left on Quinn's contract with St. Brigit's. There was plenty of time for him to make her realize she belonged here—*with him*. But first, they needed to go to her place and see if there was anything left.

"One step at a time," Milo muttered as he stepped onto the beach.

"How bad is it?" Quinn's voice was ragged.

She turned to him as she brushed a tear from her cheek. The single tear tore his heart. Had he ever seen Quinn cry? No.

Quinn refused to show that weakness. Even when her parents had been awful, and then when they'd passed and the opportunity to ever achieve some reconciliation had evaporated, no tears had spilled from Quinn's eyes. He'd known that the bungalow meant a lot to her, but Milo hadn't realized how much the place had touched her.

She wrapped her arms around his waist. "Just tell me."

"I don't know." He laid his head against her head, wishing he could put an end to the unknown. Hating that this horrible situation she was facing gave him an excuse to touch her.

He dropped a kiss to the top of her head without thinking and was grateful when she didn't pull away. If they could stand on the beach holding each other forever, he'd be the happiest man ever. But life called, and they needed to see to the next steps. "That was just the notification that the fire is contained enough for us to return this afternoon."

Quinn ran her hands through her hair and cringed. "This is the worst Schrödinger's cat situation. Is my house still around? Or do I have nothing? Nowhere to go?"

"You will *never* have nowhere to go, Quinn." Milo squeezed her tightly, wishing there was a way to take all the pain and worry from her.

How could she think about going anywhere but to his place?

"I hope your bungalow is unharmed. But Quinn—" he squeezed her tightly "—you will always have a place with me."

"I know." Quinn smiled, but it didn't quite reach her eyes. The wind caught her hair as she stared at him. "I'm just worried and trying to bury my neediness."

Her eyes widened, and Milo doubted she'd meant to say that. "Being worried about your home isn't neediness, Quinn. And everyone is needy sometimes."

"Thank you," she sighed.

"Miranda called, too. Looks like we've worked our last shifts at my parents' clinic. The fire is contained enough for everyone to make it safely to St. Brigit's." The words were sooty in his mouth. He'd enjoyed working at Ocean-side again. Loved being near his family.

"Well, right now, I am trying to figure out how to get back to the town house without dragging sand everywhere. Standing in the ocean seemed like such a good idea a few minutes ago."

Milo had worn sandals down to the beach. This was something he could fix. "Hop on!" He turned and pointed to his back.

"No!" Quinn laughed. "I'm too tall and heavy."

"Are you calling me weak?" Milo grinned as he looked over his shoulder at her. These were the moments he lived for; being with her, making her laugh even as life's chaos twisted around them. He wanted years of laughter and fun with her.

"Very funny." Quinn glared at him.

Another wave rolled over her feet, and he hopped just far enough away to keep his feet from getting wet. He was going to have a bit of sand on his sandals, a small price to pay for living so close to the beach.

Except you don't live here anymore, his brain reminded him.

"Either you're going to have to walk through the sand with wet feet, or you'll have to get on my back. Come on, Quinn."

"Fine. But if I break you, you can't complain about it." Quinn wagged her finger before accepting his offer.

"You could never break me," Milo stated with more bravado than he felt. Quinn was light enough on his back. But she had the power to destroy him.

They were best friends, but so much more. She was the person who knew him better than anyone else. The woman who had made him smile when his marriage had failed. The person who'd answer his phone calls no matter which time zone she was in. She could tell his moods and always find a way to make him feel better. Quinn was the other part of his heart.

But what if she didn't feel the same way?

Milo pushed that worry away.

Hope slipped away as Quinn stared at the ashes around them as she and Milo made their way toward where her bungalow should be. The hills that had once been dotted with older homes and small lawns were now unrecognizable. Quinn was grateful that Milo had insisted on driving. Not only because her hands were shaking, but because she wasn't sure she could have found her way here.

All the landmarks she'd associated with the area were

gone. She could have relied on GPS, sure, but she prob-ably wouldn't have thought to turn it on until she'd been turned around a few times. Quinn had worked in multiple disaster zones, seen people deal with the trauma of losing everything, but she hadn't been prepared for this. No one could be.

Milo's hand reached for hers and Quinn held it tightly. "I am so sorry, Quinn."

As he slowed the car, Quinn realized they'd turned down her street. Everything was gone. A small sob escaped her lips. Her parents hadn't allowed her to have many posses-sions as a child. At least, not things that mattered to a small child, like drawings from school or pictures she liked. She'd never developed a desire for worldly goods. But seeing what little she did have turned to gray dust stung.

She had renter's insurance and—thankfully—had added wildfire protection, but the pictures of her and Milo all dressed up for their undergraduate graduation, pictures and notes from friends around the world, the few memen-tos she'd saved from her childhood. No amount of insur-ance could replace those.

She leaned her head against the headrest. Her body was heavy. Quinn had thought she was ready for this. She'd known what might happen when the mandatory evacua-tion had been issued. But seeing the destruction sent waves of panic through her.

What was she going to do?

"Do you want to go?" Milo's voice was gentle as his fingers stroked hers. "We don't have to look through the ashes. At least, not today. If anything is left…" His voice died away, but he didn't release her hand.

She wanted to run—wanted to get away from the week's stresses and hurts. But the sooner she got through this part, the sooner she could start to grieve for what was gone.

At least Milo is here.

"No, let's get this over with. I don't think I can do this alone." The confession slipped through her lips. She'd traveled the world, landed in new places and handled all of life's challenges alone. It was something Quinn took pride in.

But her ability to control herself, to lock away her emotions, had evaporated. Her face heated, but she kept her eyes firmly closed. It was the truth, and her walls were piles of ash at this point anyway.

"You never have to do anything alone, Quinn." Milo's arms suddenly enveloped her. "Never."

The car was small, and the action felt awkward, but comfort swam through her. She only allowed herself a cycle of breath before she pulled back. "Thank you."

Gripping the door handle, she looked at the destroyed lot that had once been her bungalow. "Let's go see if the fire left anything. Then, do you mind dropping me at a clothing store? I'd like something other than Bianca's leftovers."

"Of course." Milo nodded. "But I am not dropping you anywhere. If you need to go to twenty different stores, I will go to each one with you."

She should say something, thank him for the kind statement, but her tongue was heavy and her brain lacked words. Opening the car door, she let out a soft cry. The world smelled of smoke and destroyed dreams.

But Quinn forced her feet to move forward. She could do this. Had to.

Walking up the singed cement walkway, Quinn stared at the fallen stucco walls and wet soot. She stepped over a pile of debris as she stood in what was once her living room, though there was nothing to identify it.

Swallowing, she turned to find Milo. His face was long, but he was pushing at the ashes with his feet. She needed to do the same, to see if there was anything that she might be able to salvage. But where to start?

The garage… The boxes she'd set there and then forgotten in her rush to get to Molly's delivery had been full of papers and trinkets that wouldn't have stood a chance in the blaze. But she had to check.

Please...

The metal door frame that had led to the tiny garage was still standing. A spooky host to a door that had burned. A doorway to nowhere. Quinn shivered despite the afternoon's heat. Watching her step, she moved toward the marker.

Squatting, she brushed away the ashes that had once been her most precious things. Biting her lip, Quinn sucked in air. They were just things... The phrase felt hollow. They were her memories, and now they lived entirely in her mind.

Her fingers caught on something sharp and Quinn let out a small cry. Pulling her hand back, she looked it over. No blood or scratches.

"Quinn?"

Milo's voice carried across the damage, but she ignored him. Something besides soot and ash was there. It was probably part of the ceiling or a chunk of wall, but...

An ironwork frame emerged from the destruction and she let out another low cry. This time her heart was rejoicing. The frame was singed, and the glass darkened, but there in the frame was the image of her and Milo holding up her nursing diploma.

Her family hadn't attended her graduation. Her father had claimed a big work meeting that he couldn't miss and her mother had made an excuse so ridiculous that Quinn had long ago dumped it from her memory. But Milo had waited for hours before the civic hall opened to make sure he could sit in the front row.

Her lip trembled as she stared at the photograph. It was dirty, the corners burned. It would never look pristine again, but it was safe.

"I still remember how big your smile was when you

walked across the stage." Milo's voice was low as he knelt next to her. "You were radiant. I remember the exact moment your gaze caught mine." Milo smiled as he looked at the photo.

Radiant... Her throat tightened as she clasped the picture to her chest. *What was he doing?*

She kept that question buried in her heart as she stared at the rest of the debris pile. "I think this is the only thing that survived."

"I found a few pots, though they are a bit less cylindrical now. And one spoon." Milo wrapped an arm around her shoulders. "But I didn't make it back to your bedroom. Did you have any pictures there?"

"No." Quinn blinked back the moisture coating her eyes. She was not going to cry, "I put all the photos I treasured by the door. When Molly went into labor, I left. Guess I figured I'd get another chance."

Milo's nose scrunched. She pressed her hand against his cheek, not caring about the soot stain she was leaving. Quinn needed to touch him, needed to ground them. "What's wrong?"

He raised an eyebrow. "Speaking of another chance—" Before he could finish, a scream went up from the house, or what was left of it, a few doors down.

"Help!" The call was cracked and laced with terror.

Milo took off. Quinn laid the picture down and raced after him.

Mrs. Garcia was hovering over her husband near the front steps of what had once been their well-maintained porch. Her hands were covered in blood.

Milo reached them, and Quinn pulled out her phone to call 9-1-1 as she turned and raced back to the car. There was water there, and they'd brought their midwifery bags with them. They had sterile gauze and a few supplies that might be useful until the ambulance arrived.

By the time she returned, she had a stitch in her side, but Mr. Garcia was sitting up. The right side of his face was streaked with blood, and the cut running up his leg would need to be cleaned at the hospital and closed with at least a dozen stitches. It was still seeping blood.

"Is it slowing at all?" Quinn asked as she slipped in next to Milo.

"No." He took the water and hand sanitizer she offered. It wasn't much, but it was better than nothing. Milo laid several gauze pads across the wound before pulling off his T-shirt and pressing it against the wound, as well.

She glanced at Milo as she sanitized her own hands and donned gloves. His muscles were taut as he kept pressure on Mr. Garcia's wound. He hadn't hesitated to act. His quick thinking would have been a benefit in many of the field hospitals she'd served in.

And they were a giant benefit here, too.

"The ambulance is at least fifteen minutes out." Quinn kept her voice low, but she heard Mrs. Garcia whimper. In an area with well-known traffic issues, fifteen minutes wasn't terrible. Still, everyone knew that it might take longer.

Milo nodded. "I think the bleeding is slowing, but there is at least one vein open, up by the knee."

Pulling out the surgical tape that they carried in their bags, Quinn wrapped it tightly around the shirt. She and Milo needed both their hands. This way, pressure would remain on the wound.

"What happened?" Milo asked as he moved his attention from Mr. Garcia's leg to his head.

"He insisted we come back for some silly trinket that he forgot to pack." Mrs. Garcia bit her lip as she stared at her husband.

Quinn offered her a forgiving look. "I think Milo was asking about what happened with the injury."

"I…" Mr. Garcia huffed as he gestured to the house and started over. "The steps were loose and crumbled when I stepped on them. Guess the fire was hot enough to weaken the cement." He blinked and moved to touch his face before Milo caught his arm.

"Let me." His voice was low and soothing, but still authoritative. Even in this destroyed area, shirtless, with nothing but a midwifery bag and bottles of water, Milo was the consummate professional.

Quinn bit her lip as Milo carefully cleaned the cut on Mr. Garcia's head. His gentle touches made Quinn's heart clench. She'd loved working with him. It wasn't St. Brigit's, or the wonderful work being done there, that had called her home. It was Milo and how complete she felt when she was near him.

Milo was the reason her walls were in such shambles. She'd never kept them up around him. She'd always been herself. Maybe it would be safer for her heart to find a way to erect them, but Quinn didn't want to. Not now or ever.

"And it wasn't a trinket." Mr. Garcia's voice was strong as he looked at his wife. "It was your anniversary present. I spent months making…"

He looked over Quinn's shoulder. "I didn't expect this level of destruction. Even with the news reports, somehow…" He closed his eyes.

Mrs. Garcia's eyes widened. "We are here for an anniversary present? I could throttle you." Then her gaze softened. "Right after I kiss you."

"I almost lost you once, honey. I won't risk it again." Mr. Garcia's eyes were full of love as they looked at his wife.

"Almost lost her?" The question slipped from Quinn's lips as she checked on Mr. Garcia's leg. It was still bleeding, but blood wasn't seeping through Milo's T-shirt. Though Quinn had waved to Mrs. Garcia whenever she saw the woman puttering around in her yard, they were not close.

Certainly not close enough for her to pry into their private lives.

Mrs. Garcia laughed as she folded her arms. "It's his running joke. I asked him out first. I was very brazen in my youth, although I'm more so now, if I may say so." She winked at her husband. The silly gesture felt oddly intimate. The kind of inside joke that long-married, happy couples enjoyed.

"Gumption," Mr. Garcia corrected. "She had—*has* so much gumption."

"Anyway…" Her eyes never left her husband's face as she retold what was obviously a well-discussed memory between them. "I asked him out, and he said no."

Milo's breath hitched and Quinn's chest tightened. She made sure to keep her face averted.

What was he thinking?

"I was so surprised that the prettiest girl I'd ever seen wanted me. I thought it was a joke. Biggest mistake of my life." Mr. Garcia sighed as he stared at his wife.

The sirens rang out in the distance, and Quinn saw Mrs. Garcia's shoulders relax. She understood. She'd be glad when they were on their way to get his leg properly looked at, too.

"It took me almost a month to work up the courage to own up to the mistake." Mr. Garcia wrapped his hand around his wife's wrist.

Quinn felt moisture form along the ridges of her eyelashes—again. She was in danger of becoming a real watering pot.

She saw Milo catch her gaze and watched an unknown emotion play across his face. She wanted to believe that it was desire, hope for a different future than they'd discussed on the beach. A second chance…

She'd played his little touches and jokes from this morning over in her head. She was almost positive he'd been flirting. Milo never did anything without thinking it out.

There'd been so much going on the day she'd kissed him. What if she broached the topic again when life wasn't so hectic? When he could think about it for a few minutes? If he turned her down then, at least she'd never wonder what-if—even if it left a crater in her heart.

"What was the present?" Milo's question stunned her as he waved to the incoming paramedics.

Mr. Garcia shook his head. "If I tell you, it won't be a surprise, son. I figure I got a few months to recreate it. Maybe in time for Christmas."

Milo laughed as he stepped to the side and started talking to the paramedics.

"Your boyfriend is quite the looker." Mrs. Garcia smiled at Quinn.

"He's not my boyfriend." The words tasted like soot as she stared at Milo. He made her feel important. He wrapped her in comfort and had always cheered her on, no matter the places she traveled or the jobs she took. And he'd guided her home. "He's my best friend."

But those words didn't feel right anymore as Quinn wrapped her arms around herself. Milo was her compass, the person who kept her on course.

Mrs. Garcia raised an eyebrow but didn't say anything before hustling off after her husband.

Quinn wasn't needed here anymore. Letting out a sigh, she walked back to her destroyed bungalow. She picked up the photo and smiled at the happy memory before turning her focus to the ruins around her.

It was all really gone. Outside of filing insurance paperwork, this wasn't her home anymore. The one place she'd felt like she could let all her walls down, be herself.

Strong arms wrapped around her, and Quinn leaned back against Milo.

"Ready to go?"

"Are you sure you want me to stay with you, Milo? I'll admit, the idea of walking to St. Brigit's from your apartment is nice." Quinn turned in his arms. She should step back, but she had neither the strength nor the desire to. This was where she felt safe. "But I doubt I will be great company."

"You'll be you. And that is priceless." Milo rested his forehead against hers for a moment. "We'll figure out all the details when we get to the apartment. I actually have a plan I want to run by you."

"A plan?" Quinn let out a soft giggle despite herself. Of course Milo had a plan for what happened if she couldn't come home. "I can't wait to hear it."

"It may be my best plan ever." He smiled, and warmth crept through her belly.

CHAPTER SIX

QUINN'S HAIR WAS WET, and her new tank top clung to her waist as she pulled out the chair at his kitchen island. She smiled as she accepted the glass of wine. Her eyes closed as she took a long sip.

Milo stared at her neck. He wanted to plant kisses there, trail them down her shoulder and lower. Wanted to hold her, to wake up next to her. He wanted so many things.

"So, what is your plan?" Quinn's voice carried through the kitchen.

Her dark eyes called to him. He'd looked at them so often, he knew where each of the gold flecks were.

Quinn called to him.

Her spirit made Milo's soul cry out with need. Her unfailing desire to help, to run from her destroyed home to aid a neighbor... Her ability to pick up and start anew... Everything about her made his heart leap.

"Milo?" Her hand ran along his knee, and he jumped.

"Sorry." Quinn's voice shook. "I... I..." Her eyes raced across his face. "I didn't mean to scare you."

"You didn't." Milo shook his head. "No, you did. But not just now. I mean, I jumped, but..." He shut his mouth. Rambling was not how he'd meant to have this conversation.

"When you kissed me..." Milo bit his tongue. He'd planned this talk and now he was starting in the middle?

"I scared you when I kissed you." Quinn's fingers reached for her wineglass, but she didn't look away.

Milo looked at her and his heart cracked as her bottom lip trembled. His script had flown from his memory. Taking a deep breath, he started again. "I made a mistake." The words were simple, but they were the truth.

"A mistake?" Quinn took another sip of wine before setting her glass down. "Do you want me to leave? I can…"

"No." He reached for her hands. As her fingers wrapped through his, his soul calmed. Quinn grounded him. "I am saying all the wrong things. And I even had a plan."

He gulped and started over.

"When you kissed me…" Quinn looked away, and Milo couldn't stand that. Running a finger along her cheek, Milo waited until she looked at him to continue. "I've dreamed of kissing you for years. Since our undergraduate days. Even before. The time never seemed right to ask, or maybe I was just worried you'd say no. But when it finally happened, my brain went into overthinking mode. Because—"

Quinn laid a finger against his lips. "Years?"

"Years," Milo confirmed.

Quinn's mouth fell into the cutest O shape.

God, she was adorable.

"I want you. But not for just a night or a few months, Quinn. I've spent the last two days trying to figure out how to get you back into my arms. I have a whole plan, but honestly, you've driven it from my mind. All I can think of is kissing you." He leaned forward. "I want to kiss you. Desperately. But if you need time to think—"

Her lips were on his before he could finish.

Quinn…his Quinn.

Pulling her to him, Milo deepened the kiss as the chairs they were sitting in locked together. Quinn in his arms was simply right. Life slowed as he reveled in the taste of her.

The feel of her heat pressed against his chest. All of it was intoxicating.

There was more to discuss, to figure out. But when she was in his arms, none of it seemed to matter. Her fingers traced up his neck and Milo let out a low groan. How had he waited days to have this conversation? Years? Those were days, hours and minutes of kisses he'd thrown away.

"Quinn." Milo let his fingers travel down her sides. "I want you. But if you don't want me to carry you to bed right now, we need to stop."

She pulled back momentarily.

He meant it. If she wanted to take their physical relationship slowly, he'd wait as long as she needed him to.

"I've wanted you since the moment I landed in LA."

The sultry words undid him. There would be time to discuss his plans later. Right now, he needed Quinn.

Sliding from his chair, Milo wrapped his arms around her and lifted her. She let out a light squeal and he kissed her neck. "I've got you, Quinn."

And he was never going to let go.

He dropped kisses on her lips as he carried her to his bedroom. He laid her gently on the bed before reaching for the small lamp. The first time he made love to Quinn was not going to be in the dark.

Her fingers reached for his shirt and he let her pull it off, relishing the desire pooling in her eyes. Had anyone ever looked at him like that? Like they needed him and only him?

Sitting beside her, Milo ran his fingers under her tank top, listening to every tiny change in her breathing. Cataloging where she responded. When his fingers finally worked their way to her breast, Milo's heart raced. He didn't want to rush this, but his body was taut with need.

Quinn's eyes met his as she lifted her shirt over her

head. She wore no bra. She bit her lips as she stared at him. "Milo…"

"You are so beautiful," he murmured as he stared at her. He wanted to know exactly how she liked to be touched, the noises she made. But he could see an emotion hovering in her eyes that he couldn't quite read. "Do you want to stop?"

"No." She kissed his chin.

"Tell me what you're thinking, then." Milo licked the hollow at the base of her neck, loving the groan that echoed in the room.

"That this doesn't feel weird." Quinn's hand trailed along his stomach and down his thigh. "After so many years of friendship—this feels right."

"And how, then—" Milo kissed her lips "—does this feel?" Dipping his head, he sucked one nipple before turning his attention to the other.

"Amazing…"

Quinn's voice, was threaded with need, and it made Milo's own desire pulse more.

She was so beautiful.

Gripping her shoulders, Milo guided her onto her back. Lowering her shorts, Milo let out a soft groan. She wasn't wearing any panties. Quinn, his perfect Quinn, was naked on the bed.

"I don't sleep in underwear," Quinn stated as he ran a finger up her thigh.

"That is something I didn't know." Milo held her gaze for a moment before lowering his head. "I love learning new things about you. Like how you taste…"

His senses exploded as he savored her. Her body arched, pushing against him.

This was perfect.

"Milo." He doubted there was a sweeter sound than his name on Quinn's lips when she was in the throes of passion.

He let his fingers trail her calves as he teased her, driving her closer to the edge with his mouth. Her hands running across his shoulders, rolling through his hair, were enough to make him want to bury himself deep inside her. But he was determined not to rush this. They had all night—and all the days after.

"Milo." Quinn gripped his shoulders, and he felt her reach the edge. "Please, Milo. Make love to me."

The plea undid him.

He dropped his jeans to the floor, grabbed a condom from the side table and returned to her.

Quinn's arms wrapped around his neck as she pulled him close. "I need you."

Her mouth captured his as he drove into her. "Milo!" Her fingers raked his back and he held her tightly.

Nothing in the world mattered more than this moment. This perfect moment. He felt her start to orgasm again and, this time, he didn't hold back. "Quinn."

Her fingers traced his back as he lay in her arms afterward. "That was…" She sighed against his shoulder. "Not sure the words exist." Her voice was lazy with pleasure and exhaustion.

"I agree." He kissed her, his hand caressing her chin. She was so wonderful, and she was here in his arms.

His Quinn.

The sun was rising over LA as Quinn stood in front of the planning boards in Milo's study. He'd outlined his life for the next fifteen years. Something that her parents would have been impressed by. *And* it was impressive—and daunting.

He'd said that he'd worked out a plan for them. But her name was nowhere on any of the lists. So, where did she fit? And did she really want everything planned out? *Controlled?*

She'd lived like that for years. Plans and schedules were

one of the things she'd left behind when she'd fled her parents' home. Quinn only planned for her current job and one follow-on assignment. There had been a few times when she hadn't known what was going to happen, yet she'd found that life generally worked out. But she knew Milo needed these.

Lifting the mug of coffee to her lips, she took a deep breath and tried to reorient her mind. She'd spent the night in Milo's bed, though they hadn't slept much. Her body tingled as she remembered the feel of Milo's fingers on her skin. His kisses trailing along her belly. Last night had been lovely. So why was she standing in his study before dawn, unable to quiet the chatter in her mind?

Rolling her neck, Quinn let out a sigh. Milo planned. He thought things through. And he followed through with his plans, no matter what. When he'd decided to resign from the Oceanside Clinic, nothing she or his mom had said had mattered. He was determined.

It was one of the things Quinn loved about him. The word had floated around her last night as he'd held her. Quinn loved Milo. Loved his thoughtfulness, his open heart, his determined spirit. When had her love shifted from that of a cherished friend to romantic?

Did it matter?

Milo had wanted her—had said he'd wanted her for years. But what if she failed to fit into his plans like she'd failed to fit into her parents'?

Her knees trembled. No. Milo was not her parents, and she was not going to imagine the end of this relationship before it even began.

She wasn't.

Quinn forced herself to walk into the kitchen. Placing the mug on the counter, she moved to grab the coffeepot. She poured the coffee then turned to rinse out the pot. Yawning, she reached for her mug, but her fingers didn't quite catch it. The cup tumbled to the floor and she let out a cry. The ceramic shattered at her feet, the sound echoing through the room.

Heat raced along her toes as coffee splashed. "Shoot!" She hopped onto the counter. The coffee spreading across the tiles, clinging to the previously perfect grout.

"In his apartment for less than twenty-four hours and already destroying stuff." Quinn sighed. Somewhere her mother's ghost was saying, *Told you so...*

"I don't care about a mug, Quinn." Milo spoke from the doorway. He wore only boxers, and he looked from the floor to where she was perched on the counter. "Are you okay?"

"Burned my toes, but otherwise fine." Quinn looked around the kitchen. She'd kept towels in the drawer by the sink at the bungalow, and Milo knew where everything was. But she had no idea where he kept his towels.

Because she'd avoided his upscale apartment.

Avoided things that reminded her of her past. But Milo was part of her past, and good. So good. And she was done running.

She was...

Her heart beat with a certainty her brain didn't quite feel, but the rush of emotion was enough to propel her mentally forward. "Where are your towels?"

Milo didn't answer as he started toward her.

"Wait!" Quinn held up her hands. "You're barefoot. The shards..." She didn't want him hurt. And she could see the same emotion wavering on his face. "I promise to stay right here while you get shoes."

He raised an eyebrow as he looked at her. "If you get down, we will have our first fight."

First fight... They were silly words, but they made her smile. She wanted a whole world of firsts with him.

Milo returned quickly. "You're smiling."

"You mentioned our first fight. I am pretty sure that we had our first major fight over your refusal to sit as a subject in my art class in high school."

Milo chuckled as he walked over and pulled two towels from a drawer. He dropped them on top of the mess before lifting her off the counter and carrying her into the other room. "You were mad at me for almost a month. All because I didn't want to pose in a toga."

"It seemed important at the time. Although, if you want to pose for me now…" She kissed the delicate skin behind his ear, enjoying the soft groan that escaped his lips as she slipped down from his arms. Flirting with Milo was fun and easy. But they needed to get the mess she'd made cleaned up, and then discuss what had happened last night.

"I don't think any of the ceramic shards traveled this far." Her fingers tousled his hair as she leaned against his chest.

"I like holding you." Milo sighed. "Though I guess we do need to clean up the mess."

She slipped her flip-flops on and followed Milo back into the kitchen. "I really am sorry. I guess I wasn't too far off when I said I'd make a mess of your place."

"Don't do that." The broken pottery clinked as it hit the bottom of the trash can, but Milo didn't break her gaze.

"Do what?"

He raised an eyebrow before bending to grab the towels from the floor.

Quinn bit her lip. She knew what. He'd gotten on her for years about her self-deprecating jokes. She'd used them to survive in her family, and now her brain just automatically supplied them.

"I know." Quinn shook her head. "My coping mechanism is not the best."

Milo pulled her into his arms and kissed her forehead. "You've had a lot to deal with over the last few days. But you belong here with me. I don't care if you destroy every single mug in the cabinet." He paused for a moment before adding, "Except my favorite mug. It's special."

Milo opened a cabinet and pulled out a slightly mis-shapen mug.

Her mouth fell open as he held it up for her inspection. "You kept it!" Quinn laughed. The mug was the only thing to survive the twelve weeks of pottery courses she'd taken years ago.

The traveling nursing agency she'd contracted with had mandated the three-month sabbatical after she'd worked in three different disaster zones in nine months. She'd rented a small unit over a pottery studio and taken classes each day—never managing to make more than one lopsided cup.

Drawing and painting were skills that came more or less naturally to her. Her work was pretty, and she'd even sold a few pieces. But no matter what she'd done, the clay refused to turn into anything. The cup was too short, and its handle was misshapen.

"I can't believe you kept that." She'd given it to Milo right after his marriage had ended. He'd held it up and smiled. The first smile she'd seen on his lips for weeks. She'd meant the cup to be a joke, a brief spotlight of hap-piness before it landed in the trash. But it was in his hands now, being held with such reverence that she thought her heart might explode.

"You worked hard to make this. I remember you cursing about the 'stupid pottery wheel.' Very colorful language, if I remember correctly." Milo put the mug away and then pushed a piece of hair away from Quinn's eyes. "You can break everything in this place, Quinn, and it still won't make me think you don't belong here."

"You never told me your plan." Quinn looked up and the emotion traveling across Milo's face made her heart race. "We got distracted." Quinn grinned. "A few times."

"Yes, we did." Milo dropped his lips to hers.

Quinn's skin tingled as he deepened the kiss. She'd been in relationships; but this sense of rightness, of being in the arms of her match, had never been present. Even during her short engagement, Quinn had never reacted to James the way she reacted to Milo. Her body sang every time he touched her.

"Was your plan to only be distracted a few times?" She held her breath.

"No." Milo's tone was firm as he stared at her. "And after last night, if you still think we're better off as just friends, then I have a whole other plan to make you change your mind."

Her words from the beach felt like another lifetime ago. And maybe they were. She'd kept a part of herself locked away in every relationship. Even James had complained that Quinn never let him all the way in. He'd said that if she loved him, he wouldn't have to guess what was going on in her mind. Though *he* hadn't loved *her* enough to stay faithful, to choose her. The wounds across her heart may not bleed anymore, but they'd never fully healed.

But this was Milo, and he already knew so much about her. She could let him into the few places she kept only for herself.

She could.

Grinning, she ran a finger along the outside of his thigh. "I want us to try being us."

"How did you manage to make the word *us* sound so intimate?" Milo's eyes sparked as he pushed another wayward strand of her hair behind her ear.

Milo bent his head, but she stepped back. There was clearly still something she needed to say. "I have two conditions, which I probably should have laid down last night. But you are very good at distractions."

"Name them," Milo stated. "Whatever they are, I'll do it."

"Really?" Quinn raised a brow. If she said she wanted to take a job a few thousand miles from here, what would he say?

No! That was the fear she'd always let worm its way into her brain. *Look for the way you might get hurt, how it might end.* Then she could be prepared. Protected. But she refused to do that with Milo.

"No matter what happens, we stay friends." Quinn gripped his fingers. "I couldn't stand it if I lost you forever. I want this to work. But if it doesn't…" Her breath caught as Milo pulled her forward.

"I want it to work, too." Milo's lips grazed hers. "But I promise, Quinn. No matter what, I am in your life forever. What's the other condition?"

"You can't plan out everything." Quinn paused as a shadow passed over Milo's eyes. "I don't want to live by an outline, Milo. Let's see where these feelings take us— with no plan."

"No plan?" Milo's voice was tense. "I am not sure I can do that, Quinn. What if I make you a deal?"

She tried to ignore the button of fear in her belly. "What's the deal?"

"I can plan a week at a time—that at least gets us a date night once or twice a week," Milo countered.

"A week at a time…" Quinn nodded. "Deal, but if something fun comes up, we are jumping at it—even if the weekly plan says we're booked."

Milo shook his head before smiling, "Do we settle this with a handshake…or?" Wrapping his arms around her waist, Milo's lips captured hers. "Or would you prefer another action to seal the deal?"

She sighed as he deepened the kiss. If there was a better way to start the morning than kissing Milo, she didn't wish to find it.

She moved her lips down, kissing the delicate skin along

his neck. She loved the way Milo responded to her touch. "Do you want breakfast? Or are you up for more 'distracting'?"

Milo kissed her, his hands wandering to her hips. "I plan to spend most of the day 'distracting' you."

Quinn sighed as his lips trailed to her chest. She kept her gaze off the coffee stain on the kitchen tile. She'd make sure the lingering evidence of her mishap was mopped up later. It wasn't important right now.

CHAPTER SEVEN

THE LAST WEEK had flown by in kisses and a fog of happiness. Quinn smiled as she exited the employee lounge. She couldn't seem to stop smiling.

It was intoxicating and a bit unsettling. Milo raised his head from the end of the hall before heading into a patient's room. The subtle acknowledgment sent a burst of happiness through her.

Glancing at the next patient's chart on her tablet, Quinn frowned. Tara Siemens had checked the "extreme stress" box on the survey they gave to all their patients before their appointments, which didn't make sense to Quinn. Tara was one of her happiest clients.

Many first-time mothers got worried toward the end of their pregnancy. Still, extreme stress could have detrimental effects on the mother and child. Quinn sent an electronic note to Milo, requesting he stop in if he was available. Milo and Dr. Greg had both done additional training on maternal mental health care. It was therefore standard procedure to ask one of them to see any patient who'd checked the extreme stress box.

Quinn opened the door and a sob echoed from the room. "Tara?" Setting aside the tablet, Quinn grabbed the rolling chair and slid in front of her patient.

Her eyes were swollen and red. She wiped at her nose and then took the box of tissues Quinn offered. "So...sorry."

Quinn tapped Tara's knee. "You don't need to apologize. All feelings are allowed in here. What is going on?"

"Brandon." Tara hiccupped and closed her eyes.

Quinn slid her eyes to Tara's hand and noticed her engagement ring was gone. Brandon had attended a few of the appointments with Tara. He'd seemed distracted, but he wasn't the only partner that Quinn had thought was less than enthusiastic about the prospect of parenthood. Most of the time it was nerves, or a coping strategy, particularly in the early days, in case something went wrong. Sometimes, though...

"I am so sorry." Quinn made sure to keep her voice low and soothing. There was never a great time to end an engagement, but when a child was involved, it added a significant amount of stress.

"Want to take a look at your baby?" When a mother was frantic, or concerned, seeing her child often offered a bit of calm. When Tara had checked the stress box on the survey, it had ensured she was placed in one of the rooms with a portable ultrasound machine.

Tara nodded and leaned back on the table. She let Quinn raise her shirt, but silent tears still streamed down her cheeks. "Brandon said he liked the fact that we were so different."

The phrase caught Quinn off guard as she grabbed the gel. She wanted to calm Tara, but relationship discussions were not Quinn's forte—even with the few people she knew well. She made a low noncommittal noise as she dropped a bit of gel against Tara's belly.

"Opposites attract. That was the joke he made when he proposed. He liked my need to order my life, said it balanced his free spirit. Until it didn't..."

The baby's strong heartbeat saved Quinn from trying to find an answer. What was she supposed to say? Opposites sometimes attracted—look at her and Milo. But they'd only just started dating.

"That sounds like a strong heartbeat." Milo's deep voice echoed through the small room. "And you look gorgeous as always, Tara." His voice was soothing as he met Tara's gaze.

"If you like snotty noses and red eyes." Tara sniffled into her tissue.

"Your daughter looks very healthy," Quinn added as Tara stared at the monitor. The monitor that Quinn had hooked up as she'd readied the ultrasound machine showed Tara's heart rate was slowing, too.

Milo caught Quinn's eye, and she carefully rubbed her ring finger. He looked from her hand to Tara's, and she saw recognition flare in Milo's eyes. This wasn't the first time a couple had broken up before the birth of their child, but it was never easy.

"Did you eat breakfast this morning?" Milo asked.

"Egg sandwich," Tara answered.

"Good." Milo nodded. "I had a giant plate of pancakes!"

It was a lie. Milo had eaten a granola bar and a yogurt-to-go, the same as Quinn, as they'd raced out of his place this morning. But he was putting the patient at ease as he asked a series of questions designed to assess her well-being without raising suspicion. Tara's shoulders started to relax as Milo talked to her.

He was gentle but made sure that Tara answered the questions. Pregnancy was a stressful time. Add in trying to find a new place to live and getting over a broken engagement, and you were dealing with issues that could feel overwhelming.

"I think you are going to be just fine," Milo said. "But we are going to give you an emotional check sheet before you leave today. Most people are aware of postpartum depression, but some women will suffer from antepartum depression or depression during pregnancy. Major life changes and the hormone changes going on in your body can make you more susceptible to this kind of depression. And there is nothing wrong with you if it happens."

"Nothing," Quinn reiterated. Many women believed they were supposed to be happy no matter what during their pregnancy. That line of thinking could be dangerous.

Milo nodded. "I need to see to another patient. I enjoyed our chat, Tara."

Quinn talked to Tara about the rain that had started this afternoon and their plans for dinner as they wrapped up the appointment. Easy topics, but Tara didn't cry. That was a good sign.

"You think she'll be okay?" Milo caught Quinn as he exited another patient's room. His thumb rubbed against the back of her wrist.

"I hope so." Quinn quickly straightened the collar of his shirt.

How had he not noticed that?

"She seems so heartbroken."

"Breakups are never easy." Milo flipped through a few screens on his tablet before looking at her.

"She said her ex loved the fact that they were opposites... until he suddenly didn't." Quinn huffed out a breath. It was ridiculous to make comparisons, but she'd always imagined that was how her family had seen her. A perfect, dark-haired opposite to them...until that wasn't good enough.

"Well, that old wisdom that opposites attract is pretty inaccurate."

"It is?" Quinn's heart spun as she stared at him.

If he thought that, what were they doing together?

She picked up and moved when the call came. Milo had moved less than a hundred miles from where they'd grown up. She loved bright, obnoxious decorations and letting life take her where she was supposed to go. Milo liked neutrals and planning everything. He had one-year, three-year, five-year, ten-year and twenty-year plans written on his wall in the study. Quinn didn't even know what three years from now would look like for her—except for the certainty that she wanted Milo in her life.

Milo pushed a piece of hair behind her ear, "I've always thought so. Eventually, the differences drive you apart. Unless the partners can adjust."

"Adjust?" Quinn's skin felt like ice. How was he so casually discussing this? *With her?* Did he not see how different they were? Was the first hint of emotional intoxication overwhelming his rational planning self? And when would he decide that her differences were too much?

"Sure. Everyone adjusts in a relationship. But in an opposites situation, the adjustment has to be larger. I don't know many couples that can overcome that. Though, ideally, you figure that out before starting a family. Plans…" He shrugged. "But life happens." Milo looked at her, his smile gone.

Was she part of life happening? Something that went against Milo's plans? Her mouth was dry as she tried to think of something to say to turn this conversation to something else. Anything else…

"Quinn?" Milo's hand reached for hers. He grasped it briefly before he dropped it. The floor knew that they were dating, but professionalism still needed to be maintained. "I know what you're thinking, but we balance each other. And we have a lot in common. We both love bad movies, hate cooking, love our jobs. We make each other laugh."

But were those enough?

"You're right," Quinn finally murmured, trying to stop the twist of her stomach as it rumbled. "Those pancakes are sounding better by the moment."

Milo raised an eyebrow, but didn't call her out on shifting the topic. "Do you want to do breakfast for dinner? We can make pancakes drizzled with maple syrup, and I am pretty sure that I have some bacon in the fridge. But we could also swing by the market before we go home."

Home. That was a word that struck Quinn. She wanted a home, and Milo including her in the simple statement meant the world to her. But what if their differences set them apart eventually?

"Quinn?" Milo's voice broke her woolgathering.

"Pancakes for dinner would be lovely." The words slipped from her lips without much thought.

"Okay." Milo squeezed her hand one more time before he turned to head to his next patient's room.

Quinn crossed her arms as she watched him go. Milo was right; everyone had to make adjustments in relationships.

They could make it work...couldn't they?

"I'll see you when I get ho—back." Quinn kissed his cheek as she carefully held on to her to-go cup of coffee. She'd purchased the travel mugs the day after she'd spilled the coffee across the kitchen. At least today, she was actually going somewhere with it. No matter how many times Milo told her that he didn't care if she dumped coffee on the floor each morning, she refused to use the ceramic mugs.

It was a silly thing to worry about, but Milo couldn't press the fear from his throat that Quinn was maintaining a bit of distance. Not much, just a thin veneer around her heart—enough to protect herself. Like she didn't think this was permanent. Like *he* might not be permanent.

This wasn't Quinn's home. Milo understood that. And if her bungalow hadn't been a casualty in the fire, they wouldn't have transitioned to living together so quickly—though he'd probably would've stayed at the bungalow as often as possible.

He enjoyed having her here. Loved waking next to the tangle of dark hair on the pillow beside him. But he hated the fact that Quinn didn't feel completely comfortable in his home. Hated that the gray walls brought forth ghosts better left buried.

With Quinn in residence over the last two weeks, he'd watched her carefully slip into the quiet, palatable Quinn she'd been when living with her parents. Her Quinn shell.

That was the term he'd coined years ago. It had made Quinn laugh, though he knew that she hated that it was necessary to maintain the peace in her home. She'd dropped her defense mechanism once she'd moved out. And he hated that it was currently being used on him—even if she didn't realize she was doing it.

He wanted the real Quinn. The woman who'd bloomed in her own space. Who wore what she wanted, not outfits selected by her mother. The woman who flew wherever was necessary and served everyone. The woman he was in love with.

Love... The word struck him. He'd been dating Quinn a few weeks; that couldn't be right. It was too soon. He'd been with Bianca nearly six months before they'd broached the topic of love.

But as the word settled around him, Milo let it warm him. He loved Quinn. *Loved Quinn.*

He'd never considered theirs a short-term relationship, but as the word rattled around his brain, Milo felt the completion of it. The joy such a simple phrase projected into all the pieces of his soul.

Still, it was too soon to tell her. Quinn had briefly dated a banker in Georgia, and he recalled her breaking it off the minute the guy had hinted at seriousness. She'd said, "Relationships need to be cultivated, not rushed." He was not going to screw this up by moving too fast. Though he wasn't planning to wait too long, either.

Despite her edict to only think one week ahead, his brain had instantly started putting plans together. In another month, it wouldn't seem too rushed if he announced his love. Hopefully, that would give Quinn enough time to realize that they belonged together. If not...? Well, Quinn was worth waiting a lifetime for.

But right now he needed to find a way to make this place feel more like a home for Quinn. Make her realize that he didn't see it as a temporary space for her. He wanted— *needed*—her to want to stay in Los Angeles. With him.

Particularly since Miranda had decided to interview the senior OB from Valley General. Milo had quietly reached out to a colleague in the unit and inquired about potential openings. They'd told him that they expected an opening in the next few months, which suggested that Dr. Torres was planning to leave, even if she didn't get the position at St. Brigit's. All Milo's plans were falling into place; he just had to make sure Quinn wanted to stay.

Crossing his arms, Milo stared at the kitchen. An idea flew into his mind. And with Quinn on a ten-hour shift, he had just enough time to pull it off.

Picking up the phone, he dialed his sister's number.

"It's not even eight, Milo! Some of us start our mornings a little later." Gina yawned, but she didn't hang up.

"I need paint. Bright yellow paint and sunflower pictures." His fingers itched to get to work. To make the feelings bursting through his heart erupt onto the walls.

"You are calling before eight to talk about redecorating. I thought you wanted all calming tones in your place. Yellow—"

"Is bright and fun. *And* Quinn's favorite color." Milo smiled as he stared at the kitchen walls. The bungalow was gone, but he could bring a bit of it here for her. His chest swelled as he mentally ran through the checklist. This was perfect, and Quinn was going to love it.

"Quinn." His sister sounded much more awake now. "I'll make some calls."

"I'm headed to the hardware store. You know where the key is." Milo grinned as he said a quick goodbye. He loved Quinn, and this was going to make her smile.

Quinn belonged in a yellow kitchen with bright pictures. And she belonged with him.

Quinn flexed her shoulders, glad her shift had finally ended. She'd overseen two deliveries that had begun long before her ten-hour stint had started. Both mothers were fine, but they'd labored for more than twenty hours and were exhausted, as was the staff. And she'd wished Milo had been there to help.

It was silly to miss him when she'd seen him just this morning. She'd known a few people who claimed working with their significant other was stressful, but working with Milo was invigorating. He challenged and supported her.

Her stomach grumbled. The two deliveries had kept her from being able to run out to the food trucks that always parked across from the medical park that housed St. Brigit's, and the few items of questionable sustenance she'd procured from the vending machine had not staved off hunger for long.

Her belly growled again, and the gentleman on the other side of the elevator car looked at her. So many people didn't realize that hospital employees rarely got full lunch or dinner breaks. This wasn't the first time she'd come home with an empty stomach. But it was nothing that a sandwich and a hot shower couldn't fix.

The door to the apartment opened as she stepped out of the elevator. Milo leaned against the door frame, exhaustion coating his eyes, too.

"Are you okay?" Quinn asked as she kissed his cheek. "And how did you time opening the door for me when I got off the elevator?"

"I'm great." Milo dipped his lips to hers just as his

stomach rumbled. "A little hungry. I lost track of time and missed lunch. And I asked Jamison to let me know when you got here."

"You asked the doorman to look out for me?" Quinn smiled. "What did you get up to today?" Her stomach growled again. "And please tell me it involved cooking dinner."

"It didn't." Milo grinned. "But the pizza and beer I ordered were delivered ten minutes ago."

"Bless you." As Milo moved aside, Quinn stepped into the apartment and stopped. Her purse slipped from her fingers, landing with a thud.

She covered her heart with her hands as she stared at the bright yellow kitchen and the sunflower pictures hanging above the sink. It was the exact same color as her kitchen at the bungalow. Her pictures had been ones she'd painted, but these were wonderful, too.

All thoughts of her grumbling stomach flew from her mind as she looked at the happy kitchen.

This *gesture was...*

Her brain couldn't find the right word. It was the most thoughtful thing that anyone had ever done for her.

Turning, she stared at Milo. "You painted the kitchen." Her lip trembled as she looked at him. How did she thank him for this? It was too much and so perfect.

His smile was huge as he stepped closer to her and wrapped an arm around her waist. His lips brushed her lips as if he couldn't stand another minute of being apart, either.

Running her free hand over the countertop, she gazed at his hard work. He'd spent the entire day doing this—*for her*. "How did you manage to paint and decorate this all in one day?"

Milo dragged a hand through his hair as he looked at her. "I had a bit of help. I called my sister, and she found the drawings for me. Gina used a few of her designer con-

nections and had them delivered while I was painting."
Milo opened the cabinet. "She even found some of those
sunflower mugs that you had." He paused. "I know it's not
quite the same—"

Quinn kissed him. It wasn't her bungalow—it was better. It was a gift. The most perfect gift. Happiness raced
through her, a delirious sensation after a long day. She
deepened the kiss, enjoying the low moans echoing in Milo's throat.

He pulled back and gave her a warm smile. "I'm glad
you like it. Maybe we should paint the bedroom, too."

She laughed as he held her close. How could she not love
it? "Blue and green can be very relaxing."

Milo traced kisses along her jaw before capturing her
mouth.

She could melt into him, sink into the wonderful feelings
racing through her. Quinn threaded her fingers through his
hair. "Thank you."

He dipped his head to her neck. "I need to hop in the
shower before I eat. You don't have to wait for me. I won't
be long."

"Or I could join you." Quinn laughed as he grabbed her
hand and headed for the bathroom.

"This is one room that I wouldn't change a single thing
about." Quinn sighed as she watched Milo lean in to turn
on the shower. His backside was a work of art.

She licked her lips as she slid her hands down his tight
butt before unbuttoning the top of his jeans. She unzipped
his pants and loved the shift in his breathing—loved knowing that she turned him on so easily. Quinn stared at him
as she pulled his pants off and stroked him.

Milo's fingers grazed her stomach as he tugged her T-
shirt off. Her bra dropped to the floor next. "If you want
to focus on a shower, you need to step into it—now." His
voice was deep as he ripped his shirt over his head.

"And if I don't want to?" Quinn smiled as she kissed him and then slowly trailed her mouth down his magnificent body.

"Quinn…" Milo's moan sent goose bumps across her skin. She enjoyed nothing more than the sound of her name on his lips as she turned him on.

She kissed her way along his thighs, coming close to his manhood, but then moving away each time. Quinn smiled as Milo's large hands cupped her head.

"Quinn, love…"

She took him in her mouth then, loving the control. She gripped his butt and sighed at the sounds of pleasure echoing through him. He pulled her up and kissed her.

"God, Quinn." Milo shuddered as he sat her on the counter. "You are too amazing."

"Imagine if you'd let me finish." Quinn was surprised by the boldness in her voice. She had never been a bold lover, but with Milo, everything felt so easy.

Milo kissed the tender spot below her ear he'd found their first night together. "I have every plan to finish," he vowed, his thumb pressing against her nub as he watched her. Milo took one of her nipples between his lips as he continued to use his fingers to drive her closer to the edge.

"Milo…" Quinn's body moved against his. The way he was teasing her felt glorious, but it wasn't enough. She needed him. All of him…now.

"Milo," she repeated.

His tongue flicked her nipple, and her body erupted. "Want something?" His eyes dilated with pleasure as he met her gaze. "All you have to do is ask. I'll give you anything, Quinn. Anything."

"I need you." Quinn ran her hand down his length. "Now!"

Milo grabbed a condom from the drawer and sheathed himself quickly. Pressing against her, he captured her lips.

He put one hand around her waist and pressed the other to the mirror as he buried himself deep inside her.

Quinn gripped his shoulders, completely lost to the oblivion that was she and Milo.

"There's a new patient asking for you," Sherrie said, nodding to room six.

Quinn looked toward the room, then back at Sherrie. Patients often asked for specific midwives, but St. Brigit's had a rule that all midwives and OBs saw all patients because when a woman went into labor, a particular midwife or doctor might not be on call.

"A new patient?" Quinn looked at Sherrie. "Why is she asking for me?"

Sherrie shrugged. "Not sure. But her husband asked if they could speak to you before they left. I can always have Heather tell them you aren't available when she goes in to schedule their next appointment. But figured if you had a moment, I'd pass along the request."

"I have a moment." Quinn smiled. Maybe a friend from overseas had moved into the local area. More likely, one of her former patients had recommended St. Brigit's because of working with Quinn.

She opened the door and froze. A woman with curly dark hair was sitting on the edge of the exam table, a brilliant smile on her face. But it was the presence of the man in the room that kept her feet planted at the entryway.

"Quinn." Her brother's voice faltered a bit, but his eyes were soft as they met hers. "It's good to see you."

"Asher." Quinn stepped into the room and shut the door. Her chest was tight, as if she couldn't get enough oxygen. He'd been a teenager when their parents had cut contact with Quinn. She'd briefly hoped they might reconnect after Asher had divided their parents' estate, but her phone calls and texts had gone unanswered. She'd looked him up on social media a few times since, though not recently. But she'd never reached out—it was clear from his silence that he hadn't been interested in having a relationship with her.

What was he doing *here*? *Having a baby.*

They'd never been close, not even as children. She couldn't remember them playing together more than a handful of times. It could have been a survival technique. Since her parents' focus had always been on what she did wrong, Asher had had a bit more freedom. Now that he was here, all that distance didn't seem to matter so much.

He had a brilliant smile as he looked from Quinn to the woman on the table. "This is Samantha." Asher gestured to the woman before gripping her hand. She wasn't visibly pregnant, but St. Brigit's typically started seeing patients around the ten-week mark. "My wife," Asher added, beaming as he looked at her.

"Congratulations," Quinn murmured. She meant the words. No matter what, she would always want the best for her brother. And she couldn't remember ever seeing him smile like this. It made her smile, too.

"I couldn't find your address or phone number when we were sending out invitations. It was a tiny ceremony, about two years ago." Asher rubbed the back of his head. "Family stuff has never been my strong suit." His jaw hardened as he squeezed his wife's hand. "Though I'm learning."

They'd hardly had good role models to follow. "It is good to see you, Asher. And to meet you, Samantha." The moment was awkward, but how could any moment with a sibling be normal after so many years of no contact?

He swallowed. "I know this isn't the time or place for a reunion. But I saw your picture on the wall in the waiting room and I couldn't believe it." Asher shrugged. "I thought you were overseas. I checked a few times online. Even started a letter to you once, but I didn't know what to write."

So she hadn't been the only one unsure how to reach

out. Pushing through the discomfort, Quinn smiled. "I was. But I've been back for almost a year. It is good to see you, Asher, but I can't treat your wife. Not as a family member." Quinn looked at Samantha. "Not that I wouldn't like to…"

The door to the room opened and Milo stepped in. His fingers pressed briefly against her back as he said, "Asher." His tone was polite but firm.

"Milo." Asher nodded at him. "I must have been too focused on Quinn's picture to notice you worked here, too. This is my wife, Samantha."

Samantha waved. "It's nice to meet both of you, but we've probably taken up enough of your workday."

Samantha was right, but Quinn didn't want to waste the opportunity. She grabbed a paper towel, and wrote down her number. "Just in case."

Asher smiled as he stared at the number. "I'll text you. It was really good to see you, Quinn."

"You, too, Asher, and nice to meet you, Samantha. Your midwife will be in to see you in just a moment."

Once outside the exam room, Quinn leaned against the closed door for a minute before she looked at Milo. "Running to my rescue?"

"Yes." Milo dropped a quick kiss on the top of her head. "Though you seemed to have it under control."

"My heart is racing, and my brain still hasn't fully figured out what is going on. So much has happened so quickly."

Her hands were shaking, but she felt good. Surprisingly good. "I think I'm fine. Guess I'm going to be an aunt! Though I'm not sure how much Asher will want me to be involved. Probably not much."

"Or maybe he would love for his children to get to know their beautiful, smart, fun aunt Quinn. He didn't tell Samantha they should cancel their appointment and run when he saw your picture. Focus on the potential good outcome. At least for now."

Milo offered her a quick hug before rushing off down the hall to his next appointment.

So much had happened in the last month and a half, Quinn was realizing that LA could be just as much of an adventure as any of the places she'd worked before. Her skills were just as useful here as they'd been anywhere else. She smiled as she watched Milo duck into another patient's room. Her heart had been right to pull her here. Despite the fire, the sweet definitely outweighed the sour.

"Did he call?" Milo knew the answer as Quinn looked away from the phone and plastered on a fake smile. If Milo could thrash Asher, he would. "I'm sorry, Quinn."

What was wrong with her family? Why couldn't they see the incredible woman she was?

"It's fine." Her voice was tired as she slid down beside him on the couch. Her shoulders sagged. "At least he sent me his number. Maybe asking if he wanted to grab dinner was too much." Her lip trembled as she flipped her phone over. "No one ever wants to keep me."

The final phrase was so quiet Milo didn't know if Quinn realized she'd said it aloud. But it ripped through him.

How could she think that?

Her family, and that lout James, may have thrown away one of the best things to happen to them, but so many others hadn't. "That is *not* true," he whispered as he kissed her forehead.

Milo sat up and pulled her hands into his lap. He waited until she looked at him. "I have always kept you. Ever since you started that food fight, it's been you and me."

"Pretty sure *you* started that food fight." She smiled, but it didn't quite reach her eyes.

"I'm not the only one, either." Milo kissed the tip of

her nose. Her parents' desire to make her into something she wasn't, to force her into their mold and then withhold love when she didn't meet their impossible standards and routines, bordered on evil, in Milo's opinion. Especially because they'd doted on Asher. They had been capable of being loving parents and yet had chosen not to be with Quinn.

"Thanks, Milo." She kissed his cheek. "I shouldn't have said it, and certainly not to you. You're always there for me."

But her voice wasn't steady and the tears he saw her trying to hide nearly broke him. She didn't see herself the way others saw her, and that ended tonight.

"Your phone has the number for the head of Doctors Without Borders, right?"

"Yes, because I worked a few missions for them." Quinn shrugged.

"No. Julio has your number because you bonded late one night in some out-of-the-way place while he was still just one of their regular physicians. He calls you to ask your opinion because of how impressed he was with you." Milo paused. "And what about the hospital in Boston that has twice offered you a position as a senior midwife in their unit? And that's just in your professional life…

"There have been cards arriving here for the last two weeks from your friends around the world sorry to hear that your bungalow burned. Not to mention the box of clothes and photos that arrived yesterday, from someone named Christine, to replace some of what you lost."

Quinn's lips captured his, and Milo held her for a minute before pulling away. "Trying to silence me with kisses?"

Her lips tipped up as her dark eyes held his. "Maybe." Quinn leaned her head back. "It's uncomfortable to hear so many good things about myself."

Particularly when you grew up hearing so many bad things.

Quinn left those words unstated, but Milo knew she was thinking them. "If Asher doesn't want a relationship with you, that is *his* loss." Milo kissed the top of her head.

"I know." Quinn leaned against him. "I really do know that—objectively." She was silent for a minute before adding, "But he's my family, and it just hurts."

Rubbing her arm, Milo held her close. He'd grown up in a loving family. They'd supported him and never made him feel like he was anything other than a beloved son. He'd never felt like his mom loved him more or less than his sister. In his mother's eyes, they were equal.

"I'm here for you," Milo added, hoping it was enough.

"Thank you." Quinn sat up and smiled. "I lo—"

Her cell interrupted her, and Milo glared at it. What if Quinn was going to say I love you? But if Asher had interrupted... Well, it would be worth it to make Quinn happy. Though he'd give the man a hard time about it at some point.

Quinn answered, and he saw her eyebrows twitch before she smiled. It wasn't the giant smile that always sent such a thrill down his body, so it probably wasn't Asher. At least someone else had brightened her mood. She kissed his cheek and then stood up, walking into the kitchen as she continued the call.

"Florida?" Quinn laughed before looking over at him.

Florida? Milo's mind spun into overdrive. This was the call that he'd been terrified of since they'd started dating. She'd made connections all over the world—literally. It had always been only a matter of time before her phone rang again with news of a new opportunity, a new adventure.

Milo hadn't been kidding when he'd spoken about how many people wanted to work with Quinn. Even if her family had been unable to see the wonderful woman she was, her colleagues admired her greatly.

"I'll think about it."

Those words sent a splash of pain racing through him. Florida was on the other side of the country. An all-day plane trip away from him. His stomach knotted as she grinned and put her phone in her pocket.

"How do you feel about the Atlantic Ocean?" Quinn asked, handing him a beer.

"I've never really thought about it." That wasn't completely true. He'd rolled the idea of living and working somewhere else around his brain a few times since they'd started dating. He'd even stood in front of his wall of plans a few days ago. But the image of his father's face and his hand pointing to the nameplate kept floating in Milo's mind— a beacon that stayed his hand whenever he picked up the eraser, thinking about changing his plan.

"But I like California." That was true. He'd always felt his path was here, even as he watched Quinn plot her course around the world.

Quinn held up a finger. "Don't worry. I'm not actually planning on taking this position."

His heart lifted with joy before crashing. *This position.* She hadn't said that she wouldn't consider moving at all. His gaze flew to the yellow kitchen, and he racked his brain, trying to think of a way he could compete with the likely possibility that an offer would come that she would want to take.

"Why?" He hated the selfish thoughts running through his mind. But that didn't stop his need to know the answer.

Quinn paused as she looked at him. She opened her mouth, but closed it a second later. Then she shrugged. "Because I like where I'm at right now."

That wasn't what she'd thought about saying; he was nearly certain. Milo's heart yearned to hear what had been on the tip of her tongue before she'd swallowed it. He should be happy, thrilled, but the words *right now* pounded in his brain.

Quinn's gaze wandered to the window behind him. "But I have always wanted to run my own unit…"

"Is that what the job is? Does that mean you *are* thinking about it?" Milo tried to gauge the look in her eyes. She almost looked like she was trying to talk herself out of it.

"No, I'm not considering it. But thinking about running my own unit makes me smile." Quinn tapped his knee. Her voice was bright, but he could hear the bit of longing in it. "But I'm not moving to Florida. So, you don't need to worry about it. Florida's not high on my list of places I want to work."

List of places?

His throat constricted as he looked at her. How long was that list? His brain was spinning as he tried to focus.

"But you said you'd think about it?" Milo knew he shouldn't press, but there was something about the glint in her eye when she'd mentioned running her own unit. The head of St. Brigit's had at least another ten years before she retired. That was a long time to wait. If Quinn really wanted to run her own unit soon—it wouldn't be here.

"Terri is persistent!" Quinn laughed. "If I'd said no right away, he'd say I hadn't thought it through and my inbox would be full of emails detailing the wonders of Orlando. I bet he'd even offer Disney World tickets."

"Anaheim is less than thirty miles from here. We can see Mickey anytime." Milo hated the defensiveness in his tone.

"When did you become such a Disney fan?" Quinn smiled as she set her beer down. "I seem to remember you complaining about the ticket prices, parking and lines when we went as teenagers. It was a very grown-up complaint, if memory serves." Her lips pressed against his cheek as her fingers tracked his thigh.

"The lines *were* long, and it *was* hot. But we still had a great time." Milo had taken her for their sixteenth birthdays, excited to be able to drive them there himself. For a moment that day, he'd considered kissing her. He'd looked at Quinn and wondered what if...? But the moment had passed.

But she was here now. Her fingers slid up to the waistband of his jeans, and the memory flew from his brain. "You're trying to distract me," Milo murmured as Quinn placed light kisses along his jawline.

"There is nothing more to discuss. I'm not interested in the Orlando job. What I am interested in..." Her fingers slid inside his pants, and Milo lost his ability to reason. There would be plenty of time to work out a plan.

Plenty of time.

CHAPTER EIGHT

"Quinn!" Opal called from the registration desk. "Can you do a quick review of this transfer chart?"

"Sure." Quinn took the tablet from Opal's outstretched hand. It was unusual for a patient to transfer their care from St. Brigit's, but sometimes the facility wasn't a good fit. Or, if the pregnancy was high risk, they'd recommend delivering at a nearby hospital instead. But before they transferred a patient's records, a midwife or OB had to do a quick review of the chart to make sure everything was in order.

Her stomach shook as she stared at the name on the chart: Samantha Davis. "I can't do the review." Even if it wasn't against policy for her to review her brother's wife's chart, Quinn couldn't have stomached it. Why had Asher asked to see her if he was just going to ghost her again?

Pain trickled across her skin. She knew it wouldn't be visible to anyone, but her whole body ached at th…th… the… Her heart screamed *betrayal*, but her mind refused to accept the word. *Denial*.

Asher had never spoken up on her behalf. Never interjected to support her as she'd argued that she didn't want to do the activities her parents thought were best, even though she'd seen him roll his eyes at her mother's daily schedules, too. She could forgive him for not realizing how differently their parents treated them when they were children—no child should think their parents capable of only loving one of their children—but the inequity in their family had been so glaring, he had to have seen it as a teenager and as a young adult. And yet he'd said nothing; he'd just accepted it.

She couldn't have treated his wife. As a family member, the relationship was too personal.

Even for a family that never spoke.

But apparently just being in the same facility as Quinn was too much. The hurt spun through her as she stared at her brother's name on the forms. They had the same last name, had lived in the same house for sixteen years, but that hadn't been enough to bind them.

"Quinn?" Opal's question drew her back to reality. "Are you okay?"

No. She was going to lose it, and she couldn't do that here. Not now. "Yes, but Samantha Davis is my brother's wife. So, you will need one of the other midwives or doctors to review this before the transfer." She was impressed that her voice didn't break, even as a piece of her spirit shattered.

"Ah-hh." Opal's eyes widened. "I didn't know you had a brother."

Why wouldn't your brother want his wife to deliver here? That was the question hovering in Opal's eyes, but Quinn knew she wouldn't ask it. At least, not to Quinn. This was going to be fodder for gossip, but what answer could Quinn give?

"Oh, Dr. Russell." Opal's eyes brightened as Milo joined them. "Since you're here, can you do a quick patient review for me?"

Milo's gaze slid to Quinn. She saw the recognition flash across his face as he made the logical leap to why she wasn't the one reviewing the records.

Milo knew Asher hadn't returned her invitation to dinner. Hadn't even texted a polite "too busy." He knew it hurt, even if Quinn tried to pretend that it didn't. His hand brushed her back as he leaned over to take the tablet. It was a small motion, one that no one else would notice, but it sent a flood of comfort through her, and her heart clung to it.

He'd been a bit odd after Terri had called to offer her the job in Orlando, though she'd tried her best to quiet his fears. Before coming back to California, Quinn would have jumped at the offer—the adventure of running her own unit.

But moving didn't hold the appeal it once had. Milo's closeness settled her. From the moment she'd arrived at LAX, the pull of the road had relaxed. The driving need to move, to find a new place—her place—had almost vanished.

Her place was here.

That probably would have terrified her if it wasn't for Milo. Maybe his need to control life's chaos really did balance her need to be propelled by her emotions and gut instinct.

The idea of running her own unit was appealing, but another opening would present itself eventually. That was one lesson she'd learned. Life had a habit of providing opportunities that surprised you. Maybe not always with happiness and joy, but those things would be mixed in, too.

"Molly is in room two for a postpartum follow-up." The nurse's aide's voice was taut as she walked toward them, looking from Quinn to Milo. "She checked off three items on her postpartum depression survey, and she's trying to hold back tears."

"Okay." Quinn took the tablet and headed toward room two. At least this gave her something to focus on. More than fifteen percent of women suffered from postpartum depression, but many still felt there was shame in admitting it.

In Quinn's experience, if a recently delivered mother was acknowledging there was a problem, that was a win. But if they checked more than two boxes, they were also probably experiencing additional symptoms.

"Molly." Quinn smiled as she walked into the room. Her son was asleep in his carrier and Molly was chewing on a fingernail. "How are you feeling?"

"Fine!" Molly's response was too bright. Her hair was unkempt, and there were bags under her eyes and spit-up on her clothes. All symptoms of having a newborn at home. But the watery eyes, anxious glances at her son and nail biting sent a bead of worry through Quinn.

"It's okay if you're not."

Molly's eyes darted between Quinn and the door.

"What's going on?"

She tapped her chewed fingernails against her knees before letting out a sigh that was nearly a sob. "I wanted to be a mother for so long." Molly's lips shook. "Then we adopted Owen. It was amazing. *Is amazing.* But when we found out I was pregnant..." Molly closed her eyes and hugged herself tightly. "It felt like I was going to get to experience something I missed with Owen." Molly hiccupped and wiped a tear away.

"If I can't be happy now, what kind of mom does that make me?" Molly looked at Quinn, and the dam of emotions broke. Tears cascaded down her cheeks, and she sucked in a breath.

"It makes you a mom who is dealing with the stress of having two children and a body that's been through a trial, because birth is hard. There's a reason we call it labor!" Quinn patted Molly's knee. "This is not uncommon. It isn't."

"I want to run away when Adam cries." Molly's cheeks flamed as she told the dark secret. "I never felt that way with Owen. And Owen is clingy, which I know is to be expected with the new baby. But after what feels like marathon breastfeeding sessions with Adam, snuggling with Owen is too much. That isn't how a good mom responds."

"Yes. It is, sometimes." Quinn looked at Molly. "This is

postpartum depression, and you cannot just force it away. There is no shame in saying it. You're very brave for telling me these things."

"Owen is into everything, and I am trying to make sure he doesn't feel left out, but Adam is up all the time, and breastfeeding hasn't been super easy. My mother took Owen last weekend to give us a bit of a break. It's easier with one." Molly let out an uncomfortable laugh as she stared at her son.

That statement cut at Quinn's heart. She'd heard the same from countless mothers. The fact that her own mother had only wanted one, and would have liked to return her adopted daughter, didn't have any bearing on what was going on with Molly.

"I bet it was," Quinn agreed and nodded when Molly's mouth gaped.

"I'm terrible." Molly wiped a tear away.

"No, you're not." Quinn kept her voice level but firm. "There is nothing wrong with the truth, Molly. You've gone from having a wonderful, lovely toddler—who, by your own description, is into everything—and added a newborn to the mix. And your body is still healing. How did you feel when Owen was gone?"

"A little more relaxed. But I missed him terribly. He only stayed one night before I asked Mom to bring him home." She ran the tissue under her nose and then sighed. "I can't stop crying, and I feel like a failure."

Reassuringly, Quinn tapped Molly's hand. "You are a good mother. Do you know how I know?"

Molly shook her head, but didn't answer.

"Because you love your children. That is what matters. It's what they…" Quinn swallowed the lump that had unexpectedly materialized in her throat. "It's what they remember most—the love."

Especially if it isn't given.

But she left that last thought unstated.

"Now, let's get *you* taken care of."

"Are you okay?"

Milo's question hit her as she stared at the charred hill in the distance. She didn't have an easy answer. How had it been less than two months since she'd sat and avoided looking out this window while her home burned? And how had so much changed?

"I don't know." The truth slipped through Quinn's lips. After discovering that Asher and his wife had transferred their care, and dealing with the emotions of Molly's post-partum issues, Quinn felt drained. Her tank was empty.

Milo's arms wrapped around her, and Quinn sighed but didn't step away. "We're at work."

"And you've had a long day," Milo kissed the top of her head as he released her. "I am sorry about Asher."

"It's not just him." Quinn hugged herself.

"Is it the Orlando job?" Milo's voice was tight.

"What?" Quinn frowned. This was the fourth time he'd brought it up over the last three days. Why would he not drop it? She'd sent a polite refusal to Terri this morning. Though he'd sent back the standard request to give it one more thought, Quinn knew Terri wouldn't press. "No, it's that Molly has postpartum depression. She made some comments about it being easier with only one kid. She loves her children, and with medication and the support group Sherrie set up several years ago, she is going to be fine. But with Asher's refusal to contact me and her having an older adopted son, my brain is just spinning."

"That's to be expected," Milo stated. "The last two months would have overloaded anyone. It doesn't make you weak for being tired—and maybe even a little furious at the universe."

She shook her head as he offered her a lopsided smile.

"Maybe I need to get away." She looked at the hills and sighed. A small holiday would be nice, and they both had a healthy amount of vacation days stocked up.

"Away?" Milo's voice caught as he looked at her.

"Sure, running away—" The unit alarm interrupted her. She looked at Milo. "Who is in labor?"

"No one," Milo called as he raced for the door.

Was there no time for anyone to breathe?

Maybe it was too soon, but they were going to take a vacation together. Maybe she could convince Milo to throw a dart on a map and just go.

"It's time to push," Milo ordered as Tien gripped Quinn's hand. The woman had labored at home for almost nine hours and she'd been eight centimeters when she'd walked in. Her husband had boarded a plane on the east coast as soon as he could once her labor started, but he was still at least two hours out. Milo understood why she was so distraught, but babies waited for no one.

"My husband isn't here." Tien let out a wail as Quinn helped her get into position. She'd repeated that line every few minutes since arriving. Probably hoping that the mantra would either speed up his arrival or delay the baby's.

"I know." Quinn's voice was soft as she held Tien's gaze. "I know he wants to be here, too."

That was true. Milo had served as Tien's primary OB over the last nine months. Her husband had been to every appointment but the last one, when his job had sent him to DC for a week, but he'd video-called. Tien had still had four weeks before her due date—but babies rarely adhered to scheduled dates, unfortunately. If Milo had been a betting man, he'd have bet that Tien had at least two more weeks before delivering her first child.

Quinn pressed a cloth to Tien's forehead. "Your son or daughter is going to be here soon. And then you'll get to introduce your new child to your husband when he arrives." Quinn took a deep breath. "But right now, it's time for you to do your job. Dr. Russell and I are here for you."

Her voice was the perfect mix of comforting and authoritative. Tien let out a small cry as she sat up.

Milo nodded to Quinn. She was impressive. Even after the long day, and the shock of learning that Asher's wife had requested to transfer her care, Quinn was taking care of another mother. With no hint of the turmoil that Milo knew she must be experiencing.

"All right, Tien. Push!" Milo ordered.

Milo found Quinn cooing over Tien's tiny daughter as she sat with the new mother. They'd been off the clock for almost two hours, but traffic from LAX was so bad that Tien's husband still hadn't made it to the hospital. So, she'd stayed at St. Brigit's to keep her company while Milo ran home to get some dinner ready.

He'd done his best to make sure everything at home would be just right when he finally managed to get Quinn to leave St. Brigit's. Her quip about running away was still sending chills through him. After the day she'd had—hell, the last several weeks she'd had—he could understand the sentiment, but it still frightened him.

They both needed a hot meal and a full night of sleep. Quinn should be dead on her feet after the day's emotional roller-coaster ride, but you would never be able to guess it from the happy laughs coming from Tien's room. How was he so lucky to have found such a terrific partner?

Milo's heart ached as he watched Quinn take the little girl from Tien. She cuddled the baby, and he saw her shoulders relax just a bit. She'd discussed children a few times over the years. Always wistfully, like she didn't know if she'd ever get the chance.

But staring at Quinn with a child in her arms, Milo felt

the future tug at him. She'd be an excellent mother. She'd fight for her children and make sure they never doubted her love.

And he wanted to be the one standing next to her through all of it. Wanted to plan a life that included family and fun, and endless happy memories.

"Dr. Russell!" Tien's husband, Jack, ran toward him with a man who was nearly his mirror image. "Where's Tien?"

"Deep breaths, son," the other man said.

"Room five." Milo nodded toward the doorway.

"Thank you." Jack's father grinned as he watched his son run into the room. "The nurse at the front desk told him the same thing, but I'm not sure his brain fully heard it in his rush."

"Understandable." Milo nodded to Quinn as she exited the room and gestured to the employee lounge before heading to grab her things.

Jack's father leaned over and peered through the door. "I can't wait to meet my granddaughter, but I think my son and daughter-in-law deserve a few minutes before Papa intrudes." The pride radiating off the man was intoxicating. "Not sure there's a better moment than seeing your son hold his own child."

The words hung in the space around Milo, pushing at him as he watched Jack's father wipe a tear from his eye and turned to go meet his new granddaughter. This was a moment Milo's father had never had—and would never get. The small ache that never left him throbbed and a wave of unexpected grief passed over him.

For a moment, Milo was a kid again. Reaching for his dad. But the memory was foggy, like so many of them were. And his voice refused to come to Milo.

Quinn's hand was warm as it slipped into his. "What's wrong?"

The quiet words drew him back to the present, and her

presence grounded him. How did you explain that you'd lost your dad's memory? That it was easier to draw his face to your mind only after you looked at his picture? That you felt like a failure for not keeping his memory closer?

The right words didn't appear, and Milo wasn't certain he was strong enough to utter them if they did.

"Long day." He threw his arm around Quinn's shoulders. "But it's nothing a plate of hot food, a shower, and a night in your arms won't fix."

She raised an eyebrow, and Milo could see her desire to call out the lie. Instead, she patted his chest just over his heart and kissed his cheek. "Let's go home."

Quinn was curled on the couch reading when Milo's phone buzzed. He'd been in his study for most of the afternoon. He'd said he was catching up on paperwork, but the two times that Quinn had peered in the door, he'd been staring at his planning boards. She'd asked if he needed any help, but he'd just kissed her and told her he was fine.

Ever since coming home after Tien's birth, Milo had been… Her brain searched for the right word. *Reflective.*

If she asked, he said it was nothing, but she knew that wasn't true. Something was bothering him, and he hadn't told Quinn what it was. It felt like he was actively keeping it from her.

Milo had maintained his planning boards for as long as Quinn had known him. They gave him a sense of peace, of control. He only adjusted them when he was certain of the plan he wanted to follow.

And her name hadn't appeared anywhere on them.

It was selfish to want it when she'd ordered him not to plan out their relationship. Told him not to focus too far into the future. But she was surprised by how much she wanted the confirmation that he saw her there, wanted the security of knowing what five years from now looked like. It was terrifying for a woman who'd spent the last decade care-fully avoiding any sort of long-term plan. Yet she couldn't force the desire away.

When the phone buzzed again, she pushed away the prickle of panic as she answered. "Hi, Diana. Milo is in his study doing…" Quinn hesitated. She had no idea what was keeping him so long. "Something," she finished lamely.

Milo's mother let out a soft laugh. "Knowing my son, he's probably planning something. Or adjusting a plan, or thinking about adjusting a plan."

Quinn chuckled, too, but the sound was false, even to her own ears. She was certain that was what Milo was up to, and part of her wanted to ask what changes he was mak-ing. Most important, if they included her.

They'd moved in together before they'd even officially started dating. They were happy. *They were!* But occasion-ally he looked at her and she could see the doubt hovering in his eyes. And it had been there several times since she'd been offered the job in Florida.

Was he waiting for her to leave?

Pushing the thought to the side, Quinn stood up and wandered to the kitchen. "I suspect you're right about the plans. It's his favorite hobby."

"Yes," his mother stated, an underlying note to the word that Quinn couldn't place.

"Is there something I can do for you?"

"Felix and I are having a barbecue this weekend. We usually try to plan these things out. Otherwise, Milo or Gina—or both—are busy. But the weather is going to be so nice."

There was something she wasn't saying… Quinn was almost certain, but then she shook herself. Now she was looking for things to worry about with Milo's mom? She needed to get control of herself. "We aren't on call this weekend. What should I bring?"

"How about some dessert? Gina's already promised the dip—which I know Milo hates."

Quinn laughed. "Well, dessert is easy enough."

"Wonderful!" She could hear Diana's smile through the phone. "I can't wait to see you, Quinn—and Milo, too."

Diana had been thrilled when they'd told her they were dating. Quinn had always felt comfortable around his mother and sister, but they were really making her feel like part of the family.

An important part, not just Milo's girlfriend.

"Your parents are having a barbecue this weekend," Quinn stated as soon as she stepped into his study.

Milo turned in his chair, and Quinn looked at the wall behind him. The plans hadn't changed. There was still nothing to indicate he saw her as part of his five- or ten-year plan.

Stop it!

Her heart pounded at her brain's warning. She was not going to fall into the trap she'd fallen into so many times. She wasn't going to look for things that might mean she'd get hurt.

She wasn't.

"And I'll bet Gina's bringing that dip I hate. Well, this time, we'll bring our own," Milo said with a rueful shake of his head.

"I already promised we'd bring dessert." She giggled as he threw his hands in the air. Quinn had heard his dip rant several times over the years. She wasn't even sure Gina liked the dip she brought, but she loved seeing Milo act overly put off by it. And Milo enjoyed the show as much as his sister.

What would life have been like if Quinn and Asher had had inside jokes like that? Had made silly games that annoyed their parents but made each other laugh? Had been partners *and* siblings? It would have been a whole different world. A fun world.

If Milo and Quinn had kids, she hoped they'd be friends, too.

The air rushed from Quinn's lungs as she stared at Milo. Children were a topic Quinn had always tried to push to the back of her mind, but whenever she held a newborn, part of her briefly wondered what it would feel like to cuddle her own.

And now, even though she and Milo had only been dating a few weeks, she could already imagine him snuggling with a little one that had her dark hair and his nose. Could imagine him playing games and encouraging their kids to get along and be friends.

"You okay?"

Milo pulled her close and she sank into his heat. Her heart pounded as the desire for a family—her family—nearly overwhelmed her. "I feel like I should be asking you that."

Milo kissed her cheek, but didn't comment.

"Maybe one day I'll have an inside joke with the Russell family, too."

Milo chuckled and dropped a kiss across her temple. "Challenge accepted."

She laughed as she laid her head against his shoulder. It was a simple statement, but she heard her future in it. Her name might not be on any of those boards—yet—but one way or another, she was going to add a few items to those boards. Items that would fulfill both their dreams.

"You look so happy." Milo's mother squeezed his hand as she looked at Quinn.

Quinn was rocking a friend's baby on the porch. He felt his mind start calculating. If he told her he loved her in three weeks, proposed in six months, then they married six months from that, they could be parents in the next three or four years.

He'd almost adjusted his list a few times over the past week. But each time he'd raised his eraser, his hand had refused to move. Quinn had a list of places she wanted to work. Milo had *a* place he needed to work. There had to be a way to reconcile the two, but he hadn't found it yet.

His mother started pulling fruit trays from the refrigerator. She looked out the window over the sink and smiled. A faraway look came over her features as she stared at the gathered mass outside. "I love having everyone here. Love having the entire weekend off."

"It's nice," Milo agreed as he took a sip of his water. Her distant tone sent shivers along his arms, but he didn't know why.

"I want to do it more often." His mother crossed her arms and looked at him.

He looked out the window and grinned. Today had been close to perfect. The weather had been fine, the food delicious. He wasn't sure he could have planned a finer day if he'd had weeks to do it.

Milo shrugged. "Sure. A little more planning might be a good idea. We got lucky this time, but there is no telling when we might all have the day off again. Babies don't generally hold their deliveries for barbecues."

"Sometimes it's nice not to plan." She looked at him and leaned close. "I want to clear my schedule a bit."

Milo looked at his mother. Her smile was bright, but she was bouncing on her heels.

What was going on?

"Meaning?"

"Felix and I are planning to retire."

"Really?" Milo was stunned. His brain clicked through a multitude of responses as it reeled at the news. This couldn't be—his mother and Felix loved their clinic. They'd just started the birthing center. "I'm…" His mouth seemed stuck. "Stunned," he finally managed.

"I know. But we don't want to work for the rest of our lives. And it seems like the right time to start dialing back."

"Wow," Milo breathed out. He'd always seen his mom at the clinic, had always thought of it as hers. He'd never considered that she and Felix would want to move on. In his mind, that was where they belonged. *Always*.

"So, what are you doing about the clinic, the birthing center?" His throat burned, and Milo took a sip of water to force the uncomfortable sensation away. His mother had taken the job at Oceanside Clinic just after his father died. Her professional relationship with Felix had bloomed into friendship that had eventually turned to love. Milo couldn't imagine Oceanside without them. Didn't want to imagine a stranger running such a special place.

"We were hoping you might want to take it over." His mother's eyes shimmered as they looked at him.

He could see the hope in her gaze. The need. She expected him to take it. To want it. And part of him did.

"I know your father would like the idea, too."

The words set his heart racing. He tried to pull on that thread. Tried to imagine what his father might say, but all he could pull up was the trip to Valley General. His dad bending close to him, saying something about running the unit. Even now, with everything his mother had said, the shadowy image sent chills down his back.

"Milo, you are the best person I can think of to run Oceanside Clinic." His mother smiled. "You helped design the birthing center. It should be you."

Why was she making this so difficult?

She rubbed his hand, and hundreds of memories of them working together at Oceanside jumped into his mind. His first and last day, the babies they'd cooed over, the difficult days when everything had gone wrong. He had a lifetime of memories there.

And only one solid one of his dad.

His mother nodded toward the window. "The birthing center needs a head midwife, too." Her eyes were bright. Maybe she'd expected him to scream no immediately. He should put her hope aside and explain his decision, but the words were caught in his throat.

"Nancy only planned to get it off the ground. She's been talking about retirement for the last three years. I'd planned to talk to Quinn about the position—even before I knew you were together. She's perfect for it."

"She is," Milo agreed. His tongue felt tied. He knew Quinn would love being the head midwife at the birthing center, and that she'd excel at it.

"I know you've dreamed of running a big hospital unit—"

"I haven't *just* dreamed of it," Milo interrupted, and immediately felt heat travel up his neck, but he continued. He had to make his mother understand why his answer had to be no. "I feel called to it. Led to it…by dad."

His mother sighed, but she didn't look away. "Are you prepared for everything you will have to sacrifice?" His mother's eyes darted to the back patio.

Turning his head, Milo couldn't stop the smile spreading across his face. Quinn was dancing barefoot in the grass with the neighbor's granddaughter. She was laughing as they spun around, and his heart expanded as she collapsed on the grass with the young girl.

"I'm not going to have to sacrifice anything." Quinn knew about his plans. She'd seen his boards. She knew what a life with him looked like.

Didn't she?

"With the right plan, you can avoid—"

"Life doesn't always care about your plans," his mother

snapped. "As you are so fond of saying, babies don't care about schedules, or birthdays or anniversaries. Children don't care that you're on call. They have dance recitals, baseball games, all sorts of activities. As a physician, you are already going to miss some, but if you run a large unit…" She shook her head. "At Oceanside, you and Quinn could control more of your schedule, your life."

Why was she pushing this? How could his mother not understand? "If you could have seen him that day at Valley General, felt what I felt—what I still feel—you'd understand."

"Milo, you are allowed your own dreams." She smiled. It was the look she'd used when he was a kid and she was trying to coax him into finding the right answer on his own.

"This is my dream." Milo shook his head. How could she not understand? Part of him needed this. And it was larger than the unruly piece of his heart that screamed he belonged at Oceanside Clinic.

"Is it?" She stepped closer. "Or are you trying to make up for something that was never your fault?" Her hands trembled, and she wrapped her arms around her waist. "Listen to me. Your father died in a car accident. That was *not* your fault."

"If I hadn't put off my science fair project…" He hated how small his voice sounded. How it made him face the feeling of failure that had never fully left him.

His mother's warmth seeped into his chest. He wasn't sure when she'd reached out to hug him. Still, he let her hold him as the energy and anger drained from him.

Milo blew out a breath. He loved his mother. But the hole his father's death had left could never be filled. That was the way it was with his grief—it never fully went away. He just learned to move around it, to walk with it.

After several minutes, she raised her head and stroked his cheek. "Milo, for the hundredth time, it wasn't about a poster board. And it wasn't about the flowers he went to get because of our fight, either. It was bad timing, and another person's poor decision-making." She held him tightly.

"Your father loved every minute of his life. He loved you and me and Gina. And he understood that you don't get guarantees." She smiled as she looked at Milo. "The last thing he would have wanted was for you to be unhappy."

Milo shook his head. "I'm not unhappy." It was true. He enjoyed his work at St. Brigit's, was looking forward to competing for the Valley General position when it opened. Just because he loved Oceanside didn't mean he had to give up the dream he'd had for so long.

She kissed his cheek. "Your father would have loved Oceanside, too. He sometimes talked about owning his own practice."

"He did?" That revelation stunned him. He racked his brain, but he couldn't think of a single time he'd heard that before.

His mother sighed, and her eyes drifted to the side. "Parents are always more than their children see, at least when they are young." Her hand wrapped around his. "On rough days, your dad even talked about becoming a full-time writer. I always thought he was joking, but there were three unfinished fantasy manuscripts at the bottom of his filing cabinet that I found…" She bit her lip and waved a hand. "The point is, he had many dreams. And he would want you to live yours."

Running the Valley General unit was his dream…wasn't it? The thing that promised him comfort? The thing he wanted terribly? It was. "My career is in LA."

Her fingers patted his cheek before she turned to grab the fruit platter. "I know that's what your plans say, sweetheart. Just make sure it's what *you* really want." Then she headed back out onto the patio, leaving him alone with his thoughts and memories.

CHAPTER NINE

MILO HAD KISSED her and then disappeared into his study as soon as they got home. Did he know that his mother had talked to her about running the birthing center at the Oceanside Clinic? Surely, she'd discussed it with him. But each time Quinn had tried to broach the topic on the ride home, Milo had changed the subject.

He hadn't even attempted to be subtle about it. She knew he liked working together at St. Brigit's. But he wasn't going to stay there forever. He'd brought up St. Brigit's new hire and the empty spot left at Valley General only once, but she knew how much he wanted that position.

If she accepted Diana's offer, they could live halfway. But that meant at least an hour and a half commute with traffic for each. And if they were on call, it would be easier to stay at the hospital than to come home.

How long could they last living that way?

She preferred the hominess of birthing centers. The personal care she got to give with only having a few women giving birth on any one day. She'd been at hospitals where she'd helped deliver a dozen babies during her shift. There wasn't time to enjoy the newborn's snuggles, to help a new mom acclimate to breastfeeding, or to answer the dozens of questions that arose in the first hours of new life.

None of those needs had gone unseen. But *she* hadn't been able to take her moms from prenatal to postpartum care. And Quinn loved that aspect of the job. It was what put the bounce in her step when she went in for each shift.

Milo loved it, too. Loved watching the joy that came with new life. And he was going to miss it terribly if he ran the ob-gyn unit at Valley General and had to focus much of his time on the minutia of making a unit run well.

Resolved, she started for the study. If they were to have a future together, they needed to get on the same page. And Quinn was done letting him change the topic…and done avoiding it herself.

He didn't turn around as she entered the study. He'd been in here for almost an hour, but none of the tension she'd seen in the car had leaked from him. Whatever was going on, she could help him—talk him through it, like he'd talked her through so many things in the last few weeks alone.

"So, I take it my mother told you that she and my stepfather are planning to retire?"

His voice was distant as she stepped up beside him. Quinn knocked his hip with hers, trying to push a bit of the rigidity from him. "She did. I expect that we shall be getting a lot more barbecue invitations in the future."

He nodded, but his eyes never wavered from the wall before them. "They want me to run Oceanside Clinic when they retire."

The words stunned Quinn. Diana hadn't mentioned that when she'd discussed the midwife job with her. Her heart pounded in her chest. That would solve all the problems she'd been worrying about for the past ten minutes. "Really! That would be perfect. You would be so good—"

"I told her no." Milo's words were flat as they fell between them.

Quinn was shocked. "No? Just no? Without even telling her you'd think about it?" She knew he had his plans. But this was the chance to run his own clinic. A place he loved.

"I don't need to think about it." A nerve twitched in

Milo's jaw as he stared at the wall of goals in front of him. "I've already made the necessary decisions about my future," Milo said, gesturing to the words scrawled in front of him.

"Your future?" The words slipped through Quinn's numb lips.

Not *our* future...

Stepping between him and the boards, Quinn waited for Milo to look at her. Her chest was knotted, but her voice was steady. "These are whiteboards. Do you know what is wonderful about them?" She ran her hand across one and held up her finger stained with red ink. "You can figure out what you want and alter the plan."

She trembled as she stared at him. She'd never touched his boards. They were sacred to him. A physical homage to his father. She'd crossed a line, but she couldn't go back now.

Her heart stung as she looked at him. Her parents had been rigid. Milo wasn't a rigid person—he planned, liked to know what he was doing, but he could adjust.

Couldn't he?

"Why can't you even consider changing them for this opportunity?"

"Because I'm not impulsive! Not..." Milo pulled his hand across his face.

"Not flighty. Is that what you mean? Never flying off to parts unknown for a position, right?" Her lips trembled as she wrapped her arms around her waist.

"That wasn't what I was going to say." Milo's voice was firm, but he still wouldn't look at her.

She wanted to challenge him, and her heart ached as he stared at the erased marks on his board. They were just notes, writings that could be replaced.

She waited a moment longer, wishing he'd look at her.

Just her. Then she turned. If she spoke, Quinn worried it was going to be something hurtful.

Bottling up the pain pushing through her, she headed for the door. She knew he wouldn't follow her, and that crushed her spirit a bit further. They each needed some time to blow off steam, but she still wished that he would run after her.

Her cell phone rang as she grabbed her keys. She hit Ignore as she walked out. She didn't have a goal in mind—she just needed to be somewhere else.

Anywhere else.

She'd walked through the small park by the apartment three times before her phone rang again. It wasn't Milo's ring, and her heart seized when she saw her old traveling nurse agency's number. Swallowing, Quinn answered. It never hurt to listen, to think about possibilities, to have a backup plan.

A backup plan...

The simple thought crushed her soul. But she pressed Answer on her phone.

"Quinn! I have the perfect position for you!" Isla didn't wait for Quinn to say hello. The staffing adviser was one of the bubbliest individuals Quinn had ever met. "It's in Maine, and you don't have to be there for three months. It's a six-month rotation as the lead of a midwifery unit, while the head midwife is out on maternity leave."

Quinn puffed out a breath. It was as far from Milo as she could get and still remain in the continental US. She looked up at the high-rise complex and rubbed a tear away. "I'm not sure. Can you give me a few days?"

"Of course. But there is actually another position I need to fill, too. Do you know a Sherrie Foster? She works at St. Brigit and applied a few months ago. She's very qualified for the other midwife position at this unit. The traveling nurse there now plans to rotate out in a few months, too."

"She's wonderful." Quinn wrapped an arm around her

waist. Sherrie had mentioned applying. Quinn had told her that she'd be a reference, but Sherrie hadn't mentioned it again. "She'd be a good fit for the head position, too, if I decide to turn it down."

Quinn kicked a rock. Could she take the position at Oceanside if she and Milo weren't destined for forever?

No.

The word resounded in her head. Her phone beeped, and she quickly told Isla that she'd let her know in a few days.

Come home...please. Milo's text sent chills racing across her heart. Was it her home? All of this had happened so quickly. And she'd erased part of one of his boards.

What had come over her? Fear.

She wanted Milo to choose her. To rewrite his plans or to at least include her in discussions about the future. She needed to know that he saw her dreams as part of his future, too.

Milo paced back and forth, trying to calm himself. His brain had panicked when Quinn had held up her ink-stained finger. No one erased his boards. They were his connection to his father—erasing them felt almost like betrayal.

But in his frustration, he'd lashed out. Impulsive might not sound like a horrid thing to fling into a conversation, but he'd known how she might take it. And then he hadn't been able to do anything but stare at the blank spaces she'd left. She'd wiped it all away so easily.

How different would his life be if he could do that? And why hadn't he chased after her already?

Milo wanted her home. And with each passing minute, his stomach sank further. He'd gone to the door three times, thinking he'd heard her, only to be met with the curious stare of his neighbor.

He'd called, and she hadn't answered. Then he'd sent the text. He looked at his phone. Quinn had read it twenty minutes ago and hadn't responded. What if he'd driven her away for good? He didn't want to lose Quinn.

Pressing his hand to his forehead, Milo hit Call on his phone again. He heard Quinn's phone ring in the hallway outside and tripped over a shoe in his rush to get to the door. His knees collided with the tiled floor, but Milo didn't care. Quinn was here.

"I am so sorry."

"I'm sorry."

They each said the words at the same time as Quinn rushed to his side. Milo stood, ignoring the pain in his knees as he held her. "I should not have let you think that I thought you impulsive or flighty, and I should have immediately come after you. I am so sorry."

"I shouldn't have wiped away part of your board." Quinn rested her head against his shoulder. "I know how much those mean. I just…" Her words were firm. "I just wanted you to think about it."

Milo stiffened. He had thought about it. Maybe not today, or at least not as much today, but years ago. Even if he wasn't trying to honor his father. Oceanside wasn't what he wanted.

At least, it wasn't the only thing he wanted—was it?

Why did his brain keep coming back to that thought? Milo had charged down this path for years. With the potential opening at Valley General, it was finally within his grasp—finally, he could be close to his dad again.

So why did it feel like his heart was leaning away from it now that the opportunity was here?

"What if I consider it for a few days?" He hadn't meant for the question to exit his mind.

Quinn's eyes met his. An emotion he feared was doubt hovered in them. "I promise to think about it, Quinn. It's just… I've had my career path laid out for years. I swore I'd do this for my dad."

"What about what you want?" Quinn's voice was quiet, but he felt her stiffen in his arms.

Leaning back, he looked at her. Why did his heart have to want so many conflicting things? "Give me a couple of days to think about it."

She smiled, but it wasn't quite full. "That's all I'm asking."

She kissed his cheek, but the fear coating his heart didn't disappear.

Was that really all she was asking? And what if he didn't change his mind?

Milo kept those questions buried inside. She was back—in his arms. That was what mattered tonight.

Milo nodded as he handed Quinn a tablet chart. Dark circles underlined his beautiful eyes, and the strum of tension that had connected them over the last week hummed as her fingers touched his. He grinned, but it was taut. When was the last time she'd seen him smile? Really smile?

They'd always remained professional during work, but the little touches and stolen conversations were gone. There was an uncharted space between them now.

And neither wanted to address it.

Quinn wished there was a way to go back to the early days of their relationship. Then she scoffed. They'd been together less than three months. These *were* the early days.

And if they were already at an impasse?

Since they were teenagers, Quinn had talked to Milo about almost everything. During the first weeks of their relationship, she'd relished how easy it was to talk to him as a partner. To already know his tells.

Now it was a curse. Quinn knew he was stressed. But when she asked about it, he just said it was nothing. And she was hiding things, too. She hadn't taken the job in Maine, hadn't turned it down, either. And she hadn't told Milo— yet. Her heart ached at all the unsaid words between them.

She bit her lip. She and Milo had managed to get through the last few days by ignoring the giant boulder between them. She wanted to run the midwifery unit at Oceanside, and he wanted to be the head of Valley General's obstetrics program.

Were those two things really so at odds?

Quinn tapped a pencil on the nurse's station and tried to catch her breath. Were relationships supposed to be this hard to navigate?

"You okay?" Sherrie asked as she leaned over the nurses' station and placed her tablet on the charging pad.

"Yes." The lie weighed on her heart, but if she opened up about it, Quinn worried that she would burst into tears. Or maybe rage at what she feared were Milo's unyielding dreams.

Sherrie raised an eyebrow, but she didn't press her. "If you decide you want to talk about it, I'm available."

She was pleased by the kind offer. "Thank you."

Her friend nodded. "I suspect Keena will be delivering by the weekend, but Hanna is at least another week away. We might need to start talking about what happens if we need to do an induction."

Quinn smiled as the conversation turned to work. This was an area where she was comfortable. She didn't doubt herself inside these walls. Didn't doubt that she had a place. In the midwifery unit, she knew what to expect and trusted herself.

Babies might keep to their own schedules, but Quinn knew there were patterns you could recognize, once you'd been a midwife for long enough. "Hanna will not be thrilled with an induction. She's already overdue, and she had to be induced with her first. I remember when she was here for her twelve-week appointment. She wanted to know what she could do to avoid it happening again."

"I know," Sherrie said. "I mentioned it to her today, and her reaction was what you'd expect. After a few sniffles, she squared her shoulders. Pitocin is no one's first choice, but she said whatever is best for the baby."

Quinn smiled. "Right answer. She still has at least another week before we need to start worrying, though. Maybe the little one will grant his mother some grace."

"Maybe." Sherrie turned off her tablet, but she didn't look very confident. "I'm off for the night. And Quinn—" Sherrie crossed her arms "—if you need anything, let me know. I owe you. Particularly if you turn down that head nurse position in Maine."

"They told you they'd offered it to me, huh?" Quinn rolled her eyes. "Isla is bubbly and happy, but she is not known for her discretion. One day it's going to get her in trouble. What if you'd wanted to battle it out with me?" Quinn laughed.

"If you want it, the job's yours. I know that." Sherrie said it with such confidence that Quinn's head popped back. "You've worked all over the place and literally fled a wildfire while successfully delivering a patient. Of course, you're their first choice."

Quinn let out a breath. "My résumé is certainly unique."

"I've never left California. I'm excited about the opportunity." Sherrie swallowed before continuing. "Though it would be nice to know someone in Maine." She waved as she headed toward the employee lounge. "Oh, I didn't see you there, Dr. Russell," Sherrie said as she stepped around Milo—who had appeared at an exam room doorway—and disappeared down the hall.

Milo's face didn't give anything away, but Quinn wrapped her arms around herself as she stared at him.

Had he heard?

Quinn had meant to discuss the Maine offer with him several times, but the tension between them was already high. The time was never right, and the last thing she wanted to do was to make him think she was fleeing. It was just a backup plan—one she wasn't going to use.

She wasn't.

She'd checked his study each day, hoping to see some sort of change on his board, some indication that he saw her as permanent. But nothing had changed. What if she told him about the job offer and he told her to take it? That would make his choice about the Oceanside Clinic and Valley General so much easier.

Before she could gauge his reaction, Tara Siemens walked into St. Brigit's and immediately doubled over, clenching her belly. Quinn and Milo reached her at nearly the same time.

"How far apart are the contractions?" Milo's voice was light, but she could see the small tremor in his jaw. He'd heard Sherrie. Worry cascaded through her, but there wasn't time to deal with it now.

"Five… minutes…" Tara panted. "I tried to get Brandon to come. But he wouldn't answer my calls."

Fury floated across Quinn's skin. It didn't matter what the differences were between Tara and her ex-fiancé—to not answer the call of your pregnant ex when you knew she was close to delivery was horrible. Sucking in a quick breath, Quinn squeezed Tara's hand as Milo led her back to a delivery room.

"My parents are gone, and my sister lives on the other side of the country. She's going to come out for a few weeks next month, but she has two under two so…" Tara looked out the window and wiped away a tear as she rubbed her belly. "Brandon was all I had."

"Well, soon you're going to have a new little member of the family. And Quinn and I will make sure you are never alone." Milo's voice was soft as he started hooking up the monitor to measure Tara's contractions.

Never alone...

Milo had made the promise so easily. At St. Brigit's or at Oceanside, it could be effortlessly accomplished, but such a promise would be a stretch at a large facility like Valley General.

The buzzer on Quinn's hip went off. "I need to see another patient, but I'll leave you in the capable hands of Dr. Russell for now, and I'll be back shortly."

As Quinn stepped to the door, she glanced back at Milo. He was talking with Tara about movies while watching the monitors, fully focused on his patient, on making sure she'd be okay delivering without a loved one. In a larger facility, he wouldn't have the luxury to take his time like this.

He laughed at something Quinn couldn't hear, and she watched his shoulders relax. A facility like St. Brigit's or Oceanside would make him happiest. It was where he belonged. How could he not see that?

Quinn had been offered a position across the country.

And she hadn't told him.

The thought ricocheted around his mind as he stepped out of Tara's birthing room. He'd managed to trade off care with Quinn during Tara's labor as he wasn't sure how long he could be around her without begging for answers.

Tara smiled as she walked past him. Her contractions had remained five minutes apart for the last two hours, so one of the nursing aids was walking the halls with her now, trying to move labor along.

"I talked to Tara's ex." Quinn's voice was low as she motioned for Milo to follow her into the employee lounge.

His heart leaped as they stepped into the room together. They were at work, but his palms ached to touch her. His arms wanted to pull her close. To kiss away the worry lines marring her forehead. To plead for answers about the Maine job. But none of those things was possible right now.

"You called him?" Milo was stunned. He'd thought Brandon was acting immaturely. Hopefully, he'd change his actions after his child was born. If not before. But there were rules and procedures that had to be followed.

Quinn's eyes widened. "Of course not."

He saw the hurt flash across her features. The words he'd said to her these past few days always seemed to be off. The easiness that had flowed between them had evaporated once the offer to run the Oceanside Clinic had been thrown into the mix. If only she could understand that his plans didn't include a return to Oceanside.

He needed to focus. "Sorry, Quinn." She was an excellent midwife and nurse. She knew the rules regarding patient information.

Her face relaxed a bit, but she didn't touch him. All the little touches, the small smiles, that he'd taken for granted had disappeared. He craved them.

She sighed as she leaned against the bay of lockers. "He's called the admitting desk every thirty minutes since she arrived." Quinn shook her head. "If he's so concerned with her condition, then he should be here…which is what I told him."

Milo let out a soft chuckle. "And how did he take that?"

"Told me they were too different and hung up the phone." Quinn sighed. "Differences may keep them apart, but they are bound by a child forever. Shame he can't see that right now."

"Differences have a way of piling up." Milo's voice was tight. For a moment, he wasn't sure if he was talking about Tara and Brandon or him and Quinn.

Partners didn't have to be exactly the same. But they did need to want the same things. And if she could still consider taking a job with her traveling nursing agency... The thought tore through his soul.

Why hadn't she immediately told her old agency she wasn't interested in the new job?

Quinn's eyes held his, and he could see the questions hovering there. But now wasn't the time to discuss them. Besides, he was terrified of the answers. Terrified that she wouldn't choose his plan.

Wouldn't choose *him*.

"Tara's contractions are picking up." The aid slipped back from the employee lounge door before either Quinn or Milo could respond.

He watched Quinn swallow before he nodded at the door. "Shall we go see about a baby, Dr. Russell?"

Dr. Russell? He would focus on what that meant later.

"Are you coming to bed?" Quinn rubbed her arms as she stood in the doorway of Milo's study. Tara's labor had finally proceeded, and she'd delivered a healthy baby boy. But she'd been alone. Her ex had answered when she'd asked Milo to call and tell him he had a son, but Quinn didn't know if he would come visit the baby. She hoped he would.

There was so much for Quinn and Milo to talk about, but he'd grabbed a quick snack and retreated almost as soon as they'd arrived home. It stung. He was pulling away from her. And Quinn had no idea how to draw him back.

How did she compete with plans he felt he owed his father?

Should she?

That was the question that tore through her the most.

Life without Milo had never seemed like an option before. They'd sworn when this started to remain friends. Quinn now saw how laughable that was. As if there was a way she could act as though her heart wouldn't always cry out for him.

She loved him. Always would. But if this ended, their friendship would be a casualty. Her heart tore as she stared at his back. "Milo?"

"When were you going to tell me that you were considering moving to Maine?" His voice was rough as he looked over his shoulder.

Quinn went cold as she tried to find the right words. They needed to talk. Needed to figure out what was next. If anything...

"I should have told you. But they called after our—" her voice caught "—disagreement the other night, and the timing wasn't right." She felt her throat closing, but she pushed through. "I haven't accepted the position."

"Have you turned it down?" His voice was rough—*hurt*.

"No." Quinn bit her lip, wishing there was a different answer, but it was the truth. "I always think about job offers for a few days." That was her routine. He knew that. She'd always talked to him about where the agency had open positions and gotten his thoughts, though he'd commented more than once that she always went with her gut, so why ask him?

"So what does your gut say you should do? Is the job calling to you more than LA?" The lines around Milo's eyes were deep as he dug his fingers into his folded arms.

"That is *not* fair," Quinn shot back. They were exhausted, too exhausted to have this argument now. "We should get some rest, then we can discuss the Oceanside Clinic, Maine, and everything else."

"I'm not going to take my mom's offer. It's not what I want."

What about what she wanted? What about their future—together?

She had wanted to put off for a few more hours what now felt inevitable. It would be his plan that mattered. His choice that reigned.

"We need to figure out our plan."

"Now, it's *our* plan?" Quinn wanted to shake him. She'd wanted him to start including her in his plan weeks ago. For a man who plotted everything out, she should have seen some sort of change on his whiteboards. Or some mention of their future. So where was she? Where was her place amid his dreams of running Valley General's OB unit?

And if she stayed, would he keep looking at her like she was a flight risk? "Are you expecting me to leave? Ever since Terri offered me the position in Orlando, I feel like you've been waiting for me to say I'm packing my bags."

Milo shrugged, and Quinn felt her heart crack.

"I've been looking for the signs that you're about to leave ever since you moved back. That's what you do, Quinn. You leave. But me? I can't go anywhere. The job for senior OB at Valley General opened yesterday."

So, she hadn't been the only one keeping career opportunities secret.

"And if you don't get it?"

"I will," Milo stated.

To be so confident…

"But if you don't, will you consider your mother's opportunity then?" Pain dug into her palms and she forced her fingers to relax.

"If I don't get it, then I'll look at Mercy General. Valley hires out of there regularly."

Pain ripped through her as she looked at his infernal boards. He'd never thought she was staying—no wonder Milo hadn't adjusted his plans to include her.

Instead, he'd painstakingly rewritten the words her hand had erased two days ago. Though the ink looked different. Her heart sank as she stared at it.

Why didn't it have the silky look of Dry Erase markers?

Stepping up to the board, she ran her finger along it. It came away clean.

She held it up for his inspection. "I was a traveling nurse for more than a decade. It was a job I loved, but I never considered leaving St. Brigit's until you refused to even consider Oceanside Clinic. To consider something different, some other way to honor your father, your dreams, and mine. It doesn't just have to be Valley General, Milo."

"If you had seen his face, Quinn. Felt what I felt—what I still feel. I know objectively that my actions weren't the reason he passed. But I need this, and it is within my reach. If not now, then in a few years."

How did one compete with a ghost?

"I need this."

More than he needed her?

Quinn couldn't ask that question. Couldn't bear the answer.

Her hand shook as she pointed at the boards. "I understand, but these aren't *our* plans, Milo. They're yours. And in the last forty-eight hours, the only change you've made to them is to write the notes in permanent marker."

Quinn closed her eyes and rocked back on her heels. "If this isn't what I want, then I don't fit in to these plans, do I? My desire to run a unit, Oceanside…" Her lip trembled, but she refused to break. Not yet. There would be plenty of time for that later. *Forever.*

"Of course you fit in. You love being at St. Brigit's. And you'd love Mercy General or Valley General." Milo's nose scrunched as he looked at her.

"So, if I make all the adjustments. Change all my plans…" Quinn shuddered.

How come her dreams were so easy to dismiss?

And why was this happening with Milo? The one person who knew her better than anyone.

"You go from position to position, trusting your gut." Milo stared at her. "That isn't a plan."

She'd had a lot of positions over the last decade, but each

one had added a valuable piece to her résumé. And each had taught her what she really wanted, and it wasn't to be another face in a large hospital.

"Trusting my intuition on job choices doesn't mean that I don't think things through. Just because I don't need to list out every move for the next five or fifty years doesn't make my choices less valid. It doesn't mean I don't know what I want." Quinn brushed away the lone tear that refused to listen to her mandate.

"I want to belong, to be chosen. For who *I* am. I don't want someone who has to fit me in. I want a man who stands beside me and sees me and my dreams in his future. Who is willing to change his plans if it's what's best for us." Quinn stared at him, willing him to change his mind. To say he wanted her. No matter what.

"Your dreams matter to me. But I need this. I need Valley General," Milo countered, and the final piece of hope died inside her.

"Why? It's just a place. Why does it have to be the only place?" Pain tumbled through her, but she needed an answer.

"I've thought about it for years. I've researched everything." He pushed a hand through his hair.

It wasn't an answer, not really. But she'd heard similar words before, so many times.

Our plan is best, Quinn. We've done all the research and work, so you don't have to. Why can't you just get in line?

"Where do I fit on that list, Milo? Or your family? Or children? What if we don't fall in line with the plan?" Quinn gestured to the boards.

Love, real love, didn't ask you to adjust for it. It accepted you.

"Life can't be outlined like a book. Chaos and change are inevitable." Her heart wept as she stared at him. It had to be this way, but she hated it.

She wished she'd paid more attention to the last time they'd kissed. Wished she could remember the last time he'd held her more clearly. If she'd known it had been the last time, she'd have made sure to let it seep into every edge of her soul.

Pushing the pain away for a moment longer, she met his gaze. "I want you to get everything on your list, Milo. I really do." She tried to force out a goodbye, but her heart refused to provide any words as it broke.

She turned without looking back. If she looked at him, she'd break.

If he had chased after her, she'd have pledged whatever he'd wanted. But he hadn't. He'd stayed in the study while she'd packed the small number of belongings she'd accumulated during their relationship, the door firmly closed to her dreams and wishes.

She hung her key on the ring by the kitchen and forced her eyes to stare ahead as she closed the front door behind her. It was time to move on. To find the next adventure, even if it never excited her as much as these last few months with Milo had.

CHAPTER TEN

MILO SAT ON the floor of his living room and stared at the bright yellow kitchen as the sun rose. He'd spent the entire night trying to figure out how everything had gone so wrong. How his deepest dream had evaporated in a matter of minutes.

He looked at the small box on the coffee table. After Quinn had left the study, he'd stared at the window, trying to find the right words to explain why he'd rewritten everything in permanent marker. To explain that after his mother had offered him the chance to run Oceanside, he'd rewritten it so he couldn't change his mind. So, it wouldn't seem like an option to derail him from his father's memory. It was ridiculous and childish. But Milo had felt better after the small gesture.

Then he'd stared at the boards rather than run after her. Trying to find an adjustment, so they both got what they needed. A way that didn't feel like he was letting down his father or Quinn. But nothing had come to him.

Finally, he'd grabbed the box from the drawer where he'd hidden it weeks ago. He hadn't planned to buy it. It had happened by accident. *By impulse.* He'd walked past the jewelry store and had just been pulled in.

But after the purchase, he'd started second-guessing himself. Wondering if it had been too soon. If he should have spent more time researching to find the perfect symbol of his devotion. He'd spent so much time worrying over it that he hadn't even managed to figure out the best plan for asking the woman he loved to be his wife.

And then he'd been unable to give her what she'd really wanted—needed—when she'd asked. A chance to be included in his future—fully. Her dreams and his, blended in harmony.

He'd wanted her, but on his terms. By the time he'd grabbed the ring—the symbol that he wanted her forever— Quinn was already gone. And she hadn't answered any of his calls or texts since.

He didn't blame her. Quinn had only wanted to know that she was part of his life. That she'd have a say on their future. And he'd dismissed her dreams. Dismissed her gut feelings.

Dismissed the woman he loved.

He'd clung to an idealized version of a memory and lost the person that made him happiest as a result. And now he had no idea where she was.

Milo laid his head back against the couch and tried to force air through his lungs. She was gone, and he was alone. Everything hurt.

How was he supposed to get through the rest of his life without Quinn? From the moment they'd met, he'd felt like she was family. She'd been his constant. A place of sanctuary. His person. Why hadn't those words materialized when they'd been arguing?

Fear.

Milo pressed his palms against his closed eyes. As soon as she'd landed in LA, Milo had been afraid that Quinn would leave. Feared that he wouldn't be able to compete with the adventures she'd already had and could have in the future. She wanted to work at Oceanside now, but what if, in a few years, another phone call came, offering something even more exciting?

He pressed his palm to his forehead. He had spent all his time calculating how she might leave...but what if she stayed? Milo had never fully considered that. And he'd never forget the look in her eyes when he'd confessed that he'd been looking for signs that she'd leave for almost a year—or the selfish hope that had wanted her to promise that she wouldn't. Relationships took adjustments, but other than painting his kitchen, what adjustments had he made for her?

None! his brain shouted. He'd held back, hoping she'd make all the changes. That way, he wouldn't have to examine what he really wanted. What he really needed. He could just float by on the path that he thought might bring him some form of closure with his dad.

Even if he wasn't sure it was what he really wanted.

God, Quinn was right to leave.

He dialed her number again and bit his lip as the call immediately went to voice mail. What had he expected? She'd asked to have a say in the dreams they followed, and he'd stayed silent, terrified to embrace a future that might mean letting go of the past.

He called St. Brigit's. He wasn't on shift today, but he needed to take some additional personal time. He couldn't see Quinn. At least not yet.

Not until I have a *plan*. The thought ran through his mind, and Milo wanted to bang the rigidity out of his brain.

He'd lost Quinn because of his incessant need to organize his life, to pretend he had some say in life's chaos. Yet, that was where his brain wanted to go, wanted to leap to: the security of plans.

Except nothing in his plans had prepared him for such heartbreak.

He called HR and asked for two weeks off. He doubted his heart would ever heal, but maybe by then the simple act of forcing oxygen into his lungs wouldn't be so difficult.

Standing, he ignored the pain in his legs. He'd been on the floor for too long, but Milo didn't care. He couldn't stay here, couldn't be where everything reminded him of Quinn. Grabbing his keys, he raced for the door. He didn't have a destination in mind, but anywhere had to be better than the emptiness here.

Quinn stared at the gray walls of her hotel room. When had gray become such a popular color? At least the sad color matched the feel of her soul. The hotel was the first one she'd passed after leaving last night. It wasn't much, but with the rental insurance from the fire and staying with Milo, her nest egg was quite healthy.

Milo…

Her lungs burned, but her eyes were finally dry. No matter what she did, his name kept popping into her mind. Even now, it felt like he was everywhere. Milo had seeped into her soul years ago, and there was no way to remove him. No matter how much it hurt.

Her phone rang, but it wasn't Milo's ringtone. Milo had called repeatedly after she left, but Quinn hadn't trusted herself to answer. As soon as she'd closed the door to the apartment, she'd wanted to turn around. Wanted to say that it didn't matter that his life plan was written in permanent ink—without her—she could accept it.

But she couldn't. She'd lived like that before, and she hadn't been able to bend enough to fit. If Milo ever looked at her like her parents had, like she was intruding…

She wasn't sure she could survive it. It was better to leave before that happened. Quinn tasted blood, and belatedly realized that she was biting the inside of her cheek.

Milo wanted a different dream. It wasn't wrong, and he should have it because he'd worked so hard to make sure it happened. She just hoped it brought him all the peace he sought, and wished she'd realized that he would never walk away from his dream before she'd lost her heart so completely.

Each time she heard his ringtone, she'd burst into tears, wishing he'd leave her be. When the calls had stopped, she'd cried again. Nothing felt right anymore.

The phone rang again, and she flipped it over. Her fingers froze, but she managed to answer just before it shifted to voice mail.

"Asher?" Quinn kept her voice level.

"Quinn." Asher's voice was rigid, and immediately she knew something was wrong.

"What's wrong?"

"Samantha's been hospitalized. They're trying to stop her labor." Asher let out a soft whimper. "She's only twenty-two weeks along. If she delivers…" Asher's voice broke.

"Where are you?" Quinn slid from the hotel bed. They weren't close, but she could hear the pain in his voice. And Samantha would be understandably terrified.

"Valley General," Asher stated. "You don't have to come." But she could hear the plea in his voice.

"I'm on my way."

"I think you probably don't need me anymore." Quinn stood and stretched. The hours had passed in a stream of nurses, monitors and checks. The doctor had decided Samantha would spend at least the next two days being monitored, and then be on strict bed rest for the rest of her pregnancy. But, at last, it seemed like Samantha was out of danger.

"Thank you so much for coming," Samantha said as she held out a hand. "Asher, why don't you see Quinn to her car?"

Quinn started to protest, but she caught a look between the two and held her tongue. She and Milo had been able to do that, too. To communicate so much with just a small look.

Her heart bled as she started for the door. Focusing on

Asher and Samantha's issues had allowed her a brief respite from her own brokenness. The idea of heading back to her small hotel room held no appeal, but staying here didn't seem like an option, either. Quinn had hovered long enough.

She let her brother follow her to the waiting room then turned to him. "I know that Samantha wanted you to see me out, but it's really okay, Asher. If you have any questions about bed rest or what to expect, you can call."

"I should have called you back." Asher's voice was low as he stared at her. His lip stuck out, and he sighed. "Should have jumped at the chance to have dinner or coffee."

Quinn's heart twisted as she looked at him. It would be easy to offer a platitude. To tell him that it was fine that he'd left her wondering what she'd done wrong and waiting patiently for a response that never came. But her heart wasn't in it. "So why didn't you?"

Her brother pursed his lips before he stuck his hands into his pockets. "I started to, so many times. But I had no idea how to say all that needed to be said. That should be said." Asher rocked back on his heels. "No matter how Mom and Dad tried to change you, you resisted. They tried to mold you into their image, and you refused." Asher ran a hand through his short hair. "You're my hero."

Quinn felt her mouth fall open. Hero? None of that made any sense. "Asher, I think you're remembering everything a bit wrong."

His cheeks heated as he shook his head, "No, I'm not. I gave in to everything they wanted. It was easier—God knows they rewarded me for it—but even after they passed…" He pushed a hand through his hair again. "I became a lawyer just like they wanted me to. Did so many things because—" his lip trembled as he met his gaze "—I didn't know who I was until a few years ago."

His eyes burned through her, but Quinn had no idea what to say.

"You were yourself. No matter how Mom tried to make you blend in, you stood out. You figured out what you wanted in life and left to get it."

"Sure of myself? I was terrified." Quinn shook her head. She'd never felt like she belonged. "I literally ran away."

"Could have fooled me," Asher lightly scoffed. "You set off on an adventure. And then another. And another... I was always in awe of your ability to escape. You never needed anyone."

Never needed anyone? The words struck her. She'd needed Milo, but had she ever told him that? The world spun around her as she tried to steady herself.

Her brother continued. "You see what you want and you go for it. No matter where it means you have to go."

She'd loved being a travel nurse, loved going new places. But it had been lonely, too. Never staying in one place, keeping people at a distance because you weren't sure you'd ever see them again. That was one of the reasons she'd come back to California.

To Milo.

She'd never said it was permanent, though. Milo had been waiting for her to pack her bags because she'd always packed them before.

Even her furniture had been rented.

But she hadn't wanted to get away from Milo.

Had she ever told him that? Ever told him that he was what grounded her, gave her the roots she desperately needed?

No.

Because she'd wanted him to change first. Wanted him to adjust his plans for her, rather than seeing if there was a way they could join their dreams together. Blood rushed through her ears as she tried to focus on her brother.

Asher's warm hand pressed into hers. "I just didn't know how to say how sorry I was for not standing up to Mom and Dad. For just following the safety of the plans laid out before me."

He huffed out a deep breath. "I was jealous of you."

"Jealous?"

He smiled. "When Mom and Dad said they wouldn't pay for nursing school, you told them that you'd already filled out the paperwork for scholarships and applied for a loan. I was in awe of your courage. You set a goal and didn't let anyone distract you or talk you out of it."

Like wanting to run the birthing center at Oceanside. She'd decided that was her next goal—her next adventure. And yet, when Milo hadn't immediately altered everything, she'd run.

Just like he'd feared she would.

But Milo wasn't her parents. His plans hadn't been designed to trap her. *She'd* set that trap, and stepped into it herself.

She knew how important plans were to him. How safe they made him feel. How they brought him closer to his father's memory. Yet she'd asked him to change everything. And it had cost her the person who made her feel whole.

Quinn's heart melted as she embraced her brother. "None of this is your fault. We each made mistakes, but that's in the past now." She meant the words. They'd been children in a home with impossible rules. And each had adapted in their own way. She was too old to keep running from past pains.

"I know it's selfish," Asher said, "but I kind of hope you're planning to stay in the area. At least for a little while. I'd love for our child to spend as much time as possible with Aunt Quinn."

Her heart pounded as she nodded. "I've actually been

thinking of making my California residency permanent." The words felt right. She smiled as her brother beamed.

The Oceanside Clinic had four cars in the employee parking lot as he pulled in. But none of them belonged to his mother or Felix. At least he wouldn't have to immediately explain why he was there.

He'd driven here without thinking. But when he'd finally arrived in Oceanside, Milo hadn't wanted to go to his town house. The memory of Quinn kissing him there was imprinted on his brain. Instead, he'd sat on the beach, just thinking until the sun had finally started to sink over the ocean.

Kelly, the nurse at the front desk, smiled as he walked through the front door. "Dr. Russell." She started to stand, but he motioned for her to stay where she was. "We don't have any patients in labor, two patients and their little ones are sleeping, and Dr. Acton is on call. It's her last month before she moves." Kelly stopped chatting. "Sorry, slow night shift."

"I understand. The shifts drag when there's no one to help. I…" He looked at the pictures he'd helped his sister pick out. "I just needed to see this place."

The words left his mouth and he felt a weight lift from his chest. He needed to walk through this center he'd helped design, needed a chance to say goodbye.

Kelly gave him a strange look, but she didn't say anything as he started down the hall.

Once his mother and Felix retired, he doubted the new physician would want to keep him on as a very part-time employee. His head hurt as he realized he would no longer have a connection to the place.

The thought that this would be someone else's pride and joy felt like a rock in his stomach. His mother and Felix had supported the idea of the birthing center, but it had been Milo's baby. He'd pored over the architect's plans, spent hours researching and investigating how to let mothers birth in complete comfort.

The door to his mother's office was open, and Milo slipped through it. This could be his. *Should be his.*

The thought held him, and Milo exhaled. Peace settled through him. His father wasn't at Valley General. His dad was with him no matter where he served, because Milo carried him with him always. Memories faded, but love carried through time and space. Why had it taken him so long to see that? To accept it?

His cell buzzed, and he smiled as he answered. "I'm surprised it took Kelly this long to let you know I was here."

"Is everything okay?" His mother's voice was tired, but he knew she'd come to the clinic if he said he needed it.

"No," Milo answered honestly. "But it will be. I'm going to run this clinic, Mom."

"And Quinn?"

Just her name was enough to make the blood rush to his ears as his heart ached. He swallowed as he stared across the hall at the office that should be hers. "If I can convince her, this will be our greatest adventure."

"If anyone can figure out a plan for that, it's you."

Milo smiled. "Maybe. But I need a favor."

"Name it!"

He could see his mother's smile in his mind. He hoped that he hadn't pushed Quinn too far. That she'd want to take this new path with him.

CHAPTER ELEVEN

"WHY IS MILO not on the schedule for the next two weeks?" Quinn's soul shuddered as she looked at Martina. He wasn't supposed to be on the schedule today, and she'd been grateful for the extra day to figure out how to tell him she was staying. And that she wanted to be with him, no matter what his plans were.

She'd turned down the position in Maine last night. For years, Quinn had picked up and moved on when life got tough. She'd controlled life by running from hurt. When she'd faced setbacks, she'd reached for the comfort of knowing that she could escape. But her heart didn't want an escape. There was nowhere better than wherever Milo was. Quinn Davis was done running. She was putting down roots.

The news that Milo was taking an extended vacation had been the talk of the employee lounge when she'd arrived this morning, everyone wondering what he was doing and commenting on the fact that he never normally took leave. She'd caught more than a few side glances her direction, too—though no one had worked up the courage to ask her directly if she knew where he was.

Thank goodness.

"He called in yesterday and asked for some leave." Martina leaned closer. "I bet he's interviewing for the position over at Valley General. If he gets it, he has a lot of unused leave he's accumulated here that he either uses or loses."

"Valley General." Quinn nodded. "Of course."

Martina held up her hands. "I suspect he'll get it. I still remember him telling me his five-year plan during his interview. That man had it all outlined—even then." She shook her head. "I've already put out a few feelers. But if you know anyone who might be interested—send me their name. Oh, and we need to start thinking about your contract, too. We would love to retain you. Let's set up a meeting next week to go over the details."

"I'll get it on your calendar." Quinn smiled.

Her phone buzzed and she froze as Milo's name jumped across the screen.

You left something at my place. Can you come by after your shift?

Left something? Quinn wasn't sure what he'd found, but it couldn't have been anything major. Was this his way of trying to talk…or of pushing the last remnants of her from his life?

I'll be there as soon as my shift ends.

She hit Send and then forced herself to focus on work. Time would move faster if she stayed as busy as possible.

The knock at the door sent tingles across Milo's skin. Quinn was here. She was finally here.

When he'd sent the text this morning, Milo had been prepared to wait exactly one day for her to respond before he took more drastic measures to seek her out. But she'd answered almost instantly. He'd wrapped his mind around all the potential outcomes this afternoon, but he was not going to focus on those now.

Sliding the door open, he took her in. She wore jeans and a loose T-shirt. Her dark hair was pulled into a low ponytail. His body ached with relief as his eyes drank her in.

Quinn...

"Are you going to invite me in?" Her voice wavered a little as she looked past him.

"Oh my gosh!" Milo jumped to the side. "Yes, of course. It's just so good to see you. My brain stopped working." Her lips tipped up, and Milo released the breath he'd been holding. "I was worried you might change your mind about coming."

Her dark eyes raked across him.

Did she want to touch him as much as he wanted to touch her? He refused to examine that thought. There was too much to say.

"You said I left something." Her head swiveled as she looked around the living room. "Where is it?"

"Here." Milo placed a hand to his chest as he let the words flow. "You left my heart."

Milo stepped toward her, grateful when she didn't move away. "It's yours, Quinn, and it always will be. I should have said so many things the other night. I should have promised you forever. I thought my plans grounded me, but they were just a cover for my fear that everything can be ripped away. My life has revolved around plans and control since Dad died. They were my talisman—my protection against the world of unknowns. And my way to keep him close." Milo swallowed, waiting for the grief he always felt when he thought of his dad, but it didn't overwhelm him this time.

"That's understandable."

"Maybe." Milo reached for her hand, unable to keep from touching her. Her fingers wrapped through his, but there was still so much to say. "But I can't lose my dad—he's part of me. And I never meant to make you feel like you weren't part of my future. *You* are my plan, Quinn.

"I know you like to travel—" Milo let go of her hand to trace his fingers across her chin "—but I'm hoping that I can convince you to stay local. I love it here. Love being close to Mom and Felix and Gina. Even if she does make the worst vegetable dip in history. But if you need—"

"I owe you an apology, too." Quinn closed the bit of distance between them as she interrupted.

"No."

Her finger landed against his lips. "Let me finish."

Milo nodded as he relished the heat from her other hand slipping into his. His heart steadied as Quinn held him. For the first time in two days, the pressure in his chest finally evaporated.

"You were right." Quinn pressed her lips to his cheek. "Maine was my backup." A tear ran down her cheek. "After I wiped away your plans…" She sucked in a breath. "I worried that maybe I wouldn't fit into your life. Wouldn't have a place. And I panicked. But I'm done running."

He pulled her close and just held her. Pressing light kisses to the top of her head, Milo waited until she looked up at him. Pushing the tears from her cheek, Milo held her gaze. "I will always choose you, Quinn. Always."

Then his lips captured hers, and her arms wrapped around his neck as she deepened the kiss.

"I love you, Quinn Davis."

"I love you, too."

He got down on one knee and smiled as her fingers covered her lips. "I bought this weeks ago. When you asked me to show you that your dreams were part of my future, I should have pulled this from the drawer and gotten down on one knee then. You are my plan, Quinn. From now until forever, please say you'll be my wife."

Lowering herself to her knees, Quinn put her hands on either side of his face as she dropped a kiss against his lips. "Yes. Yes." She giggled as he placed the diamond on her finger. "It's perfect."

"There is one other thing we need to discuss. About St. Brigit's…"

"Martina mentioned my contract today. And that you might be taking a position at Valley General." Quinn squeezed his hand.

"You didn't sign a new contract, did you?" Milo's voice was rushed, and he shook his head. "It's just, I made one plan without talking to you. Well—two, but that's all. I promise."

Quinn raised an eyebrow. "What have you done?"

"After you left, I couldn't stay here. I went to Oceanside. I meant to say goodbye to the facility, but…" Milo smiled. "It's where I belong. I want to run the clinic and the birthing center. Do you want to run the midwife unit?"

"Yes!" Quinn's scream echoed in the room, and she covered her lips. "That was a little loud!"

"I loved it." Milo kissed her. "But there is still the other plan."

Quinn's brow furrowed, but she didn't interrupt him.

"I got my mother and Felix to agree to put off their retirement for six months." Milo pushed a loose piece of hair behind her ear.

"Why?" Quinn's eyes were wide as she stared at him.

"In case you wanted to go on one more tour with Doctors Without Borders. You mentioned getting away a few weeks ago. Once we take over the clinic, that option will not be something we can do—at least not without a lot of pre-planning. And if we have a family, then it becomes even harder."

"We?" Quinn's voice was low as she ran her hand along his cheek.

"Figure it might be a good time for an adventure."
Milo's heart exploded as she launched into his arms.
"I love you!" She peppered his face with kisses.

EPILOGUE

QUINN BREATHED THROUGH her contractions as she smiled at Robin. She'd been walking with the young woman down Oceanside's hallways for the last hour, hoping it might speed up Robin's contractions. But all it appeared to have done was bring on Quinn's. When she'd said she planned to work up until she delivered, she hadn't meant it so literally.

She looked toward the clock and frowned. The last three had been exactly five and a half minutes apart.

Milo strolled through the front door of the birthing center as she and Robin rounded the nurses' station. He grinned before stepping aside and letting Kelly through, too. Neither of them was supposed to be on rounds today.

"Who told on me?" Quinn squinted as Kelly took Robin's arm.

"So, you are in labor?" Robin grinned.

"I run to the restroom for five minutes…" Quinn sighed. "I thought I was covering it well, too."

Robin let out a sheepish laugh. "You squeezed my arm almost every seven minutes, then every six. At least our little ones will have the same birthdays." She laughed again before a contraction overtook her.

"I was going to call you as soon as I hit five minutes." Quinn beamed as Milo dropped a kiss on her forehead.

"Right now, all I can think about is that our daughter

will be here soon. I brought the birthing bag." Milo's smile spun up her spine as he held up the bag.

They'd packed it weeks ago. Actually, he'd packed it—carefully going over each item on his list. Quinn had laughed and said all they really needed was an outfit for the baby and car seat, but he'd insisted.

"I think this little one is a bit anxious." Quinn gripped Milo's arm as she breathed through another contraction. "Her due date isn't for another three days. She isn't following the plan."

Milo laughed before he kissed her. "Some plans are meant to be broken."

* * * * *

AWAKENING
THE SHY NURSE

ALISON ROBERTS

PROLOGUE

'Who's that?'

'Nothing.' Annalise Phillips tried to fold the sheet of paper and stuff it back in the envelope at the same time. Her nonchalance didn't quite work and her younger sister Abby narrowed her eyes suspiciously.

'That's envelope's got a window. It's a bill, isn't it?'

'It's nothing to worry about. I've got everything under control.' Lisa watched as Abby manoeuvred her wheelchair to the other side of the kitchen table. She'd always been able to convince Abby that she could manage and that had turned out to be an accurate prediction for so many years that it had become an automatic and genuine reassurance. So why was Lisa aware of a nasty edge of panic approaching this time?

'Look…' It was good that there was a distraction on hand. 'There's a letter here for you as well. No window.'

'Really?' Abby transferred her laptop from her knees to the table and reached for the letter. 'Oh… maybe it's confirmation of my date to sit my driver's licence.' She grinned at Lisa. 'I still can't believe you managed to find that funding for my modified car. It's the most exciting thing ever…'

It felt good to be able to smile and tap into the glow of having achieved something that had been such a long time coming. Abby didn't need to know that Lisa hadn't exactly found funding from a charitable community support organisation and she had, instead, taken out a huge loan against the house to pay for the modifications the car had needed to accommodate a paraplegic driver. Or that the first repayment of the loan was now due at such an unfortunate time when she was between jobs, having been forced to resign from her nursing home position due to a merger that would have meant she had to move to another city.

'Oh...*oh*, you're not going to believe this...' Abby sounded as though her new car had just been demoted from being the most exciting ever. She handed her letter to Lisa. 'There's a room available at the uni hostel. Ground floor, with an en suite bathroom—one of the ones that are only available to disabled students. And get this... it's an unexpected vacancy because a student has pulled out of her course so I can move in next week!'

'Next *week*?' Lisa took the sheet of paper but she couldn't focus on the words. 'But...but...' She had to swallow hard. She wasn't ready for this after all.

Abby was waiting for her to look up. 'You knew this was coming, Lise,' she reminded her gently. 'I've had my name down for one of those rooms in that hostel ever since I started uni and that's years ago.'

'I know.' Lisa tried to find that smile that seemed a million miles away now. 'And it's wonderful. You're going to be completely independent and I'm so proud of you and...and...would you like a cup of tea?' Lisa got to her feet quickly to escape her sister's watchful gaze. 'Wait, no...we should be having a drink to celebrate, shouldn't we? Have we got any wine?'

'We never got round to opening that fizz when you found out about your new job. You said that seeing as you weren't starting for more than a month, we might as well keep it on ice, but maybe now is the perfect time.'

'Mmm... I think it is.' Lisa busied herself finding the bottle in the back of the fridge, getting glasses down from the high cupboard and then opening the sparkling wine. It certainly seemed like a good idea. Abby wouldn't know that she might be drowning her sorrows instead of celebrating, would she? Or panicking because she needed to find enough money to pay a rather large bill in the very near future?

But, of course, her sister knew her better than that. How could she not, when Lisa had been pretty much her principal carer for as long as she could remember? Her only family since their grandmother had died nearly ten years ago now.

'What's really up, Lise?' she asked quietly.

What could Lisa say? That she was beginning to wonder if she'd made a big mistake applying for that desk job as a junior manager in another nursing home just because it had regular hours and was close to home and would make life a lot simpler? That living alone in this little house they had inherited from Gran suddenly seemed like the loneliest prospect ever and it would give her far too much time to worry about how Abby was coping. Worse, it would be more time to revisit the guilt that it was her fault in the first place that her sister was having to cope with so many more challenges in life?

No. She couldn't go there. They'd agreed long ago that it was so far in the past it was a no-go subject. That you could destroy your future if you didn't leave your past behind...

But she couldn't be dishonest either. 'I'm going to miss you,' she told Abby.

'I'll only be on the other side of town. I'll drive you crazy with how often I visit.'

'And I'm only a phone call away.' Lisa nodded, taking another sip of her wine. 'If...you know...'

'If I fall out of my chair, you mean?' Abby laughed. 'I can manage. It's a long time since I've needed you hovering around like a helicopter parent.'

It was meant as a joke but Abby must have realised it stung a bit because she reached out to touch Lisa's arm. 'It's not that I don't appreciate everything you've done, you know that, don't you?'

Lisa nodded. And took a longer sip of her wine.

'You've been—and still are—the best sister ever but it's time we both got to live our own lives. It's the next step for me and then I'll really be able to have a place of my own. Where I can bring my boyfriend home. Or you can bring yours, at least.'

Lisa's jaw dropped. 'You've got a boyfriend?'

'No, silly.' There was a beat of something very dark in the way Abby avoided her gaze. Avoided allowing a memory any hint of the light of day in the hope that it would stay buried for ever. It was another reason that Lisa felt the need to stay close to Abby to be able to protect her. If she hadn't come home when she had that night, they both knew what would have happened because Abby had been unable to defend herself.

'You'd be the first to know if I did.' Abby's tone

was too bright. 'I've been way too busy getting my Master's in occupational therapy to want the hassle of a man in my life again. And now I'm well into my postgraduate course in hand therapy so I'm still too busy but, for heaven's sake, Lise—you're nearly thirty and you haven't had a proper boyfriend yet and it feels like that's at least partly because you think you have to keep looking after me.'

'I have had boyfriends,' Lisa protested. If Abby was determined to deal with her past trauma by burying it, then all she could do was support her. She made her own tone light and bright as well. 'I've had lots of them. There was Michael. And Stephen. And...um... what was his name? Oh, yeah... Geoffrey. I guess he doesn't really count...'

Abby was laughing again. 'None of them count. They were all the most boring men on earth. Stephen wore socks and sandals and the most interesting thing he had to talk about was his worm farm. Michael was so skinny and tall and bald he looked like one of the test tubes in his laboratory and...oh, my God... I'd forgotten about Geoffrey. Wasn't he the one whose mother turned up on your first date?'

The wine was definitely helping because Lisa was laughing now, too. 'I think he'd booked a table for three all along.'

They'd seemed like such nice men, though. Safe...

'You're right,' she had to admit. 'I have a talent for picking boring men.'

'Being bored is bad,' Abby declared. 'I think that's your problem at the moment. You haven't got enough to do until you start your next job. You should go on a holiday.'

Lisa's breath escaped in a huff of laughter. As if. She'd never been on holiday in her life and she certainly wasn't about to start now. Not when money was so tight it was scaring her.

'What I *should* do is find a job for a few weeks.'

She didn't realise that she had voiced the thought aloud until she saw the frown on Abby's forehead.

'Why? Oh…it's because of my car, isn't it? I *knew* it cost too much…'

'No.' Lisa shook her head. 'It's because I need something to do so I don't die of boredom. I'll go crazy rattling around here by myself for weeks after you move into the hostel. I might end up on your doorstep every day.'

'Can't have that.' Abby feigned horror. 'Fill up those glasses again.' She opened her laptop and started tapping keys. 'I'm going to see what's on offer for a supertalented nurse who only wants a few weeks of work. Hmm…we need a high-end medical locum agency, don't we?'

By the time Lisa had their glasses brimming again, Abby was looking triumphant.

'I've found the *perfect* thing. Tailor-made. It's work but it's a holiday at the same time. And it's legit. This agency—London Locums—is obviously highly rated.'

'What is it?'

'A cruise. More specifically, a Mediterranean cruise. Oh…' Abby's sigh was heartfelt. 'It starts in Spain and then goes to places in the south of France and Italy and some Greek islands before finishing up back in Spain again. How romantic is that…?'

The countries and islands were fantasy destinations.

A cruise ship even more of a fantasy but not one that Lisa had ever considered desirable.

'I couldn't do that. Cruise ships are full of self-indulgent people who have too much money and just want to float around having a good time, eating and drinking far too much. It would be disgusting.'

It certainly went against the values Lisa Phillips had embraced since she'd been no more than a child.

'There's nothing wrong with having a good time occasionally.' Abby was watching her sister again. 'It might be fun. They need a nurse in this ship's well-equipped infirmary, just for a two-week cruise, to fill in a gap in a team of two doctors and three nurses. You'll get time off to go on shore at some ports of call and accommodation and all meals are provided. And they'll pay top rates for the right person. Why don't you give this woman a call tomorrow? Julia, her name is...'

Lisa's attention had certainly been caught. Not so much by the idea of shore excursions in foreign parts or shipboard accommodation or even the novelty of working in a completely different kind of environment. There was, however, something that made this feel like it might be meant to be—probably the words "top rates".

'Show me...' She leaned closer as Abby turned her computer so she could see the screen. 'Oh, wow... they're paying *that* much? And it doesn't start until after next week so I'd be here to help you move.'

Lisa pulled in a deep breath. 'I think you're right. It *is* perfect...'

CHAPTER ONE

WEARING JEANS HAD been a bad idea.

It was much hotter than Lisa had expected in Barcelona and, by the time she climbed out of the taxi after her trip from the airport to the port, it felt like the denim was actually sticking to the back of her legs. Even her short-sleeved white shirt felt too warm, despite her having removed her light cardigan. She could only hope that the uniform Julia from London Locums had told her would be supplied for her temporary job as a ship's nurse was better suited to a late summer Mediterranean climate.

The friendly taxi driver opened the boot of the car to retrieve her small, bright red suitcase. 'Here you go, *señorita*.'

'Thank you so much.' Lisa dug in her bag to find her wallet. 'I don't suppose you know which of the ships here belongs to the Aquamarine cruise line?'

Her driver shrugged. 'It's no problem. See that big round building over there?'

Lisa looked over her shoulder and nodded.

'That's the World Trade Centre. Your ship will be one of the ones berthed around it.'

Lisa could see the massive ships docked around the

building. They looked like floating cities and one of them was going to be her home for the next couple of weeks. Maybe those butterflies in her stomach weren't solely due to the nervousness that came from starting any new job. Maybe they were due to something she didn't have that much experience of...like excitement? She could feel a smile tugging at the corners of her mouth as she turned back to pay her driver but for a split second her gaze snagged on what was happening over *his* shoulder.

Another taxi had pulled up. The rear door was open and a man had stepped out. A tall, lean, *ridiculously* good-looking man... He was wearing light, casual clothing and looked as though he'd just spent a very relaxing day of sightseeing and highlighting those streaks of sun-kissed blond in his hair. To add to the impression of sheer pleasure, she saw the long, long legs of his companion emerging from the back seat of the car. Slim, elegant arms went straight around the man's neck as the woman got to her feet and he leaned in to kiss her with a leisurely grace that suggested it was by no means a first kiss and more like a continuation of a sexy, afternoon romp.

'Um... Here you are. Is that enough for a tip?' Embarrassed, Lisa was fumbling with the notes and coins. The embarrassment wasn't just because she didn't know about tipping practices in Spain. It was more to do with what was going on just a few feet away from her. That *kiss*... It was still going on. And on. For heaven's sake, it was broad daylight. Those two needed to get a room. Again...?

'Enjoy your time before you set sail,' her driver instructed. 'You can walk to Las Ramblas from here in less than fifteen minutes. If you have time, take a tour on the bus. This is the most beautiful city in the world.'

Lisa nodded her thanks for the advice but she knew she wouldn't be exploring Barcelona today. Arrangements for her urgent passport hadn't been finalised in time for her to join the cruise along with all the new passengers in Malaga a couple of days ago so it felt like she was playing catch-up already. She was due on board her new place of employment at four p.m. and that was…she glanced at her watch…less than twenty minutes from now, which didn't give her that much time to identify the correct ship to board. Being late was the height of rudeness as far as Lisa Phillips was concerned.

As her taxi pulled away she noticed that *that* kiss was finally over and the leggy blonde was—reluctantly—getting back into her taxi. As Lisa pulled the long handle out of her suitcase the man lifted his hand in a farewell wave and then turned, his gaze locking onto Lisa's a heartbeat later. He had to know that she'd seen what he'd just been doing but he didn't seem remotely bothered. If anything, that quirk of his eyebrow seemed like nothing more than a flirtatious invitation. Perhaps *she* might like to find out how good at kissing he was?

Lisa could feel colour flooding her cheeks as she snapped the handle of her suitcase into place and then tipped it so she could start dragging it behind her. She'd already had a sneaking suspicion that it wasn't just the sightseeing and unlimited food and drink people took cruises for and that had just been confirmed. Some people clearly found a cruise an opportunity for unlimited sexual adventures as well. A "what happens on board stays on board" kind of thing.

'Can I be of some assistance?'

Oh...dear Lord... The man's voice was just as gorgeous as the rest of him. Deep and sexy and with a hint of laughter that went with his whole, laidback look. It had to be the overly warm air she was dragging into her lungs that was adding to the heat Lisa could feel in her cheeks. And in the pit of her stomach, come to that. A rebellious corner of her brain was melting in that heat as well. Otherwise, why would it come up with the absurd idea that maybe she *would* rather like to find out how good this man was at kissing?

'No,' she said firmly, without looking up, so he wouldn't notice her fiery cheeks. 'Thank you, but I'm fine. It's not heavy and I'm perfectly capable of managing by myself.'

'No problem.' That hint of laughter was more pronounced now. 'Enjoy your cruise.'

A group of women, in flowing maxi dresses and floppy sunhats were coming towards them. Amidst the giggles, a call came that sounded more like a command.

'Hugh... You must see these photos we took at the beach today. Wait until you see Scout's new bikini.'

He'd already slowed his pace so it took only seconds for Lisa to leave him behind with the young women. Fellow passengers from the same ship, she decided. Hopefully not hers. She quickened her own pace, heading towards the first ship that was towering over her more and more as she got closer. There was a covered gangway sloping up to a door on the side of the hull and a desk shaded by a canopy at the bottom, staffed by uniformed people who might well be able to help her. If this wasn't her ship, they could no doubt point her in the right direction.

Well, well, well… So there were still women in the world who blushed?

Hugh Patterson was intrigued, he had to admit, as he strolled along the marina, having finally extricated himself from the group of overexcited young women that he really didn't have the energy for after a long lunch with his Spanish friend, Carlotta. Well acquainted with the tourist circuit of the Mediterranean for a couple of years now, Hugh had friends in many of the popular cruise ship destinations.

It wasn't just sailors that had a girl in every port these days, he mused. Ships' doctors could be just as privileged and if you were that way inclined, it was the easiest sex life ever because anybody involved knew that it was never going to be anything serious. It was just intermittent fun. Living life for the moment and enjoying every minute of it.

That young woman he'd made blush at the taxi rank had looked as if she needed to learn to let herself enjoy the moment. Fancy being so uptight you wouldn't even let someone help with your suitcase? Or even make eye contact with them when they offered? Maybe it was actually irritating rather than intriguing? Being dismissed like that was not something he was used to.

'Hi, Hugh. Had a good day?'

One of the team welcoming people back on board the ship after their shore excursions saw him heading for the gangway.

'Fabulous, thanks, Simon. I love Barcelona. I had a picnic with a friend in Parc Guell.'

'Oh…lucky you, not having to work today. I don't get a day off on shore until Santorini this time. Or it might be Mykonos. One of the Greek islands, anyway.'

'I know… I'm lucky. We only need one doctor on board at all times when we're in port so, with two of us, we can take turns.'

He did feel lucky. What other doctors got to do their work in what could seem like an endless holiday but still got to practise enough real medicine that it didn't get boring and it was also possible to keep one's skills honed? Okay, he'd probably want to settle down sometime in the future but not yet. Maybe never, in fact. He'd almost done that once and look what a disaster that had turned out to be.

'I'm about to go and take over from Peter now, though,' he added, heading towards the gangway. 'That way he can at least get out and stretch his legs on land.'

Hugh took the stairs rather than the elevator to get to the lobby atrium of the ship, which was one of the most impressive areas on board with its marble floors, glittering chandeliers, huge potted palm trees, and the grand piano that was always providing some background music for the crowds taking advantage of the boutique shops and bars that circled the lobby on several levels.

Except old Harry wasn't playing his usual repertoire of popular classics. He wasn't playing anything at all but standing beside his piano stool, looking down at a knot of people at the base of one of several staircases that curved gracefully between the atrium levels.

What was going on? Hugh's pace increased as he

got close enough to see that someone was on the floor in the middle of the group. An elderly woman, who, despite what had to be well over thirty-degree heat today, was wearing quite thick stockings. One of her shoes had come off and was lying beside someone that was crouched at the woman's head.

'Let me through, please,' he said calmly. 'I'm a doctor. What's happened here?'

The crouching person looked up and Hugh was momentarily startled to see that it was the blushing girl from the taxi rank. Right now, however, she was supporting an elderly woman's head in a manner that suggested she knew what she was doing to protect and assess a potential cervical spine injury.

'She fell,' he was told. 'From about halfway down these stairs. Her neck seems to be okay, though.'

'Did you see it happen?'

'Yes… I was almost beside her going up the stairs.'

'Please…' the victim of the fall raised her hands. 'Just help me up. I'm fine… I really don't want to cause such a fuss.'

'We need to make sure you're okay first,' Hugh told her. 'My name's Hugh and I'm a doctor and this is…' He raised his eyebrows at the young woman who had, he couldn't help noticing, rather extraordinary eyes—a golden hazel shade but the edge of the iris had a dark rim around it, as if nature had been determined to accentuate the design.

'Lisa,' she supplied. 'My name's Lisa and I'm a nurse.'

No wonder she was giving the impression of competence, Hugh thought, as he focused on his patient. 'What's your name, love?' he asked.

'Mabel…'

'Is anything hurting, Mabel?'

'I… I'm not sure… I don't think so, dear.'

'Can you take a deep breath? Does that hurt?'

'No…'

'Is someone with you?'

'Frank…my husband…he's coming shoon. We need to shee about our…our…'

Hugh frowned. Mabel might look to be well into her eighties but that didn't mean she might not have been having a drink or two this afternoon. But slurred speech could very well be an indication of something more serious as well—like hypoglycaemia from a diabetic emergency or a head injury, which was not unlikely given the hard marble flooring beneath her.

'Was she knocked out?' he asked Lisa.

She shook her head. 'I don't think so but, if she was, it would have only been for a moment because I was beside her by the time she got to the bottom of the stairs. I tried to catch her but I was just a split second too slow, unfortunately.'

This Lisa might be small but Hugh could imagine her leaping into action to try and help someone. She was still clearly determined to help.

'She didn't just fall,' Lisa added. 'She looked dizzy. She was already holding the railing but she let go and…' Lisa was watching the elderly woman carefully. 'Mabel? Do you remember that?'

'No…pleashe…let me up…'

Hugh was holding Mabel's wrist, finding her pulse rapid but very pronounced, so her blood pressure couldn't be low enough to explain any dizziness.

'Move back, folks.' Old Harry, the pianist, had come

down from the stage and was trying to move people further away. 'Let's give them some space.' He caught Hugh's gaze. 'I'll go to the infirmary, shall I? And get some help?'

Hugh nodded. 'Yes, thank you.'

Mabel pulled away from his hand and moved as if she was making an effort to sit up.

'Don't move, Mabel,' Lisa said. 'Let us look after you for a minute, okay?'

But Mabel tried to roll and then cried out with pain.

'What's hurting?' Hugh asked.

'Look...' Lisa tilted her head to indicate what she had noticed. 'That looks like some rotation and shortening of her left leg, don't you think? A NOF?'

Fracturing a neck of femur was a definite possibility given the mechanism of injury and they were often not that painful until the patient tried to move, but Hugh was impressed that Lisa had picked up on it with no more than a glance.

'Try and keep still, Mabel.' Lisa leaned down so that Mabel could hear her reassurance. 'It's okay... we're going to take care of you...'

The warmth and confidence in her voice was as distinctive as her eye colouring. She sounded absolutely genuine—as if she was well used to taking care of people and doing it extremely well. If Hugh were unwell or injured, he would certainly feel better hearing that voice. Mabel was trying to respond but seemed to be having trouble getting any words out and that was when Hugh noticed the droop that was now obvious on one side of her face. Lisa's observations that it had appeared to be a medical event that had caused the fall rather than a simple trip and the other symptoms like the slurred speech now were coming together to make it urgent to get this patient into hospital.

It was a relief to see the other ship's doctor, his colleague Peter, coming into the lobby, with the emergency kit in his arms. One of their nurses was following and she carried a pillow and a blanket under one arm and an oxygen cylinder under the other. Hugh had another flash of relief that they were currently docked in the port of a major city. They might be very well equipped to deal with emergencies on board but someone who was potentially having a stroke and had fractured their hip in a fall would have needed evacuation to a land hospital as quickly as possible. At least they wouldn't need to call in a helicopter this time.

'We need an ambulance,' he told Peter. 'Not just for the NOF. We've got signs that the fall might be the result of a CVA.'

'We'll get them on the way.' the older doctor nodded.

'Mabs?' An elderly man was pushing his way through the concerned spectators. 'Oh, no…what's happened?'

He crouched down beside Lisa, who moved to let him get closer to his wife. Hugh turned to reach into the emergency kit as Peter opened it. They needed to get some oxygen on for their patient, check her blood glucose level, get an IV line in and some pain medication on board and to splint her hip. They needed to talk to Mabel's husband, too, and find out about her past medical history and what kind of medications she might be taking. It was only when he looked back to start talking to Frank that he realised that Lisa had disappeared. Did she think she might be in the way now that the rest of the ship's medical staff were on scene?

It was a shame she'd gone, anyway. He would have liked to have thanked her. And to tell her how helpful she had been.

Lisa should probably have introduced herself to the ship's doctor and the nurse who'd come in with him and she should have offered to keep helping, but after she'd moved to let Mabel's husband get close enough to comfort his wife, the nurse had moved in front of her and it just hadn't been the right time to say anything that might interrupt the focus on their patient so Lisa had let herself slip into the background to let them do their work. She would have expected that good-looking passenger who also happened to be a doctor to stand back and let the people in uniform take over but it almost looked as if he was still in charge of the scene.

Moving further back brought Lisa to the bottom of the staircase and she took a few steps and then paused to watch what was happening. She might be doing this herself very soon, dressed in pale green scrubs with a stethoscope hanging round her neck like the nurse who was currently taking Mabel's blood pressure. The doctor, in a crisp, white uniform with epaulettes on the shoulders of his shirt, was attaching electrodes to monitor Mabel's heart and the extra doctor… Hugh… was sorting something from what looked like a well-stocked kit. IV supplies, perhaps?

She could only see Hugh's profile but she'd been much closer to him only a minute or two ago and she'd been aware from the instant he'd appeared that this was a very different man from the one who might have been flirting with her near the taxi rank earlier.

It wasn't that he was any less good looking, of course. Or even that that relaxed grace that came from an easy enjoyment of his life had vanished. It was more that there was a focus that made it obvious this man was intelligent and he knew what he was doing. Lisa could respect that. She could forgive him for being some kind of playboy, in fact. After all, doctors were just like any other professional people and there were no laws that prevented them going on holiday and letting their hair down occasionally, were there?

Onlookers were being asked to leave the area and make space as a team of paramedics arrived with a stretcher. Lisa found herself in a flow of people that took her to the next level of the atrium but she knew she needed to find an elevator or internal stairway. Not that there was any point in finding the ship's medical centre to introduce herself when she knew the staff were busy here for the moment, but her suitcase would have been delivered to her cabin by now so it would be a good time to find out where that was and freshen up before she went to meet her new colleagues.

She did know she had to go down rather than up. Crew members didn't get cabins with balconies. They were possibly right in the middle of the ship and might not even have any portholes. Lisa had to hope that she wasn't prone to seasickness. Either that, or that the Mediterranean was a very calm sea.

An hour or so later, Lisa was heading for the middle of Deck Two, where a helpful steward had told her the medical centre and infirmary were located. She had showered, swapped her jeans for a more formal skirt and brushed her short waves of auburn hair into a semblance of order. A large red cross painted on a steel door told her that she had found her destination and a sign below that gave the hours the medical facility was open and phone numbers for the nurse on duty for out of hours. So, it was a nurse rather than a doctor that made the first response to any calls?

Lisa's heart skipped a beat as she went into an empty waiting room. She was going to be one of those nurses for the next two weeks, with possibly more responsibility than she'd ever had before if she was going to be the first responder to something major like a cardiac arrest or severe trauma. This time she knew that that internal flutter was definitely excitement. She was stepping well out of her comfort zone here, and... well...she couldn't wait...

'Hello?'

The desk at one side of the waiting room was empty. Lisa peered around a corner and walked a short distance down the corridor. There were consulting rooms, a room labelled as a laboratory where she could see benches covered with equipment that looked like specialised blood or specimen testing machines and a closed door that had a sign saying it was the pharmacy. An open door on the other side of the corridor showed Lisa what looked like a small operating theatre. Surprised, she stepped into it. There was a theatre light above the narrow bed in the centre of the room, a portable X-ray machine, cardiac monitor and ventilator nearby and glass-fronted cupboards lining the walls that looked to be stocked with a huge amount of medical supplies.

A movement in her peripheral vision as she entered the narrow corridor again made Lisa turn, to see the back view of the white pants and shirt of the ship's doctor's uniform as he stood at the desk in the waiting room.

'Hello...' she said again, walking towards him. 'I was starting to wonder if I was all alone here.'

The doctor turned and Lisa could actually feel her jaw dropping. If she'd thought this man was good looking when she'd seen him kissing his girlfriend, it was nothing to how attractive he looked in uniform. Especially *this* uniform, with the snowy, white fabric accentuating his tanned skin and making those brown eyes look remarkably like melted chocolate. He also looked as startled as Lisa was feeling. They both spoke at precisely the same time.

'What are *you* doing here?' Lisa's voice was embarrassingly squeaky.

'It's *you*...' His tone was more than welcoming. It was almost delighted.

They both stopped speaking then and simply stared at each other. Lisa was confused. Why was Hugh wearing the same uniform as the ship's doctor? And, now that they were nowhere near someone who needed medical attention, why was it that the first thought that came into her head as she looked at him was the image of him kissing that woman so very thoroughly? To her dismay she could feel heat creeping into her cheeks.

It was Hugh who finally broke the awkward moment, his mouth curving into a lazy smile. 'You're blushing.' He sounded amused. 'Again...'

Oh, help... So, avoiding eye contact with him out on the pier hadn't been enough to disguise her beetroot-coloured cheeks, then. Lisa closed her eyes as she sighed. 'I'm a redhead. It kind of goes with the territory.' She opened her eyes again, frowning. 'I thought you were a passenger.'

'But you knew I was a doctor. We've just been working together.'

'Yes, but... I thought you were a doctor who was on holiday.' Good grief...the look she was getting suggested that it was Hugh who was confused now. He probably thought that she was an idiot. 'I'm Lisa,' she added. 'Lisa Phillips. I'm a—'

'Nurse,' Hugh put in helpfully. 'Yes, I remember. A good one, too, I think. Thank you for your help earlier. With Mabel.'

'It was a pleasure.' The compliment about her abilities was making her feel far more proud of herself than it merited. 'Do you know how she is?'

'I believe she's doing well. She's scheduled for hip surgery later this evening but the better news was that her neurological symptoms had virtually resolved by the time she reached the hospital.'

'So it was a TIA rather than a stroke?' A transient ischaemic attack could present with the same symptoms of a stroke but they were temporary. A warning signal rather than a critical event.

'So it would seem.' The quirk of Hugh's eyebrow told her that he was impressed by her medical assessment but then his smile reappeared. 'Now...what it is that I can help *you* with, Lisa Phillips? I hope you're not unwell...or injured...'

Along with a very genuine concern in his voice, there was a gleam in those brown eyes that made Lisa remember that kiss all over again. Or rather the moment he'd caught her gaze after the kiss and they'd both acknowledged what she'd seen. There was also an acknowledgement of something on a different level—one of mutual attraction, perhaps? Oh...help... Lisa looked away. Any attempt to return the man's smile evaporated instantly. She'd never expected to see him again and things were about to get even more unsettling.

'I'm a nurse,' she explained.

'Yes, I know. A nurse on holiday.'

'No... I'm here to work. Through London Locums. I believe I'm replacing someone called Amanda who needed time to support her mother who's having surgery?'

There was another moment of startled silence. 'You're our *locum*? Why didn't you say something?'

'Why would I? I thought you were a passenger.'

'But you didn't say anything when Peter turned up.'

'Peter?'

'Our other doctor. And Janet was there—one of our nurses.'

'Well...it didn't seem quite the right moment to be introducing myself.'

'I guess not. Let's do that properly now, shall we?' Hugh was holding out his hand. 'I'm Hugh Patterson. Pleased to meet you, Lisa. I look forward to working with you for the next couple of weeks. And it will be me you're working with mostly because you're filling a gap on my Blue Watch.'

'Oh?'

Lisa had taken his hand automatically but, instead of shaking hers, he simply held it for a moment and then gave it a slow squeeze, and that did it. Like a switch being flicked on, an electrical jolt shot from

Lisa's hand and raced up her arm—an extraordinary tingle she had never felt before in her life. It was enough to make her pull her hand free with the kind of instinctive reflex she might have had to touching something that was hot enough to burn her badly.

How weird was that?

And this Hugh Patterson was looking forward to working with her?

'Yes,' he said, as if confirming her silent query. 'I'm Blue Watch. Peter's Green Watch. It just means that we'll be working together. Probably having the same days off as well and you should be able to get some shore excursions if there's space. Do you have a favourite place to visit around the Mediterranean?'

'This is the first time I've been out of England,' Lisa confessed.

'Really?' Hugh sounded astonished. 'You don't like travelling?'

'I've…um…never really had the opportunity, that's all.' Lisa wasn't about to tell him the reasons why. He didn't need to know about her family responsibilities and he certainly wouldn't be interested in hearing about financial hardship. This Hugh Patterson looked like one of life's golden people who never had to worry about anything much. Someone from a completely different planet from her own, which made her wonder how well they might be able to work together. Perhaps he was thinking along the same lines now because the look she was receiving made her feel as if she was being seen as someone very unusual. Someone…interesting?

The prospect of her new working responsibilities pushing the limits of her professional comfort zones were nothing in comparison to how this man was pushing the boundaries of anything she considered personally safe when it came to men.

No wonder she'd snatched her hand back as if she was about to get burned.

Anyone who had anything to do with Hugh Patterson could be playing with fire. Lisa could feel herself releasing her deeper than usual breath carefully. It was nothing to worry about because she never played with anything dangerous. Never had. Never would. That there was even any temptation there was enough of a warning that she wasn't about to ignore.

'I'm looking forward to working here as well,' she heard herself saying with commendable calmness. 'And, if you've got a moment, I'd appreciate a bit of a tour, if you've got time, that is. I'd like to get up to speed as soon as possible—preferably before my first shift tomorrow morning.'

Lisa was edging back a little as she spoke. Even though she had broken the skin contact between them well over a minute ago, she could still feel that odd tingle it had provoked. It was almost as if she could still feel the warmth of his skin, filling the air between them, and when he spoke both his words and his tone made both those impressions even more noticeable.

'No problem,' he said. Those dark eyes were watching her so closely Lisa had the horrible feeling that he knew about that tingle. That he knew that she thought he was dangerous.

'Come with me,' he added, with that lazy smile that was already beginning to feel familiar—the one that suggested he was finding this all rather amusing and he intended to enjoy the entertainment as much as possible. 'I'm all yours, Nurse Phillips.'

CHAPTER TWO

OH, DEAR...

It was going to be too tempting not to tease this new colleague a little. There was something about her that made her seem much younger than she probably was. First appearances were giving him an interesting impression of someone being well educated and intelligent but possibly naïve at the same time. Hugh had never had a little sister, but if he had, he was quite sure he'd feel like this in her company. He could appreciate the fact she was gorgeous without being remotely attracted, feel proud of her ability to do her job well and perhaps recognise that there were things he could teach her. That, in the interests of being a kind, big brotherly sort of person, he had a duty to teach her, even.

Like persuading her that life could be significantly more enjoyable if she relaxed a bit? She was so tense. So eager to give the impression that she could cope with anything she might be asked to do. It seemed that this Lisa not only liked to be able to manage on her own when it came to carrying a suitcase, she was determined to get all the information she needed to be able to achieve the ability to manage alone in her professional environment if that should prove necessary.

'So...do you follow a standard protocol for resuscitation in cardiac arrest?' Lisa was clearly familiar with the model of life pack for cardiac monitoring and defibrillation that was on top of their rapid-response/resuscitation trolley. 'Thirty to two compressions to ventilation rate until an advanced airway is secure? Immediate shock for documented VT or VF and then every two minutes?'

Hugh nodded. 'You've got a recent Advanced Care Life Support qualification, I assume? That's one of the standard requirements for working on board a ship.'

Lisa mirrored his nod. 'I've had experience with laryngeal mask airways and administration of adrenaline but I'm not yet qualified for antiarrhythmic drugs or intubation.'

Something in her tone made Hugh curious. Or maybe it was the use of that qualifying 'yet'.

'What made you decide to go into nursing and not become a doctor?' he asked her.

There was a flash of surprise in her eyes that made him wonder if she wasn't used to people asking her personal questions—or that she discouraged them because she preferred to guard her privacy.

The response was no more than a verbal shrug, however. 'Why do you ask?'

'I just get the impression you'd like to be doing more. Like intubating someone in a cardiac arrest?'

Lisa's glance slid away from his. 'I always wanted to work in a medical field,' she said. 'Nursing was the most practical option at the time.' She turned to touch another piece of equipment that was close. 'Does this take digital X-rays?'

'Mmm...' Hugh was still curious but he knew when

someone wanted to avoid talking about something. Had
Lisa become a nurse because she hadn't been able to
afford the time or costs to go to medical school? 'It can
be helpful to be able to transmit an image, either for a
second opinion—which we can get via internet links
to all sorts of international experts—or to get the right
treatment available as soon as possible if we transfer
someone to a land hospital, by chopper, for instance.'

'Do you go with them?'

'Sometimes they might need a doctor on board if
they're critical. If someone local doesn't come with the
evacuation crew we might send Tim, who's qualified
as both a paramedic and a nurse and covers a lot of our
night shifts currently. Or you might even go as a medical chaperone, depending on what else is going on.'

It was a true statement but Hugh was telling her
that she might be involved because he wanted to see
her reaction and, sure enough, there was a gleam of
interest in those amazing eyes at the prospect of being
choppered off the ship and back again. A glow of excitement even, and that gave him an odd little kick in
his gut. So, she was up for a bit of adventure, this Lisa,
even if she was uptight. This was good. It could make
teasing her even more enjoyable.

'And do you ever do actual surgery in here? It looks
more like an operating theatre than an assessment or
treatment area.'

'It is, at times.' Hugh told her. 'We have to be able
to deal with every situation you could imagine and
sometimes we're out of range of emergency transport
for some time. We've got anaesthetic and ventilation
gear along with the digital X-ray and ultrasound and

a full range of surgical instruments, though I haven't had to use too many of them yet.'

'But you've got a surgical background?'

'I've mostly specialised in emergency medicine and critical care but I've got both surgical and anaesthetic diplomas as well. How 'bout you?' Hugh led the way out of the room. 'What's your background?'

'My early experience was working in A and E,' Lisa said. 'Which I really loved. But my last job as head of a nursing home team gave me a lot of scope for first response and medical assessment and that was interesting, too. I'm…between jobs at the moment, which was why a locum position was ideal.' She had paused to look through the door of the laboratory. 'What range of tests can you do on board?'

It seemed like asking Lisa a question only made him want to ask more—like why she'd gone to work in a nursing home if she'd loved the emergency department so much? And, if she'd had so much experience already, why did she give off this impression of…well, it was almost innocence. Unworldliness, anyway, and that certainly wasn't something Hugh normally came across in the women he met these days. He was curious, he realised. A lot more curious than he usually was when he met someone new.

'Again, we have to be prepared for as many things as possible. We can test for cardiac enzymes if we suspect a heart attack, infections, arterial oxygen levels and blood glucose levels and a dozen or more other things. Janet's our expert and she can give you a rundown on how to do the tests but it's mostly automatic so it's easy. And, speaking of Janet, she's in our little two-bed infirmary at the moment because we admitted a woman with a severe migraine earlier today for monitoring so let's go there and I can introduce you.'

'That will be great, thank you.'

Hugh watched as Lisa took a last, slow glance back over her shoulder towards the areas he'd already shown her, as if she was mentally cataloguing and memorising everything she'd learned so far, and he was almost tempted to give her a quick quiz but then her gaze ended by catching his and there was a note of surprise there. Or maybe it was criticism because she had expected him to be moving by now and taking her to the next source of information about her new job.

She could turn out to be bossy, he decided, once she had settled in and was confident of her surroundings and responsibilities, but he took the hint and led her towards the hospital end of the medical centre.

"Bossy" was the wrong word, he decided moments later. "Feisty" was probably a more accurate prediction. His internal correction made him smile.

Hugh liked feisty. He liked it a lot.

If he was any more laidback, he'd be horizontal.

But Lisa knew that this relaxed impression of complete confidence with a streak of an impish desire to liven things up a little was just one side of the coin as far as Dr Hugh Patterson was concerned. She'd seen him morph into a completely focused professional dealing with an accident scene and she saw the coin start to flip again as they entered the ship's hospital at the other end of the medical centre. There were two small four-bed wards, one for passengers and one for crew, separated by a nursing station currently staffed by the team's senior nurse. Janet was older, with a friendly face and a Scottish accent but they had no time for more than a brief introduction before Hugh picked up the chart for their inpatient.

'She's responded well to the treatment,' Janet told him. 'She's had a good sleep, her headache's down to a two-out-of-ten pain score and she hasn't vomited since her first dose of anti-emetic.'

Lisa saw the frown line of concentration that appeared between Hugh's eyes as he rapidly scanned the information on the chart of medications administered and observations taken. Then he walked towards one of the only two beds in the room, the frown line evaporating as his mouth curved in a reassuring smile.

'Rita, isn't it? I'm Hugh Patterson, one of the doctors on board. It was my colleague Peter who saw you this morning, yes?'

The woman on the bed, who looked to be in her early forties, was nodding. 'I feel ever so much better,' she told Hugh. 'Those pills have been wonderful.' She was staring at Hugh. 'Have we met somewhere before?'

His smile was charming but fleeting. 'I don't think I've had the pleasure but I'm very glad you're feeling better. I suspect the main thing that's helped was to give you something for the nausea and vomiting and fix the dehydration that was making things worse. This wasn't your first migraine, was it?'

'No, but I haven't had one for ages. I know to stay away from triggers like chocolate and red wine.'

'Are they the only triggers that you know of? Flashing lights and loud noises can do it for some people. You haven't been out partying in the nightclubs on board till all hours, have you?' His tone was teasing.

'I should be so lucky.'

Rita was smiling now. And blinking more rapidly, Lisa noticed. Good grief…was she trying to flirt with her doctor? Batting her eyelashes even? If so, at least Hugh wasn't responding with anything more than a hint of his earlier smile.

'Might be an idea to keep avoiding anything like that for a day or two. I'm sure you don't want to be stuck in here and missing out on any more shore excursions.'

'No…my friends all went out for a horse riding trek today and I was so looking forward to doing that. Oh…' Rita's eyes widened. 'I remember now. I *do* know you. You're *that* Hugh Patterson…'

'Oh?' Hugh was looking wary now. 'Which one would that be?'

'Your mother was Diane Patterson, yes? The District Commissioner for the Windsor pony club and you used to have a three-day event on your family estate every year. I rode in it more than once—oh, ages ago now but I remember you used to be on the quad bike, doing errands like delivering coffee to the judges.'

Wow… His family had an estate in Windsor? Somehow that didn't surprise Lisa. That laidback, making the most of good things approach to life often went hand in hand with extreme wealth, didn't it?

'Mmm… Ancient history.'

His clipped tone made it very clear that he had no interest in pursuing this line of conversation and Lisa dropped her gaze instantly when his glance slid sideways so she could let him know she wasn't interested in hearing personal information like this. She could understand perfectly well why he might be embarrassed at having his family's financial situation made

common knowledge and she could sympathise with
that. She might be completely at the other end of the
financial spectrum but she wouldn't want strangers
knowing about hers either.

'We'll be setting sail in the next hour or so.' Hugh
was scribbling something on Rita's chart. 'What we'll
do is take your IV line out and give you some medications to take with you.' He was turning away from this
patient. 'Don't hesitate to call if you're not continuing
to improve, though. One of our wonderful staff members will be available at all times.'

His smile became suddenly a lot more genuine as
his gaze shifted to catch Lisa's and, for the first time,
it was impossible not to smile back. He was making
her feel so welcome and as though he really did believe she would be a welcome addition to their team,
even though he had only just met her. There could
be relief making that welcome more pronounced because he could get away from a conversation he obviously didn't want to have but it didn't matter... Lisa
was going to make sure that Hugh wasn't disappointed
with his new staff member.

Janet was also very welcoming and, after she had
taken out Rita's IV line, dispensed the medication
Hugh had prescribed and discharged her, the older
nurse took Lisa to find her uniform and then continue
her exploration of the ship's medical facilities as she
heard about what her duties would entail.

It was during this additional tour that Lisa became
aware of a background hum of sound that was new and
an odd sensation that something was changing in the
air around her. Janet smiled at her expression.

'We're underway,' she told Lisa. 'I love that moment when we leave shore and head out into the freedom of the open sea. It's what keeps me coming back every season.'

Yes. Lisa could recognise that it was the distant hum and vibration of extremely powerful engines that she could both hear and feel, and the realisation hit her that this massive vessel and the thousands of passengers and crew on board were soon going to be far from land and reliant on what suddenly seemed like a very small medical team to deal with any medical or traumatic emergency that might happen.

They were also on the way to somewhere Lisa had never been in her life and the combination of potential adventure and challenge was…well…it was enormously exciting, that's what it was. The hum and sensation of movement was coalescing somewhere in the pit of her stomach in a tingle that was not unlike the one she had experienced earlier today, when Hugh Patterson had been holding her hand, but this was far more acceptable. Welcome, in fact, because it was almost completely a professional kind of excitement.

Whatever this exotic position threw at her for the next couple of weeks, she was going to do her absolute best. She always did, of course, but there was an incentive here that was a little different from anything she'd experienced before. She had to admit that part of that incentive was a little disturbing, however. While it was perfectly natural to want to do her job exceptionally well for the sake of anybody who was ill or injured on this ship, and she'd always had that determination wherever she'd worked, what was different this time was why it seemed almost more important to impress her new boss.

* * *

I found your ship online. Looks amazing!

It's totally unreal. There are bars and restaurants open all night, shows like you might see on Broadway, fitness clubs and dance classes—you name it, it's happening on board this ship.

I found a page with pictures of all the important people who had lots of stripes on their shoulders.

They're the officers.

Lisa was curled up on her bunk, typing rapidly in the message box on her laptop screen. Conversations with Abby were both more reliable and a lot less expensive this way than by phone.

The ship's doctors were there too.

They're considered to be officers as well. The nurses get privileges too. We can go anywhere we like on board and not just keep to the crew quarters for meals and things.

Who's the doctor with the beard?

That's Peter.

And who's the other one? The really *really* good-looking one?

Hugh. He's the one I mostly work with.

Oooh… Lucky you.

A string of emojis with hearts instead of eyes made Lisa shake her head before she tapped back.

You're just as bad as every other woman on board. We had four of them in the clinic yesterday, all trying to outdo each other to get his attention and…get this… two of them had come in to ask for the morning-after pill because things had got "out of hand" the night before at some party.

Wow…not the best line to take if you want to get somebody interested, I wouldn't have thought.

Lisa was smiling as she responded.
No. And anyway there are strict rules about the crew fraternising with the passengers.

What about the crew fraternising with the crew???

It was a winking face at the end of Abby's message this time.

Not going to happen.

Why not? Is he single?

I haven't asked him.

Why not?

I'm not interested.

Oh…yeah…right… Why not? Because he's too good-looking? Doesn't wear socks with sandals?

Lisa leaned back against her pillow and closed her eyes for a moment. She'd been busy enough settling into her new environment in the last couple of days so that she could concentrate purely on her work and find her way around this enormous ship. There was a lot of work to do during the often busy open surgeries at the medical centre, which ran for a couple of hours both morning and early evening, where she was responsible for triaging any patients that arrived and dealing with minor cases that didn't need to see a doctor, like small lacerations or medication needed for seasickness.

Between those hours, there seemed to be plenty of administration to take care of, new people to meet and calls to what had so far proved to be easily managed situations in cabins or public areas of the ship.

But now that Abby was teasing her, there was no getting away from the fact that she was not immune to Hugh Patterson's charms, however confident she was in being able to resist them. Not that she'd had to resist them, mind you. He was both charming, friendly and great to work with, but it was patently obvious that she was a curiosity to him and she knew why. She'd seen one of the type of women he was attracted to, for heaven's sake, and she couldn't be more different to the sophisticated, confident and sexy blonde that had accompanied him back to the port in Barcelona.

The woman that he'd been kissing with such… thoroughness…

Oh, no…there it was again. That tingle that she thought she had actually conquered over the last busy days. Distraction was needed.

Lisa opened her eyes and started tapping again.

How are things for you? Do you still like the hostel?

Love it. It's so much easier to be close to campus like this and the food's great. Miss you, though.

Miss you, too. Got a date for your driver's licence test yet?

Next week. And guess what?

What?

I'm going to try out for a wheelchair basketball team. I need some more exercise, what with all the great food in the canteens.

Hope that's not as dangerous as wheelchair rugby.

Lisa hit the "enter" button before she stopped to think that maybe Abby wouldn't appreciate the warning but it had always been difficult not to be overprotective of her little sister.

Sure enough, she could almost hear the sigh that came with Abby's response. And she obviously wasn't the only one who would prefer a distraction.

Stop being a mother hen. Tell me about where you are. Have you been on a shore excursion yet?

Not yet. My watch was on duty for the stops in both Corsica and Marseilles. Next stop is Nice, though—tomorrow—although we actually stop around the corner in Villefranche sur Mer because this ship is too big for the Nice port and we have to take small boats to get in to shore. We dock at dawn and then the ship doesn't sail until about ten o'clock at night and I'm just helping with the morning surgery hours so I've got most of the day and the evening to go sightseeing.

OMG...on the French Riviera? You're living the dream.

I know.

Lisa found an emoji with a huge grin.

I'll send photos but try not to get too jealous.

Don't send a photo unless it's you and that cute doctor alone in some romantic French café. Preferably drinking champagne.

LOL Lisa sent back.

Give it up, Abby. Not going to happen.

But, despite any firm intentions, it was what she was thinking about as she shut down her computer, climbed into bed a bit later and switched off her light. Champagne. Delicious food. An outdoor eatery, maybe shaded with grapevines. Someone playing a piano accordion nearby. And a companion who was only biding his time before taking the opportunity to kiss her senseless. Lisa could actually feel the tension of that anticipation. The curiosity. Desire...?

No. She pushed it away, rolling over to find a cool patch on her pillow. She'd certainly never found a kiss that lived up to that level of anticipation. It was the stuff of romance novels, not real life. It was just easier to toy with fantasy when she was temporarily "living the dream", as Abby had reminded her. Floating on the Mediterranean in a luxury cruise ship. Heading for land in a country that was famous for romance as much as anything else.

And there she was again...imagining being on the receiving side of a kiss like the one Hugh had been giving the gorgeous blonde. Not necessarily with Hugh, of course...just a kiss like that.

Oh...who was she kidding? It had to be Hugh, she realised as she was drifting into sleep. She'd never even seen anyone kissing like that in real life—she'd only read about it, or seen it on a movie screen. But this wasn't real life, exactly, was it? Lisa was already deeply into a very odd mix of real life and fantasy and the lines between the two were already a bit blurred. About to indulge herself by drifting further towards the fantasy side, it was a rude shock to hear the strident beeping of her pager. She snapped on her light and reached for the small device.

Code One, the pager read. Lido Deck.

Lisa was out of bed and hauling on her uniform in seconds. There was no time to even think about what her hair looked like. Her cabin was the closest to the medical centre. She had to go and grab the rapid response trolley and head for the deck that had the swimming pools. Hopefully, someone else from the team would join her quickly but, for the moment, she knew she was on her own.

Her heart skipped a beat and then sped up as she raced along the narrow corridor towards the medical centre. This was definitely real life and not any kind of fantasy and she was on the front line. Lisa had no idea if any of the other medical staff would also be responding to this call, even if Code One was the most urgent kind of summons. She might well be on her own until she found out whether the situation was really serious enough to warrant extra staff at this time of night.

It had to be well after midnight by the time Lisa had commandeered a service lift to get her to the Lido deck as quickly as possible. Heads turned as she raced past people wrapped up in blankets lying on deckchairs. It was a movie night where a huge screen had been lowered on the other side of the largest swimming pool, the deckchairs lined up in rows to accommodate the audience. Red and white striped bags of popcorn got spilled as a crew member in a white hat jumped out of Lisa's way. She passed restaurants that were still open and she could smell the variety of food on offer—from burgers to Indian meals.

There were people everywhere, laughing and having fun, even dancing in the area that Lisa was heading for where there was another pool and two spas, which made it feel quite bizarre to find a knot of crew members and others around a figure that was slumped against the side of one of the spa pools, wearing only a bathing suit.

Lisa could hear that the young man was having trouble breathing as she crouched down beside him, feeling for his pulse on his wrist. It was rapid and very faint, which suggested his blood pressure could be low.

'I'm Lisa,' she told him. 'One of the ship's nurses. Can you tell me your name?'

He opened his mouth but all she could hear was the harsh sounds of him trying to move air through obstructed passages.

'His name's Alex,' someone told her. 'We got him out of the pool because he started coughing and couldn't stop.'

'Are you asthmatic, Alex?' Lisa was pulling open drawers on the resus trolley. She needed to get some oxygen on her patient and probably a nebuliser to try and help him breathe.

'He's allergic.'

Lisa looked up at the young woman in a red bikini. 'To what?'

'Strawberries. He told me when he didn't want to try my strawberry daiquiri.'

'He said he had an adrenaline pen in his pocket,' A crew member added. 'But we haven't found where he left his clothes yet.'

'Okay…' Lisa slipped an oxygen mask over Alex's face. 'I'm going to give you an injection right now,' she told him.

Her own heart rate was well up as she located the drug she needed, filled the syringe and administered the intramuscular injection. An anaphylactic reaction could be a very satisfying emergency to treat if it responded rapidly to adrenaline and the frightening swelling in the airways began to settle, but it could also be a situation that could just as rapidly spiral into something worse—potentially life-threatening.

Waiting the few minutes to see if a repeat dose was needed gave Lisa a chance to take some vital signs and check Alex more thoroughly, and that was when she noted the diffuse, red rash that was appearing all over his body.

'You didn't drink the daiquiri, did you, Alex?'

He shook his head. He was holding the oxygen mask against his face and his eyes, above the mask, were terrified. Even through the plastic of the mask, Lisa could see that his lips were swelling.

'I kissed him.' The girl in the red bikini burst into tears. 'This is my fault, isn't it? He's not going to die, is he? You have to *do* something...'

She did. Nebulised adrenaline was the next step, along with a repeat dose of the drug by injection but, even if that started to make a difference, Lisa was going to need help and, as if she'd sent out a silent prayer, the figure that pushed through the group of spectators was the answer she would have wanted the most.

Hugh Patterson.

'Fill me in,' was all he said. 'I've got some crew bringing a stretcher.'

'Anaphylaxis to strawberries,' Lisa told him. 'Diffuse rash, hypotensive, tachycardic and respiratory obstruction with stridor—oxygen saturation currently eighty-eight percent. First dose of adrenaline was about three minutes ago but there's no improvement.'

'No worries.' His nod let Lisa know that he'd absorbed all the information and he knew how serious this was. His tone was still laidback enough not to alarm anyone else, however. 'Let's get another dose on board. And can you set up a nebuliser as well?'

Lisa drew up the medication as Hugh put a hand on their patient's shoulder. 'We've got this, okay? But we're going to take you down to our medical centre where we've got all the bells and whistles. I'm just going to pop an IV into your arm while we wait for your transport.'

Lisa knew her way around the trolley drawers by now so she was able to hand Hugh everything he needed before he had to ask. A tourniquet to wrap around Alex's upper arm, an alcohol wipe to clean the skin, a cannula to slip into a vein and then the Luer plug and dressing to secure the access. Lisa prepped the bag of saline by puncturing the port with the spike of the giving set and then running fluid through the tubes to eliminate any air bubbles. Hugh was attaching the line to the Luer plug as the crew members arrived with the stretcher and then helped lift Alex onto it.

'Carry that bag, please, Lisa. And squeeze it. We need to get that fluid in fast.'

They moved swiftly through an increasingly sub-dued crowd of people on the Lido deck, into the lift and then down to the deck they needed. Lisa was re-lieved that they would soon be in their well-equipped treatment room. She was even more relieved that she had Hugh by her side. They had just been working seamlessly, side by side, to stabilise this patient and she was sure that they would have things under con-trol in no time.

'On my count,' Hugh said to the crew. 'Lift on three. One, two...*three*...'

Alex was being placed smoothly onto the bed as Lisa reached up to flick on the overhead operating the-atre light and she caught her breath in a gasp of dismay as it went on. Alex's head had flopped to one side and his chin had dropped enough to close his airway completely. He had clearly lost consciousness.

Hugh heard her gasp and his gaze locked on hers—only for a heartbeat but it was enough for a very clear message to be shared. Their patient's condition had just become a whole lot worse. They were in trouble and Hugh was counting on Lisa's assistance. She could also see the determination not to lose this battle in those dark eyes.

Lisa tilted her head instantly in a nod to let Hugh know she had received the message. That she would do whatever she could to help. That she shared his determination to succeed. And then she took a very deep breath.

CHAPTER THREE

IT WAS VERY likely that other members of the medical staff on board were already making their way to help with a Code One emergency but the non-medical crew members who'd helped transport their patient were dispatched to make sure that Peter knew what was going on. In the meantime, the situation was escalating so quickly that Hugh and Lisa were the only people available to deal with it and they would have to work fast to save this young man's life.

The bag of IV fluid that Lisa had been squeezing to administer it more quickly was empty so she reached for a new one. Fluid resuscitation was an essential part of dealing with anaphylactic shock. As was oxygenation. As she worked to set up the new bag of saline she could see how smoothly Hugh was working to tilt Alex's head back to try and open his airway and then, using one hand, to shift his stethoscope over all lung fields to listen for air movement.

'He's still shifting some air but it's not enough.'

Lisa checked that the clip on Alex's finger was secure and looked at the screen of the monitor, below the overly rapid spikes of the ECG. 'Oxygen saturation is down to seventy five percent,' she told Hugh.

The automatic blood pressure cuff was deflating at the same time. 'His BP's dropping again. Seventy-five over forty.'

'Come and take over here. We'll swap the nebuliser mask and use an Ambu bag and a hundred percent oxygen. I'll get another IV line in and start an adrenaline infusion. I'm not going to wait if things deteriorate any more, though. We'll go for a rapid sequence intubation.'

Lisa could feel the fierce concentration when Hugh took her place by Alex's head a minute or two later to try and insert a breathing tube through the swollen tissues in their patient's mouth and throat. A lot of doctors might have panicked when not only the first but the second attempt failed. Hugh only looked more focused. He caught Lisa's gaze as she moved back in with the bag mask and tried to deliver oxygen to Alex's lungs.

'Oxygen saturation's down to seventy percent,' he said quietly. 'We're in a "can't intubate, can't oxygenate" situation. Have you ever assisted with a surgical cricothyroidotomy?'

'No.' Lisa held his gaze. 'Do you want me to find Tim? Or Peter?'

'There's no time.' Hugh hadn't broken the gaze either. 'You can do this. I'll talk you through it.'

And, within what felt like seconds, when they were both gloved and Hugh had unrolled another kit, that was exactly what he was doing as he palpated the front of Alex's neck around his Adam's apple after swabbing it with antiseptic.

'I can feel the thyroid cartilage here and this is the cricoid cartilage. I'm aiming for the space between them, where the membrane is, and I've got a good grip on it all so nothing moves.'

With his free hand, Hugh picked up a scalpel and made first a vertical incision and then a horizontal one. Because Alex was now deeply unconscious and this was such an urgent situation, there was no time or need for local anaesthesia but Lisa found herself holding her breath at Hugh's confident, swift movements.

'I can feel the "pop" so I know I'm in the trachea now.' Even his voice sounded calm. 'I'm going to put my finger in when I take the scalpel out but what I need you to do is pick up that tracheal hook, put it at the top end of the incision and retract everything for me.'

Lisa had never been this hands on in such a dramatic invasion procedure but, amazingly, her hand wasn't shaking and she had no problem following Hugh's clear instructions. She watched as he widened the incision, inserted a bougie as a guide for the endotracheal tube that followed and then inflated the balloon around the end of the tube that would help secure it. He attached the Ambu bag to the tube and squeezed it.

'Good chest rise,' he said quietly. 'I'll have a listen to be sure and then we can take that hook out and secure the tube properly.'

Lisa could tell that the tube had been correctly placed because the concentration of oxygen in Alex's blood was already increasing and his heart rate slowing a little. They had got through a crisis that could have killed an otherwise healthy young person and, when Hugh looked up and smiled at Lisa, while he was still listening to lung sounds with his stethoscope, she knew that he was just as happy as she was.

They had done this together. She could hear other people arriving in the medical centre now, with rapid footsteps coming towards the treatment room, but it was Lisa and Hugh who had done the hard work here. They were the only ones to have shared that rising tension, background alarm of the ticking clock of a limited amount of time available and the nail-biting stress of a dramatic procedure to deal with it. So they were the only ones who got to share this moment of relief. Joy, even.

Along with something else. A knowledge that they could work together this closely under extreme circumstances. That they could trust each other. That they were in exactly the same place when it came to how much they cared about their patients and how hard they were prepared for a fight for something that really mattered. The moment of connection was only a heartbeat before others rushed into the room but the effect lingered as Lisa stepped back to let Peter and Tim close to their patient. It was Tim who was tasked with securing the tube and Peter assisted Hugh in setting up the portable ventilator.

'We'll need transport to the nearest hospital. He'll need intensive care monitoring for a while.'

'Chopper?'

'Possibly. We might be close enough to shore for a coastguard vessel. I'll get hold of the captain.'

'I can go with him, if he needs an escort,' Tim offered.

Hugh nodded his acknowledgment of the offer but his gaze shifted to Lisa, one eyebrow raised. Was he asking if she wanted that drama? Maybe he was even suggesting that they both go to look after the man who had been a patient they had both been so invested in saving. Suddenly, it felt like the connection they had just forged was strong enough to make Lisa feel flustered. Unsure of which way to jump and it was a well-practised habit to find a safe option as quickly as possible. Ignoring the unspoken invitation was a first step. Removing herself from the situation was the second.

'We'll need more details, won't we?' she said. 'I could go back up to the Lido deck where we found him. They might have found his clothes and his medication. He'll need something more than a swimming suit when they discharge him.'

'Good thinking, Lisa.' It was Peter who was nodding now. 'We can get Housekeeping to go to his cabin and pack a few things for him as well. I'll get someone to meet you.'

By the time Lisa got back to the medical centre with Alex's suitcase, she found the entire team were ready to escort their patient up to helipad at the very bow of the ship.

'None of us need to go with him.' Hugh had a clipboard in his hands and must have been working fast to have written up what looked like a very detailed report. 'They're sending an intensive care doctor and a paramedic to take him back.'

'Come and watch,' Janet said. 'It doesn't happen that often and it's pretty exciting, especially in the middle of the night.'

'Does the ship have to stop?'

'It's already slowing down but I've seen them land even in fairly big seas when the ship is going fast. If it's too dangerous to land, they'll winch the patient up. They're amazing.'

It was an opportunity not to be missed. Lisa followed the entourage and waited with them to watch as the helicopter got close enough to glow in the flood-lit area of the helipad located right at the bow of the ship, overlooked by the bridge, as it hovered and very slowly sank until its skids were on the deck. Two of the French crew ducked their heads beneath the still whir-ring blades of the aircraft and came to meet Hugh, who was standing at the head of Alex's stretcher, holding the clipboard, raising his voice to give a verbal hando-ver to the new health professionals in charge.

'Bonjour, messieurs. Voici Alex, qui a eu une réac-tion anaphylactique sévère...'

The fact that Hugh was doing the handover in French was not only astonishing, it completely took Lisa's breath away. That he was already such a charm-ing and good-looking man had been quite enough to deal with in terms of being happy to keep herself at a safe distance. That he seemed to be at ease speak-ing what had to be the most beautiful language on earth took his attractiveness to another level and, on top of that, there was now that moment of connec-tion they'd shared tonight that made Lisa think that the social planets they inhabited might not be that far apart after all.

Minutes later, she also had to wonder whether the butterflies that had taken over her stomach were due solely to the excitement of standing here as the heli-copter lifted off and swung away right in front of her, the beat of its rotors vibrating right through her body. It was quite possible that these unfamiliar sensations had even more to do with the man who was standing right beside her.

It was no wonder that Lisa found it impossible to go back to bed and try to sleep after the tension and excitement of the last few hours. Even though it was nearly three a.m. she decided she needed to go and walk off the adrenaline or whatever it was that was still bubbling in her veins and making her brain race in an endless loop of reliving those fraught minutes of working to save Alex's life. The beat of fear when she'd believed she was facing the challenge alone. The relief when Hugh had arrived. That feeling of someone moving close enough to touch her soul when they'd shared the joy of success and, possibly the most disconcerting recurrent thought, how she'd felt when she'd heard him speaking French so fluently.

Yes…that very odd, melting sensation that was happening every time that part of the loop resurfaced was the best reason of all to go for a brisk walk and get some fresh air outside.

Lisa headed for the stairs that would take her to the deck she wanted that had a running track available. They were right beside a set of elevators and the doors on one slid open as she walked past. She heard the giggle of an obviously inebriated woman and she probably would have heard her voice even if she was halfway up the stairs.

'But you *are* coming to my cabin, aren't you, darling? You promised…'

'Yes, I did. And I will. Oops-a-daisy… I think you'd better hang on a bit more tightly…'

It was the sound of the male voice that made Lisa turn her head and slow her feet enough to count as a long pause. A deep, sexy voice with that note of muted amusement she was rather familiar with. She knew she was staring. She knew her mouth was gaping and she was probably looking as appalled as she was feeling.

For one long, horrified moment she held Hugh Patterson's gaze. And then she all but fled up the stairs because, quite honestly, she couldn't get away fast enough. Not that she had any intention of trying to analyse why she felt so…disappointed? Because she suspected that there might be a corner of her mind that could justifiably taunt her with the notion that she was jealous.

Oh…*man*…

It had been all too obvious what Lisa Phillips had been thinking when she'd seen him holding up that drunk woman in the lift. She probably wouldn't believe him if he told her that he'd found the woman rather too worse for wear when he'd gone back to the bar on the Lido deck to reassure the staff who'd been so worried about Alex, and he'd offered to make sure she got safely back to her own cabin. What was his nurse still doing up, anyway? He had the excuse of having been waiting for an update from the hospital that had taken their patient and then spending time with the staff on the Lido deck, but Lisa should have been in bed long before now.

As if he'd ever take advantage of an inebriated passenger. Or any passenger, for that matter. Okay, it was not unpleasant to have an endlessly changing number of beautiful women who were often remarkably uninhibited in advertising that they'd like to add to their holiday pleasures by including a dalliance with him but he very rarely had any desire to do more than a bit of harmless flirting.

He'd practically been a monk, for heaven's sake— apart from that first cruise when he'd been a passenger and not a crew member, of course, and when he'd needed a lot more than the on-board entertainment to distract himself from the betrayal of the woman he'd believed had loved him as much as he'd loved her. A woman he'd been on the verge of committing to for the rest of his life, in fact.

His friendship with Carlotta, in Barcelona, was the closest he'd come to in any kind of relationship since then and they both knew that it was no more than a friendship with occasional benefits.

It seemed a bit ironic that the first time he'd seen Lisa she'd been watching him kiss Carlotta and he'd been well aware that she'd been somewhat shocked. Well…she'd looked more than shocked when she'd seen him in the elevator tonight. She'd looked positively disgusted, and the worst thing about that was that a part of Hugh's brain could see himself through her eyes only too easily and…he had to admit, it looked shallow.

He looked like a pleasure-seeker with a job that might provide the occasional medical challenge, as tonight had done, but was mostly delivering a kind of private general practice, catering for an elite group of people who were wealthy enough to take luxury holidays. It was also a job that could obviously provide a playground for unlimited sexual adventures.

Hugh didn't like the thought that Lisa would think so little of him. But, then again, he didn't like the idea that she was judging him either. She knew nothing about why he was here or how much satisfaction this job could deliver on a regular basis. She was only here for a couple of weeks anyway, so why the hell should it matter *what* she thought?

But it seemed that it did. Having found a female crew member who had helped him get the passenger back to her cabin and taken over the responsibility of getting her into bed and checking on her later, Hugh didn't go straight back to his own cabin. He needed a bit of fresh air, he decided. A moment to take a breath and dismiss whatever unpleasant vibe that look on Lisa's face had left him with.

It was unfortunate that he chose that particular deck to go out onto. Or that his new colleague had still not retired to her cabin and was looking over the railing at the stern of the ship, watching the moonlight sparkle on the impressive foam of the wake stretching back into the inky darkness of the sea. It was even more unfortunate that, when she finally noticed him walking in her direction, she chose to try and make some sort of negative comment about his sexual prowess.

'That was quick,' she said. She sounded surprised but there was a smile tugging at the corners of her mouth, as if the idea of him being terrible in bed was somehow unexpected but amusing.

'Excuse me?' Hugh stopped. He took a breath, trying to put a lid on how defensive he was feeling, but the lid didn't quite fit. 'I take it that you're assuming I jumped into bed with the passenger you saw me with?'

'The invitation was obviously there.'

'And you think I would have been unable to resist? That I sleep with every woman who offers invitations for sex even if they're not sober or if it might jeopardise the position I hold here?'

Her gaze slid away from his. 'It's none of my business,' she said. At least she had the grace to sound uncomfortable. She might even be blushing, although it was hard to tell in this light, but Hugh wasn't about to let her off that lightly. For some inexplicable reason this mattered.

Maybe that was because he was feeling something other than defensive. Something like disappointment? Working with Lisa tonight and especially that moment when they'd both acknowledged how amazing it was to know that you'd saved someone's life had given Hugh a feeling of connection with a woman that was different from anything he'd ever experienced before.

A chink in his armour even, where he could feel what it must be like to be with someone you could really trust. Someone who could share the important things of life—for either celebration or encouragement to conquer. And maybe he had felt that way because he'd seen himself in a big brother role, which gave Lisa the status of family—someone it was safe to care about.

But she was judging him and his lifestyle now and any glimmer from that chink in his protective armour was nowhere to be seen. Lisa wasn't family. She was a stranger and, while she might be damned good at her job, she was uptight to the point of being a prude.

'At least I know how to relax occasionally and enjoy myself,' he heard himself saying. 'What's *your* problem, Lisa?'

'I haven't got one.'

She sounded as defensive as he had been feeling and Hugh could see that her hands were gripping the railing so tightly her knuckles were white. Was she *scared* of something? Hugh contemplated the ship's wake for a long moment and he could actually feel his negative thoughts getting washed away and disappearing into the night. There was something vulnerable about Lisa. She was the one who needed encouragement right now, even if she didn't realise it. He injected a teasing note into his voice as he turned to lean his back against the railing so he could watch Lisa's reaction.

'Are you a virgin?' he asked.

That shocked expression he'd seen on her face when she'd seen him propping up that passenger in the lift was back again.

'*No*... Of course I'm not.'

'But I'm guessing you don't like sex that much?'

Her breath came out in such an incredulous huff he could hear it over the hum of the engines and the sound of the churning water far below them.

'Just because I don't approve of jumping into bed with total strangers?' Her chin came up. 'I think sex is an important part of a relationship, if you must know. But I also happen to think there are more important things.'

'I'm not talking about a relationship.' Hugh was keeping his tone light. He was curious about how far down the list sex would come on the list of important things in a relationship for her but that could wait for another conversation. Right now, all he wanted to find out was just how tightly this woman kept herself under control.

'I'm just talking about sex,' he added. 'Enjoying a physical activity. Like dancing.' This seemed inspired. Did Lisa ever let herself go enough to dance? 'Do you dance?'

'No.' Lisa was resolutely keeping her gaze on the

endless wake, although he had the feeling that she knew how closely he was watching her.

Hugh could feel a frown line appearing between his eyebrows as he leaned a little closer so that he could lower his voice. 'What about eating some amazing meal? Or drinking champagne? Do you like drinking champagne, Lisa?'

She shrugged. 'I've never tasted real champagne.'

Wow…she'd never tasted a lot of things, it seemed. Hugh's annoyance had long since vanished. He was watching Lisa's profile—the way the wind was playing with that short tumble of waves, the freckles he could see dusting her pale cheeks and that delicious curve at the corners of her mouth that looked like an embryonic smile, even though she was clearly not that happy at the moment.

Hugh leaned even closer. So close he could feel the tickle of a windblown lock of hair touch his forehead.

'What *do* you enjoy, then?' he asked.

He hadn't really intended to use his best flirtatious tone that he knew women loved. He hadn't actually intended to be this close to Lisa and he certainly hadn't expected the punch in his gut when she turned her head slowly and he found himself so very close to those remarkable eyes. They were a very dark shade of golden brown right now, with the pupils dilating rapidly towards that intriguing dark rim.

Hugh knew exactly what that punch in his gut was telling him. He also knew by Lisa's reaction that she was experiencing the same thing. Whether or not she was prepared to acknowledge that shaft of desire was quite another matter and Hugh knew he should move before she even had the time to think about it. He should step back, say something about it being far too late to be out and about and escape before this odd moment turned into something they might both regret.

Except he left it a split second too late. Just long enough for his gaze to catch something other than the expression in Lisa's eyes. He could see the way her lips were parting... The way the tip of her tongue appeared to touch her bottom lip. It was mesmerising, that's what it was. Hugh was unaware of any movement from either of them but their faces were even closer now. Close enough for their noses to touch as his mouth hovered above hers.

And then their lips touched. So lightly it was no more than a feather-light brush—not dissimilar to the touch of the wind that Hugh could feel caressing the bare skin on his arms and neck as he bent his head. A scrape of a touch that was also similar to a match being struck and it certainly created a flame. It was impossible not to repeat the action and, this time, Hugh could feel the response.

He might have expected Lisa to be shocked. He was shocked himself, to be honest, but it seemed that even that gentlest of touches contained something far too powerful to be resisted. On both sides. There was nothing for it but to *really* kiss her, Hugh decided as he covered her lips with his own and began a conversation that he might have had a thousand times already in his life but he'd never found one quite like this.

Ever...

Oh...dear Lord...

She'd wondered what it might be like to be kissed by this man from the moment she'd first clapped eyes on him kissing another woman. She'd imagined how it might feel. She'd even dreamt about it but she'd had *no* idea, had she?

It wasn't the first time she'd been kissed by any means but it *felt* like it was.

Who knew that there were such infinite variations in pressure and movement that a kiss could feel like listening to the most amazing music with its different notes and rhythms? That closing your eyes would only intensify other senses and there'd never been anything that tasted like Hugh's mouth and that the silky glide of his tongue against hers would trigger a sensation that felt like the inside of her whole body was melting...

She could feel the absolute control that Hugh had but she could sense the strength behind it and she wanted more. So much more. If a kiss with this man could be like this, what would sex be like?

Any judgement she might have had about people on cruise ships who were intent on finding as much pleasure as possible in the shortest amount of time were disappearing—getting buried under the weight of curiosity. No...make that a kind of desire that Lisa had never, ever experienced before. Hugh hadn't been that far off the mark, had he, when he'd suggested that she didn't like sex that much? She'd never been kissed like this, though. Or felt desire that was more like a desperate need to discover something she might otherwise miss out on for the rest of her life.

It was a subtle change in the engine noise beneath them that finally broke that kiss. Or perhaps it was a need for more oxygen because Lisa knew she was breathing far more rapidly than normal as they pulled apart. Her lips were still parted as well, and her eyes drifted open to find her gaze locking onto Hugh's.

His smile grew slowly. 'I take it back,' he said.

'Take what back?' The thought that he was already regretting that kiss was like a shower of cold water in her face.

'Thinking you were so uptight,' Hugh said. 'Where did you learn to kiss like that, Lisa Phillips?'

She couldn't say anything. Because she'd have to admit that she'd never learned to kiss like that until he'd taught her? Or because she was processing the fact that he'd considered her to be uptight? Lisa could feel herself taking a step back to create some more distance between them.

Was Hugh laughing at her? She couldn't let him know that that kiss had, quite possibly, been life-changing for her when it was probably no more than an everyday occurrence for Hugh. He'd think she was immature as well as uptight, wouldn't he? Had he just been amusing himself all along by kissing her in the first place? Or…and it was a horrible thought…had she been the one who had initiated that kiss? Lisa could feel her cheeks reddening in one of her hated blushes so she turned away so that she could catch the breeze on her face.

'We're slowing down.' Hugh broke a silence that was on the verge of becoming really awkward moments later as the engine noise dropped another note. 'We can't be that far away from docking. I expect we'll have a busy clinic in the morning. When most of the passengers have gone ashore, it gives a lot of the crew a chance to visit us.'

He was talking like her boss, which prompted Lisa

to shift her gaze to catch his again. Was he dismissing that kiss as something that shouldn't have happened between people who had to work together? Or was he warning her that it couldn't go any further? It was more like there was a question to be seen in his eyes than a warning, however. Maybe he was wondering if he should say something about that kiss? Or was he waiting for an indication from her that she'd enjoyed it as much as he had? That she wasn't that "uptight" after all?

Well…she didn't have to prove anything. And she didn't want to talk about it either—certainly not with someone who thought sex was just something to enjoy as a physical activity, like dancing or drinking champagne. She'd already let Hugh know how much she disapproved of people who simply jumped into bed with each other for no other reason than giving in to lust.

Okay, she might have just gained a disturbing new insight into how it could easily happen but, now that she'd had a moment to catch her breath, she could remember that she wasn't that type of person herself. That she knew it was dangerous to break rules or step too far outside the boundaries of what you knew was the right thing to do. The safe thing.

Maybe what Hugh was really asking was if she'd like to pretend the kiss had never happened. Or that it was no big deal—which it obviously wasn't for someone like Hugh. It was the first thing she'd ever seen him doing, after all. Perhaps he'd mentioned work because it was a safer topic and a place where they had discovered a professional connection and that was absolutely something Lisa could use as a life raft when her head was such a whirlpool of jumbled sensations and emotions she was in danger of drowning. She grabbed hold of it.

'And it's late,' she added briskly, turning away. 'Don't know about you but I need some sleep before I turn up for work. See you in the morning, Hugh.'

CHAPTER FOUR

How the hell had that happened, exactly?

Okay, he'd been pushing her a bit after being irritated by that unimpressed comment that he had interpreted as judgement on his performance in bed. Deliberately being in her personal space as well as he'd prodded that barrier Lisa seemed to have between herself and the good things in life, but he'd certainly never expected it to end in a kiss. He hadn't even been attracted to her, given that she was so not his type. Was that what had made that kiss seem so different? Why it had haunted his dreams in the few snatched hours of sleep he'd managed later and why it was still lurking in the perimeter of his consciousness this morning?

Hugh arrived early at the medical centre, despite his lack of sleep, but moving around his familiar environment as he checked that everything had been thoroughly cleaned and restocked in the wake of managing their dramatic case of Alex's respiratory arrest due to anaphylaxis in the early hours of this morning, he was aware of an unfamiliar tension.

He might not understand how that kiss had happened exactly but there was no getting away from the fact that it *had* happened and now it felt like it was going to be more than a little awkward working with Lisa. Most women he knew would be happy to either dismiss that kiss as fun but naughty, given they had to work together, or to enjoy a bit of sexual tension and have fun playing with it for a while. But Lisa wasn't like any of the women he knew and Hugh wasn't confident he would know how to respond to a different, less relaxed reaction.

Sure enough, when she arrived a few minutes before morning surgery was due to begin, she avoided any direct eye contact with him when he gave her a friendly greeting and said that he hoped she'd had enough sleep, given her extended working hours last night.

She merely nodded, still not meeting his gaze as she reached for a stethoscope to hook around her neck. 'Shall I set up in the second consulting room to do the initial obs?'

'Yes, please.' So she was going to pretend the kiss had never happened? That was a bit "head in the sand", but he could go along with that. And it was always useful to get an idea of what a patient was presenting with, along with baseline observations that let him know whether they had any signs of infection like a fever or any problems with their blood pressure or heart rhythm. A competent nurse could also deal with minor stuff herself, like dressing a burn or closing a small laceration with sticky strips or glue.

It was a walk-in clinic that didn't require appointments and the knowledge, based on experience, that they might be very busy for the next couple of hours should have been enough to focus Hugh's attention completely on his job.

Except it wasn't quite enough. He was watching

Lisa from the corner of his eye as she moved swiftly around the medical centre for the next few minutes, collecting supplies like the plastic sheaths for the tip of the tympanic thermometer, a new roll of graph paper for the ECG monitor and dressing supplies and antiseptic ointments that might be needed to deal with minor injuries that didn't need a doctor's attention. How hard was she finding it to pretend that the kiss hadn't happened?

Was she thinking about it as much as he was? Those unwanted flashes of memory that were strong enough to interfere with anything else he might be trying to focus on? Did she have the same, disturbing idea that it could be tempting to do it again or was she avoiding even looking at him directly because she really was wishing it had never happened in the first place?

He found himself listening in from the treatment room as he made sure the electronic equipment like the X-ray machine was turned on and ready for use, when Janet arrived to help with the surgery by manning the reception area and triaging to get the most important cases seen first.

'Tim's been telling me about all the excitement last night. Can't believe something like that happened when I'm not even on call.'

'It was a memorable night, that's for sure. Possibly a once-in-a-lifetime experience.'

Hugh flicked another switch to turn the steriliser on. Was Lisa making a reference to the case...or the kiss? Not that it mattered, because maybe he agreed with her—on both counts.

'You could be right. I've never seen a cricothyroidotomy done on land, let alone at sea.'

'I'd never seen one done either and I've worked in ED a lot. It was amazing. *Hugh* was amazing. He saved that guy's life…'

'*We* saved that guy's life.' Hugh couldn't eavesdrop any more when he was the subject of the conversation.

Perhaps it was because she was startled by his sudden appearance or the genuine compliment he was offering that Lisa finally looked at him properly and something in Hugh's gut did an odd little flip as her gaze met his. The last time he'd seen those eyes had been very close up indeed…

'Lisa was first on the scene,' he added, 'and I couldn't have handled his airway later without her excellent assistance.'

'So he actually arrested?' Janet was open-mouthed.

'Close enough. His oxygen saturation got down to below seventy percent at one stage and he was unconscious.'

'Wow…'

'Have you had any update on his condition?'

Lisa shifted her gaze swiftly as he looked back to answer her question. The way she was biting her lower lip was another sign that she was finding any interaction between them awkward this morning and that had the effect of making whatever that was in Hugh's gut flip back the other way. Yep…this was awkward all right and Hugh was aware of a beat of another, unfamiliar emotion.

Guilt? He'd imagined himself in a big brother kind of role with Lisa, hadn't he? Well…nobody would trust him to take on that kind of role again, would they? Had he really asked her if she was a virgin? And suggested that maybe she didn't like sex? How insulting had that been? Plus, he'd told her how uptight he'd thought she was as well and that had been an unkind thing to say. No wonder Lisa had backed off so fast. She probably wasn't looking forward to working with him at all and he couldn't blame her.

'Alex is fine,' he said aloud. 'They monitored him in Intensive Care for the rest of the night but everything had settled by the time I spoke to someone an hour or so ago. They're going to patch up his neck, give him a course of steroids for a couple of days and have advised him to wear a medic alert bracelet and make sure he has his auto-injector within reach at all times. He should be back on board before we sail this evening.'

A late sailing, Hugh remembered, turning to head into his consulting room as Janet moved to open the doors to their first patients. And after this morning's surgery he had the day to himself in one of his favourite parts of the world, which was just what he needed. A chance to relax and soak up some of the very best things in life. The kind of things that Lisa didn't seem to be at all familiar with. That he'd thought he could help her discover. Maybe he could try and step back into that helpful role.

He turned back. 'What are you going to do with your first onshore leave, Lisa?'

If nothing else, he could provide some recommendations for things she could see or do and that might get them past this awkwardness.

'I'm not sure.' Lisa's gaze skittered away from his again. 'One of the team on the excursions desk told me about a walk that was lovely around the Cap d'Antibes but what I'd really love to see is one of the medieval towns.'

'Get up to Eze, if you can. It's an outstanding example of a medieval village. Or St Paul de Vence, although that could still be pretty crowded on a lovely day like this. It's a shame we won't finish in time for you to tag along with one of the organised bus tours. They're always keen to have someone from our team available as medical cover but a taxi probably wouldn't be too expensive. Less than fifty euros, probably.'

The expression on Lisa's face suggested that their ideas of what wasn't too expensive were poles apart. She was the one to turn away this time but he caught the hint of smile that felt like an acknowledgement of his effort to restore their working relationship to its former amicability. Not that it seemed to have worked particularly well.

'I expect I'll just take a walk around Villefranche sur Mer from where the tender boat drops us,' she said. 'Or I can find the bus that goes into Nice. I'll explore the old town and then find somewhere lovely for a late lunch. I'm sure it will be gorgeous.'

Oh…*help*…

The first time Lisa had been in this reception area and had realised that she was going to be working with Hugh, she hadn't been able to dismiss the memory of having seen him kissing that leggy blonde woman.

Now she was totally unable to dismiss the memory of having been kissed herself. And it was so much more than merely a thought. She could actually *feel* it happening again. The soft press of his lips on hers. The taste of his mouth. The fierce lick of desire that sent an electric buzz to every cell in her body and made her knees feel distinctly weak.

Biting her bottom lip hard enough to hurt helped. So did avoiding any more than a split second of eye contact. Even better was being able to focus on the patients that started arriving within the next few minutes. Hugh had been right—they were in for a very busy few hours and, best of all, there was plenty for Lisa to do in her consulting room and she wasn't being asked to assist Hugh in any way.

An hour in and she was starting to feel a lot more confident that they could continue working together without the awkwardness of that kiss hanging in the air between them. A purely professional exchange presented no problems at all after the first couple.

'This is Elaine.' Lisa handed the clipboard to Hugh as she took her tenth patient into his consulting room. 'She's running a fever of thirty-nine point six, has frequency and pain on urination and the dipstick test was positive for blood in her urine.'

It would be a quick consult for Hugh to double check the history and any other health issues that Elaine had and then prescribe the antibiotics and other medications to ease the discomfort of a urinary tract infection for their patient.

Jeff, the next patient, only needed a certificate to be signed by Hugh to give him a day away from his job as a kitchen hand.

'It's a second degree burn but the blisters are still intact,' Lisa told him. 'I've cleaned it, put antibiotic cream on and a non-stick gauze dressing and I've told Jeff to come back tomorrow for a dressing change so that I can make sure it's not infected. If it's looking okay, I think he'll be able to work as long as he wears gloves and keeps it dry.'

Hugh scrawled his signature on the certificate. 'How's the waiting room looking?'

'Still quite full. I've got someone with chest pain to do an ECG on now, but he's a dancer in one of the cabaret acts and I suspect he's pulled a muscle.'

'It should start to slow down soon.' Hugh handed back the piece of paper and smiled at Lisa. 'You're doing a great job,' he told her. 'Thanks…'

She tucked the praise away as she went back to Jeff to give him his final instructions on how to look after his burn injury today and sort out an appointment for a dressing change tomorrow morning. Hugh's words made her feel good, she decided, but they hadn't undermined the relief of stepping back into the purely professional interactions between herself and her boss. If anything, they were giving what had happened in the early hours of today a dreamlike quality—as if that kiss couldn't possibly have happened for real.

The final patient that came in turned out to be the real test of whether things were back to normal. A tall, brusque Scotsman in his fifties, he was reluctant to admit to having anything wrong.

'But if it gets any worse, I'm not going to be able to do any more of these tours, Nurse,' he said as he limped from the waiting room. 'I can barely put any weight on my foot now.'

His anxious wife was by his side. 'We're supposed to be doing a tour of St Jean Cap Ferrat that includes lunch at that amazing hotel that was in a movie we saw recently. The *Abolutely Fabulous* one? It would be such a shame to miss out.'

Lisa had a look at the sole of the man's foot. He had

a reddened area just below his middle toes that could be a deep blister.

'Let me just run a couple of checks and then we'll get the doctor to have a look.' Lisa wrapped a blood pressure cuff around his arm. 'You haven't been doing a lot of walking in a new pair of shoes, have you? Going barefoot more than usual? Could you have had an injury that you might not have taken much notice of, like a stone bruise?'

She went in with her patient to give handover to Hugh a few minutes later. 'This is Gordon,' she told him. 'He's presenting with nine out of ten pain when he tries to put any weight on the ball of his left foot. Vital signs are all normal. He had an injury two weeks ago when he was replacing boards on his deck and fell through a rotten part but he was treated in his local ED and discharged.'

'Oh? What did they do for treatment?'

'Cleaned out a small cut but it wasn't anything to worry about.' Gordon shook his head, dismissing the incident. 'They X-rayed my foot, too, in case I'd broken something but they said it all looked fine. They gave me a tetanus shot and some antibiotics.'

'And it's only started to get painful again now?'

'It's been sore ever since.' It was Gordon's wife who spoke. 'He's just been putting a brave face on it but when he got up this morning it was suddenly a whole lot worse. He almost fell over.'

Lisa had been about to leave Hugh to deal with his patient and go and finish up her own paperwork but he caught her gaze.

'Could you set up the treatment room for us,

please?' he asked. 'I think we'll have a look with the ultrasound.'

'Why would you want to do that?' Gordon's wife echoed Lisa's first thought. 'I thought ultrasounds were just for when you were pregnant.'

Lisa had seen that kind of smile on Hugh's face many times already but this time she noticed the crinkles around his eyes as well. It wasn't that he was making fun of a layperson's lack of medical knowledge in any way. This smile held understanding rather than amusement and it was also reassuring. Lisa knew that the people in front of him would be confident that he cared about them. That he was doing what he believed might help.

'There are some things that don't show up on X-rays,' he told them. 'It could be that there's something in your foot, like a piece of glass or a splinter.'

Sure enough, there was something to be seen on the screen as Hugh gently examined Gordon's foot.

'The entry wound's healed over now,' Hugh warned. 'We'll need to do a bit of minor surgery to open it up and see what we can find. Are you happy for us to do that or would you like a referral to an emergency department of a local hospital?'

'I'd rather you did it, Doc. That way we can get it over with and we might make our posh lunch after all.'

'Oh...' His wife didn't look so happy. 'I can't watch. Not if there's going to be blood...'

Hugh's smile reappeared. 'Don't worry,' he said. 'We'll get Janet to make you a nice cup of tea while you wait. Lisa and I have got this covered. We're the A team, aren't we?'

Reopening a wound to explore it for the presence

of a foreign body was a walk in the park compared to making an opening in someone's neck to establish an emergency airway. Lisa found herself smiling back at Hugh in total agreement. They most definitely did have this covered and it could prove to be a very satisfying end to their morning clinic. Even better, it seemed that the awkwardness had finally evaporated.

This was fun.

Minor surgery was an unexpected finale to an ordinary clinic but Hugh really was enjoying himself. He'd already known that Lisa was someone that he could rely on in a tense, emergency situation but this time he could relax and appreciate her skilled assistance even more. As he filled a syringe with local anaesthetic, he watched her setting up everything he could need on a tray and then swabbing the skin of Gordon's foot and arranging sterile drapes to protect the area.

'This is going to hurt, isn't it?' Gordon's stoic expression slipped a little.

'Not once the local is doing its job,' Hugh assured him. 'Bit of a sting just to start with. Lisa, can you hold Gordon's foot steady, please?

It wasn't the easiest area of the body to be working on and it was frustrating to be able to feel the tip of whatever it was embedded in his patient's foot but be unable to grasp it firmly enough to extract it. Hugh could feel Lisa watching him as he pressed a little deeper into the wound and opened the forceps a little wider. Then he took a grip and held it and this time he could feel something shift. The dark object slowly came out through the skin and just kept coming. With a silent whistle of how impressed he was, Hugh held up an enormous triangular splinter between the teeth of the forceps.

'Look at that.'

He didn't need to tell Lisa to look. She was staring in disbelief that anyone could have been walking around with something that size buried in their foot. Her gaze only had to shift a fraction to catch Hugh's, given that he was watching her reaction, and he wasn't disappointed. Her astonishment morphed into delight. Or maybe it was just professional satisfaction but it didn't matter because just watching the change was a joy. The note of connection might pale in comparison to the satisfaction they'd shared in getting a secure airway into Alex last night but this was significant in its own way because it felt like that awkwardness between himself and Lisa had gone.

She certainly sounded happier. 'You're not going to believe how big this splinter is,' she told Gordon. 'You've been walking around with a log in your foot.'

Hugh showed their patient what he'd pulled out and Gordon grinned. 'That's a piece of my deck, that is. No wonder it was a wee bit sore.'

'I'm going to clean out the wound thoroughly now,' Hugh told him, 'and then we'll get you patched up and bandaged. You might want to keep the weight off your foot as much as you can today but there's no reason you can't go and enjoy your lunch.'

As he intended to enjoy his own. It was nearly two p.m. by the time Hugh had taken one of the tender shuttles to get into the port of Villefranche sur Mer and he was delighted to find that his arrangements for the afternoon were in place. He picked up the keys to the classic car he'd hired, and when the powerful engine of the gunmetal-grey nineteen-sixties E-type Jaguar purred into life a short time later he just smiled and listened to it for a moment, before pulling onto the road.

It was a sparkling blue day with that soft light and warmth that he loved about the French Riviera. He was going to put the roof of this convertible down and drive up towards the mountains and one of his most favourite restaurants ever. He might even indulge in a glass of the best champagne they had on ice.

Lisa Phillips had never tasted champagne...

The thought came from nowhere but with an intensity that let him imagine exactly what she might look like when she did taste it for the first time. He would see that surprise in her eyes and be able to watch it shift and grow and light up her whole face with the pleasure of something new and delicious. Kind of like the way he'd seen her satisfaction with her work but better somehow. More like what he'd seen in her eyes after that kiss? Until he'd ruined the moment by telling her how uptight she was.

Why had he done that? It was almost as if he'd been trying to push her away as a form of self-protection but that was ridiculous. Even if Lisa had been completely his type of woman, he had absolute control over how involved he ever got with anyone. He wasn't about to make the mistake of falling in love again.

But, hey...maybe he could bring a bottle of champagne back with him as a way of making up for being a bit of a jerk.

Or...

Maybe there was a way he could not only make it up to Lisa but reassure himself just how in control of his own feelings he was.

He was moving slowly down the street now, towards a new group of people who'd just been ferried from the cruise ship by the tender. Heads were turning to admire the car he was driving but he was focused only on the solitary figure amongst them. Lisa was wearing a pale yellow T-shirt, jeans that were rolled up to mid-calf, and sensible-looking shoes on her feet that would be just right for a lot of walking as she explored the medieval centres of either Villefranche or Nice. She was clutching her shoulder bag as if she expected a pickpocket was already following her and, as Hugh got closer, he saw her pause and look around. He could even see the way she was taking a deep breath as if she might be a little overwhelmed by the prospect of a solo adventure but he could sense her determination as well. She was going to make the most of whatever new experiences were in store for her in the next few hours.

His foot pressed on the brake as he made the decision to go with that flash of inspiration he'd just had. The car was right in front of Lisa as he stopped, and Hugh leaned across the empty passenger seat to open the door. Then he put on what he hoped was his most charming smile.

'Perfect timing,' he said. 'Hop in.'

He couldn't see the expression in her eyes because she was wearing sunglasses but he knew it would be surprised. Possibly shocked. Definitely hesitant.

'You won't regret it.' He caught his own sunglasses, pulling them down enough that she could see his eyes. 'I promise...'

CHAPTER FIVE

LISA OPENED HER mouth to say, *Thanks, but, no thanks*.

Getting back to a working relationship that wasn't full of lingering tension had been hard enough in a professional environment where there'd been any amount of distraction. Spending time with Hugh when he was looking like some celebrity about to do a photo shoot with a vintage sports car would take her right back to square one when she'd just been kissed senseless and hadn't known which way was up.

The words didn't emerge from her mouth, however, because another thought occurred in the same instant. Maybe spending time with Hugh could do the opposite and reassure her that she wasn't someone who ever lost total control. There seemed to be a tacit agreement between them that they were both going to pretend that kiss had never happened after all.

Or…and it was quite hard to silence that naughty whisper in the back of her mind that was wondering if accepting this invitation might actually lead to another one of those extraordinary kisses. Trying to stifle that whisper made Lisa take hold of the open door of the car, ready to push it shut. It would be far less stressful to go exploring on her own.

But now Lisa could actually hear Abby's voice in her ear. And see an imaginary message that could be her sister's response to news of what her day out had involved.

You went driving around on the French Riviera in a vintage sports car with the roof down? With that gorgeous man driving? That's more like it, Lise... Live the dream...and remember...don't send me a photo unless you're with him in some romantic French café. Preferably drinking champagne...

She'd want to know about every detail and it would make her so happy. It might even go a long way towards finally erasing some of that guilt that Abby could never quite let go of—that she had somehow held Lisa back from doing what she really wanted to do in life.

It wouldn't hurt to live the dream just for an afternoon. As a bonus it would give her enough to tell Abby about that her sister wouldn't be able to pick up that Lisa was keeping something to herself as she had no intention to confessing anything about that kiss. Or letting it happen again, despite that whisper. She was in control. She'd learned very early in life to stay in control and not be seduced by anything because that was where danger lay.

If she hadn't stopped to gaze dreamily at that doll in the toyshop window that day, she would have been holding onto Abby's hand far more tightly. The toddler would never have been able to pull away with a gleeful chuckle and run straight onto the road...

Lisa had tested her resolve to stay in control countless times since then. This might be another test for her, but it was nothing more than a friendly gesture on Hugh's part because, clearly, he'd already dismissed as unimportant what had led to their awkwardness this morning. Or maybe it was even an apology that it had happened in the first place? If Lisa declined the offer, that awkwardness might be there again the next time they had to work together and she didn't want that to happen. The hand Lisa had been about to use to push the door of this extraordinary car shut pulled it further open instead and she settled herself onto the smooth, red leather of the passenger seat.

'Hold on to your hat,' Hugh told her. 'You're about to get blown away.'

He wasn't wrong. Lisa was blown away by far more than the wind in her hair. It seemed that Hugh knew these mountains and their villages like the back of his hand and Lisa was whisked from one amazing view to another until they finally stopped, hours later, in a walled, medieval town that sat high on a hilltop with what looked like a view of the entire Côte d'Azur. Ancient stone walls gave way to rippling acres of forest and, in the misty distance, the deep, deep blue of the Mediterranean. The same stone was underfoot on the terrace of the restaurant Hugh took her to. Vines scrambled overhead to provide shade and frame the view from what had to be the best table available. Lisa shook her head.

'So, is this what usually happens when you rock up in a car like this? You get the corner table with the best view? Even if you're with someone who's wearing jeans and whose hair must look like a complete bird's nest after being out in the wind like that?'

Hugh just laughed. 'You look great,' he told her. 'This is a very relaxed place and they only care about providing the best food and wine. Plus…' He winked at Lisa. 'I booked this particular table. I've been here before. Several times.'

Lisa could believe that. She could also believe that he hadn't been here alone on his past visits and, without warning, she was aware of a beat of something that felt like…envy? Jealousy, even?

No. How ridiculous was that? She was only here as a colleague of Hugh's but, even if she had been here in a far more intimate capacity as his date, it would be stupid to feel jealous of other women in this man's life. There must have been dozens of them in the past and there would no doubt be dozens more in the future because Hugh obviously liked to play hard. He loved dining out and dancing. Champagne and…sex…

Oh, *help*…

Lisa could feel her cheeks heating up. Looking around for a distraction—any distraction—she found herself watching the maître d' of the restaurant approaching with a white cloth over his arm, a bottle in one hand and two fluted glasses in the other. A waiter was following with an ice bucket.

A short time later, Lisa found herself holding her very first glass of real French champagne.

'Chin-chin.' Hugh held up his glass. He took a sip of the wine but he was watching Lisa over the rim of the glass. Waiting to see her reaction?

She closed her eyes as the bubbles seemed to explode on her tongue and then almost evaporate before she could swallow the icy liquid. As her eyes flew open in astonishment she saw amusement dancing in Hugh's steady gaze.

'I knew you'd look like that,' he murmured. 'Tastes nice, doesn't it?'

'Unbelievable.' Lisa took another sip and then she had to reach into her bag for her phone. 'Sorry,' she muttered. 'I hate it when people take photos of what they're eating or drinking but Abby's not going to believe this without some proof.'

It was exactly the photo she'd requested, wasn't it? The romantic café. The "cute doctor". The champagne.

'Abby?'

'My sister. Well, she's my half-sister, actually, but we're…um…really close. And I know how much she would love this place.'

'You'll have to come back one day, then, now that you know where it is. You can bring your sister.'

How amazing would that be? Lisa would give anything for Abby to have the joy she'd had today of cruising mountain roads in a spectacular car, exploring cobbled streets and vibrant marketplaces and cooling off in the shadows of an ancient cathedral or two. How much harder would it be to do that in a wheelchair, though? Lisa had to blink to clear the sting at the back of her eyes as she took a photo of the frosty flute beside the bottle of what she suspected was a very expensive—probably vintage—champagne. Hugh had already told her, politely but firmly, as they'd come into the restaurant that she was here at his invitation and that this was his treat and he would be highly offended if she offered to pay for any of it.

'Let me take one of you with the glass in your hand.'

Hugh reached for her phone and Lisa blinked again, held her glass up as if she was toasting Abby and sent a silent message to her sister.

Here I am... Living the dream...

At least it would be easy to convince her sister that she wasn't on a date with Hugh. Who would go out on a date in a T-shirt and jeans?

She needed to take a picture of the view as well. She didn't let embarrassment stop her taking some of their food either. She wanted to capture every detail for Abby, including the beautifully presented salad Niçoise she had ordered, the steam rising from the ramekin of the boeuf bourguignon that had been Hugh's choice—even the basket piled with sliced baguette.

'So...' Hugh filled Lisa's glass again when he had mopped up the last of his sauce with torn pieces of the crusty bread. 'Tell me about your sister. She must be younger than you, yes?'

'What makes you say that?'

'Well...you're so well organised and you like being in charge.' The corner of Hugh's mouth twitched, as though he was supressing a smile. 'I can imagine you being a bossy big sister.'

Was it a magical side-effect of champagne that made that sound like a compliment? Or maybe it was Hugh's smile.

'I'm six years older,' she admitted. 'It was the perfect age to get a baby sister to help look after and...'

'And?' The prompt from Hugh fell into a sudden silence.

Lisa almost told him. That she'd had to take sole responsibility for Abby on so many occasions that it was like she had been another mother for that tiny baby. That she hadn't done a very good job of it either, because it was her fault that Abby was now facing challenges that would mean it would be so much more difficult for her to end up in a place like this. In a mountain village in France. Drinking real champagne...

She took another mouthful.

'And I love her to bits,' she added quietly. 'I'm missing her and I'm worried about her, to be honest.'

'Why?'

'We've been living together for her whole life but she's just moved into a university hostel and I know that she's going to be fine and that she can cope perfectly well without me. She's amazing, in fact, so I have to get over worrying about her but...'

But Hugh was frowning. 'If Abby's six years younger than you, that makes her...what...about twenty-four?' His gaze was focused intently on Lisa and she could almost see his clever brain putting pieces of a puzzle together. 'Is she...okay?'

'She got badly injured being hit by a car when she was nearly two.' There was no need to tell Hugh that it had been her fault and she'd never stop hating herself for that moment of carelessness. 'She's been in a wheelchair ever since,' she added. 'And she's always needed me. We went to live with our grandmother when Mum died a couple of years later.' Again, Lisa held back on the more sordid detail that her mother's death had been due to an overdose. 'Gran had some health issues of her own so she couldn't really manage the kind of round-the-clock care Abby needed. We always had some help but I did as much as possible myself.' Lisa took a deep breath and reached for her glass of wine again.

'Sorry... I don't usually talk about this stuff. I guess I'm missing Abby because this is the longest time we've ever been apart.' She found a smile. 'I only took this job because she talked me into it. She thought it all sounded very romantic and that it was time I had some fun.'

'And are you?' Hugh was watching her again. 'Having fun?'

Lisa couldn't read his expression but it seemed... serious. Not in that focused, professional kind of way when they were working together. Not in that flirting kind of way, like the first time he'd ever looked at her, and it was definitely not in that intense *I'm about to kiss you* kind of way. This was...just different. A new side of Hugh.

'You don't really think about "having fun", do you?' he added quietly. 'I think that maybe you've always been too busy worrying about and looking after other people to worry about yourself.'

It was a look of respect, that's what it was. Understanding, perhaps, of how much Lisa had sacrificed along the way, from the small things like not going to play with friends after school because she'd needed to get home and help look after her little sister to being excused from school trips that would take her away from home and even her career choice, because if she'd wanted to follow her first dream to become a doctor she would have had to go away to medical school. Nursing training had been available in her own city.

That Hugh might get how hard some of those decisions had been and respect her for making them made

Lisa suddenly feel an enormous pride in everything she'd done. For all those sacrifices she had made—and was still making—in order to be there for her sister. Unjustified pride, perhaps, given that it had been her fault in the first place but it was a lovely feeling, nonetheless. There was something else in his gaze as well...was he feeling sad on her behalf? She needed to reassure him. To reassure herself at the same time, or maybe it was to disguise a flash of guilt that he was only thinking so well of her because he didn't know the whole truth?

'Today has been so much fun,' she told Hugh. 'It's quite likely the best day of my life so far.'

His smile was one of pride. 'There you go. All you needed was the example of an expert. And I'm sorry I said that you were uptight. It's not true, by the way.' He took the bottle from its bed of ice again. 'Uptight people don't love champagne.' He reached for her glass. 'And you'll need to finish this because I'm driving soon. I'd better get us back to the ship before it sails.'

Lisa made a face as she took her glass again. 'Tough job,' she murmured, 'but I guess someone's gotta do it.'

Hugh laughed. 'I like you, Lisa Phillips,' he said. 'We might be total opposites but that doesn't mean we can't be friends, does it?'

They *were* total opposites. Hugh indulged in pleasure of all kinds and Lisa had learned to sacrifice anything that could interfere with what was most important in her life—keeping her sister safe. But Hugh could afford to indulge without any guilt, not only because he could obviously afford it financially—going by the personal information that patient with the migraine had revealed—but more because he didn't have anyone depending on him, did he? He was free to enjoy everything and, today, he'd given Lisa her first taste of that kind of life.

And it had been utterly amazing. It wasn't hard to return his smile. 'How could I not be friends with the person who introduced me to French champagne?'

'My work is done.' Hugh leaned back in his chair. 'If only everything in life could be sorted so easily.'

Friends.

It had been hard to persuade Abby that that was all there was to her relationship with Hugh after she sighed over the romantic photos of that mountaintop café.

'Nothing happened? Really? Not even a kiss?'

'Not even a kiss.' Lisa could sound sincere because they were only discussing the French outing, not what had happened the night before. 'Or not a real one, that is. We were running late by the time we got back and we only just caught the last tender so we were laughing about it all and then we kind of had a hug to say goodnight and he kissed me on the cheek.'

'Aha! There's still time, then. Sounds like a perfect first date to me.'

'Except that it wasn't a date. Now, tell me what's going on with you. You had your test today, didn't you?'

And fortunately Abby was too excited over the news that she'd not only passed her driver's licence test but had been accepted onto the wheelchair basketball team to try and pry any more information out of her big sister.

'Oh, and I've got my first real, hands-on session

with a patient tomorrow, to practise what we've been learning about wound care and splinting. My case is a guy who broke three fingers in a rugby game. I can't wait. I'm going to feel like I'm a huge step closer to being a real hand therapist.'

'Good luck with that. I'll look forward to hearing how it went. We'll be docking near Rome so reception might be good enough for a video call. Ring me when you're all done for the day. I'll be on duty but if I can't take the call I'll ring you back later, okay?'

Lisa did miss Abby's call the following evening. Even if she'd been aware of her phone ringing, she wouldn't have even been able to fish it out of her pocket. She was running at the time, helping Tim the paramedic push the resuscitation trolley that was kept ready to deal with any sudden collapse that could be due to a cardiac arrest. Hugh was already on scene because he happened to be eating in the same restaurant as the man who had simply fallen sideways off his chair while he had been waiting for his main course to be served.

'It's the restaurant that caters for passengers who think an evening meal with the ship's officers is a traditional part of their cruising experience,' Tim told her as he hit buttons to try and make the elevator work faster. 'They love an occasion to get really dressed up. Usually older people so it could well be a cardiac arrest. Lucky they've often got a doctor hosting one of the tables. Peter and Hugh take it in turns.'

Hugh was wearing a different kind of uniform, Lisa noticed as they raced into the small restaurant moments later. He still had a white shirt but it was paired with black trousers and jacket and even a tie. There were other people standing around wearing similar formal outfits and she recognised one as the captain of their ship, although she'd only met him briefly and hadn't been invited to have dinner at his table yet. Most of the diners seemed to have left the area but staff were looking after a distraught-looking woman.

The unconscious man lying on the carpeted floor was certainly not one of the older passengers Tim had told her about. This man barely looked any older than the doctor who was kneeling beside him, performing chest compressions. Maybe that was why there was a flash of real relief on his face when Hugh looked up to see Lisa and Tim arriving with the trolley.

'Take over compressions, will you, Tim? I've been going for more than two minutes.' Hugh pulled at his tie to loosen and remove it as he straightened up and moved to let Tim kneel. He was shrugging out of his jacket as he scrambled to his feet to get the defibrillator off the trolley. Lisa had already turned it on and taken the sticky pads from the pouch on the side.

'Find some laryngeal mask airways, please, Lisa. We'll need the IV kit and the drug roll. You can set up some saline and make sure we've got adrenaline and amiodarone ready to draw up.'

The next few minutes were controlled chaos. Hugh applied the patches while Tim kept up the rapid compressions until he was asked to stop so that they could identify the rhythm on the screen of the defibrillator.

'It's VF.' Hugh nodded. He pushed a button on the machine and the whine of the increasing charge could be heard. 'Okay, everybody clear. This is going to be a single shock at maximum joules.'

Tim put his hands in the air. 'Clear,' he responded.

Lisa wriggled back from where she was on her knees, unrolling the drug pouch. 'I'm clear,' she added.

The whine changed to an alarm. 'Shocking,' Hugh warned.

Their patient's body arced and then flopped back. He made a sound like a groan despite the mask airway that was filling his mouth and the woman, whom Lisa assumed was his wife, cried out in distress from where she was watching the resuscitation efforts.

'You good to continue compressions?' Hugh asked Tim.

'Yep.' Ideally the person doing the compressions should change every two minutes to keep the energy level high and effective but there was too much to do in a very limited time and Lisa was ideally placed to assist Hugh right now. He needed to get an IV line inserted and the first of the drug dosages administered.

'Draw up one milligram of adrenaline, please, Lisa.'

'On it.' Lisa had put everything he needed for putting in an IV line on a towel. She could watch Hugh moving as she located the ampoule of adrenaline, tapped the top to shift any liquid back into the base and then snapped off the tip so that she could fill a syringe. Hugh's movements were swift and sure. He tightened the tourniquet, felt for only a brief instant for a vein and slid the needle and cannula in only seconds later. By the time Lisa had drawn up the drug, he had secured the line and attached a Luer plug. Lisa handed him the syringe, and the ampoule so he could double check that the right drug was being given.

The first dose of adrenaline made no difference to the potentially fatal rhythm of ventricular fibrillation. A dose of amiodarone was administered, also with no effect. A two-minute cycle was ending so another shock was delivered and Hugh and Tim swapped places for compressions and using the bag mask to deliver oxygen.

'Any cardiac history?' Tim asked.

'No. He's forty-six,' Hugh told him. 'Company director from Canada. His name's Carter.'

'Family history?'

'Clear. No history of congenital heart defects or fainting episodes that might suggest an arrhythmia. He passed a medical recently and his blood pressure and cholesterol were fine. This cruise is the honeymoon for his second marriage. That's his new wife over there.'

Lisa glanced over her shoulder at the woman in a silver evening gown who was standing in complete shock, her hands pressed to her mouth. The ship's captain was right beside her and he was looking just as shocked as it became apparent that this wasn't going well.

At twenty minutes into the resuscitation attempt, with their patient now intubated and receiving continuous chest compressions, another dose of amiodarone was added to the repeated doses of adrenaline and repeated shocks but Lisa could see, every time there was a rhythm check, that the wiggly line of fibrillation was getting flatter and flatter.

News of the emergency must have travelled fast because both Peter and Janet arrived at the restaurant. They now had the ship's full medical team involved and they weren't about to give up but, twenty minutes later, when the line on the screen was absolutely flat, Lisa could tell that the doctors were trying to prepare the man's wife for bad news as they explained what they were trying to achieve with their actions as they still continued the attempt to save Carter's life.

'It's a heart attack, isn't it?' she sobbed.

'It's a cardiac arrest,' Hugh told her gently, leaving Peter to carry on as he went to stand beside her. 'A heart attack is when an artery is blocked and blood can't get to the heart. An arrest is when something is disturbing the electrical current that makes the heart beat. It can be caused by a heart attack. More often it's caused by something that interferes with the rhythm.'

'He's…he's not going to be okay, is he?'

'We've done everything we can,' Hugh said, his tone sombre. 'We've shocked him and used all the drugs we can to try and correct any electrical disturbance and we've kept his circulation going while we've tried but…we're not winning. I'm so sorry…'

Lisa bit her lip, staring down at the pile of discarded wrappers and the sharps bin where she'd been putting broken glass ampoules and needles from syringes. In a case like this, with a younger person involved, it had to be a unanimous team decision to stop the resuscitation. They had probably already gone for much longer than could have been deemed justified but nobody wanted to give up.

Nobody wanted to witness the distress of Carter's new wife a short time later when that decision was finally made. Peter took over caring for her while Tim and Hugh arranged for a stretcher to take him to the ship's morgue. Lisa and Janet cleaned up the mess of equipment and medical supplies and they took the trolley back to the medical centre to restock. It might be unthinkable but this kind of lightning could strike twice in the same place and they had to make sure that they were ready to respond.

'You okay?' Janet asked.

Lisa nodded. But the nod turned into a head shake. 'Not really,' she admitted. 'It's never nice to lose a patient but that was so sad. He was so young. And on his honeymoon...'

'I know.' Janet gave her a hug. 'The only good thing I can see is that he would have been so happy and it happened so suddenly he wouldn't have known anything about it. There are worse ways to go and things like that can happen at any age.'

Lisa nodded again. Her sister could have had a sudden death when she was only two.

'Is there someone you'd like to talk to? Hugh will be back soon. Or we could go and get a coffee.'

But Lisa was reaching into her pocket. 'It's okay,' she told Janet. 'But thanks. I promised I'd talk to my sister tonight and she'll understand.' Glancing at the screen, she saw that she'd missed a call from Abby hours ago now. Would she still be awake? Would it ruin her evening to know that Lisa was upset?

Abby rang straight back when Lisa texted so that she wouldn't disturb her if she was already asleep. It was a video call on her phone so that she could see that Abby was clearly not about to go to sleep either.

'Hey...' Lisa frowned at what she could see on her sister's face. 'What's up, Abby?'

Any thoughts of offloading onto her sister to receive the comfort and reassurance she needed evaporated instantly. Lisa might also be upset but it was Abby who burst into tears and struggled to get her words out.

'It's just... I've had...the most *awful* day.'

'Oh, no…' Lisa suddenly felt far too far away from the person she loved most in the world. All she wanted to do was hug her sister but all she could do was listen. 'Tell me what's happened…'

CHAPTER SIX

WAVE-WATCHING.

The river of churning water between the white waves on either side stretched as far as she could see into the night. How great would it be to be able to gather up any distressing thoughts and throw them overboard to get washed away and simply disappear into that endless sea?

It was an astonishingly therapeutic activity, Lisa decided, having wandered to the stern of the ship when she had finished her call to Abby. It had taken nearly an hour before Abby had started sounding anything like her normal determined and courageous self, but she'd had a real blow to her confidence today when she'd been taking a big step forward to achieving her dream of becoming a specialist hand therapist with her first clinical session.

'He thought I was there for therapy myself,' a still tearful Abby had told Lisa. *'And the look on his face when he found out I was there to treat him... Okay, maybe it might have been justified if I was there to help him learn to walk with a prosthetic leg or how to get down stairs with crutches but I was there to dress*

and splint his hand, Lise. Why do most people only see my wheelchair? Why can't they see me*?'*

It was so unlike Abby to let something knock her like this but, as Lisa had reminded her, she had a lot going on in her life. She was adapting to living independently in a new environment, coping with an intensive regime of postgraduate study towards her new speciality and...the only family member she had might as well be on the other side of the world. When Abby had finished the call by telling Lisa how much she missed her, it had been Lisa who'd had tears rolling down her face—fortunately after she had ended the video call.

She needed to be home but she wasn't even halfway through this cruise and she couldn't walk out and leave the medical team shorthanded, especially given that she was learning just how intense this job could be. There was a dead man somewhere on board this ship right now, and a grieving woman whose dream honeymoon had become her worst nightmare.

And she didn't really need to be home at all. She didn't need to do what she'd been doing her whole life and fret so much about Abby because she knew that her sister was going to be fine. Abby had already processed why the assumption had been made by her patient by the time she'd finished her conversation with Lisa. She'd forgiven the man for making it and had even laughed about it in the end, polishing up that armour that she'd built as a small child when she'd got stared or laughed at in the playground.

'I'll show them,' she'd say. *'I can do stuff too, even if my legs don't work.'*

Lisa lifted her gaze from the movement of the

churning water so far below her and looked out to sea. They must be close to the Italian coastline now but she couldn't see it. All she could see was inky-black water below and an equally dark sky above with just the pin-pricks of starlight. This massive ship suddenly seemed a tiny thing in the universe and, as a person standing there alone, Lisa felt totally insignificant.

And unbearably lonely. She wasn't as vital in Abby's life as she had been up till now and her own life suddenly seemed so much emptier, but she couldn't just turn away and take herself in a whole new direction either. She had to be very sure that Abby was safe and that meant staying close. Keeping herself safe.

'Hey...'

The voice behind her made her jump and then spin to see who was greeting her. Not that she needed to see. She'd known who it was as soon as she'd heard his voice.

'Hugh...what are you doing out here?' She was pathetically pleased to see him because it meant she wasn't alone any longer. And because they were friends. She needed a friend right now.

'Same as you, I expect,' Hugh said. 'Clearing my head. It's been quite a night, hasn't it?'

He looked exhausted, Lisa thought. He was still wearing his formal uniform but he had the sleeves of his white shirt rolled up and the neck undone, his jacket was hanging over one arm and she could see the tail of his tie that had been stuffed into a pocket of his black trousers. His hair was rumpled as well, as though he'd been combing it with his fingers. He looked more sombre than Lisa had ever seen him look, too, and that melted something in her heart.

She wanted to give him the hug that she hadn't been able to give Abby but, if she did that, she had the horrible feeling that she might burst into tears and how embarrassing would that be?

'Something like that doesn't happen that often,' Hugh said. 'And, when it does, it's usually someone in their eighties or nineties or with an underlying condition that means they're living on borrowed time. It's a lot harder to take when it's someone so much younger and apparently healthy, isn't it?'

Lisa nodded slowly, dropping her gaze so that Hugh wouldn't see her eyes fill with tears.

But he put a finger under her chin and she had to lift her face and there was no hiding how she was feeling. Hugh's gaze was searching. It seemed as if he was absorbing everything she was feeling. That he wanted to understand because then he might be able to fix something and the impression that he cared enough to do that was almost enough to undo Lisa completely in that moment.

'Come with me,' was all he said, dropping his arm around her shoulders. 'Peter and Tim are covering the rest of the night and I have something to show you.'

Lisa was aware of the weight of Hugh's arm and that her feet were already moving in response to his encouragement. She had no idea what it was he wanted to show her, but the last time she had gone somewhere with him he'd promised that she wouldn't regret it and he'd given her a memory that she would treasure for ever. It wasn't hard to trust him now.

'We did everything we possibly could, you know,' Hugh told her when they were alone in the elevator, going down to a lower deck. 'And you were an important part of that, getting the defibrillator on scene so fast. Even if he'd been in the best-equipped emergency department on land he wouldn't have survived. I'm guessing he had a catastrophic heart attack or a serious, undiagnosed cardiomyopathy.'

'He was on his honeymoon,' Lisa said. 'How sad is that?' She walked ahead of Hugh as the elevator doors opened. 'It should have been the happiest time of his life.'

The huff of sound from Hugh made Lisa turn swiftly and his eyebrows rose at the look she was giving him.

'Sorry… It's not funny at all. It's just that…well, the first time I ever came on a cruise ship, I was on my honeymoon.'

Lisa could feel her jaw dropping. 'You're *married*?' Oddly, there seemed to be a sinking sensation in her stomach at the same time. Because she was disappointed that a married man would be playing around with so many other women, perhaps?

But Hugh was shaking his head emphatically. 'Nope. Never been married. Never intend to be either. One honeymoon was enough and I did it solo.' His mouth tilted on one side. 'Apart from everyone I met along the way, of course, but I did it without a wife.'

'What happened?' The personal question popped out before Lisa could stop it but, as a distraction from her own less than happy thoughts, this was irresistible.

Hugh shrugged. 'I'd gone to my best friend's house a couple of days before the wedding to deliver his suit because he was going to be my best man. That was when I found him in bed with my fiancée, Catherine. It was a no-brainer to cancel the wedding but I couldn't cancel the cruise and I thought, seeing as I'd paid for it all and arranged time off work, I might as well get away for a couple of weeks.'

'So this was before you started working on ships?'

'It was *why* I started working on ships.'

Lisa was so fascinated by this story she simply walked through the door that Hugh had opened but then she stopped and stared.

'This is someone's cabin,' she said.

'It is indeed,' Hugh agreed. 'It's my cabin.'

It was a lot bigger than Lisa's cabin. There was a desk with its surface crowded by a laptop computer, scattered medical journals and a collection of empty mugs. The chair in front of it had Hugh's normal white uniform draped over it. There was a couch and armchairs in front of doors that led out to a generous balcony, a door that obviously led to a bathroom and a double bed that looked rumpled enough to give the impression that Hugh had just climbed out of it.

Lisa's gaze slid sideways, trying to imagine him in pyjamas. Nope... If ever there was a man who would sleep naked, surely it would be Hugh Patterson. The uninvited thought was enough to make her close her eyes for a moment as she willed her cheeks not to start glowing like Rudolph the reindeer's nose.

'Um...' She cleared her throat. 'What was it you were saying?'

Lisa looked about as uncomfortable as she had the first time Hugh had ever seen her, first on the wharf in Barcelona when they both knew she'd been watching him kiss Carlotta and then when he'd met her in the medical centre and she'd known she would be working with him for the next couple of weeks.

But, until she realised he had brought her into his private, personal space, he'd been doing a good job of distracting her from the misery that he assumed was due to their unsuccessful resuscitation efforts this evening. He hadn't seen her with tears in her eyes like that before and he suspected it would take something huge to make Lisa Phillips cry so it had induced an odd squeezing sensation in his chest that meant he had to try and fix things.

'Ah...' Hugh decided to ignore her embarrassment and act like it was no big deal that his cabin was messy and he hadn't even made his bed properly. He walked towards the sitting room corner to open the balcony doors. That way, Lisa wouldn't feel like she was trapped and it was a nice enough evening to sit out there if that helped. 'I was saying that my solo honeymoon was the reason I took a job as a ship's doctor. I had been about to take up a position in a general practice in the nice outer London suburb I'd grown up in. I was all set to settle down and move back into the family home and raise my two point four children—you know, the whole nine yards.'

Lisa was shaking her head. 'You were really in love, weren't you? It must have been absolutely devastating.'

'Better to happen then than when those two and a bit kids were involved.' Hugh kept his tone light. He also needed to change the subject because, like his privileged background, it was something he preferred not to talk about. To anyone. He *had* been devastated. He'd gone on board his first cruise ship feeling totally betrayed and crushed and, for some weird reason, he almost felt like telling Lisa every gruesome detail. Because he knew she would understand? That she would care?

'Anyway…there was an incident on board. Or rather on shore. One of the passengers was riding a donkey on a Greek island and he fell off and dislocated his shoulder. I managed to get it relocated for him and used his clothes to splint it in place, got him back to the ship and then ended up helping to X-ray him to make sure it was all okay.'

Lisa had followed him towards the balcony but now she sat down on the edge of the couch as she listened to his story.

'The doctor I was working with told me they were looking for new medical staff and it all came together. I didn't have to settle in one place or start thinking about real estate or nursery schools. I didn't need to get bored by turning up to the same place every day to do the same job. I could live and work like I was on a permanent holiday and get an endless variety of medical challenges, some of them as big as anything you'd get on land—like tonight.'

Hugh turned away, towards the small fridge tucked behind one of the armchairs. That had been more than two years ago now. It didn't feel so much like a permanent holiday any longer. He was, in fact, turning up to the same place every day to do the same job, wasn't he? And, yes, he was living the dream with all the fabulous places he got to visit and the glamour of being a ship's officer but…sometimes it all felt a bit transitory, with nothing solid to hang onto. Even friends that you made along the way—like Lisa—didn't necessarily stay in your life.

This living the dream felt pretty darned lonely sometimes, in fact...

Empty, even?

'Right.' He opened the fridge. 'This is what I wanted to show you.'

'You're kidding.' Lisa looked shocked. 'Champagne? Tonight—after how *awful* it's been?'

Her voice wobbled a little on the last few words and Hugh felt that squeeze in his chest again. He opened the freezer compartment of the fridge to pick out the frosty glasses that lived there and then went to sit beside Lisa, putting the glasses on the coffee table in front of her.

'Have you heard of Napoleon Bonaparte?' he asked casually.

'Of course. I loved history at school.' Lisa looked surprised at the random question but there was a hint of a smile on her face as she played along. 'Short guy, born in Corsica, married Josephine and crowned himself emperor of France. He was famous for saying that an army marches on its stomach, I believe.'

Hugh nodded. He was removing the foil and twisting the wire around the cork on the bottle. 'He had something to say about champagne, too.'

'Oh?'

'Yep. He said that in victory you deserve champagne but in defeat you *need* it.' As if to applaud the statement, the cork shot towards the ceiling with a satisfyingly loud popping sound. The sound of Lisa's laughter was even more satisfying.

'You're incorrigible, Hugh, you know that?'

'I'd agree if I knew what that meant.' Hugh suppressed a smile as he filled a glass to hand to Lisa.

'But it's a good thing, yes?' He touched his glass to hers. *'Santé,'* he murmured.

'You know perfectly well what it means.' But there was genuine amusement in her eyes before she closed them as she took an appreciative sip of her sparkling wine.

'It's just as good as the first time,' she said. 'Maybe even better. That doesn't often happen, does it?'

'Some things actually get better the more often you do them,' he said, 'And some things you never want to do for a second time. Once burnt, forever shy.'

'Mmm...'

He could feel Lisa's gaze on him and, as soon as he turned towards her, he knew she was thinking about the spectacular crash and burn of his wedding plans. He could feel the moment her thoughts changed from sympathy to something else, though. She was thinking about the kinds of things he had done often enough to become expert in. Like kissing... Any second now, she was going to go back to that assumption she'd made that he fell into bed with every willing woman who tried to attract his attention.

He held her gaze steadily, making a silent statement that she was completely wrong in that assumption. That there were actually very few women he had fallen—or wanted to fall—into bed with.

But... He didn't need that spear of sensation in his body to confirm what he suddenly realised. Lisa Phillips was definitely one of those women and, at this moment in time, it felt like she was the only one.

Stunned by the realisation, Hugh put his glass carefully down on the table as an excuse to break the eye contact but he was a fraction of a second too late. He'd seen the way her pupils were dilating. She not only knew what he was thinking, she was responding to it.

Hugh pulled in a slow breath but he wasn't about to shake off the detour his brain, and his body, were determined to take. He wanted her. He wanted to see that flicker of desire in her eyes get kindled into a flame. Maybe he wanted to tease her in a completely different way from any he would have considered before now—to create enough frustration to be able to make getting tipped into paradise all the more intense. Would the expression in her eyes be anything like the first time she had tasted real champagne?

Would he be making a terrible mistake if he tried to find out? Just proving that Lisa's assumptions about his lifestyle were not wrong? Or was he right in suspecting that she might want this as much as he did?

He turned back to meet her gaze again, knowing that she would see that last question in his eyes. Maybe he didn't really have a choice here, given the way his desire was exploding now that it had been acknowledged. But Lisa did have a choice and he would totally respect that. A cold shower might well be in the cards in his very near future.

Oh…*my*… That *look*…

Lisa had to swallow her mouthful of champagne in a hurry. Nobody had ever looked at her like that. Ever. As if she was the most desirable thing in the entire world. As if he wanted to do a whole lot more than simply kiss her. And every single cell in Lisa's body was not only reminding her of what it was like to be kissed by this man but making a plea to find out what doing more than kissing would be like.

This was, she realised, the first time in her life that she actually, desperately wanted to get really intimate with someone. Oh, she'd had the usual teenage curiosity about sex but that had been mixed with doubt that the experience might not live up to expectations that had been set by some of the books she'd read and she'd been so right. Early attempts had been fumbling and embarrassing. With her more recent choices of boyfriends it had been a lot better. Enjoyable, even, but still nothing like having fireworks going off or the earth spinning on its axis or a herd of unicorns galloping off into the sunset.

She had, with the help of one of those boyfriends, come to the conclusion that the fault lay completely on her side, and in a way that had been a relief because perhaps there was a part of her that had decided long ago that she really didn't deserve that kind of pleasure. Whatever the cause, Lisa had given up believing in any of that hype about how good sex could be—as far as she was concerned, anyway.

Until Hugh Patterson had kissed her the other night, that was...

Lisa could imagine that she was standing on the edge of a precipice here. She could—and undoubtedly *should*—step back onto firm, safe ground. If she let herself fall, there were two possibilities. One was that Hugh would catch her—probably with his lips to start with—and the other was that she would just keep falling, in which case she might crash into an embarrassing heap because he would find out that she wasn't very good at sex, but...

But... There was something about tonight that felt different. Hugh had found her at one of the lowest points she could remember in a very long time. She was missing Abby and worried about her but aware that her sister would actually be able to cope perfectly well without her, which made this a turning point in her life, but it was scary because she couldn't imagine such a different future. She had been gutted by the death of their patient. She'd realised what an insignificant speck she was in the face of a limitless night sky and sea and she'd been feeling *so* lonely.

His company had been a godsend because it was exactly what she needed to counteract that loneliness. The way he'd held her face up with his finger under her chin and tried to read her face like a book had made her feel as if her well-being was important to him. That he was really seeing her. He didn't know a lot about her life, other than how important her sister was to her, but it felt like he knew more than any man ever had.

He'd shared something personal, too. Physically, as in bringing her into his private cabin, but emotionally as well, by telling her the story of how he'd been betrayed by the woman he'd loved enough to be about to marry. Above all, he'd made her laugh. He'd given her a moment that had obliterated the worry for Abby, fear for the future and the grief for the man who'd died tonight.

Right now, he was silently asking her if she wanted to be made love to and the answer was a cry that came from somewhere very deep in Lisa's soul. She felt astonishingly vulnerable in this moment but…she trusted this man and she'd never before wanted so much to be as close to another person as possible. She needed that comfort. To escape for a little while from any worries or sadness in her world. To know that she wasn't as insignificant as she'd imagined?

She still hesitated, however. Because, judging by that kiss, Hugh was an expert in all things sexual and she...well, he was going to be disappointed, wasn't he?

Oddly, the nerves in her fingers seemed to have stopped working because she made no attempt to hang onto her glass when Hugh gently took it from her and put it down beside his on the table. The nerves in her lips, on the other hand, were in overdrive as he slowly turned back, cupped her chin in one hand and touched her lips with his own in the same way he had the first time he'd done this. Such a feather-light touch, a soft rub, a tiny lick. Infinitely subtle changes of pressure as if her mouth was being not only invited to dance but being led around a dance floor so that being good at it was effortless. A tiny sound escaped her lips as Lisa let herself sink blissfully deeper into that kiss.

It was that tiny sound that totally undid Hugh.

That took him to a place he didn't recognise, in fact. He'd seen the heart-breaking vulnerability in Lisa's eyes before he'd kissed her and that had set off alarm bells like never before because he knew he was in a position to hurt Lisa. But she knew as well as he did that this was only about tonight and he could feel that her need was as urgent as his own. And...what really did something unprecedented to his head—and his heart— was that he could see the trust she was gifting him.

That sound was like the sigh of someone who'd pushed past a final barrier and could see the place they were desperate to get to. And, even more than how much his own body was craving the release of indulging this astonishingly powerful desire, that sound made Hugh want this to be something special for Lisa. She might not be a virgin but there was something that told him Lisa was nervous of sex for some reason. Afraid of it, even? He had given her the joy of her first taste of real champagne. Maybe, if he took things slowly and gently, he could give her the knowledge that sex could be just as good. Perhaps even better...

So that's what he did. He lost track of time but it didn't matter a damn how long this took. He took his sweet time getting them both naked and into his bed and then introducing himself to every inch of Lisa's body with his hands and his lips. He could feel every time she got tense or tried to please *him* by hurrying things along so he would slow her hands. Capture them and hold them above her head for a moment or two.

'Shh... It's all good,' he would murmur to reassure her, before kissing her for as long as it took for her to relax again. 'Wait... We've got all the time in the world.'

Maybe it was the gentle motion of the sea way beneath them.

Or maybe a taste of champagne on top of the emotional and physical fatigue of this evening had put Lisa into a space like no other.

Or—and this was far the most likely—it was because this was Hugh she was with. A man who clearly knew his way around a woman's body. It seemed like he knew *her* body better than she knew it herself. And whenever she had the fear that he was going to discover that she was being a complete fraud and only pretending that she was loving this, he would simply back off.

Slow the pace and force her to be patient when all she wanted to try and do was give him the pleasure of the release he more than deserved.

She'd try again in just a minute, she decided. Surely he'd had enough of trying to bring her to a climax. It wasn't going to happen and the worry was that he would guess that she was faking it, like others had, unless she could be more convincing than she had ever been before. But the flicker of doubt came and went, along with the determination to move and touch Hugh again in a way she was sure he wouldn't be able to resist. She was caught, she realised, in an escalating tension being created by the movement of Hugh's fingers.

She put her hand over his to ask him to stop but he ignored her and, in alarm, Lisa opened her eyes, only to find that Hugh's face was right beside her own and he was watching her. And that was when it happened. She was falling. Falling into wave after wave of the most intense pleasure she'd ever experienced in her life.

Her astonished gasp triggered what she'd been trying to achieve for what felt like for ever to make sure that this was good for Hugh and, even as those extraordinary waves began to recede, she heard his groan of need and then she could feel him inside her and, unbelievably, the new movement was building that tension all over again.

This time, when she unravelled, he was holding her tightly in his arms so she could feel the shudders in his body and knew that they were both falling. He was still holding her as she tried to slow her breathing afterwards, aware of the pounding of both their hearts. Aware that Hugh was watching her again and there was a question in his eyes but a smile on his face as if he already knew the answer.

'Good?' he whispered.

Lisa could feel a smile curving her own lips. 'Unicorns,' she whispered back.

The sparkle of delight in Hugh's eyes and the way his smile widened told Lisa that he understood. That he couldn't be happier that she'd found it magic and the knowledge that he was so happy that she was happy gave Lisa a whole new sensation of falling.

Falling in love?

'So, what do you reckon?' Hugh was still smiling. 'Is sex as good as or better than champagne?'

That's what this had been, Lisa reminded herself hurriedly. Just sex. One of those "good things" in life—like dancing or fine wine. It might have been the best sex she'd ever had in her life but she and Hugh weren't lovers, they were only friends. But that didn't seem to matter right now because Lisa was still under the spell of the magic and it seemed that she was stepping into a whole new world.

'I'm not sure,' she murmured. 'I might have to test that theory again sometime.'

The growling sound that Hugh made was most definitely one of approval. 'I think that's very wise. One should never jump to conclusions about important things. I'm happy to help with the research.'

But Lisa wriggled free as he began to trail kisses down her neck and onto her shoulder. Her world had just been rocked in a rather spectacular manner but reality was making its presence felt and there was suddenly a beat of fear to be found in the knowledge that she had lost control to such an extent. That, for heaven knows how long, the most important thing in her life had been Hugh and what was happening between them. She'd never let desire overwhelm her like that before. It was dangerous because it distracted you and, if you let important things slip from your grasp when you were distracted, it could ruin your life. That she could remember a lifelong mantra she had just ignored but still feel so incredibly happy was confusing, to say the least.

'I need to go,' she said. 'I think it's time I got back to my own cabin and got some sleep.'

Hugh let her slip out of his grasp. 'No problem,' he responded. 'We've got all the time in the world for that research.'

Which wasn't true, Lisa thought as she moved quietly along deserted narrow hallways a few minutes later. They had little more than another week before the fantasy of shipboard life, exotic locations and now mind-blowing sex would have to come to an end. But that didn't seem to matter either. Because, even if tonight was the only night she could ever have with Hugh Patterson, it had been worth it. She wasn't broken after all. She'd just needed a person who cared enough to show her that and, while she couldn't possibly be *in* love with someone like Hugh, she could love him for giving her that. For making her feel that perhaps she *did* deserve that kind of joy in her life.

And, even if it was dangerous to be distracted like that, it had nothing to do with her real life, did it? Abby was safe. Lisa was here, earning extra money to make sure she could maintain that safety for both of them. So the distraction was confined. And limited. It could only last a matter of days, until this cruise was finished and she flew back to her real life. A handful of days was just a blip in anyone's lifetime.

Could there be any real harm in enjoying it while it lasted?

CHAPTER SEVEN

SO…SEX WAS one of the things that got better the more often you did it.

Or, she should qualify that, Lisa realised, because it was only sex with Hugh that continued to surprise and delight her on new levels every time. The total opposite to her past experience in relationships, in fact, when sex had become progressively more predictable and dull. Anxiety inducing as well, because she'd known she wasn't performing as well as expected.

She knew why it was so different, of course. Hugh was the complete opposite to anyone she had ever chosen to get close to in the past. The bad boy versus the sensible, safe kind of man. Not that they were in a relationship. They both knew that this was never going to be any more than a friendship and that their time together was limited. Perhaps that was why they were both making the most of it.

Keeping it secret was part of the thrill as well. Maybe that was making it safer to enjoy because it confirmed that this was a friendship with hidden benefits rather than a relationship that carried responsibilities. Or perhaps it really was frowned upon for crew members to hook up, but whatever the reason was, the agreement was tacit and became more enjoyable as the days ticked past. There were a couple of long days at sea as the ship sailed around the bottom of Italy to the Greek Islands on the itinerary and then back again.

They both became very good at the game of working together without betraying how close they were, resisting the urge to hold eye contact a little too long, or engineer moments when their hands or bodies might touch as they moved in sometimes confined spaces. They were being careful not to be seen visiting each other's cabins and spending only a part of each night together, and they could make it appear that they went on shore leave separately but meeting up as soon as they were out of sight.

Like they had for a delightful day on the island of Mykonos, where they had met up at a private beach that was not on the usual tourist radar. There were small fishing boats in the nearby port, pelicans that seemed to be expert in posing for photographs and a waveless beach that was like the biggest swimming pool ever.

And like they had again today as they'd reached the second-last destination of this cruise and it was Blue Watch's turn to have shore leave, having stayed on the ship for the visit to Santorini.

With the cruise ship docked in the port of Salerno as they reached Italy again on the way back to Spain, there had been multiple choices for a day's outing. There were buses going to Naples, to Sorrento with a boat trip to the island of Capri, and a tour that took in both Mount Vesuvius and the ancient city of Pompeii.

They were all destinations that took Lisa's breath away so why did she avoid every one of them?

Because Hugh had offered her something far more

enticing. Another day alone with him and somewhere that no one else would be likely to be going.

'I know this walk,' he told her. 'It's called The Valley of the Ancient Mills. And it's right under everybody's noses but they'll be jumping on the buses to go further afield. This valley is quiet and green, and full of the ruins of old mills and a river and waterfalls, and we can walk up the hills towards a gorgeous village called Ravello, but on the way is another little village. I don't even know the name of it but it has a restaurant with a terrace and a view and—'

'Stop…' Lisa pressed her finger against Hugh's lips. 'I'm sold. How could I go past a restaurant with a terrace?'

She couldn't. Not after the most romantic evening ever, in that French restaurant, even though there had been nothing romantic happening between them yet. How much more fabulous would it be to have a setting like that when you were with your lover? Well, okay, she couldn't—and didn't—think of Hugh as her lover and she knew there was a definite limit to this fling and that this outing today would be almost the last, but she was making memories here, wasn't she? And memories could be woven into a fantasy that she could enjoy for ever. A private fantasy. She hadn't confessed the new development in her life to Abby, although her sister had guessed something was going on.

'You just look so…different, Lise. So…happy. I've never seen you kind of glowing like this before.'

'I'm happy you're okay. That that last clinical session was the total opposite of that horrible first one. She won't be the first patient to see you as an inspiration.'

But Abby hadn't been convinced. *'It's more than that. You look like, I don't know, a kid on Christmas morning.'*

'I'm loving this cruise, that's all. I could go to Pompeii on our next stop, if I want. Or walk up to the top of Mount Vesuvius. How incredible is that?'

She had convinced Abby that her excitement was at the prospect of seeing such famous sights but the real reason was far simpler.

'Actually, you had me at the name of the valley,' she told Hugh. 'It sounds very...romantic.'

And it was. It was as green and quiet as Hugh had promised and the shade was welcome in the increasing heat of a late Italian morning. There were wild cyclamen making a carpet of pale pink beneath the trees, the buzzing of bees and bird calls nearby and the refreshing ripple of the river not far away. There were moss-covered ruins of the old stone mills and, best of all, they had this track all to themselves. A private world. Hugh took Lisa's hand to help her up a rocky part of the path but he didn't let go when she was back on smooth ground.

Instead, he pulled her close and kissed her with one of those slow and, oh, so thorough kisses that Lisa was quite probably getting addicted to because they were a drug all by themselves. She could feel herself floating away within seconds towards that place where nothing else existed. Just herself and Hugh and the promise of absolute bliss...

But Hugh broke the kiss too soon this time, albeit reluctantly.

'We need to keep going,' he said. 'We've got a bit further to go and this weather's not going to last.'

'I heard that there was stormy weather coming but I thought it was a few days away yet.'

'The big storms probably won't catch us until we're somewhere between Sardinia and Malaga on our way home but it's going to get overcast later today and will probably rain by tomorrow.'

Lisa didn't want to think about arriving in Malaga, which was when she would be leaving the ship to fly back to England. 'I hope the sun lasts while we have lunch on that terrace,' she said. 'I can't wait.'

'I hope it lasts a bit longer. If we've got time and enough energy, we can walk further up to Ravello and go exploring and then get a taxi or bus back to the ship. There's an amazing old villa in Ravello called the Villa Rufolo and it's well worth visiting.'

'You know so many places to go.'

'I've done it so many times. Too many, perhaps. I usually try to find something new to see at every destination but…' he smiled at Lisa. 'It's actually a lot more fun sharing the things I already know with you because… I don't know…it makes them more special.'

His words made Lisa feel special. In fact, knowing that Hugh was getting genuine pleasure from sharing things that he liked with her was giving her an even stronger connection to this man who had the most gorgeous smile in the world. It gave her a bit of lump in her throat, to be honest.

They finally left the beautiful valley and its mills behind and followed a path that gave them wonderful views past forests and lemon groves and terraced fields of tomatoes to where the town of Amalfi nestled right beside the sparkling blue of the Mediterranean. The path led through stone archways that were charmingly decorated with old wicker baskets and unusual-looking utensils.

By the time they reached the restaurant, they were ready to rest and enjoy a meal. They both ordered an *insalata caprese*—a salad of delicious slices of fresh local tomatoes, mozzarella cheese and basil leaves that was drizzled with olive oil. It came with a basket of fresh, crusty bread and was the most perfect-looking lunch Lisa had ever seen. She had to take a photo of it for Abby.

Hugh ordered Prosecco as well.

'Think of it as Italian champagne,' he told Lisa, with a wink. *'Saluti, cara.'*

Cara. Didn't that mean something like *darling* or *sweetheart*? Lisa touched her glass to Hugh's and met his gaze over the top of the glasses. The warmth in those brown eyes and the echoes of the endearment he had just used stole her breath away and it was at that moment that Lisa realised she was in trouble.

She had known right from the start that this was temporary. That it was just a shipboard fling that was going to end very soon and it was highly unlikely that she would ever see Hugh Patterson again. But she also knew that it was not going to be easy. At this moment, if felt as if it could very well be devastating.

Because she'd fallen in love with him. It had probably happened, without her even realising, that night when he'd managed to make her laugh when she'd been feeling so awful. When he'd taken her to his bed and changed her life for ever. When she'd mistakenly analysed her feelings as lust rather than love, but this was so much deeper than anything purely sexual. Lisa wanted the closeness and connection they'd discovered to last for ever. She wanted, in particular, to freeze this moment in time when it felt like she could fall into that gaze and never want to come up for air.

Maybe it was an omen that a shadow noticeably darkened this idyllic scene as a first bank of clouds drifted overhead to obscure the sun. It was Hugh who broke that eye contact to look up at the sky.

'Uh-oh,' he murmured. 'Maybe that storm's on its way a bit quicker than they predicted.'

'Mmm.' But Lisa wasn't thinking about bad weather as she made a concerned sound and even suppressed a shiver. She was thinking of something that was going to be a lot less pleasant to endure.

Saying goodbye to Hugh...

Had Hugh really thought that Lisa Phillips was uptight and controlling?

That she wouldn't trust anyone else enough to even help her carry her suitcase?

That she was the complete opposite of the type of women he could ever be attracted to?

Oh, man...how wrong could a person be?

As if she'd picked up on his thought by telepathy, Lisa turned from the window of the bus to catch his gaze. There was awe in those amazing eyes, thanks to the view down the mountainside to the town of Amalfi they were heading back to, but there was also a bit of fear at the speed at which the bus driver was taking these hairpin bends on the narrow road.

'I guess he knows what he's doing,' she muttered. 'He must have done it plenty of times before.'

That was so like Lisa, wasn't it? She might be afraid to some degree and she might be determined to excel in everything she did but she was still prepared to trust someone else, which gave her a very endearing, almost childlike quality.

She trusted *him* now. On a very different level from anything he would have imagined them sharing.

He had wanted a certain level of trust from Lisa as soon as he'd realised they were going to be spending a lot of time together for a couple of weeks. He'd wanted to tease her and make her a little less 'uptight'. He'd wanted to show her that there were things in life that were meant to be enjoyed and she was missing out on most of them.

What he hadn't realised was that sharing those things with her would make them so different for him. He'd been drinking champagne and having sex with beautiful women, travelling to amazing places and just getting the most out of his life for a very long time now, but doing exactly the same things with Lisa was like doing them himself for the very first time because they felt *that* different.

The bus was leaning as it took another bend and Hugh could feel the pit of his own stomach dropping as he looked over Lisa's shoulder to the drop below the side of the road. The bus seemed to be clinging to the road by the edge of its tyres but Lisa's squeak of terror was half excitement and the way her fingers clutched his arm so dramatically made him smile.

Maybe this was what it was like when you had a child, he thought, and you got to see the world all over again from their perspective. You could experience the sourness of a lemon perhaps as you laughed at the face they made. Or the joy of feeling your body fly through the air that was enough to make you shriek with glee when someone pushed you on a swing for the first time. Perhaps what made this so different with Lisa was that it was an adult version of rediscovery.

The sex had been a revelation every single time. So familiar but so new as well—as if everything had suddenly become colour instead of just black and white. The joy on her face today, when she'd had to stop and simply gaze at the beauty of that walk past the ancient paper mills, and her eyes closing in bliss when she'd had her first mouthful of that mix of tomatoes and cheese and basil...

Hugh had never tasted a salad that good himself and yet he'd eaten an *insalata caprese* countless times before. It wasn't that those astonishingly bright red local tomatoes had that much more flavour. Or that the olive oil was especially good. Hugh knew that it was being with Lisa that was making things so different and that was more than a little disturbing.

Because it was true that she wasn't his "type" at all. That when he had first met her, when he had actually been with the sophisticated Carlotta—who was exactly his type—he wouldn't have dreamed of asking Lisa out. The notion that he might be able to make love to her time and time again and feel like he could never get enough of her would have been a joke. If he'd had a premonition that doing something as ordinary as sightseeing with her could be so delightful he would have known he needed to stay well clear. He had invented what he thought of as his type because those women were safe. They didn't want loyalty or commitment or to risk betrayal any more than he did.

It had been too long, hadn't it? He'd become complacent and hadn't realised that it was even possible

for anyone to get past his protective barriers. He'd
considered himself to be completely safe from feeling like this again. That *pride* in being the one to provide something that gave joy to someone else. That
desire that had nothing to do with sex but was a wish
to keep providing things like that. To protect someone
and cherish them.

That was what falling in love was all about, wasn't
it?

He'd started out seeing Lisa as someone who could
be the little sister he'd never had. How could this determined but naïve, petite, shaggy red-haired woman
with unusual eyes and freckles to match their hazel
brown have become the most beautiful person Hugh
had ever known? He'd been in love once before but
how he was starting to feel about Lisa had the potential to blow that past love out of the water and make it
barely worth remembering.

That was a little terrifying, he had to admit.

Except that Lisa was nothing like Catherine, his
ex-fiancée, was she? This was someone who had actually sacrificed probably more than she was letting
on in order to care for someone she loved—her sister
Abby. Lisa would have that kind of loyalty to anyone
she loved, if she ever let someone in to that degree,
and she wouldn't lie about how she felt either. Or, if
she tried, he would be able to see immediately that she
wasn't being truthful because he could read her face
like a book now thanks to watching it so carefully in
her unguarded moments.

And that meant he could trust Lisa. On a level that
he'd never thought he would ever trust a woman again.
But what, if anything, should he do about that? There

was a clock ticking here. In a matter of only a couple of days this woman was going to walk out of his life and back to her own. If he didn't want that to happen he would have to make some big decisions in a hurry. But not yet... He might recognise that he was feeling the way you did when you fell in love but that didn't mean it had actually happened yet, did it? Or that Lisa even felt the same way.

They were nearly back at sea level now, passing the first houses of Amalfi, and they'd need to hurry to get a taxi back to Salerno and back on board the ship in good time before they left the port. There would be no time for a while to give such a serious matter the amount of thought it needed and Hugh could feel himself releasing his breath in a sigh of relief as they climbed down the steps of the bus. He could just stop thinking about it and enjoy the present for a bit longer. He'd lived this way for long enough to know that it could work.

The smile on Lisa's face as she skipped a step to catch up with his long stride was enough to make it well worth thinking only about the next few hours. Getting back on board, an evening surgery, dinner and then... Hugh held Lisa's gaze for a long moment as he sent a silent invitation for her to come to his cabin later tonight. The way her smile faded as the colour in her eyes changed from golden brown to something more molten was enough to let him know that the invitation had been received and accepted.

He couldn't bring himself to break that gaze. He opened his mouth and he knew that the words that were about to come out would change everything.

Three little words.

I love you...

They were there. In his head. On the tip of his tongue. But something stopped him. Maybe it was the tiny frown line that appeared between Lisa's eyes when she heard a sound from her phone. She dived into her bag to find it.

'That's Abby texting me. She was going back to the house to check things for me today. I hope everything's all right.'

Hugh could sense that Lisa's attention was a very long way away from him now. She was back in her real life for the moment. Away from her working holiday fling. In a place he would never belong.

'Everything okay?'

'She's stressing because she's found a pile of mail behind the door and she's wants to know if she should open it. I've told her to leave it where it is. I'll deal with it all when I get home.'

Her glance was apologetic, as if she understood that her real life had nothing to do with him. Or that she didn't want it to have anything to do with him? Hugh took a deeper breath and he could feel his mind clearing noticeably. He was certainly going to miss Lisa when she left the ship in Malaga but he could cope if he had to and that would be a lot easier than grappling with concepts he had given up even thinking about a very long time ago. Things like settling down to a more ordinary job somewhere. Getting married. Having a family.

Good grief... Hugh turned away from Lisa and hurriedly raised his arm to flag down a taxi. Had the thought of getting *married* actually entered his head in that flash of muddled thoughts? The sooner they were back on board his beloved ship and in his familiar environment the better. He had to put a stop to this before he did something really crazy.

Like asking Lisa to marry him...

Something had changed but, for the life of her, Lisa couldn't put her finger on quite what it could be.

They'd had such a lovely day together with that walk up through the valley and the delicious lunch and then exploring the mountain town and that crazy bus ride back to the coast. She was quite sure that Hugh had enjoyed the day as much as she had but he seemed a little edgy when they opened the medical centre for the evening surgery. Was it because the wind had picked up as the ship had eased out into more open sea? Lisa could feel the gentle roll of bigger swells beneath them, although she wasn't finding it alarming at all.

'Is it likely to be a problem, getting a storm while we're at sea?'

'Hard to say. Sometimes the captain can navigate around the bad weather and modern ships have stabilisers that help a lot, although it's surprising to a lot of people how rough the Mediterranean can get. Usually they just blow past with nothing more than a lot of people getting very seasick or complaining that some decks and the swimming pools are closed. Thanks for the reminder. I'd better check our supplies of anti-motion-sickness medications.'

'What do you use?' Lisa followed him into the pharmacy room.

'We give out the usual over-the-counter remedies to anyone who asks and they're also available in many of the shops if there gets to be too much of a queue here. The shops also have things like different forms of ginger and peppermint, which we often advise people to try. Other advice includes eating something, like dry crackers, getting some fresh air on the balcony or deck or going to the centre of the ship where it's more stable.'

'And if it's serious?'

'We've got good stocks of promethazine and metoclopramide.' Hugh shut and locked the glass-fronted cupboard he'd opened. 'And plenty of saline if someone gets really dehydrated. Here...' He scooped a lot of small packages out of a drawer to hand to Lisa. 'Let's keep these supplies of Dramamine at the front desk. If they're mild cases you can dispense this and send them home when you're triaging.' He glanced over his shoulder as he led the way out of the pharmacy. 'You're not worried about this storm, are you?'

'Um...no...' But Lisa bit her lip. 'I did find some videos online, though, that looked a bit scary. Restaurants with all the tables and even a piano rolling one way and then the other and taking people out on the way.'

Hugh was smiling. 'Have you seen that movie with the ship and the iceberg? That's a good one, too. It's just as well that we don't get many icebergs in the Mediterranean.'

Lisa loved that smile so much. She loved the way there were crinkles of amusement on either side of those gorgeous brown eyes but, most of all, she loved that he was checking how she was feeling about something and was trying to make her laugh to ease any worry. She *did* laugh and, suddenly, whatever tension had been in the air this evening evaporated, along with any nerves about stormy weather. She was with Hugh. They could handle whatever came their way.

Including a patient she was worried about the moment she walked into the medical centre and had to snatch a breath even while she was introducing herself.

'You're sounding very wheezy, Michelle. Are you asthmatic?'

The young woman nodded. 'It's not getting better... so I thought... I'd come in...'

'Good thinking. Come with me.' Lisa led her straight to the treatment room. 'I'm just going to check your blood pressure and heart rate and the oxygen level in your blood.' She put the clip on his finger. 'Have you been using your inhaler?'

'Yes...lots...'

She got Michelle to blow into a peak flow meter as well.

'What do you normally blow?'

'On a good day...four hundred.'

She was down to a lot less than three hundred now.

'I'm sure the doctor will want to start a nebuliser at least. Let's give you another pillow or two to keep you a bit more upright and I'll go and find him.'

Hugh was with another patient who had run out of his high blood pressure medication a week ago but had thought it wouldn't matter until he'd started getting bad headaches, but one look at Lisa's face and he stood up.

'Wait there, Jim,' he told his patient. 'I'll be back very soon. We're going to admit you to our little hospital here for a while so we can keep an eye on you while you have some intravenous medication to bring your blood pressure down in a controlled manner.'

Jim's wife had come to the appointment with him. 'I

told you it was serious,' she growled. 'Don't you dare move. I'm going back to the cabin to get your pyjamas and toothbrush. You're going to stay here until the doctor says you're okay.'

Hugh was right beside Lisa as she sped back to the treatment room. 'I'm worried that her asthma isn't responding to her inhaler. She's not speaking more than three to four words per breath and her oxygen saturation is down to ninety-six percent. Respiration rate is twenty-five, heart rate is one twenty, and peak flow is not much more than fifty percent of normal for her. Do you want me to set up a nebuliser?'

'Absolutely. We might need to start some IV corticosteroids as well. And get an arterial blood gas measurement.'

By the time Hugh had listened to Michelle's chest, Lisa had a nebuliser mask ready, with medication in the chamber and oxygen running through at a high enough rate to produce a good vapour. She slipped the elastic over the back of Michelle's head and rearranged her pillows to make it more comfortable for her to sit upright.

She worked with Hugh to find and hand him everything he needed to set up an IV line and then the more difficult procedure of inserting a cannula into an artery in Michelle's wrist so that they would be able to get a far more accurate indication of how much circulating oxygen she had in her blood. It couldn't be something that Hugh had to do very often but he made it look easy, from putting in some local anaesthetic to find a vessel that was much deeper than a vein, inserting the cannula and then controlling the spurt of blood under pressure as he attached and taped down the Luer plug. He filled a tiny, two-ml syringe with the arterial blood.

'I'll page Janet or Tim to pop in and show you how to use the benchtop ABG analysis,' he told Lisa when he headed back to his other patient a few minutes later. 'We're also going to need a hand for a while. Might see what Peter's up to. I need to get Jim's blood pressure down so we'll have two patients that need close monitoring for some time.' He held her gaze. 'We could be in for a long night.'

'I wasn't planning on being anywhere else,' she responded.

Except that was only partly true. She might have been planning to be with Hugh tonight but it hadn't occurred to her that they might not be able to leave the medical centre and spend any time alone together. Not that it mattered. Except that that was only partly true also. There was no question that their patients had complete priority while they were on duty, but they only had a very limited number of nights left that they could find that kind of private time so losing one of them was actually quite a big deal. It felt as if there was a giant clock nearby that might be invisible but Lisa could hear the loudness of its ticking slowly increasing.

She was the kind of person you would want right by your side in any crisis but Hugh had already known that, hadn't he? It was one of those trustworthy things about Lisa Phillips. Like the way she had devoted herself to caring for her sister. And the way she not only always gave a hundred and ten percent in everything she did but she did it with intelligence and good-humoured grace even when she had to be rather tired by now.

Hugh was feeling a little weary himself. They'd put in quite a few miles of uphill walking today and work had been full on ever since the start of the evening surgery. They'd been kept very busy, despite calling in the extra team members, until the surgery hours were over. Now he and Lisa were alone in the medical centre and ship's hospital. Janet had gone to bed and Peter and Tim were going to be on call for anything else that happened on board overnight.

Jim's blood pressure had responded well to the intravenous medications and had dropped slowly enough not to cause any complications. Hugh wanted to keep him under observation till morning but he didn't need to be wakened for another check for an hour so he was sleeping peacefully. His wife had gone back to their cabin.

Michelle's condition had, thankfully, started to improve once the extra medications had taken effect. Hugh wasn't going to let her go in a hurry either. He was going to keep a very careful eye on her blood oxygen levels, which meant another arterial sample needed to be taken soon and they would continue to give her both oxygen and nebuliser therapy every few hours.

The roll of the ship was more obvious now as the night wore on. It didn't bother Hugh at all—he rather liked a bit of rough water, in fact, and he had been pleased to see that it didn't seem to be affecting Lisa either. He was concerned about what her level of fatigue must be like by now, though, so he went to the tiny kitchen in the medical centre on the other side of the reception area and put the electric jug on to boil water so he could make Lisa a mug of coffee.

He left the door behind him ajar because this room was not much bigger than a cupboard and, as he gathered the mugs and spoons he needed, he could hear that someone had come into the reception area. He turned his head so that he could see through the crack of the door, hoping that it wasn't a new patient arriving. It wasn't. Lisa had obviously come out of the treatment room so as not to disturb Michelle by taking a phone call.

'I can't talk long,' she was saying. 'I'm monitoring a patient. What on earth are you doing up at this time of night anyway?'

Hugh heard the soft ping of the jug announcing that the water had boiled. He should step out of the room, he thought, and let Lisa know he was nearby. But he hesitated, probably because it was a little disturbing how much he wanted to step closer to her, having heard that note of anxiety in her voice. The urge to protect this woman and to fix things that might be a problem for her was getting steadily more pronounced.

'I told you not to open that mail, Abby.'

There was a note of something like panic in Lisa's voice now, even though she had lowered it, and that need to try and make things better for her was so powerful it squeezed his chest tightly enough to be a physical pain.

'It's not a problem, okay?' Her voice was firm now after a short silence. 'I'm dealing with it. That's why this job was such a great idea.'

Hugh could feel a deep frown creasing his forehead. What wasn't a problem? And why would being on this cruise be a way of dealing with it? Was there something she'd needed to get away from for a while? Or some*one*?

'It's only money,' he heard her say then. 'I've got this—I've got a plan. Don't worry. Look, I'll be home in just a couple of days and I'll explain everything. Now, I've really got to go. Talk soon, yeah?'

Lisa had her back to the kitchen door and she walked back to the treatment room as soon as she'd ended the call so she had no idea that Hugh had been eavesdropping.

He couldn't tell her, of course. Which meant he couldn't ask her what kind of problem she had or what the solution she was planning was all about. If it was money she needed, he had more than enough. He could help…

Or maybe not. Maybe he shouldn't try to find out what was going on and risk getting sucked into an even deeper involvement in Lisa's life.

It had been the mention of money that was changing things. Setting off warning bells that he couldn't ignore, despite the fact that they were taking him straight back to a place he had no desire to be. Back to those dismal days right before the wedding that had never happened. Back to the time when he'd lost both his fiancée and his best friend in one fell swoop.

Back to the worst moment of all. When Catherine had turned away from him to walk out of his life for ever with the words that were going to haunt him for ever.

'I never really loved *you*, Hugh. I just loved your money.'

CHAPTER EIGHT

THE STORM BUILT through the night.

By the time daylight broke, the huge ship was riding some dramatic swells that only seemed to get bigger as the day wore on. The Lido deck was closed and the view from the windows was of a such a dark grey sea it was almost black, so the contrast of the white foam of countless breaking waves was even more breathtaking. The feeling of your stomach dropping when a swell had been crested was alarming and the crunch of the change at the bottom before another climb was also breathtaking. Wind howled through windows that weren't closed tightly enough and people were tilted sideways as they negotiated corridors around the ship.

It was like riding a roller-coaster in very slow motion and Lisa had never wanted to ride any kind of roller-coaster. Or do any thrill seeking, for that matter. Hugh, on the other hand, was actually enjoying this.

The medical centre was busier than Lisa had ever seen and, despite having only managing to catch a few hours of interrupted sleep after caring for their inpatients overnight, she and Hugh were there along with Peter, Janet and Tim, dealing with not only the normal kind of workload but minor injuries that were arriving at an increasing rate due mainly to falls caused by the ship's rolling. They were also handing out huge quantities of anti-motion-sickness medications, trying to reassure overly anxious passengers, and they still had their inpatients.

Michelle seemed to be well over her frightening asthma attack but, for everybody's peace of mind, they were going to keep monitoring her for a few more hours. Jim's blood pressure was down to an acceptable level and he could be discharged as soon as a crew member was available to make sure he got back to his cabin safely.

On top of what was keeping the medical centre so busy, they were also fielding calls to various parts of the ship. Tim had just rushed off to a cabin where it sounded like an elderly person had fallen and hit their head to cause a frightening amount of bleeding when another call came in.

'It's in the gym,' Hugh announced. 'Another fall but they're having trouble breathing so I might need a hand.'

Lisa came out from behind the desk instantly. She was on Hugh's watch so it was obvious that she was the one to accompany Hugh.

But he wasn't even looking in her direction. 'Janet?'

Janet put her hands up in front of her. 'Not unless I have to. I'm okay here but if I go forward and that high I'll get sick.' She was the one to turn to Lisa. 'You're not prone to motion sickness, are you?'

'Haven't noticed anything yet.' Lisa tried to smile but there *was* a knot in her stomach that could turn into nausea down the track. Anxiety about the storm had

just been augmented by anxiety about why Hugh had
chosen Janet to go with him rather than her.

'Be a good test for you, then.' Hugh still wasn't
looking at Lisa as he picked up another one of their
first response packs. 'The gym's right at the bow. And
we need to cross the Lido deck if we want to get there
fast. Here, put this on.' He handed Lisa a bright yellow sou'wester. 'Even if it's not raining, there's enough
spray to get you soaked almost instantly.'

They needed to get there fast if someone was having difficulty breathing and that meant running up the
stairs to avoid both waiting for an elevator and the risk
of getting caught if there was a power outage.

There were people pressed against windows as they
reached the interior part of the Lido deck and the col-
lective cries of mixed awe, alarm and excitement only
added to Lisa's anxiety.

'You ready?' Hugh had his shoulder against the door
that led to the deck. 'Brace yourself.'

They only had about twenty metres to go to get to
the outside entrance of the gym on the other side of
one of the swimming pools. Lisa was unprepared for
the blast of wind as she went outside, however, and
could feel herself losing her footing. She could get
blown overboard, she thought. Or into a swimming
pool that currently looked like something out of one
of those horrific videos she'd seen where the grand
piano was flying across a room. The water in the pool
was tipping towards one end and then sloshing back
to form a small tsunami that spilled out and washed
across the deck with enough force to send deck chairs
sliding into a heap against the railing.

For one terrible moment Lisa thought she might

be going to drown and all she could think of was that she wouldn't be there for Abby when she was needed in the future. It had been bad enough not to have been there for her sister the other day when the upsetting incident with the patient had happened but at least she'd been able to talk to her and it had been enough. Not being there in any form would be even more of a failure than having been responsible for Abby's injuries in the first place.

How could she have been so irresponsible to have put herself in danger like this?

Except, in that same terrible moment, Hugh reached out and caught Lisa's arm. He was leaning into the wind and she could feel how stable his body was. He'd done this before. He was, in fact—judging by the grin on his face and the sparkle in his eyes—loving every moment of it.

Nothing could have demonstrated more clearly that they were—as Hugh had commented on during that, oh, so romantic dinner when they'd decided they could be friends—total opposites when it came to their approach to life.

But… Lisa was clinging to Hugh until they reached the doors that led to the relative safety of the gym. Opposites attracted, didn't they? Sometimes they could even make a long-term relationship work. If both sides wanted it to work, that was.

It was feeling more and more like Hugh was losing interest, however. Something was very different today but it wasn't until they were halfway through assessing the crew member in the gym who'd lost his balance and gone rolling across the floor to land against the metal handles of a piece of equipment that Lisa realised what it was.

The feeling of connection had vanished. As suddenly as a switch being flicked off.

Ever since their first night together, they'd been playing that game when they were working together. Frequent eye contact that was held just short of being a beat too long. Accentuating the kind of situations that meant they came into physical contact with each other, like their hands brushing when Lisa helped to shift the crew member's shirt to expose the painful area of his chest.

The tingle had gone. That awareness. Something was broken and Lisa didn't know what it was but it scared her. Okay, she'd known that her time with Hugh was coming to an end and it would be difficult but she'd thought they would make the most of it for as long as possible and then part as close friends. That they could stay in touch and might even see each other again one day. But maybe that was breaking some unspoken rule. That what happened on board ship simply ceased to exist when the cruise was over, and perhaps Hugh was thinking it was a good idea to wind things down as preparation so he wouldn't have to deal with tears or something when they said goodbye.

Or maybe what was really scaring her was being out in the open sea in weather like this. She could understand now why Janet had wanted to stay in the centre of the ship. Right up at the bow like this made the falling into the trough of a swell even more stomach-dropping and she could see the impressive wall of spray that came up to flood a lower deck when they hit the bottom of the dip between waves.

'Try and take a deep breath for me,' Hugh told their patient as he gently palpated an area where bruising was already becoming evident.

'Can't.' The young man's voice was strained. 'Hurts... *Ow...*'

'Sorry, mate. I think you might have cracked a rib or two. Let me listen to your chest and then we'll give you something for the pain and get you down to the clinic so we can so some X-rays.' He unhooked the stethoscope from around his neck. 'You didn't hit your head as well, did you?' He looked up at another member of the gym staff. 'Was he knocked out?'

The other personal trainer shook his head. 'He just went flying, along with a bunch of gear. We've closed the gym now, which is a shame, because we're going to be stuck at sea for an extra day. Have you heard that Sardinia's been cancelled? We're heading straight back to Malaga.'

What a way to end a cruise.

You had to feel sorry for the passengers but, for Hugh, it was a blessing. He loved being flat out like this, facing a challenge that threatened to tip them past the point of being able to cope. He loved the thrill of riding waves like this but, best of all, it was the perfect excuse to totally ignore the mixed messages in his head concerning Lisa.

He was being given the chance to step right back and see what was going on from a perspective that wasn't getting sabotaged by spending personal time with her. Just being alone with Lisa was enough to make him want to trust her. Enough to make it preferable to block his ears to any alarm bells ringing. It was a bonus that fate was going to ensure they didn't get a chance to make love again because that would be even harder to resist and might make him want really stupid things, like being able to wake up with her in his bed for the rest of his life.

How could you feel so strongly about someone you'd only met a couple of weeks ago? He didn't really know Lisa at all, did he? Not that it probably made much difference in the long run. He'd known Catherine for two years, for heaven's sake.

As another bonus, there were the other medical staff around. It was Tim who helped Hugh glue the scalp wound that he'd found on the patient who'd been bleeding in her cabin. Peter took the X-rays that confirmed the broken ribs that the personal trainer had suffered but had also been reassuring that there was no underlying injury like a punctured lung.

He also X-rayed a Colles' wrist fracture that came in a little later and Lisa was tasked with helping splint the arm with a plaster slab underneath which kept her well out of Hugh's way for some time.

He hadn't missed the occasional puzzled glance that came his way from her from time to time but it was as though he wasn't actually in control of the growing distance between them. It was simply happening and he wasn't exactly enjoying the process himself.

He was missing Lisa already.

The medical staff took turns to have meal breaks by themselves or had food delivered by room service to ensure that they were caring for their inpatients, that someone was available at all times to see people that turned up at the clinic and that they had enough staff to respond to calls from other parts of the ship as well.

That would need to continue overnight, although the forecast was that the weather would have settled by the time they were due to dock in Malaga tomorrow morning. Even if that was the case, however, everybody was going to be exhausted by the time they reached their final port but at least Hugh and the rest of the team would have a couple of days off before a new cruise began—a three-week one next time—and Lisa would be heading home and would no doubt have plenty of time to rest before going back to her real job.

And her real life that didn't include him. Maybe it couldn't include any permanent relationship given that her sister was her first priority. Ironically, that was one of the things he loved about Lisa. The thing that made him feel like she was completely trustworthy and that was what was doing his head in enough to make it impossible to sleep when he was given a break in the early hours of the morning.

Instead, he went walking around the ship because, finally, the seas around them were subsiding. He might as well get a coffee, Hugh decided, because there was little point in trying to sleep for what was left of the night. They would be busy as soon as they docked as well, making arrangements for transport for the people who needed hospital care, like the woman who'd broken her wrist.

There were staff in the bar on the Lido deck that was now open again and it seemed like something was drawing Hugh into it.

'Just a coffee, thanks, mate.'

'Bet you've been busy, Doc. It's been kind of a wild ride, hasn't it?'

'You're not wrong there. Just as well you were

closed for the day, I think. You've had enough drama in this bar for one cruise.'

Hugh took the coffee but decided not to stay on the bar stool to drink it. The reminder of the drama in this bar early on in this cruise was a reminder of something else and he was too weary to cope with any addition to the confusion he had going on in his head. It had been right here when he'd first properly worked with Lisa Phillips as they'd responded to the crisis of Alex's anaphylactic reaction. He'd never be able to come into this bar again without thinking of her, would he?

He walked to the edge of the deck instead and stood by the rail. He could see down onto a lower deck from here and there were obviously plenty of crew working overtime tonight to start the clean-up process that was part of the aftermath of bad weather. The kitchens and dining rooms would be even worse than the decks. Hugh had already treated a few lacerations from people dealing with bucketloads of broken glass. The deck chairs were one of the main issues outside. They got blown around or washed into corners to end up in a tangled heap. Someone was walking around one of those piles right now. A small figure in a bright yellow sou'wester.

Lisa...

Was she on the way to a call or just getting some fresh air? Hugh leaned over the rail, tempted to call out. Tempted to invite her to come and have a coffee with him just because he wanted to be closer to her. As he opened his mouth, however, he saw Lisa turn suddenly and then stoop to pick something up from amongst the jumble of deck-chair legs.

It was a wallet. He might be well above Lisa and it

was the middle of the night but she was standing directly beneath a light so it was easy to see just how full of notes that wallet was when she opened it to have a look, and then touched the wad of notes as if trying to estimate its value. Hugh could also see the astonishment on Lisa's face and the way she instantly looked around, as if she expected the owner of the wallet to be nearby. Or was she wondering if anyone had seen her? The only person on that section of the deck was a crew member who had his arms full of folded deck chairs and he was walking away from Lisa to join his colleagues so he hadn't seen her. She looked over her shoulder again and then, with what almost looked like a shrug of her shoulders, Lisa folded the wallet and slipped it into the pocket of her coat.

He knew perfectly well that Lisa wasn't stealing that wallet. That she would be taking it to someone who would know what to do about finding its owner. He knew that with the same conviction that he knew how much she loved her sister. What that little scenario did do, however, was give Hugh a glimpse of an escape route back to a safe place. Because he had buttons that could be pushed quite easily when it came to women who cared too much about money—buttons that had clearly already been primed by overhearing that conversation Lisa had had with her sister. And because that button being pushed automatically pushed another one, that made him also easily remember the pain of making oneself vulnerable by loving someone so much that they had the power to break your heart.

That kind of pain was what was very likely to happen if he allowed this fling with Lisa to get any bigger than it already was. He could get hurt again. And, if that wasn't enough to convince him to pull the plug on what was happening between them, there was something else that was even less acceptable. Lisa was going to get hurt. And, okay, she might be going to get hurt anyway but this was about damage limitation now, wasn't it? For her sake even more than his own. Because that's what you did when you cared enough about someone else. They would both get over this. It had just been a shipboard fling, after all.

It wasn't exactly the end to this cruise that Lisa had imagined or that she would have wished for.

She was on deck as dawn was breaking and this massive ship was edging into port at Malaga. In a matter of only a few hours, she would be walking down the gangway and away from the most extraordinary job she'd ever had.

Away from the most extraordinary man she'd ever met.

She'd hardly seen him since that storm had peaked and they'd gone to that call in the gym together. She'd known that something had changed but she couldn't understand why. Unless she'd been completely wrong in the kind of man she believed Hugh Patterson to be? Maybe that very first impression of him had been the correct one. That he was one of those shallow, wealthy, pleasure-seeking people who were up for unlimited sexual adventures with no intention of getting involved or thought of hurting others along the way.

No...that wasn't going to work. She knew perfectly well that Hugh was one of the most genuine and caring people she'd ever met.

In fact...that was Hugh walking towards her right

now and the expression on his face was exactly that. Genuine. Caring. She knew that her own face must be showing a lot of what was happening inside her. Joy in seeing him but puzzlement about why he'd apparently been avoiding her. A need to snatch any last moments they could enjoy together but sadness in knowing that they *would* be the last.

Maybe Hugh could see all that and maybe that was why there was no need to say anything. Why he took her into his arms as she turned away from the rail towards him. Why he kissed her with such...thoroughness...

But it felt different. So heartbreakingly tender it could have been a final farewell.

Somebody walked past, which was enough to make them break the kiss, but Lisa couldn't bear to move out of the circle of his arms yet so she put her head into the hollow of his shoulder, where she could hear the beat of his heart. The way she had done many times now, when they were in bed together and desire had been sated, at least temporarily.

'I feel like I haven't seen you for so long already,' she murmured. 'I was missing you, Hugh.'

'I was up here a few hours ago.' Hugh's voice was a rumble beneath her ear. He sounded incredibly weary. Almost sad, in fact. 'I saw you on the lower deck. It looked like you'd dropped something?'

'Not me.' Lisa closed her eyes so she could soak in how it felt to have Hugh's arms around her like this. 'Somebody must have lost their wallet in the storm. It's crazy how much money some people carry around with them.' Not that Lisa wanted to talk about this. There were far more important things she wanted to talk about. Like whether or not she might ever see Hugh again. 'I…um…handed it in.'

'Oh…' It seemed like Hugh's grip tightened around her for a moment but then he let her go. 'Of course you did.'

There was something odd in his tone. Something that made Lisa look up to catch his gaze, and she couldn't interpret what she could see in his eyes but it looked as if it was mostly something sad. Disappointed even?

Perhaps he was feeling the same way she was. That she was about to lose something very precious. Lisa took a deep breath and summoned every bit of courage she had.

'I'm going to miss you, Hugh,' she whispered. 'I… I love you…'

He held her gaze. She could see the way his face softened as he smiled. 'I'm going to miss you, too, Lisa. It's been fun, hasn't it?'

Lisa swallowed hard. *Fun*?

He wasn't going to say it back, was he?

Because he didn't feel the same way. He'd just been having *fun*… Already she could feel the rush of blood to her cheeks. The heat of mortification…

Hugh broke their gaze to look over the railings of the deck. 'We'll be finished docking soon,' he said quietly. 'Our cruise will be officially over.'

And the cruise wasn't the only thing that would be officially over, obviously. Lisa was cringing inside now and she knew she must be the colour of a beetroot by now. She'd just told this man she loved him and he was about to tell her that he never wanted to see her again?

'I know,' she said quickly. 'And it'll be time to say

goodbye. These cruise things…well, they're like holiday flings, I guess. Better to leave them as a good memory than turn them into dust by trying to make them into something they're not, yes?'

Why on earth was she trying to make this so easy for him? Or was it that she was just trying to make it less painful for herself? To give herself a chance to get away before he could see just how devastating this was for her?

'Especially for people like us.' Hugh's tone seemed to hold a sigh of relief. 'You're a family person through and through. It's been hard for you to be away from your sister, hasn't it? Me—I could never stay in one place for long.'

Or with one person. Lisa could easily add those unspoken words. She'd known that right from the start. Had she really thought that maybe she would be the one to change his mind?

She really did have to escape.

'I'd better go and start packing.' She actually managed to sound cheerful. Excited about the prospect of going home, even? 'I'll come down to the clinic to say goodbye properly before I go onshore.'

Hugh wasn't in the clinic when Lisa went in to make her farewells. He had intended to be there, of course—it was the polite thing to do—but he'd left it too late because he'd gone back to that bar on the Lido deck now that he was off duty, to do something he would never normally do at this time of day.

'Another coffee, Doc?'

'No. I've been up for so long it doesn't feel like

morning any more. I'll have a glass of champagne, thanks.'

Because, in defeat, you needed it?

So here he was, watching the swarm of people leaving the ship far below him, with his glass almost empty, and that was when he realised he'd left it too late to say goodbye properly to Lisa Phillips, because he could see her on the pier, dragging her bright red suitcase behind her as she headed for the taxi rank.

She'd told him she loved him.

And he'd had to exert every ounce of his strength not to say it back. If he had, they would have stayed there in each other's arms, making plans for a future together that could never have worked. This was the life he loved and he was nowhere near ready to give it up. Lisa would never want to work on a cruise ship on a more permanent basis because that would take her away from her beloved sister. A sister who needed her to be close because she was disabled. He couldn't compete with that although Lisa might have agreed to work at sea with him if he'd asked. Because she loved him and he could feel the truth of that in a way he never had with the woman he'd almost married.

And he loved her which was why he'd pushed her away. Because if you felt like that about someone, you did what was best for them, not for yourself. He could never ask Lisa to give up caring for her sister to be with him. No matter how much she loved him, a part of her would be miserable and that would undermine every-thing. He would hate himself for making her miserable and maybe she would even hate him in the end. And, if he'd given up the life he loved in order to be with her, he would have been miserable and the end result would have been the same. It could never have worked so it was better this way. It just didn't feel like it yet.

It was easy to recognise Lisa down there on the pier but Hugh knew she wouldn't be able to spot him. It felt like she could, though, when he saw the way she stopped and turned to stare up at the ship for the longest moment.

It felt like a piece of his heart was tearing off.

CHAPTER NINE

ABIGAIL PHILLIPS WAS increasingly worried about her older sister.

She could understand that there would be a period of readjustment from the excitement of that amazing couple of weeks she'd had working on a cruise ship and then having to settle into a new job as a junior care home manager but it had been another couple of weeks now and, as far as Abby could tell, this new job was a complete disaster.

She'd never seen Lisa looking so miserable.

In an effort to cheer her up, Abby had not only picked up their takeaway dinner, in what they'd agreed would be a weekly tradition now that they weren't living together, she had a special gift for Lisa.

'Put the food in the kitchen and we'll heat it up soon. Come and sit in the lounge with me. I've got something for you.'

An advantage to being in a wheelchair was that you could tuck things in beside you and keep them hidden. It was a little harder with the bottle-shaped something that Abby had on her left side but she'd hidden that with her big, soft shoulder bag. The small, flat package on her right side had been easier to conceal.

Lisa opened the wrapping and then froze as she stared at what was inside the package. Abby's heart sank like a stone.

'It's that French café,' she said. 'The one you sent me the picture of. I thought you'd like a memory of being in the most romantic place on earth.' And that was why she'd chosen a silver frame with heart-shaped corners for the print of Lisa, sitting beneath grape-vines, with the most beautiful view in the background, holding up a glass of champagne in a toast, she'd later labelled *Here's to living the dream!* when she'd sent it to Abby. Seeing even an echo of that kind of joyous smile on her face was what Abby had been aiming for this evening. What actually happened was that Lisa burst into tears.

'Oh, heck…' Abby manoeuvred her chair and put the brakes on so that she could transfer herself to the couch and put her arms around her sister. 'I'm sorry… I've done the wrong thing, haven't I?'

'It's not you.' Lisa was making a valiant effort to stifle her sobs. She scrubbed at her eyes and sniffed. 'I…love the photo…'

'It's that new job of yours, isn't it? I know you hate it.'

'It's not that bad.'

'But you hate it, don't you?'

'I just need to get used to it. Being in an office that doesn't even have a window instead of working with any patients myself, you know? The closest I get is helping the family fill in their pre-admission forms or organising medical appointments for the residents that can't be managed in our treatment rooms.'

'You'd rather be back on that ship? Dealing with

exciting things like that guy who stopped breathing? Going to romantic places like this café?'

But Lisa was shaking her head with such emphasis that it was almost despair and Abby finally twigged.

'Oh…my God,' she breathed. 'You *did* have a fling with that cute doctor, didn't you? That was why you started looking like a kid on Christmas morning.'

Lisa caught a slow tear that was trickling down the side of her nose. 'It was a really bad idea. I knew what he was like. The first time I ever saw him he was kissing another woman, for heaven's sake.'

'He *cheated* on you?' Abby could feel a knot of anger forming in her gut. Whatever the guy had done, he'd hurt Lisa and that was unforgivable.

'You can't cheat on someone if you're not in a relationship,' Lisa said. 'And we weren't. We both knew it was only going to last as long as the cruise and, no, I know that he wasn't interested in anyone else while he was with me. He just…switched off being interested in me at the end. Like it hadn't been anything important…or even special…'

Abby watched as Lisa screwed her eyes tightly shut to try and ward off any more tears. 'You fell in love with him, didn't you?' Her own heart was breaking for Lisa. 'You went for the first non-boring guy ever and you fell for him.'

Lisa nodded miserably. 'It was entirely my fault. I knew it wasn't safe. I knew I was playing with fire and there was a good chance I'd get burnt. And that's exactly what happened.'

'Takes two to tango,' Abby muttered.

'It wasn't as if it was anything that could have become something more and we both knew that. That day, in that café in the picture, we'd agreed we could be friends even if we were total opposites and then…and then he made me laugh when I was feeling really crap.'

Abby shook her head. 'Yeah, that'll do it. What is it that's so powerful about someone making you laugh?'

'Maybe it's because it's something that shows you want someone to feel better. And that there has to be a connection, whether you've known it was there or not, to make it work.'

'Hmm…you could be right.' But Abby frowned. 'Why were you feeling so crap?'

'We'd lost a patient. A cardiac arrest in a guy who was on his honeymoon. We tried to resuscitate him for nearly an hour but we were never going to win.'

Abby's eyes widened. 'You never told me about that.'

'Well, you were having a hard time yourself. It was the same day that you'd had that patient assume *you* were a patient as well, not his therapist.'

'Oh…so you were already feeling bad and then I heaped all my crap on you and you spent your time trying to make me feel better but didn't even let me know how you were feeling so I couldn't try to make *you* feel better.' Abby really was angry now. 'How do you think that makes *me* feel?' She reached to pull her chair closer, intending to get off the couch and away from Lisa before they revisited an argument that would ruin the evening—the one about how Lisa had always done too much for Abby, who was never allowed to reciprocate in any meaningful way. 'And, as for that guy, what was his name?'

'Hugh…' Lisa's voice was a whisper.

'Yeah… *Hugh*… Well, he's just a bastard and you're

better off a million miles away from him. Man, I wish I could tell him exactly what I think of him.'

It wasn't possible to shift herself onto the cushion of her chair until she'd pulled her shoulder bag off the cushion. Oh...and that bottle of champagne. She would have hidden it from Lisa but it was too late. She'd seen it and she was crying again. But she was laughing through her tears and suddenly that made the prospect of a big fight evaporate instantly. It was Lisa who put her arms around Abby this time, to give her a fierce hug. They'd been through far worse times than this and survived. They would always survive because they had each other as support, even if the giving had always been too heavily weighted on Lisa's side.

'How did you know?' Lisa asked when she finally pulled herself free of the hug and wiped her eyes.

'Know what?'

'That, in defeat, you need champagne.'

'What on earth are you talking about, Lise?'

Lisa got to feet. 'I'll find some glasses,' she said. 'And then give you a wee history lesson about Napoleon Bonaparte.'

'It's lovely to see you, Hugh. Or it would be, if you weren't looking so...wrecked.'

'You mean I look older?' Hugh shrugged. 'It's the end of a three-weeker and we had some challenging passengers on board. Hypochondriacs, mostly. Very demanding ones.'

He hadn't enjoyed the last three weeks nearly as much as he usually enjoyed his job but maybe that was due to the fact that he'd enjoyed the previous cruise so much more than normal—up until the end of it, anyway. Because he had been sharing it with Lisa and that had made everything seem new and far more meaningful. He'd taken her to some of his favourite places. Worse, he'd taken her to his bed and the effect of sharing that with Lisa had been the same. New. Far more meaningful.

But he'd been right to let her walk back to her own life without the complications that would have come if they'd tried to keep their connection. Lisa wasn't the kind of woman who'd be happy to see him for an afternoon here or there when he happened to be in London. She deserved someone who could offer her the same kind of loyalty and commitment that she would give to someone she loved. The kind she was already committed to giving to Abby who—as she'd said herself—was the most important person in her life.

It should have been a lot easier than this to have turned back to embrace the lifestyle that had been so perfect for the last couple of years. Not much more than a month ago he'd been looking forward to spending an afternoon with Carlotta in Barcelona. He could remember how much he had enjoyed kissing her and maybe that's what he really needed to distract him. Hugh raised his hand to signal the waiter that he was ready to pay the bill for their lunch. Now they could go somewhere more appropriate for some more intimate time together.

He found what he hoped was a seductive smile, although it felt rather more that he was leering at his companion.

'You, on the other hand, look as gorgeous as ever, Carlotta. Shall we go somewhere more comfortable?'

'Of course...' But Carlotta was looking at his full glass. 'You don't want to finish your wine first?'

'I think I might have gone off champagne.' There were too many memories associated with it now, that was the problem, and every one of them included Lisa Phillips.

So many wonderful memories, like the way she would glow with the pleasure and wonder of a new experience, like tasting champagne for the first time or soaking in a fabulous view or enjoying a delicious meal or...or...dear Lord...the way she used to look when she was coming apart in his arms...

Man, it was hot here today. Hugh was wearing an open-necked shirt and yet he had an urge to loosen his tie or go in search of a sea breeze. Was his face as red as it felt? Surely he wasn't blushing, the way Lisa had been unable to prevent herself doing so furiously when she was uncomfortable or embarrassed. Like the way her cheeks had gone such a bright colour after she'd told him she loved him and he hadn't said it back...

Okay...knowing that he'd hurt Lisa wasn't such a good memory. But neither was the one that sprang to mind when Hugh opened his wallet to extract a note or two to leave a tip for their waiter. It was sad, he decided as he put his hand on Carlotta's lower back to guide her between tables, that it only took one less than happy memory to take the shine off so many of the better ones.

Carlotta slipped her arm around his waist as they left the restaurant and it was enough for him to stop and turn towards her. She put a hand on his cheek then and raised her face to kiss him. But Hugh found himself breaking the contact of their lips almost instantly. Lifting his head with a jerk.

'I'm sorry,' he said. 'But I can't... I don't know what's wrong with me today.'

'I think I do.' Carlotta's smile was knowing. 'I don't know who she is, but I think it's finally happened. You've fallen in love.'

Hugh shook his head. 'Nope. I did that once and it was the biggest mistake I ever made. I wouldn't be stupid enough to do it again.'

Carlotta's gaze was full of sympathy now. 'Oh, Hugh...it's not something you can stop happening. You can fight it, of course. Walk away from it even. But you never know...walking away from it this time might be an even bigger mistake than choosing the wrong person the first time.' She touched his cheek again before walking away with a wave. 'Thanks for lunch, Hugh. And best of luck...'

It wasn't far back to the ship and Hugh walked briskly despite the heat of the Spanish afternoon. Simon was at his usual place at the bottom of the gangway, although it was only staff he was welcoming back on board today. The passengers from this cruise had all disembarked this morning.

'Hey, Hugh...how's it going? Happy to have a day off?'

'I've got a few days off this time. I'm thinking of grabbing a flight to London and visiting my folks.'

By the time he reached the marble-floored atrium, where Harry's piano was deserted and silent, the idea of escaping the ship for a few days had become so appealing that Hugh went towards one of the desks where he knew someone could help him make his travel arrangements. Everyone on board relied on Sally to answer any questions because she'd been in the business for so long she seemed to know everything. If she couldn't give you the answer herself, she always knew where to find it.

Hugh wasn't the only one with a query this afternoon. The ship's captain was ahead of him and as Hugh got closer he was startled to hear what the captain was saying.

'I'm sure her name was Lisa. She was wearing scrubs under her sou'wester, so I assume she was working in the medical centre. It was the night of that storm.'

'Oh, I remember.' Sally nodded. 'That was some storm. Now...let me look and see if I can find who she was.'

'Lisa Phillips,' Hugh told them. 'She was just a locum nurse—only with us for the one cruise.'

Just...? Lisa could never be "just" anything. She was an extraordinary human being, that's what she was...and Carlotta was right. He *was* in love with her. She had been in love with him and had been brave enough to tell him. And he had thrown that back in her face. Even if he'd had good reason, which he'd believed he did, it was a horrible thing to have done. He hadn't even said goodbye to her, had he?

'Well, I need her address,' the captain said. 'I've got a rather large cheque to forward.'

Hugh blinked. Sally looked curious as well. 'Whatever for?' she asked.

'Someone lost their wallet during that storm. This Lisa found it and handed it in. Well, she bumped into me and asked me where she could find someone from

Security and I said I'd look after it for her. We tracked down the owner once things had settled down and, after he got home, he was so impressed that the wallet had still had a rather ill-advised amount of cash in it that he thought the person who'd found it deserved a reward.'

Hugh's breath caught in his throat. Lisa not only deserved an apology from him, she deserved the reward of that cheque. And… it gave him a perfect excuse to see her again.

He cleared his throat. 'I'm about to head to London for a day or two,' he said. 'I could deliver it personally, perhaps, if she's not too far away?'

'Marvellous idea.' The captain handed him the envelope. 'Get some flowers to go with it, lad, and tell her that we all appreciate her honesty. She's done our reputation a power of good.'

Sally was beaming. 'Let me find her address in the system for you. Ooh, I'd love to be a fly on the wall when you turn up on her doorstep. Won't she be thrilled?'

Abby glared at the man on the doorstep.

She hadn't needed his introduction.

'I *know* who you are,' she said. 'Lisa's working late but even if she was home I'm pretty damn sure she wouldn't want to see you.'

Mind you, this ship's doctor was a lot cuter in real life than in that photo on the website. He also had a massive bunch of flowers in his arms and an expression in those rather gorgeous brown eyes that looked… nervous?

The flowers—and the man—were getting rapidly

wetter as they stood there in the pouring rain but Abby suddenly had misgivings about whether sending this unexpected visitor instantly on his way was the right thing to do. Hadn't she wanted the opportunity to give him a piece of her mind about how he had treated her sister?

'You'd better come in for a minute,' she said ungraciously. 'I don't want those flowers dripping all over my lap.' Abby swung her chair around and headed for the kitchen. 'Put them in the sink,' she ordered. 'I'll deal with them later.'

He did as he was told, which was gratifying. But then he gave her a grin that was cheeky enough to disarm her completely.

'And there I was thinking that Lisa was the bossy sister,' he said.

Abby couldn't help a huff of laughter escaping. 'She is. It's actually very out of character for me to be rude but...'

'But...?'

'I don't like you,' Abby told him bluntly. 'You've made my sister miserable.'

'I'm really sorry about that. Maybe this will cheer her up.'

Hugh took an envelope out of his pocket and handed it to Abby, who opened it. Her jaw dropped when she saw the amount the cheque was written out for. By the time Hugh had explained what it was for, she had a lump in her throat that made it difficult to swallow.

'She only took that job on the ship because she was desperate for a bit of extra money,' she told Hugh. 'Because of *me*... She got a loan to get a specially modified car for me but it was a real struggle for her to meet the payments, especially when she had to find a new job after being made redundant. She even missed a mortgage payment on the house—I opened a threatening letter from the bank when she was away, which was really scary. Anyway...' She put the cheque back into its envelope, so that Lisa could get the same surprise that she'd had. 'I shouldn't be telling you any of this but I guess it's just as much my fault as yours that she's miserable now.'

He didn't say anything but when Abby looked up, she could see how carefully he was listening. How important this was to him. He also looked as though he was concerned for Abby. Perhaps he could sense how close she was to crying?

'You'd better sit down,' she said. 'Would you like a cup of tea?'

'You knew about me, didn't you?' she asked a short time later as she put a mug of tea on the kitchen table in front of Hugh.

'I knew you'd had an accident when you were very young that left you in a wheelchair. That your sister is about six years older than you and is completely devoted to you and that she was worried about not living with you any more.'

'Did you know that she's my half-sister?'

Hugh nodded. 'She did tell me that. In almost the same breath that she told me how much she loves you.'

'So she didn't tell you that we had different fathers because my mother had drug and alcohol problems that meant her relationships never lasted? That Lisa was more of a mother to me than our mother ever was, even though she was only a kid herself? That she's always blamed herself for my accident because she wasn't holding my hand tightly enough and I escaped and ran out in front of a car?'

Again, Hugh said nothing. He looked as though he had no idea where to find the words he might need but Abby wasn't going to help him. He needed to know more.

'For her entire life she's put me first,' Abby said quietly. 'She's done it out of love but she's also done it out of guilt and that's something that's really hard for me to live with. She was only a kid herself, for God's sake. She's got nothing to feel guilty about but she chose her career so that she could stay close to home. She wanted to be a doctor but that would have meant going to a medical school away from home so she did nursing training instead.'

'I kind of guessed that.' Hugh nodded.

'She never went to parties when she was a teenager. Never spent money on herself or took a gap year to do any travelling. She took over the mortgage on this house when Gran died and said it was worth it because it would keep us safe. I reckon she chose her boring boyfriends because they were safe options that weren't going to interfere with her life. I don't believe she's ever been in love either. Until now. Which means this is her first broken heart and...and it might be *my* fault she met you in the first place but that...that's down to *you*...'

Again, Hugh nodded. 'It might not be my first broken heart,' he admitted. 'But it feels like it is. And I can't argue with you because it is down to me. I've wrecked the most amazing thing I've ever found and I have no idea what to do about it. I'm sure you're probably also right about Lisa not wanting to see me.'

'Are you saying what I think you're saying?' Abby waited for Hugh to meet her gaze so that she could gauge how genuine he might be. 'That you're in love with Lise? That you really *want* to be with her?'

'For the rest of my life,' Hugh said softly. 'I'm never going to meet anyone else like your sister. I don't think there *is* anyone else in the world that lights up when she's happy quite like Lisa does. I want to see her that happy for the rest of *her* life. I want to be the one who creates some of that happiness.'

'Oh, my God…' Abby could feel a tear sneaking down her cheek. 'That's exactly what I want for her, too.'

'I'm not.' Hugh held up his hands in a gesture of surrender. 'And I realise now that being with Lisa is more important than a lifestyle that isn't exactly compatible with a long term future. I understand how important you are to her, too. I totally respect that. I love that she loves you that much.'

Abby swiped at the moisture on her cheeks. 'I'm perfectly capable of being independent, thank you. I've *told* her that. I've told her that if she wants to go and have an exciting job at sea instead of the one she hates so much here, then I might miss her but I'd be fine. I need to be independent.' Abby had found a shaky smile. 'You'd be doing me a favour if you persuaded her to go sailing off into the sunset with you for a good, long while. You can always settle down later, you know.'

'I don't think I'd be able to do that.' Hugh was shaking his head. 'She's a determined woman, your sister, and I've hurt her. It's going to take something pretty special to get her to even listen to me, isn't it?'

'Hmm...' Abby had no doubts at all about how genuine Hugh Patterson was. She could also see exactly why her sister had fallen in love with this man. But he was right. Lisa thought she had played with fire and been burnt. She wouldn't be keen to go anywhere near that heat again.

Her gaze drifted over to the flowers in the kitchen sink. And then it lifted to the window sill above them, which was where Lisa had put the small framed photo that Abby had given her last week. She turned slowly back to her guest. Biting her lip couldn't stop the smile that wanted to escape.

'I think I might have an idea,' she said.

CHAPTER TEN

'I CAN'T BELIEVE I let you talk me into this.'

'Shh… I'm busy.'

Lisa had to smile at the expression on Abby's face as her sister closed her eyes for a moment. It was sheer bliss, that's what it was.

'You don't look very busy.'

'I am. It's a big deal, you know—this living the dream stuff.'

'I know…' Her voice cracked with the emotion of it because this was exactly what she'd dreamed of for Abby, only a matter of a few weeks ago. For her to be here. In this exact spot. At this precise table, in fact, that had the best view from the terrace.

Not that she'd made it easy. Even after the astonishing good fortune of Abby winning those tickets for a weekend in the South of France in some radio competition—on top of that amazing reward that had been delivered with some flowers on behalf of the ship's captain—Lisa had initially totally refused to give in to Abby's plea to experience the most romantic place on earth. She'd even taken that photograph off the kitchen windowsill and hidden it in a drawer so she didn't have to think about it every time she caught a glimpse of the image.

'*It's the last place on earth I'd want to go,*' she'd said. '*I can't believe you'd even ask.*'

'*It's not as though you were there on a date,*' Abby had pointed out. '*It was before you hooked up with Hugh, remember? You were there as friends and you look so happy in that photo. It might help.*'

'*How?*'

'*Oh... I don't know. Like one of those reset things you can do on the computer. Where you can pick a time when you knew things were good and have all your settings revert to what they were then.*' The look on Abby's face reminded Lisa of when she'd been a small child and had desperately wanted something that she couldn't have or do because the wheelchair had made it too difficult. '*Please? For me?*'

So, of course, in the end she had agreed. When had she ever not agreed to something that Abby wanted so much?

She'd even let Abby choose her outfit. A floaty red dress sprinkled with tiny white flowers, white sandals and a little white flower on a hair clip. They might have very different shades of red hair themselves, with Lisa being a dark auburn and Abby much more of a strawberry blonde, but it had been a pact from when they were both children that they would wear red whenever they liked.

Abby's eyes opened again. 'Where's that champagne?' she asked.

'Relax. I'm sure it's on its way. We've got plenty of time. The car isn't coming back for us for hours. Have you decided what you want to eat yet?'

'I need some more time—it all looks so good. And I need to go to the loo before I think about it any more.'

'Oh…' Lisa's chair scraped on the stone of the floor. 'Of course…'

Abby's eyebrows shot up. '*You* need to go to the loo, too?'

'No… I thought…' Lisa sat down with a sigh. 'Sorry…'

'No problem.' Abby's smile was forgiving. 'And if I hadn't already checked out that they had a disabled toilet available I would probably be very grateful for your assistance. As it is, I can manage perfectly well on my own. So *you* relax. I'll be back soon.'

Watching her sister expertly manoeuvre between the tables, heading back to the reception area inside the café, Lisa managed to let go of the underlying anxiety that this might not have been a good idea. Abby had managed the travelling with ease and she was revelling in everything they had packed into this short getaway already. It had been such an amazing prize that had not only included a luxury hotel in Nice but a chauffeur-driven car for any sightseeing they had wanted to do.

Relaxing for a few minutes as she waited for Abby to return wasn't difficult. It was even warmer than it had been the last time Lisa had been here so the soft breeze drifting over the canopy of the forest beneath the café was more than welcome. The shade from the grapevine running rampant over the pergola was just as welcome and the play of shadows from the sunlight finding gaps in the leaves was delightful. It would make it harder to see when Abby was coming back, although Lisa could see a waiter standing beside the bar, putting a bottle into an ice bucket. Their champagne? She hoped that Abby would return in time to see it being opened because that pop of the cork was all part of the magic, wasn't it?

Or it had been the last time.

The first time.

From the corner of her eye, Lisa could see the waiter approaching the table now. He had a white cloth over his arm, the bottle in the bucket in one hand and two fluted glasses in the other. It was impossible not to drift back in time. To remember what it was like when those thousands of tiny bubbles exploded in her mouth and then evaporated into delicious iciness. To remember opening her eyes to find Hugh staring at her with an intensity that had taken her breath away all over again.

The same way he'd looked at her when they had been making love...

She could even hear an echo of his voice—*'I knew you'd look like that'*—with that note of happiness because *she'd* been so happy.

Oh, help...

She wasn't going to cry, Lisa told herself firmly. She wasn't going to let anything spoil this for Abby. But where *was* Abby? She was taking such a long time—maybe she did need some help after all. Lisa had to peer past the waiter to try and see if Abby had appeared again yet.

'Don't worry, she's fine.'

Lisa's jaw dropped in total disbelief as she recognised the voice of the waiter and looked up.

Hugh's smile was reassuring but the cork shot from the bottle with a sound like gunfire that made Lisa jump. He caught the escaping foam in one of the glasses.

'It was all part of the plan.' Hugh's smile had disappeared as he slid into the seat on the other side of this small wrought-iron table.

'I've been a complete idiot,' he said quietly. 'Do you think you could ever forgive me?'

This was overwhelming. Lisa suspected she might look like a stone statue because that was how she was feeling. There were just too many feelings that were too powerful.

How much manipulation had gone on to entice her here for what had clearly been a set-up? For someone who'd kept such tight control of everything in her life, including herself—in order to keep Abby and herself safe—the idea that she had fallen for it was somehow shameful.

Knowing that her beloved sister had been in on it and had kept the secret so well was so surprising it was hurtful.

The fact that it was happening here, in what she herself had described as the most romantic place on earth, had the potential to take the magic away and make it simply a stage set and not real at all.

But running beneath that horrible mix of impressions that made her want to get to her feet and run was something else. A bright, shiny thread of what felt like hope. That something precious was about to be offered to her and all she had to do was to be brave enough to accept the gift.

Finally, she found her voice. 'Um…whose idea was this?'

'Abby's,' Hugh admitted. 'Although I have to say I thought it was brilliant and you know why?'

'Why?' There were plenty more questions to ask about how and why Abby had been colluding with Hugh but they could wait. There was something far more compelling about the expression in those brown eyes Lisa loved so much. Whatever he was about to say was so important he wasn't going to let her look away.

'Because this was where you had your first taste of champagne. Where I saw that joy of it in your face. And maybe I didn't realise it at the time—okay, I probably would have run a mile if I *had* realised it—but I think that was the moment I started to fall in love with you, Lisa.'

Oh, yes…that shiny thread of hope was glowing now. Shining so brightly that it was casting a shadow over everything else.

'I told Abby how much I was in love with you. That I want to see that kind of happiness in your face as often as possible for the rest of your life and that I want to be able to do whatever I can to create that happiness for you.' Hugh's voice cracked a little. 'And you know what she said?'

Lisa shook her head. She couldn't get any words past the lump in her throat.

'She said that she wants exactly the same thing. We're friends for life now, your sister and me.'

'Oh…' There was no stopping the tears that were determined to escape.

'She told me about what happened,' Hugh said gently. 'That you've always been so determined to look after her and keep her safe. That you've held onto guilt for something that wasn't your fault.'

'But it was,' Lisa whispered. 'It was…' She swallowed hard. Maybe he didn't know the whole truth—

the worst thing about her. 'There was a doll. In the toy shop window. A really beautiful doll with curly yellow hair and I was standing there, wishing with all my heart that I had hair like that and that I could take that doll home with me… That was when it happened. I let go of Abby's hand.'

'You didn't let go, sweetheart,' Hugh said softly. 'Abby pulled because she wanted to run. She took you by surprise. You were only a little girl yourself and you should never have been given that responsibility in the first place. You've always had too much responsibility and you've taken that on with a grace and determination that's amazing. But don't you think it's about time to forgive little Lisa? To stop denying her the good things in life because you decided so long ago that maybe she didn't deserve them?'

Lisa blinked as her tears evaporated. How on earth could Hugh know those things about her when she'd only fleetingly given them any head space?

'You're allowed to want things just for yourself,' Hugh added. There was a twinkle in his eyes now. 'The things that make you feel good. Or to feel loved.' He picked up the bottle and began to pour a glass but when he held it out towards her, he paused, looking at her over the rim—like the way he had when she'd taken her first ever sip. 'Things like champagne,' he said. His fingers brushed hers as she accepted the glass and his words were a whisper that only she could hear. 'Or making love…'

Oh…*my*… Surely everybody in this café could see the glow that was about to reach Lisa's cheeks. But happiness like this was such a fragile thing, wasn't it? Irresistible but terrifying at the same time.

'I know.' Hugh was smiling at her. 'It's scary, isn't it? That was why I was such an idiot. I used my memories of the disaster that was almost my first marriage as a kind of shield to make sure I never took that kind of risk again. I took that shield out and polished it up when I realised I was getting in too deep with you. I was scared, too. I thought I'd get over missing you after you left but you know what?'

Lisa could feel her lips curling into a smile. 'What?'

'I just missed you more every single day. Until I finally realised that I had to trust my instincts. To trust *you*. As much as you were trusting me when you said you loved me. I'm sorry I got that so wrong... I wasn't ready, that's all...'

Lisa nodded. She could understand that. She could understand how hard it was to trust.

'I've never believed that the things I wanted just for myself were safe,' she told Hugh, her voice wobbling. 'They were just distractions and that made them dangerous.'

'I blame that doll,' Hugh said. 'With the stupid yellow hair.' His tone changed to something far more serious. 'You'll always be safe with me,' he said, 'if that's one of the things you want.' He drew in a deep breath. 'I love you, Lisa. Can you trust that? Can you trust *me*? Take that leap of faith?'

It was Lisa's turn to draw in a new breath. 'Could you hold my hand? So we could jump together?'

Hugh took both her hands in his. 'Always,' he murmured.

For the longest moment, they soaked in that connection. There would be time for the kind of intimate physical connection they knew would come later but the skin on skin of their entwined fingers was all they needed for this moment. The gaze on gaze of their eye contact was so deep it was a connection that felt like their souls were touching.

Nobody interrupted them but they were, after all, in the most romantic place on earth so perhaps a couple who were totally lost in each other's eyes was only to be expected. It had to stop eventually, of course, because a celebration was called for. Hugh filled the second flute with champagne. And then he reached into the inside pocket of his jacket and took out a third glass. He turned his head before he began to fill it, nodding towards the reception area of the café. Seconds later, Abby was rolling towards their table with the happiest smile Lisa had ever seen on her face.

'So you did it?' she asked Hugh. 'You proposed?'

'Oh, no...' Hugh handed Abby a glass of champagne. 'I forgot about that bit.'

Abby put her glass down. 'No champagne allowed then. Get on with it.'

Lisa laughed. '*Abby*—you can't say that.'

Abby scowled. 'But it was part of the plan.'

'It was,' Hugh agreed. 'And I had it all planned—apart from the ring because I'd want you to choose exactly what *you* want. But I just missed the perfect opportunity, didn't I?' He arched an eyebrow at Abby. 'A *private* opportunity.'

'It's not too late,' Abby said. 'Don't mind me. I want to read the menu again anyway.'

Lisa was still smiling. 'You don't have to do what she says.'

But Hugh had caught her gaze again and her smile

faded. 'We never said a proper goodbye, did we? That last day of the cruise?'

'No...' It wasn't something Lisa really wanted to remember. It was a bit shocking, in fact, to have a reminder of how broken-hearted she'd felt, walking away from Hugh.

'There was a good reason for that, even if neither of us knew it at the time.' Hugh was still holding her gaze. He'd taken hold of her hand again as well. 'I never want to say a "proper" goodbye to you, Lisa Phillips. I want you to be in my life for every day I'm lucky enough to get. Will you marry me?'

Oh... Lisa was so ready to take that leap. Straight off the edge of that cliff, and she could do it without hesitation because Hugh was holding her hand. And she knew he would always be there to hold her hand.

'Yes,' she said softly.

'What was that?' Abby raised her head from the menu. 'I didn't quite hear it.'

'Yes,' Lisa said, more loudly. She was laughing again. So was Hugh. 'Yes, yes, *yes*...'

EPILOGUE

Two years later...

IT WAS NEVER going to get old, hearing the pop of a champagne cork. Not that they did it all that often but it always made Lisa smile. Perhaps that was because there was always that moment when she would catch her husband's gaze and know that they were both re-membering that first time.

And celebrating their engagement, and later on their wedding, all in the same place, on the terrace of that magical café in the South of France. It was one of those private moments when so much could be said with nothing more than a fleeting, shared glance. It was fleeting, because they were here for something—and someone—other than themselves.

'Happy house-warming, Abby.'

'Thanks, Lise. I can't believe I'm here. That I ac-tually have this incredibly cool apartment that's been custom built just to make life easier for me. And it's all thanks to you.' She raised her glass but then grinned. 'Oh... I almost forgot. You're not even going to have a taste, then?'

Lisa shook her head, her hand protectively smoothing the roundness of her belly. As if acknowledging the touch, her baby kicked against the palm of her hand.

Abby touched Hugh's glass with her own instead. 'It's thanks to you, too, bro. If you hadn't given me the heads-up that my dream job was coming up at your hospital, I wouldn't have thought about moving at all.'

'You're going to love it at St John's Hospital. I'm coming up to a year in the emergency department there and I'm still loving it.'

'Hey, it's a specialist hand therapist position in a team that's so good, people come from all over the country to get their surgery and start their recuperation. I still can't believe how lucky I was to get the job.'

'Why wouldn't you?' Lisa was beaming proudly. 'We're not the only ones who think you're the best. And it's Gran we should toast as well. If she hadn't made a good choice when she bought that little house decades ago, it wouldn't have sold for enough to make it possible to do a makeover like this on this apartment.' She looked around at the sleek lines and open spaces that made it so easy to live in for someone in a wheelchair but it still had the character that went with the old building it was part of, like the high ceilings and feature fireplaces.

'Best of all, you're a lot closer to us now,' Hugh put in. 'For, you know…those babysitting duties that are coming up.'

The ripple of laughter was comfortable. So was the teasing. They were a family unit now and about to welcome the first of the next generation.

'It's just a shame you're not having twins,' Abby said. 'Or triplets, even.'

'You're kidding, right?' Lisa shook her head. 'Why would you wish that on me?'

'You've got all those bedrooms in that mansion of yours. You'll need to have a few more kids to fill them up. How are your parents doing, Hugh? Do they like their downsized life in Central London?'

'They're hardly ever there. It's ironic that when Lisa and I gave up working on the cruise ships, they decided that it was their favourite way to travel. They're on their way to Alaska as we speak.'

Hugh had come to stand behind Lisa and he put his arms around her, his hands over hers on her belly. The kick this time was stronger and Lisa glance slid sideways to find Hugh had done the same thing. It was another one of those private moments and it was so filled with joy that she couldn't look away.

'Oh, get a room,' Abby growled. 'No, wait...that's how this happened, wasn't it? I'll consider myself warned.'

It was a joke but Lisa could sense something in her sister's tone that made her move to give her a hug. A note of longing, perhaps? She knew Abby was thrilled with her new life that included her dream job and the perfect apartment but Lisa wanted for Abby the kind of happiness she had found with Hugh. Because it made life about as close to perfect as it could get.

'It'll be your turn one of these days,' she murmured as she wrapped her arms around her sister. 'You just wait and see...'

* * * * *

COMING SOON!

We really hope you enjoyed reading this book.
If you're looking for more romance
be sure to head to the shops when
new books are available on

Thursday 22nd
May

To see which titles are coming soon, please visit
millsandboon.co.uk/nextmonth

MILLS & BOON

MILLS & BOON

THE HEART OF ROMANCE

A ROMANCE FOR EVERY READER

MODERN — Prepare to be swept off your feet by sophisticated, sexy and seductive heroes, in some of the world's most glamourous and romantic locations, where power and passion collide.

HISTORICAL — Escape with historical heroes from time gone by. Whether your passion is for wicked Regency Rakes, muscled Vikings or rugged Highlanders, awaken the romance of the past.

MEDICAL — Set your pulse racing with dedicated, delectable doctors in the high-pressure world of medicine, where emotions run high and passion, comfort and love are the best medicine.

True Love — Celebrate true love with tender stories of heartfelt romance, from the rush of falling in love to the joy a new baby can bring, and a focus on the emotional heart of a relationship.

HEROES — The excitement of a gripping thriller, with intense romance at its heart. Resourceful, true-to-life women and strong, fearless men face danger and desire - a killer combination!

 — From showing up to glowing up, these characters are on the path to leading their best lives and finding romance along the way – with plenty of sizzling spice!

To see which titles are coming soon, please visit

millsandboon.co.uk/nextmonth

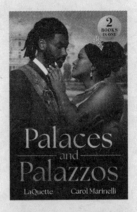

LET'S TALK

Romance

For exclusive extracts, competitions and special offers, find us online:

- MillsandBoon
- @MillsandBoon
- @MillsandBoonUK
- @MillsandBoonUK

Get in touch on 01413 063 232

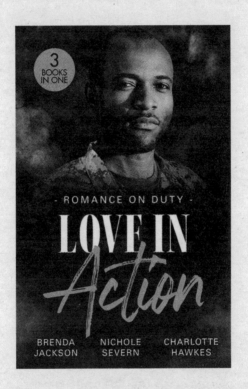

afterglow BOOKS

Afterglow Books is a trend-led, trope-filled list of books with diverse, authentic and relatable characters, a wide array of voices and representations, plus real world trials and tribulations. Featuring all the tropes you could possibly want (think small-town settings, fake relationships, grumpy vs sunshine, enemies to lovers) and all with a generous dose of spice in every story.

♪ @millsandboonuk
⊙ @millsandboonuk
afterglowbooks.co.uk
#AfterglowBooks

For all the latest book news, exclusive content and giveaways scan the QR code below to sign up to the Afterglow newsletter:

SCAN ME

afterglow BOOKS

✈ International

💻 Workplace romance

☯ Opposites attract

🚫 Forbidden love

🌶 Spicy

🌶 Spicy

OUT NOW

Two stories published every month. Discover more at:
Afterglowbooks.co.uk

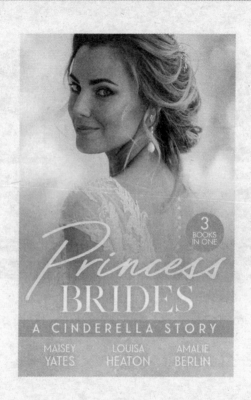

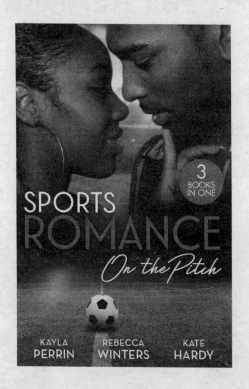

MILLS & BOON
A ROMANCE FOR EVERY READER

- **FREE** delivery direct to your door
- **EXCLUSIVE** offers every month
- **SAVE** up to 30% on pre-paid subscriptions

SUBSCRIBE AND SAVE

millsandboon.co.uk/Subscribe

MILLS & BOON

MODERN

Power and Passion

Prepare to be swept off your feet by
sophisticated, sexy and seductive heroes, in some
of the world's most glamorous and romantic
locations, where power and passion collide.

Eight Modern stories published every month, find them all at:

millsandboon.co.uk

MILLS & BOON

HEROES

At Your Service

Experience all the excitement of a gripping thriller, with an intense romance at its heart that will keep you on the edge of your seat. Resourceful, true-to-life women and strong, fearless men face danger and desire – a killer combination!

Eight Heroes stories published every month, find them all at:

millsandboon.co.uk